Danger Within

Dusty J. Miller

The Alice Ott Mystery Series

Danger in the Air (2012)
Danger at the Gates (2014)
Danger Under Ground (2017)
Danger in the House (2019)

Find all the Alice Ott Mystery series books at

DustyJMiller.com

Other books by Dusty J. Miller

Women Who Hurt Themselves:
A Book of Hope and Understanding

Addictions and Trauma Recovery:
Healing the Body, Mind and Spirit

Your Surviving Spirit:
A Spiritual Workbook for Coping with Trauma

Stop Running from Love:
3 Steps to Overcoming
Emotional Distancing & Fear of Intimacy

Danger Within

For Elizabeth, love Dusty Miller

Dusty J. Miller

CCE Publishing

Edgewater, FL

Cover photo by Cindy Casey

Published by *CCE Publishing*, Edgewater, Florida

Printed in the United States of America

ISBN 978-1-7357354-8-1

Dedication

Dorothy, always

Chapter One
Central Florida

Kori Harris replayed the call in her head, trying to think if there was anything that should make her nervous. The caller's voice was soft, tentative, and perhaps fearful that someone might overhear him.

"I got two names for you. Meet me at Lil' Bessie's, you know, that barbecue place on Canal and 14th?"

"OK," Kori said, hesitating a moment. She wasn't even sure if she was talking to a man or a woman. "Can you give me your name? Some way to reach you in case I get lost or I'm running late or something?"

"You show up at six o'clock tonight, I'll have those names." The phone connection ended.

Kori made a call-back attempt, knowing it was futile.

She was uneasy about this meeting. She didn't like going alone to meet with someone she didn't know anything about. If Charles hadn't called so late to bail on her, she might have tried to postpone the meeting. But it was only an hour before she had agreed to meet the caller. They just needed one or two more employees ready to tell the truth and they could go ahead with the lawsuit. She could manage without Charles.

At five thirty, Kori drove by Lil' Bessie's. It took her awhile to locate it, even though she was gradually learning her way around the West Side. There were small businesses tucked in between houses: barber shops, rib joints, auto repair shops, and childcare signs at homes with tiny fenced-in yards, bars, hairstyling signs, and churches so small you could miss them if you were searching after dark.

It had been a good idea to start early looking for the barbecue place. She was less sure of herself on the West Side without Charles, who grew up here. But now she was sitting in the parking lot of Lil' Bessie's with a half hour to kill, and she didn't think it was wise to go into the place thirty minutes ahead of schedule. If the caller wanted to keep their meeting private, she could mess things up by getting too chatty with folks in the restaurant before her informant arrived.

She thought about driving back over across U.S.1 to the upscale end of Canal Street where she could get a coffee and maybe even one of those mega chocolate chip cookies from the ice cream shop. Kori decided against that; she preferred to patronize the West Side businesses as much as she could. She opted for a walk by the river to use up the extra half hour. It was a healthier choice, she told herself.

When she got back to Lil' Bessie's, Kori was feeling more relaxed. But when she walked into the barbecue place, once again she felt uneasy. There were two elderly men at a little table at the back, and she could see someone in the kitchen. Looked normal enough, but it didn't smell right. There were no mouth-watering smokey barbecue smells. No one was in there enjoying themselves, laughing and drinking beer and chowing down on pulled pork sandwiches and licking fingers soaked in barbecue sauce.

"Hey, how're y'all doing?" she greeted the old men at the back table, the only customers in the restaurant. They nodded politely but resumed staring at the empty table. She hoped she wouldn't have to wait long for the person she was meeting.

A slender young man in the kitchen peered out through the service window. "You want take-out, ma'am?" he asked.

"No thank you. Ok if I just sit at one of the tables and drink a Coke or something? I'm meeting someone."

"Make yourself comfortable. Be with you shortly."

The stress of organizing the lawsuit was wearing her out. She wondered if their lawyer should have gone ahead with the number of plaintiffs they already had. Each time she met with a new informant, she was committing herself to more additional hours. She had to meet with each person two times at the minimum, listening to each TouchStone employee tell her all the relevant details of what was wrong, what was missing, what had not been there to keep them safe as they did their increasingly difficult jobs of keeping elders alive in nursing homes that should have been safe. Then she had to make sure each brave whistleblower got the information they needed about the lawsuit, about what could happen and what might never happen.

Often when she got over to the nursing home for her daily visits with Gram, she was hardly able to keep her eyes open to read the Bible verses that soothed the old woman. She had rushed her visit with Gram today, leaving before Gram's dinner arrived, worried because Charles couldn't get away from the nursing home today to go with her to meet this newest contact.

She should have said no to this last one. She checked her watch. It was just six o'clock. She hoped she wouldn't have to wait long.

The man from the kitchen brought her a glass of soda over ice. He set it down with a coaster without looking at her. Just delivered the drink and went back to the kitchen.

"Quiet tonight," Kori said, as he walked away from her.

Get up and leave! She tried to ignore the inner warning. Just nerves.

She took a sip of her drink, and pulled the phone out of her belt pack to make sure there wasn't a last minute change of plans. Nothing. She decided to send a note to Floriana about their meeting tomorrow. Flo was juggling so many things she took Kori's breath away. "Mting w whistler #25," she texted. "wrp up project tmrrow?"

She was startled when an older white man walked into the cafe and came right to her table. "You Kori?" he asked.

She nodded, staying silent.

"We best talk outside," he said, and walked back out the door.

She left a five dollar bill beside her half empty glass. No point in waiting for change; her informant was too anxious to get back outside. She followed the man out to the side lot where his truck was pulled up next to her car.

"I have two names written down for you," he said. "Come on over here and I'll get the paper out of the truck." He looked around anxiously, and she wondered if it was his fear of being in a Black neighborhood.

She needed to find out something about him. She had learned the hard way that some who came forward with information were gaming her, just in it for the money. She'd gotten so she could tell when someone was either unwilling or unable to give her verifiable information.

How was she supposed to trust some names written on a piece of paper? If she didn't like the way the conversation was going, she could always tell him she needed to think about whatever he said. She could hop into her own car if he got into badgering her about information she wasn't yet at liberty to give everyone, or if he started arguing over the terms of the agreement negotiated with every plaintiff. He wouldn't be the first person she had to say no to.

She followed him to the driver's side of his truck, and dropped her mask a moment so he could see her face. "What's your name?" she said, her smile friendly as Christmas morning.

He opened the cab door of the truck and reached for something on the seat. Kori inhaled a small gasp of surprise as he pivoted back toward her and grabbed her arm, pulling her toward him. Before she could cry out, his fist came at her and it felt like her head was exploding.

Chapter Two
Western Massachusetts

Alice was flummoxed. She wished she could just stay home and read the Gazette, the cat sleeping peacefully on her lap. From everything she'd learned about the pandemic over the past months, she believed that she and Gerard really had to decide whether or not they could live together.

She and her dashing French lover had never dreamed they would be reunited after forty years apart. Since they had found each other and fallen in love all over again, they had been gratefully taking one day at a time. So far, they had been able to manage each life choice as it happened. As far as Alice was concerned, it had been blissfully easy.

Over the eight years since their reunion, they hadn't chosen to live together. Although Gerard had asked her in the first rosy glow, to marry him, she had gently refused. As far as she could tell, they had been enjoying a satisfying relationship without having to become an old married couple. Inviting Gerard to move into her home seemed to make sense, yet she still felt hesitant.

Why rock the boat? At their age, moving in together was a multi-layered decision, one that they had avoided so far. It would take a real commitment for them to do the work of moving everything into one home or the other.

And then what would happen if they discovered that cohabiting wasn't their cup of tea? The question rattled around in her head, unsettling her more than she wanted it to. If the experiment didn't work, going back to their normal lives might no longer be possible.

Just the phrase "normal life" made Alice blink back tears. Would their familiar daily lives ever return?

For too many months now, she felt shadowed by danger.

They had to plan how to safely get groceries and cope with medical needs that, before COVID-19, were met simply by a trip to the market or the doctor's office. Occasionally, one or the other had ended up in the hospital, but that was to be expected at this age. Now, living alone and not worrying beyond the needs of the day no longer seemed possible. The immediate urgency to join forces to be safe, required a real shift in lifestyle.

Their once easy decisions, whether or not to meet for lunch, or choosing between this movie and that one, were now memories, part of a lost world. She paced back and forth between her computer and the bookcase where her beige landline phone sat fossil-like on the top shelf.

Mother Jones was watching her alertly. The cat always took interest in any activity that might indicate a refill of her food bowl. Or perhaps that intense stare was a communication about something far more consequential than kibble. Alice would never know.

The loud buzzing of the cell phone provoked a disapproving glare from Mother Jones. Alice stepped over to her computer table to scoop up the pesky little phone. Grasping the cell firmly, she studied the caller ID.

Oh dear! She considered not answering. Taking a call from Bernice would mean interrupting her already complex decision-making process. But if Bernice showed up at her door in the next minute or two, ignoring the call could become embarrassing. She didn't want to give up the extra time it would take to smooth her friend's ruffled feathers.

Just pick up and deal with it, Alice!

"Yes, Bernice?" She attempted to sound welcoming. She lowered herself into the computer chair, preparing for her friend's report from the outer world. Bernice was often the first to have her finger on the pulse of the entire village buzz, from local crime to natural disasters. What Alice most appreciated was that her friend could always give a full report on Mama Maya's soups and pastries du jour.

"I hear that the governor might establish a stay-at-home and mandatory mask order for the entire state!" Bernice said. "And you better believe there were arguments breaking out around town! That billionaire who bought the old Morgan farm on Loud Hill Road? He was carrying on about government takeovers, telling everyone at Mama Maya's that it was their patriotic duty to resist tyranny. He says everyone should refuse to wear masks or stay at home as an act of political protest!"

"Yes, I had heard this morning on ... " Alice was cut off almost immediately. Bernice was not skilled in the art of the give-and-take conversation.

"... and that waitress with biceps like a lumberjack?" Bernice continued, "she told Fancy Pants to stuff it or she'd toss her tray of coffee and breakfast specials onto his fake farmer boots! Then it got worse - "

"Bernice," Alice cut in quickly, "I need to make a call. Is there something in particular I should know?"

"I just wanted to make sure you were all right," Bernice said stiffly, the underlying hurt in her voice signaling volumes. "I called to see if you need anything. Now that the virus is spreading, you're not going to be able to go out and do your own errands, you know! I can easily pick up most anything you might need."

The offer was genuine. Bernice, generous to the core, was always ready to show up for her friends. She was especially dedicated to Alice's well-being, and Alice felt a pang of remorse. It was too easy to hurt Bernice's feelings. Now she had already caused pain, and they had barely begun the conversation.

At the same time, she was impatient to call Gerard.

"Thank you, Bernice, for your concern," she said, trying to sound extravagantly grateful. "You're right. I will have to make plans to get the provisions I need. I'm just not ready to focus on that piece of the puzzle right now. Everything seems to be changing so fast!"

"I don't know whatever happened to your travel plans with Gerard," Bernice continued gruffly, "but you know you're not going to be able to go outside the country for a long time.

"Our trip to France was postponed months ago," Alice reminded her. Why was Bernice poking at that old disappointment?

She had undoubtedly been delighted when Alice and Gerard decided not go overseas, Alice thought. When she was serving in the Marines, Bernice had experienced life beyond the U.S. borders in a very different way than Alice would ever understand. When she first heard about the long awaited trip to France, she told Alice in no uncertain terms that she herself was not a big fan of frivolous civilian travelers who risked harm in their self-indulgent pursuits of pleasure.

"Even if you tried to go," Bernice said firmly, "even if you could get yourselves over there, you and your Monsieur could be incarcerated when you tried to get back into the country! But here's an idea," she continued cheerfully. "You know Mr. Fancy Pants the anti-masker? Maybe you should ask him to fly you to Paris on his own private jet!"

Something was different with Bernice this morning, the more Alice thought about it. Bernice sounded like the actors in those TV ads for some new miracle drug for seniors that seemed to give everyone a giddiness tendency.

"That jerk would sure boost his image around town if he did something big and splashy for you, Alice," Bernice continued, chuckling mischievously. "Seriously, it wouldn't surprise me if he shows off his big bucks by offering to fly locals wherever they want to go. You should get him to take you up to Gerard's heart appointments at Dartmouth Medical Center!"

"I'll think on it," Alice said. After enduring a prolonged silence, she was more impatient to end the conversation. "Bernice dear, thank you so much for checking on me. Are you all right?"

"I'm figuring it out as I go," Bernice said. She was always close-mouthed when it came to reporting on her own life. "All righty then, you know if you need anything, all you have to do is pick up the phone."

Alice was not surprised when the phone abruptly clicked off. Bernice's capacity for social pleasantries was limited.

Now she must call Gerard before there was yet another interruption.

Chapter Three
Central Florida

"Anything I should know?" Charles asked LaTonya, the day shift supervisor, as he hung up his jacket in the staff locker room. It was the standard question when he came on.

LaTonya was in the process of trying to juggle her huge ring of keys, her large shoulder bag, a take-out meal, her cell phone, and a potted orchid plant. She was headed home, and it was already ten minutes past the time she was supposed to finish her shift.

"You can read my notes!" she told him irritably. "I got no time to make it home before my girl finishes cooking our dinner, less time even than I had before I had to stop everything to answer a bell that had been ringing for at least five minutes because Miss You-Know-Who wasn't getting off her fanny. You know how she can be! Too busy reading some book she keeps telling me I got to read, some foolishness about angels and being centered and all that stuff she's always on about. I told her I don't have time to get centered, thank you very much, because my staff is making me do their jobs as well as my own. I told her you better find yourself an armed and dangerous angel, missy, to shield you when I finally lose my center and my e-qua-nim-i-ty and write you up!"

Charles pulled down his mask for a brief instant so he could virtually embrace her with a big smile. LaTonya liked to say that one of his smiles was guaranteed to melt the heart of anyone in his path.

"I feel you!" he said. "You know I do! Go on then, go home to your baby and enjoy that meal she's making, and put those sweet feet up and have a mega huge bowl of ice cream tonight! You deserve it! I don't need a single thing from you, Ms. Super Woman, not a thing!"

LaTonya winked as she passed him. "You keep giving me those smiles, Mister Sweet Talker, and I'm just goin' to lose my train of thought and float right past home without a care in the world."

A second later, she stuck her head back into the room. "See what you can do with Miz Rosabelle, if you have time. Her grandbaby didn't stay tonight to help her with her dinner, so course she won't eat. She just keeps rocking and crying. Hope Angel Girl comes back later tonight or Miz Rosabelle won't sleep. Good luck, Charles!"

After Charles read LaTonya's notes, he strolled down the hall and stuck his head in Room 8 to see if Miz Rosabelle had calmed down. The old woman was slumped over in her recliner, moaning very softly and working the soft wool in her tattered purple shawl.

"Good evening, Miz Rosabelle!" he called softly from the doorway.

She looked up and stared at him. The moaning stopped. After a full minute, she bowed her head and began picking again at her shawl.

Charles went over and squatted down next to her chair. "You worried about your grandbaby?" he asked her gently. "She'll be here soon. You know she won't forget you, Miz Rosabelle!"

He stood up to inspect the untouched tray of food someone had moved over onto the top of the dresser. He smiled down at her. "You missing out on some good-looking biscuits and gravy here! You think you could eat a few bites if I warm this up? You want us to pray for your girl Kori that she gets herself over here now?"

There was no response. After another minute, Charles covered the dinner tray and took it down to the nurse's station. "Anybody want to record what Room 8 didn't eat?" he suggested, and went back to the staff lounge. He thought he'd see if any of the ice cream sandwiches he kept in the fridge for long nights might still be there. If he couldn't get Miz Rosabelle to eat an ice cream sandwich, he'd try something from the cafeteria later.

It was very unusual for Kori to skip the five o'clock dinner date with her Gram. Still, Charles didn't think there was anything to worry about. He knew Kori was busy meeting with the latest potential plaintiff for the lawsuit.

By nine o'clock, Charles suggested to the nurse that she give Miz Rosabelle a shot so they could all get some rest. Twenty minutes later, the pitiful sobs and whimpers had subsided and Miz Rosabelle was finally asleep.

Charles decided he would give Kori a call. He felt bad that he hadn't been able to get coverage so he could go with her to meet the newest whistleblower. He thought she should have called him by now. Suddenly he was more worried about her than her grandmother.

Chapter Four
Western Massachusetts

Alice sighed heavily. Instead of heading out for Gerard's apartment, she was dawdling, finding little things that needed doing. She knew she was putting off this conversation with Gerard. Maybe she should consult with Felicia before she talked to Gerard.

When her phone buzzed, she expected it to be Gerard. "Bon jour!" she greeted him in her most sultry tones. "Are you ready for a visit?"

Before she could listen for a response, she was jarred by loud knocking on her back door. "I'm sorry, but someone's at my door," she said without checking to see who her caller was. She dropped the phone as she propelled herself toward the door.

When Alice peered out the side window, she was very surprised to see Warp. Her heart began to race. Could something have happened to Gerard?

Her hand flew to her throat. Why would Warp be here at her back door unless something serious had happened? A phone call would have been enough for a simple message. Bolts of fear were coursing through her body, and she suddenly needed to sit down.

"Hey, Alice," Warp called through the window, "it's Warp. Hope I didn't scare you. You OK in there?"

"I'm coming," Alice called out. She was annoyed with herself for sounding so feeble. "I was just on the phone. The door should be unlocked. Come on in."

She trotted back to scoop up the phone from where she had dropped it. She turned to smile uncertainly at Warp, who was gingerly pushing open the back door. He stepped cautiously into her kitchen.

"Come right in!" she said, trying to sound as if she wasn't worried to death.

Warp was wearing his COVID mask. Where was her own mask?

She felt a sudden stab of panic. She suddenly realized that they should not be meeting inside her house. She should send him back out onto the porch. "Warp, dear," she said, "I'm afraid we really should be talking outside. And I must get my mask."

His pale face flushed slightly. "OMG, Alice! Sorry! I wasn't thinking! I'll get myself right back out the door!" In one long backward stride, he was safely back on her back porch.

Social norms had shifted and blurred as the pandemic dragged on. For several months now, no one had come into her home except Gerard. Before COVID, she would have been delighted to see Warp walking through her front door, and she would have welcomed him with a big hug.

Now she anxiously grabbed for her own mask, hanging on the hook beside the back door where she always put it.

She still felt overwhelmed by adding her mask to everything else she had to manage: her portable oxygen tank, her glasses, her cane, her hearing aids, and her purse. It was exhausting, just getting all the paraphernalia attached in the right order. Now she secured her mask, picked up her small portable oxygen tank, and moved as quickly as she could onto the back porch.

She wished that she could have given Warp the hug that she usually stretched up on her tiptoes to offer. Instead, she waved animatedly at him as if she were greeting someone at the train station. Her vigorous enthusiasm was embarrassing. The virus made it so hard to transmit even the simplest of feelings.

He was stretched out in one of her big white rockers, his legs so long that his shoes were half off the porch. Alice had a small back porch with just enough space for two rocking chairs.

The mask he wore looked to be hand-sewn, very colorful and somewhat distracting. There was a lot of black and red in the design, and the area covering his mouth had the image of a zipper in bold silver across black.

It was reassuring to see his smiling eyes above the mask.

"Tell me right away!" she said, her heart still racing, "Is Gerard all right?"

"Yup, I guess so,'" Warp said. "He's not sick or anything like that." He studied Alice thoughtfully. "Has he been talking to you about his, uh, his conspiracy theories?"

Alice stared at him. She could feel her heart settling back down, but her brain felt buzzy. Gerard had been upset about the virus like everyone else in the world, but he hadn't seemed overly preoccupied with conspiracy-related issues.

Warp was obviously worried about whatever Gerard had told him.

"I haven't heard anything specific from Gerard about this," Alice told him.

"Over the past few days, Monsieur Gerard's been calling me to talk about his theory of how the virus got started," Warp said, not quite looking at Alice.

Alice had learned to trust Warp's good judgment. She was invariably grateful that his bilingual proficiency made it possible for her to negotiate the occasional communication challenges she and Gerard bumped up against.

Fortunately, this was rare. She could think of very few times when Gerard hadn't shared something important with her. They were beyond the age when they needed to keep secrets from each other. Now, apparently, she was to be illuminated about something Gerard was rolling around in his always active brain.

"Can I fix you some coffee or tea, or bring you a glass of water?" she asked. "It sounds like we need to talk awhile."

"Nothing for me, thanks. I'll jump right in, if you don't mind. But you know, if I tried to explain every detail Gerard has been telling me, it could take hours." Even though he was masked, Alice could tell Warp was smiling. She could see the conspiratorial twinkle in his eyes.

"By all means," she urged him. "Summarize!"

"Well, he's been very worked up, for sure. I was surprised when he called and asked me to come over. When I asked if it could wait a day or two, he said no, it was urgent! So I zipped right over there, thinking he might be having some trouble with his heart. You know how he doesn't want to worry you if he can avoid it," he added, looking nervously at Alice.

She nodded quickly, gesturing for him to continue.

"So I was kind of expecting him to ask for a ride to the hospital in Greenfield. But when I got to his apartment, he took me straight out to the back porch. I figured he wasn't in a rush to get medical attention."

Alice felt unbearably impatient for Warp to get to the heart of what he wanted to tell her about Gerard.

"So, Gerard explains we have to go outside where the roar of the river will stop anyone from hearing what he's about to tell me. Then he tells me he has information about how the COVID virus started. He thinks it was stolen by scientists from a lab somewhere, maybe in Canada."

Warp gave Alice a don't-blame-the-messenger look.

"So the gist of it," he continued, "is that somehow - and he hasn't really explained that part to me yet - some scientists lost control of the virus. He says that's when it first began to infect the people in the Wuhan province in China. I can't really explain his whole theory, but he says there's been a big cover-up."

He stopped, waiting for Alice to respond. "So that's kind of the Cliff Notes version," he concluded.

Alice stared at Warp, her eyebrows raised as high as they could go. She hesitated to sound critical before she learned more, but it sounded too much like one of those conspiracy theories that Number 45 loved to generate.

"It sure has me confused," Warp said unhappily. "It's weird that Monsieur Gerard would get so intense about it, like he's got to get to the authorities before the planet blows up! I don't know, maybe I haven't been able to translate correctly. This stuff isn't, like, anything that I know anything about."

Alice was truly baffled by how wild it sounded. Before he went off to Africa, Gerard had spent many years of his life doing research on bioweapons. Undoubtedly he was basing his speculations on his expertise. Not so many years ago, he played a major role in helping her expose the U.S. anthrax letters scam, and his knowledge had been invaluable.

Still, it had been a long time since he left the military research world. Maybe he was just getting confused by the media information constantly swirling around. Could he be slipping? Maybe that good science brain of his had been fogged by too many COVID worries, and too much stress. He also had been through some serious bouts of ill health recently. Maybe she hadn't been paying close enough attention.

"Does he want to do something specific about his theories?" she asked Warp. Now she was worried. Re-organizing their everyday lives was becoming urgent, and she didn't want Gerard to get too distracted.

"Well, uh, yup," Warp said reluctantly. "He wants to reconnect with his scientist contacts from the past. He's been talking about when you were inside that military base investigating that bio-weapons mess? He's thinking maybe he could get back in there to find someone who could help him, uh, scope this out?"

Alice shuddered. "I can't imagine how Gerard could just breeze onto the base these days,'" she said. "We got in by a fluke, really. They would never let us on the base now!"

Warp ran his fingers through his long hair and stared at his feet. Alice knew that he had more than enough worries without Gerard's latest mission.

Although she didn't even know what was going on with Warp these days, she understood that he couldn't do all the face-to-face work with addicts because of all the COVID restrictions. He must be juggling so much.

"Warp," she said, "let me see if I can help Gerard so you can focus more on what to do for yourself and Ruby. I'm going over to see him now. I'll call you once I've talked to him."

"Cool," Warp said quickly. "But, like, really, no worries, Alice! You know Monsieur Gerard has done, well you know, so much for me. Always glad when I can help."

"I am grateful to you for letting me know about Gerard's new preoccupation," Alice told him. "I'll do the best I can to try to fathom what he has in mind, and if I need your help, I'll ask."

It was hard for Alice not to hug Warp as he stood up to leave.

"You know I'm always there for you guys," Warp said. "You be careful, Alice," he added, waving over his shoulder as he went down the back steps.

"Give Ruby a big hug from me," Alice called out to him. A minute later she heard the van roar down her driveway.

She gathered up all her things, admonishing herself to get herself into the car before she completely changed her mind about her invitation to Gerard.

Mother Jones eyed her thoughtfully, and yawned. Apparently, human beings were never able to just sit still and be one with their universe. She was a cat who knew this better than most, but had long since given up trying to teach her human companion anything.

Chapter Five
Central Florida

The shape beside the fence looked like it could be someone passed out. Micah didn't want to get too close, but he was curious. Maybe if the dude was out cold, he could even grab something he was needing, like some cash, or a watch or something he could sell.

He moved slowly across the patches of dirt and old asphalt in the vacant lot. If the person sat up, he could always take off.

It was too early for anyone to be out and about, so he wasn't too worried that someone would see him poking around the guy. He himself would be sleeping like the rest of the city if he wasn't up waiting for his next delivery. Couldn't count on anything being on time these days, not except Amazon.

He'd been imagining those Amazon trucks, delivery guys in those uniforms showing up with his product! It could happen. He'd seen enough TV ads to believe that anything could happen in the world's craziest country. His country, for better or worse.

A few feet away from the body, he stopped and sucked in his breath. This wasn't a dude. He was looking at a lady. She was Black, and not too much older than him. She was dressed nice, kind of a sporty look, with new-looking shoes. He checked out the lady's face, a real banged up mess. Looked to him like that was blood on her face and her shirt.

He took another step closer. Could be she was passed out. But also could be she was dead. He felt a ripple of fear. He looked over his shoulder, looked all around checking out both directions. No one yet out on the streets.

This was a situation he didn't care for.

He should check and see if she was breathing. But what if the cops drove by? They could bust him for homicide? Or if she was alive, they would put the blame on him. Could even shoot him, just like all the other brothers. Rest in peace, he said inside his head.

"I'm going to look for Big Ruthie," he said out loud so maybe she'd hear him and know that he'd be back. Then he walked back across the lot without looking back. When he turned the corner, he was sweating, then he started shivering too. He could feel himself getting all nervous, second guessing himself.

Bad as he felt, he made himself go find Big Ruthie. He'd sweet talk her into checking on the lady by the fence. Ruthie used to be a nurse, and she could tell real quick if someone was getting close to passing. "Your boy's goin' to code!" she'd warn you, and you'd know you better get something in his veins ASAP or he'd be gone.

Ruthie was sitting in the doorway of the bank where she could get shade just about all day. And no one be moving her off her spot on Sunday. Even though it was a sunny day, she was all wrapped up, her coats, plastic bags, sleeping bag. Ruthie would tell anyone who asked her that she liked being hot. "I finally got myself down South here where I didn't ever have to be cold! I said Lord, this here is my forever home!"

Micah tried for awhile to wake her up, just repeating her name. She just kept on nodding and dreaming, shooing her hand at him as if he was a fly. Finally he kicked gently at her foot.

Big Ruthie opened one eye and glared at him. "What you have to do that for?" she asked. "I was having a beautiful dream, and you interrupted! You know how I feel about interruptions, Little Brother."

"I'm sorry, Miss Ruthie, but I got an emergency. I had to wake you."

She opened both eyes so she could look him up and down. "What kind of emergency?" she asked, frowning at him.

"I got to ask you to come and look at someone over on Washington Street and Magnolia. You know that empty lot over there?"

"Tell Mr. Someone to get hisself over here and then I'll see about helping him," she said. "I'm not giving up my spot, and I'm not walking four blocks over. He needs help, he comes to me. That's how it works. You know that, Mic!"

Micah squatted down close. "It's a lady, and I don't know if she's dead or not," he said quietly. "She's not from here, I know that.

"She Black?" Ruthie asked.

"Yes ma'am," Micah told her. "She got beat up bad. Don't know nothing about her, but she might be dead and she might not. You got to get over there with me, Miss Ruthie. It will be on both of us if we leave her over there for the rats. You got to come with me."

Ruthie groaned. "You going to have to get my chair from under that pile of stuff right there, and then you got to help me get into it. Mighty big job for a little shrimp of a boy like you!" She smiled at him. "You think you up to that, Little Brother?"

Micah snorted. Why did everyone under-estimate him! He might be small but he was mighty. He wasn't really sure how old he was, but he knew that he was still growing. He took care of himself just fine, and Big Ruthie knew it.

One time when a hyper-cop was out bashing Black kids like him for no good reason, he'd got his face split open pretty bad and Miss Ruthie had stitched him back together real good. He knew what she was capable of, and she knew the same about him. They'd been good friends a few years now.

"Ok, Mama," he said, "let's get you ready for take-off!"

He pulled her raggedy old wheelchair out from under a pile of her stuff, then organized the pile so it looked almost neat. He put her special handmade poster sign on top of it: *This belong to Big Ruthie. I love my neighbors but you touch it, you in trouble, no exception!*

Getting Ruthie up into her chair was a project best done by two strong adults, but Micah pumped himself up. He heaved her up and into her chair with the skill of a professional weight lifter. "Here we go, Mama!" he said, and they took off.

When they got to the empty lot, Micah was hoping the lady would be gone, but he could see that no such miracle had happened. He pushed Ruthie across the lot to where the body lay beside the fence.

"Same," he said.

"Wheel me closer, Micah, so I can touch her. That's good. Now you got to take her arm and pull her wrist up to me."

Micah hated the thought of touching a possible dead woman, but he did what he was told. He was relieved that she didn't feel stone cold, although she was definitely cool. Too cool.

Ruthie held her wrist a long time. "I think she's still got a pulse," she said. "Faint, but I think I feel something. Now you have to do the next thing, Little Brother. You kneel down and put your head on her chest where her heart be and you listen."

Micah did what he was told. It scared him, thinking what could happen if the cops drove by. But with Big Ruthie right there, he thought it might be safer. He listened and listened. Maybe he could hear something faint or maybe not. "I don't really know," he said. "I think, yes! I hear a little tiny thump, but then I think maybe I just want to hear something."

Ruthie leaned over so far that Micah was afraid she was going to pitch right out of the chair and fall onto the body. She leaned towards the woman's face, until she could gently push up one eyelid.

A tiny sound came from the body and it made Micah pull back and jump to his feet. "I think maybe she moan?" he said. "Did you hear that?"

Ruthie sat back up. "We got to let the police know she's here," she said. "You wheel me back to my spot and then we'll get someone to make the call, or else I'll yell my loudest until some cop comes to shut me up. This poor girl hasn't yet left this world!"

Chapter Six
Western Massachusetts

Alice had just stepped into the bathroom to check herself in the mirror before leaving the house. Felicia's voice trumpeted from the back porch, startling her.

"Hello in there, Alice!" she shouted. "I've got my arms full of groceries and I'm about to drop everything!"

Alice scuttled across the room as fast as she could to open the door. Felicia was half-buried under cloth bags spilling over with edibles.

"I've just about cleaned out most of the produce section at the Family Market!" she exclaimed triumphantly. "Everyone went shopping as soon as they heard the governor's shut-down order! Not a roll of toilet paper left on the shelves! No paper towels, no tissues, and just a few packs of over-priced party napkins. I grabbed them, and then filled up my bags with dry goods and vegetables. Oh, and coffee, of course!"

Alice moved forward to help Felicia load her bags onto the small kitchen counter.

"No you don't! Not a step closer!" Felicia barked at her from behind her very chic mask, deftly side-stepping Alice's access. "You may not agree, but I believe it's not safe for you to get this close to me. Why don't you go outside and get some fresh air. I'll call you when I'm done putting the perishables in the fridge, then you can put on your mask and we'll have a visit outside."

Alice stared at Felicia in surprise. She was more than tempted to take a five minute nap. She backed slowly away and went to lie down in her bedroom. "I'm leaving the door open, Felicia," she called out, "so we may at least attempt a shouted conversation."

There was no response from the kitchen, and Alice closed her eyes to think more about Warp, and about Gerard's new preoccupation. Suddenly she did a mental double-take as she remembered the quantity of groceries Felicia seemed to be delivering.

She gasped in alarm, and sat up on the edge of the bed. "Good heavens, Felicia!" she called out. "All those groceries can't possibly be for me! We'll need to divide it up. Surely you don't think I could consume all that?"

"Who knows how long we'll be sequestered," Felicia shouted back. "Hang on a minute, Alice. I have to run the water until it gets hot. I need to wipe every item with my Au Naturel disinfectant wipes, and then I'll wash the vegetables."

Felicia had the lung power of an opera singer, Alice thought, realizing she could hear every word Felicia said.

Even though she and Felicia had been in daily contact throughout the pandemic, she hadn't realized how extremely careful her friend had become about all the wiping and washing. Alice thought it was common knowledge that this level of disinfecting groceries wasn't really necessary. Then again, nothing about the virus was completely known.

She felt overwhelmed by Felicia's presence. She hadn't planned how to stock up now that the virus had spiked again. She certainly had to give this more thought if she was to create a pod with Gerard.

Thinking more about Warp's report, she wondered if maybe Gerard just wanted to get back into his work. Maybe he felt called to do something heroic now as the whole world was becoming plagued by this terrifying pandemic. Was she being selfish to want to keep him safely at home here with her? Maybe moving in with her would seriously disrupt this renewed commitment to his call as a researcher.

She was momentarily flooded with memories. It had been long ago when she first had to make a decision about their relationship. Gerard was ready to leave the U.S. to start a new research project in Africa. Her children were teenagers, still living at home with her and coping with the inevitable complexities of the divorce. Gerard had begged her to go to Africa with him.

He wanted her to join him in an exotic new life as he began his new career. It was a moral necessity to abandon the study of biological weapons. She had been excited for him, fascinated by his new research on the environmental and social factors in understanding the health of chimpanzees.

Although it had meant giving up the most passionate romance of her life, she had refused to go to Africa. How could she go to another continent and further disrupt the lives of her three teen-agers? It was out of the question. She had to give him up.

Could she be facing another crossroads now?

Felicia's voice interrupted her memories. "Alice, if you and I were to shelter together, these provisions should be plenty for both of us for the next several weeks, if not months. I've got enough of everything here to keep us both healthy and satisfied for a good long time."

"Oh my," Alice whispered, stunned by this new possibility. The negotiations with Gerard were more than enough to prepare for, but Felicia's offer added a whole unexpected dimension.

She felt almost paralyzed by Felicia's invitation.

Maybe she should simply continue to shelter alone. Of the three of them, she was probably most vulnerable to the ravages of COVID-19 because of her fragile lungs. Living alone in her home would help her avoid contaminating Gerard or anyone else who might feel obligated to take care of her. Why hadn't she thought of this sooner?

Felicia came into the bedroom, still drying her hands from the disinfection process. "Of course Gerard must live with us too," she said matter-of-factly. "We'll bring along all his special cooking pans and baking ingredients when we go to collect him. I'm look-ing forward to daily samples of his exquisite baking! I think the three of us can manage being together under one roof, don't you?"

"Oh, dear me, I don't know," Alice said weakly. "Maybe. I just don't know."

She tried to imagine the three of them co-existing for what could be months, maybe even years. She felt a strange combination of nervousness and then an unexpected ripple of curiosity.

She treasured the quiet intimacy she had with Gerard now, the comfortable silences and the space afforded them by maintaining separate dwellings. It had been difficult enough, only minutes be-fore Felicia's bombshell, to picture giving up the ease of living alone. She had barely begun to unfurl the plan of having Gerard as her housemate. Now she had to consider the two of them.

How could she keep up with all the unexplored possibilities?

"It just came to me that we should all three live at my house!" Felicia said, sitting down companionably on the bed. "You two could have the downstairs bedroom to yourselves, and the living room. Since my bedroom is upstairs, you'll have plenty of privacy. I am perfectly capable of entertaining myself, as you know!"

Alice wondered if Felicia was at least a little ambivalent about her invitation. There was a long silence. Then she realized she needed to speak. "What a kind and generous offer," she managed to say.

"The more I think about it," Felicia said, "I believe it's the best choice for all of us. You certainly can't stay with Gerard in that third floor apartment of his. The stairs would kill you sooner than COVID!

"If Gerard stays at your house, I don't believe you can take care of him by yourself, should he get the virus. And, Alice dear, I can't see how he could take care of you if you get sick, even though he would want to do everything in his power to protect you.

"I have the biggest house," she continued, "and the best vehicle for transporting all three of us to the hospital or anywhere else we might need to go, if it comes to that. I also have a pantry full of herbal remedies and root vegetables, and plant-based proteins that will boost our immune systems. It's possible that we won't even get sick!

"As you know, I have an abundance of dried food to supplement us, not to mention what's right here in today's co-op shopping. I could carry these bags back out to the car now, and we wouldn't even have to divide it all up."

Alice was still trying to clear her thoughts when the phone buzzed. It was Gerard, his voice hearty with excitement. His buoyancy surprised Alice.

"Alice, *ma chèrie*, I have something *très, très magnifique* to tell to you!"

Alice shook her head, blinking in surprise.

"I have done the research on the ah, the *crêche* of the virus!" he explained excitedly. "Perhaps I guess the place it first grows, where is the birth home of this *petite* cell! This is good news, *très très bon*! If I am finding the answer, I can find, ah, how to say this? I perhaps make the discovery of the cure! *Ç'est* possible! You must come so I explain to you!"

Alice now felt beyond overwhelmed.

"Gerard, *mon chèr*, I will come as soon as I can," she said, hanging up before he could continue. She turned to Felicia. "Gerard thinks he can find the cure for the virus!" she said, staring wild-eyed at her friend.

"But how exciting!" Felicia trilled, her enthusiasm as robust as Gerard's. Maybe, Alice mused, if they were all living together, these two would support each other even when she herself could not rise to their peaks of intensity.

This might work out after all.

Gerard's theories about the virus would have to wait until the housing question was resolved, though. How ironic, she mused, that a toxic biological threat could be the impetus to push her and Gerard to live under one roof. It had been the mysterious anthrax virus, threatening the health of the American public, which had originally brought the two of them back together after forty years apart.

Right now, though, she had to focus on her options. What would Mother Jones choose, she wondered. That was easy. The cat would, of course, vote for Alice to remain at home alone.

Alice shook her head. She was not going to give her animal companion a voice on this question. The cat might rule the roost, but it was up to her, the human, to decide where Mother Jones's roost would be.

Chapter Seven
Central Florida

Kori could hear a voice very close to her. "Hey lady! Wake up!"

She tried to move, but she was overcome by stabs of pain all over her body. With great effort, she finally managed to open one eye. A young Black man was squatting next to her, staring at her. He looked terrified. She tried to smile at him, but he hopped backwards as if she had suddenly grown fangs.

"Hey, I didn't mean to scare you," she tried to tell him, but only garbled sounds came out. The peculiar sounds coming from her stunned her back into silence.

The young man stayed where he was. He cautiously reached toward her, but she jerked away from his hand when it made contact with her face. Everything hurt so bad!

"You gonna get help real soon," he said. "I gotta leave you before the cops come, but they're on the way. I can hear the siren now. God bless!" Suddenly he was gone, disappearing so fast she wondered if she had imagined him.

Where am I?

She heard the siren stop, then the crackle of the police radio. Soon she was looking up into the face of a white policeman kneeling down next to her. She felt someone on the other side, then a female voice. "Ma'am, can you hear my voice?"

She tried to answer yes, but the sound that came out wasn't the word she was trying to say.

"Ma'am," the woman spoke again. "I'm Officer Leandra Boudrie, and my partner here is Officer McKenna. We need to ask you a few questions, and try to determine what kind of medical attention you need, OK?"

"OK," Kori said. Once again she heard the word her brain formed transformed into something unintelligible. The male cop, whose face was very near hers, was frowning. "Can you understand what we're saying?' he asked.

Kori tried to nod but the pain stopped her.

"She could be zonked on something, or have some kind of hearing impairment," the officer said to his partner. "May not even speak English. Let's go with some simple stuff."

He addressed Kori again. "You tell us if you understand by shaking your head for no and nodding your head for yes," he told Kori.

Kori tried again to move her head but the pain was so sharp that she cried out. She could feel the woman's hand touch very lightly on her shoulder.

"Looks like you got hurt pretty bad," she said gently. "Can you blink once for yes and two for no?"

Kori blinked once.

"Good," Officer Boudrie said. "Can you understand what we're saying?"

Kori again blinked once.

"Have you used any drugs in the past twenty-four hours?"

Kori blinked twice. She felt a flicker of annoyance. Would they ask anyone that, or was it because she was Black?

"Do you know where you are?"

Kori blinked twice again.

"Are you in pain?" Officer McKenna asked.

Kori blinked once, then quickly blinked once again. She would have screamed YES if she could.

"If you were giving your pain a number, would it be a 3 for it hurts but not too bad?

Kori blinked twice.

"Would it be even higher, like a 7 or 8, like you can't hardly stand it?"

Kori blinked once.

"I don't know," the female cop said. "You're making it too complicated. Let me try, ok? Would your pain be a 9 or 10, like yes you need to go to the hospital?"

Kori blinked once. She was relieved when she heard the lady cop radio for an ambulance.

"While we're waiting for medical assistance," the man said, speaking very slowly and loudly as if Kori was hearing-impaired, "we need some kind of identification. Do you have your driver's license in a wallet somewhere on your person?"

Kori didn't know. She was trying to remember anything at all about how she got here, wherever this place was. She must have been driving. Was her wallet in her pocket? She was not about to move to retrieve it. If they moved her to look for the wallet, she knew the pain would make her cry out again.

What could have caused this kind of pain? She must have been in a car accident. But she wasn't inside a car and she didn't think she was on the pavement either. She could tell that she was on some combination of grass and hard-packed dirt.

Where was the young Black man she remembered? Where had he come from? He had called the police to come help her, she thought, but he had been quick to disappear. Was she somewhere on the West Side? How had she gotten here?

Should she be afraid? The female cop seemed to be kind enough, but the white male? There was no point in trying to think. Her head hurt way too much. Why couldn't she remember anything?

Officer Boudrie was in the passenger seat as they followed the ambulance to the hospital. "Weird, huh?" she said to McKenna. "No driver's license, beat up like a bad scene with a batterer, or hadn't paid some drug dealer. But I don't know why. Something about her doesn't seem like she fits either situation."

Officer McKenna shrugged. "Seems pretty typical to me, battered by a husband or boyfriend or by some pissed off dealer. Why not? She's in a vacant lot on the West Side, no purse or wallet, no ID. I don't see any mystery here."

Officer Boudrie snorted. "You're such a bigot, Jack! Don't you listen to any of the stuff they've been teaching in those race sensitivity trainings we've been getting?"

"All lives matter!" Officer McKenna said irritably. "I'm no racist, Lee. You know that! But let's face the facts here."

"You ever once bother to call me by my right name?" Leandra Boudrie snapped. "You start with that, you would get at least one point from me for effort. Not so hard to say, Jack. It's Lee-ann-dra! Simple! But that's not going to protect you when real shit comes down and you want me to have your back. Better get your racial sensitivity act together, Officer McKenna!"

She gave him a light thump on the bicep. "Now, do you want to learn something or you just going to hang onto your ignorant opinion?"

"OK. Miss Politically Correct All-knowing One, tell me," he

said, smiling through gritted teeth. Leandra sighed. Now he was going to be all sulky and pouty because she was calling him out.

"That young woman's got herself a good workout going on, I'd say. Very fit. And her clothes are, like, real quality but sporty, like tennis club or golf club clothes. She's gotta either be an athlete or rich or both. So what's she doing in the shady part of the West Side in a vacant lot all beat up? She doesn't look scrawny and wasted like an addict. And I just get a vibe that she's not a victim of domestic violence. Something doesn't fit, not for me."

The ambulance was pulling up to the Emergency entrance, and Officer McKenna pulled into the staff parking lot close by. "Let's see what they can figure out here," he said. "Maybe once they get her checked out, they'll even find some ID or she'll start talking."

Over an hour and two cups of hospital coffee later, the ER summoned the two officers. "Got only one piece of possible identifying evidence for you," a young woman in scrubs told them. "I can show it to you, but then I got to hang onto it so they can give it back to the patient. You take a look, take a picture if you want, then hand it back over, please. You're not planning to take her into custody, are you? The medical team's not going to let you do that today, not the condition she's in."

She handed a small multi-colored flyer to Officer Boudrie. The officers stepped away from the desk to examine the paper. It was a folded-up political flyer for Floriana Watson, a well-known African American candidate for state representative. The payoff was a hand-written message on the back. "Quit your trouble-making or you die, bitch!" The printing was rough but there was no ambiguity in the message.

"I know about this campaign," Officer Boudrie said. "Floriana Watson is running for state rep. That's a big deal. She's one more of those strong Black women showing up in politics all over the country. Everyone on the West Side knows her, and she's got a bunch of white Democrats supporting her too. That's where we should go to find out who our victim is."

"I've heard of her," McKenna said. "Do I get some sensitivity points for that? You think someone's trying to mess with her campaign? You'd have to be blind not to see those posters up all over along Canal Street and even Flagler and all the businesses on the Beach Side and West Side, and even a billboard on U.S.1. Go with Flo!"

"If this is some kind of message for the candidate, it's probably some racist crap," Officer Boudrie said, "but what kind of 'trouble-making' in a local election like this could get someone nearly killed?"

"Did Trump endorse the opponent or something?" Officer McKenna asked. "Maybe the victim got in the way of those Proud Boys or something like that! This could make the network news, you know?" McKenna looked pretty excited.

Leandra Boudrie decided she needed a little break from McKenna.

"I'm calling someone who's been working on the campaign," she said. "You feel like going to the cafeteria and getting something while I make my call?"

McKenna shrugged. "You want something?" he asked.

Boudrie smiled at him. "I want that lemon meringue pie we had last week, remember, when we brought in that dog bite guy? If they don't have it, then something like a brownie. And a black coffee, please."

As McKenna walked away, Boudrie reached her contact on the first ring. "Hey," she said, "I need to know if you have names of folks working on the Floriana Harris campaign? I need a list as close to now as possible. May be a homicide involved."

Chapter Eight
Western Massachusetts

"Felicia," Alice said, hesitating a little, "you're so kind to include Gerard in your invitation. But there's another thing. Would you consider taking in Mother Jones?"

Felicia beamed. "Well, that goes without saying! Just as I knew enough not to invite you to stay with me if Gerard wasn't part of the package. I haven't had a house pet for years now, but we'll work out whatever bumps we encounter. Of course, my dear, bring Mother Jones!"

Running her hands through her curly grey hair as she stretched out her back, she looked thoughtfully at Alice. "As a matter of fact, your cat may be the answer to my latest mouse problem in the cellar!"

Alice gave her a dubious look. "Surely you know that Mother Jones has long ago stopped providing her own meals. She's a fat cat who has no ambitions that involve exercise."

Felicia nodded, chuckling. "Now, Alice, although I know you need some time with Gerard to talk this over, the sooner we become a pod, the better for all of us. Once we're under one roof, we'll be able to help each other more easily. I have great faith that we'll be a very successful team."

"You're sure about all this?" Alice asked.

Felicia closed her eyes and began a series of tapping exercises that Alice had seen many times. Finally she opened her eyes, nodding joyfully. "This is exactly what I am supposed to be doing!" she exclaimed.

"I should head up to Gerard's now," Alice said, glancing at the kitchen clock. "We have some big changes to consider! We may have to get help from Warp to get some of his things down those three flights of stairs."

"Don't worry if you can't get everything packed up right away," Felicia told her. "We can work out ways to retrieve things bit by bit. But Alice, if possible, I'd like us to be settled under one roof by tomorrow evening. I'll zip down to the market so I can stock us with any toilet paper that might be left. We may have to sneak over the Canadian border if we run out! The Canadians are far too sensible to hoard such a thing!"

As Alice drove slowly up the winding road to Gerard's apartment, she looked at the pastures, and smiled at a small calf, well-protected by a group of grazing cows. This part of the world really was serene, virus or not.

She was starting to feel some comfort in the possibilities of her new housing option. If the three of them were living together, there would be someone to help Gerard take care of her if she was the first to get sick. And Felicia could help her take care of Gerard, if it came to that. As for Felicia, she couldn't imagine her friend getting the virus, not with all of the mental and physical health practices she was steeped in.

Thinking about all of Felicia's healthy habits, she reminded herself that she and Gerard would be subjected to a challenging diet of Felicia's healing herbs, oils, roots and other healthy edibles. At least Mother Jones would be spared new culinary challenges. Felicia had given up long ago trying to get Alice to put the cat on a vegan diet.

"Alice, you have come!" Gerard exclaimed as he opened the door. He glowed with energy. She considered herself lucky that he had left his computer long enough to let her in. Once he was caught up in a new project, he often became completely absorbed. At this moment, he seemed delighted by her arrival.

"I fix you *le café, oui? avec brioche?* and your favorite, *la confiture aux framboises!*" He ushered her into his tiny kitchen. Alice momentarily banished all thoughts of the complex world beyond these walls.

She immersed herself in the present moment, savoring the mouth-watering smell of freshly baked pastry, the aroma of dark French Roast coffee, and the delight she felt each time she was in Gerard's company. If only she could make this moment last.

Happily anticipating her coffee and straight-from-the-oven pastry, she went out to wait at the small table on the balcony. The sun was warm, and she could feel her body continue to relax. She watched the river from her perch high above the street, noticing how high it seemed as it rolled toward the bridge. The river was always dramatic in the early summer, the snow-melt from the mountains bringing it to such heights that it sometimes rose up over its banks onto the road. The run-off at the dam just beyond the bridge would be spectacular today.

She loved this view from Gerard's apartment. She wondered how long it would be before they could safely sit here again, able to enjoy whatever delicious meal he had magically created.

"Have you been listening to the radio this morning?" she asked. Gerard got most of his news from streaming Democracy Now at eight o'clock every morning. He entertained Alice by recreating his own version of the news, based on bits and pieces he absorbed as he drank his morning coffee.

"*Oui!*" Gerard told her, nodding vigorously. "The COVID, it is growing again, *oui*? Like the fires in California! *Ç'est incroyable!*"

As Gerard set out the coffee and brioches on the balcony table, Alice thought the morning's news was a good opener for the conversation. Gerard would surely agree that now the plague was creeping closer to their doorstep, they had to agree on a proactive plan. She gathered her energy to begin the conversation about Felicia's invitation.

But first, the food! With Gerard, she had learned the most basic rule of French life. Appreciating the food must happen before anything else was introduced into the conversation.

"Gerard, what a delicious repast! I have been so distracted today I don't think I ever remembered to eat my breakfast cereal." She took a large bite of her brioche to demonstrate her appetite.

Gerard beamed, his thick white eyebrows lifting as he smiled at her "*Oui, ma belle*, I feed you well so you must listen with ears open! There are secrets, *oui*, the secrets gigantique the television does not tell! I tell you something new. Perhaps, my dear Alice, I find the important secrets of the COVID virus!"

Gerard stopped to take a bite of his brioche, watching Alice intently.

She took another bite of brioche, liberally slathered with butter and homemade strawberry jam. She hesitated. She was savoring not only the food, but also this moment in time when they had not yet entered a new series of negotiations and compromises.

Gerard seized the opening and jumped back in. "In the past, you and I, we discover the secrets of the anthrax masquerade and who is responsible, *oui*?" He paused dramatically. "This was a danger to me and to you when we make the choice to investigate, oui?" He watched her face, quivering with the energy of his excitement. He was like a cat about to pounce.

Yes, Alice recalled, it had been dangerous. Having invited him into her high risk adventure, she had been horrified by the possibility that, after so many years, she might lose him again.

She quickly popped another luscious bite of brioche into her mouth. If only she could inoculate herself against the current dangers with perfect pastry, good French coffee, and a refusal to accept the reality of a world now riddled with disease and chaos.

She looked past Gerard at the rushing river. How glorious and yet treacherous it was! "Are you inviting me to join you in investigating something?" she asked, trying to keep her voice light. She had to manage the situation with some amount of playfulness so that she didn't completely deflate the balloon of excitement he was launching.

Gerard's hand shot forward, a halt signal. His demand for silence made Alice stop chewing her last delectable bite of the brioche. Danger was once again in the air. Her buttery fingers were still touching her lips as the delicious bite of pastry lost its taste. She took a large gulp of her coffee, trying to determine the sudden shift of mood.

It was clear that he was in his international spy mode. Alice knew this conversation about the virus would have to stop for now. She would relocate them. Using the gentlest voice she could summon, she suggested packing up everything, even the coffee.

"We'll drive right over to Salmon Falls, and finish our food there. The waterfall will give us privacy."

She was already on her feet, scooping up her plate, her coffee cup and the basket of pastries before Gerard could object. She knew he needed the thunderous roar of the massive waterfall to feel safe about this conversation, and it would be a good place to talk about Felicia's invitation.

The river was running very high. Unfortunately, where they sat on the bench beside the dam, the falls thundered so loudly that

Alice couldn't understand anything Gerard was trying to communicate.

"Oh dear," she said after a few minutes of frustration, "I fear we must simply give in to the roar of the water, enjoy the last sips of coffee, and talk more later." Gerard nodded as they took their last sips of coffee, then Alice gestured that they should get back into the car.

As Gerard bent down slightly to open the car door for her, Alice pulled him towards her for a quick kiss. "We'll talk about the virus investigation later," she murmured into his ear.

Just as Alice pulled into the handicap parking space in front of his apartment, her phone began to buzz. Gerard shook his head and went on up ahead of her.

Chapter Nine
Western Massachusetts

Alice sighed heavily. Bernice was calling again.

"Alice, I want you to know what I'm doing," Bernice said, sounding extremely anxious.

Alice took a calming breath. In the ever-shifting COVID world, she felt compassion for every living thing but she was not about to postpone the conversation she was determined to have with Gerard.

"Yes, Bernice," she said. "Can I call you back in just twenty minutes or so?"

"No!" Bernice gasped. "I really need you right now. This won't take long."

"What is going on?" Alice asked Bernice.

"I have just left the facility where my husband has been receiving medical care," Bernice said.

Alice was startled into complete silence. Hadn't Bernice sworn that her ex-husband could fall off the planet and she would feel nothing but relief?

"He is very ill," Bernice continued, "and because I'm still his health proxy, they called me. He seems to have the virus. They wanted me to come in and sign some papers before they intubated him."

"Oh good heavens!" Alice said, her hand flying to her heart. "Oh my! I'm so sorry, Bernice. This must be very complicated for you," she added after a sufficient pause.

"Well, I did what I had to do," Bernice said. "I've just loaded him into my car and I'm taking him home. He may well not make it, but I couldn't just stand by and let them put in a breathing tube. He didn't want anything like that. The poor man was in no position to represent his own wishes.

"They didn't do much to stop me from taking him out of there. I guess they're flooded with sick patients. They told me at least three times that he'd have to be quarantined once I got him home. So will I, of course."

"Did you say you're taking him home? Are you taking him to your home? Or do you mean the house where you lived with him?" Alice asked. Bernice had always expressed such a strong dislike of her ex-husband that Alice thought she might be mishearing.

"Yes, of course, I am taking him home," Bernice snapped. "What else could I do? I couldn't very well bring him with me to Hazel's house. Hazel's ninety-five years old and I certainly don't want her to get the virus."

Alice pictured Hazel, intrepid in the face of danger. Hazel had invited Bernice to live with her when she had nowhere to go after leaving her husband. But exposing Hazel to someone infected with COVID would be a terrible thing.

"I'm trying to figure out who could help me with his care," Bernice continued. "I can't just leave him alone to die. That's why I called you, Alice. I'm wondering if I could hire your friend Ruby Fruit, seeing as she's got nursing skills."

There was silence while Alice considered what Bernice was asking. "Ruby Starr!" she finally said quite sharply. "Her name is RubyStarr, not Ruby Fruit!" It was time for Bernice to stop calling her young friend by the wrong name.

She was startled by the request, considering Bernice's perpetual rudeness towards RubyStarr. If Bernice wanted RubyStarr to take on a situation that was obviously life-threatening, she'd better attempt a rapid attitude adjustment. Then she reminded herself that Bernice was in the middle of a nightmare.

"I'm not in a good position to ask RubyStarr for help. I'm aware of that," Bernice said, ignoring Alice's questions. "Look, I don't have time to find someone else. I don't have the medical skill to keep the man from suffering. In fact, I don't even know if I can keep him alive!

"I'm at his house now, Alice. I'm not sure I can move him inside without help. I thought of asking the neighbors to help me, but because of COVID, I can't ask anyone to help me. Plus, everyone around here knows his side of the story. I doubt anyone will trust me to take care of him. It's been three years since I left, but I figure the neighbors will still blame me for anything that goes wrong."

Bernice stopped. Alice listened to her rapid breathing at the other end of the phone.

"I'm desperate, Alice," Bernice said, her voice trembling. "I wouldn't have called you if I had other resources."

"I understand," Alice said, glancing at the clock. "I can give RubyStarr a call to see if it's OK for me to give you her number. I'll call her right now."

Alice hung up without waiting for Bernice's reply, and scrolled through her contacts looking for the number.

"Fit bit!" Alice cursed softly after getting RubyStarr's recorded message. She decided to call Bernice back and give her the number without getting RubyStarr's permission.

"Here's RubyStarr's number," Alice said as soon as she heard Bernice's voice. "Do you have something to write with?"

"Not right now I don't," Bernice said gruffly, breathing heavily into the phone. "I've got Donald onto the front porch, but I didn't find the key under the mat where we used to leave it. He's not conscious so he can't tell me where it might be. I'm going to break in through the bathroom window. You can bet somebody will call the cops on me! "

Alice took a deep breath. "Bernice, I'm sure you'll manage somehow." She was reluctant to hang up under these circumstances. "I'll try to reach Ruby again," she promised. "I'll call you as soon as I reach her. Listen," she added, "if the police show up, that might be a good thing. Maybe you should call them instead of trying to break in? They could help you get your husband into the house."

"I'll figure this out," Bernice said. "Don't worry about me."

The line went dead, and Alice breathed a guilty sigh of relief. She decided to call Gerard to explain what was going on, instead of climbing all those stairs to get back up to his apartment.

"Gerard," she said when he finally answered, "I'm sorry but Bernice is having a crisis."

"*Ah, Mon Dieu!*" Gerard replied, his voice filled with worry. Alice could picture him, tugging vigorously on his mustache. He had never been comfortable with Bernice.

"Actually, Gerard," she said hesitantly, "I want to talk about something important. We need to talk about sharing our homes."

Gerard growled miserably into the phone, the French sound of disgust or despair that no American could possibly replicate.

"Please, *ma chèrie*, please do not say you invite Bernice to move into your house!"

"What?" Alice exclaimed. "No Gerard! Not at all! I want to talk about the two of us, you and me, moving into Felicia's house. We could live there with her while there is a need for us to remain quarantined."

There! She had blurted it out.

Gerard was silent as he considered the possibilities.

"Would you like this?" he asked, after some deliberation.

"I'm certainly considering it," Alice said. "There's so much to think about right now it makes me dizzy, not even counting Bernice's terrible situation! Felicia would like us to make a decision right away. She's hoping we will be moving in by tomorrow afternoon."

"I will do whatever it is that makes you happy," Gerard said soothingly. "But please do not, ahh, do not give all your strength to Bernice."

"She's been a good friend to me, Gerard. Let me think a minute, then I'll come upstairs and we'll decide what we want to do, yes?

"Gerard, we have to change our plans. I have to get help for Bernice right now. I must go see Ruby. She might be able to help."

Chapter Ten
Western Massachusetts

Alice, OMG, I am so glad to see you!" RubyStarr exclaimed as she peered through the screen door at Alice. "But, umm, I don't see a mask! Aren't you, like, wearing a mask, like, whenever you're in public?"

"I'm afraid I forgot it," Alice said contritely. "I have several masks at home, but I seem to have totally forgotten all of them this afternoon. I wasn't planning to see anyone except Gerard, and I simply forgot to put one in my bag."

"Hold on," RubyStarr said. "I've got extras. I'll get you one. Back in a sec!"

When she came back to the door, she was wearing a medically-approved mask. She thrust another mask toward Alice.

"Here, Alice, put it on!" she said sternly. "The governor has been very clear about this. I don't mean to be sounding, like, unfriendly? I'm really happy to see you, but I'm dealing with this stuff twenty-four/seven! It isn't safe to invite you inside, of course. Can we stand out here on the porch and talk?"

She scrutinized Alice thoughtfully. "Are you, like, ok? Has something happened to Gerard?"

Alice shook her head. "No he's fine. Ruby dear, I'm sorry to have startled you."

She felt light-headed, realizing that she might be too weak to stand for long. "I'll get right to the point. I need your help because someone I care about is involved in a life and death situation. I wouldn't normally ask for your involvement, but someone may die if I can't get a medical professional to help them. You're the one person I thought I could ask."

Suddenly she realized she was so weak that if she didn't sit down, she would topple over right there on the porch. "I'm afraid I must ask if you would get me a chair, please," she added, "so I can sit for a moment while we talk."

"Oh Alice, I'm sorry! I'll get a chair, totally!"

Alice leaned on the open doorway, watching as RubyStarr hurried down the short hallway. She could see Warp sprawled on the couch, his cell cradled against his ear. She wondered if he had told Ruby about his visit to her house just a few hours earlier.

RubyStarr returned with a small kitchen chair. "So tell me more about why you're here?" she asked. "In all the years I've known you, you have never, like I mean never dropped in to visit me. Something, like, seriously complex must be going on!"

Alice needed water before she began explaining. But she couldn't sip a drink with her mask on. Yet another discombobulating experience with her mask. Alice, this is not a social call! She told herself to get to the point before Bernice's husband ended up dying.

"I'm fine," she reported, "and so is Gerard. We were headed back to his apartment, when I got a call that made me realize I had to ask you for help." She realized that she needed a little oxygen. She slipped the mask down to adjust her nose piece, then checked to make sure her oxygen was on. After a few slow breaths, she felt better.

Her phone rang, and her heart raced even before she checked the caller ID. It was Bernice again.

"Alice," Bernice said, her voice cracking, "I think he's dying right now here in the backyard. I couldn't break into the house." Alice was struggling to catch her breath, unable to respond even as she tried to speak. "I guess I'm going to have to call 911," Bernice continued. "It might be too late, I don't know. You think they will arrest me?"

Alice finally got a good breath. She tried to sound calm. "Bernice, no one is going to arrest you," she said "You just brought him home, which is what he wanted. You have done nothing wrong. Also, you're still legally married, aren't you? I believe as the medical proxy, you had the right to make the decision to bring him home."

RubyStarr was staring at her in astonishment. Alice held up one finger to signal she would explain soon.

She closed her eyes, trying to fathom how Bernice was dealing with the nightmare. "How do you know he's close to death?' she asked.

"Who is dying?" RubyStarr was not going to hesitate to interrupt.

Alice put her hand over the phone. "Bernice just took her ex-husband out of the nursing home and brought him back to their old house. Now she can't find the key to get in. She says he has the virus, and she thinks he might be dying right now."

Ruby clapped her hand over her mouth. She stared at Alice, her eyes huge with surprise. "I thought she hated the ex," she whispered.

Alice nodded. It was true. Bernice had said nothing good about Donald since the day she left him. She had made a clean break several years ago, as far as Alice knew. But today she had rescued him, for better or for worse.

Would it be worse for this man to die a painful death in the backyard of his home than to be intubated and die slowly? Even if this was the better outcome, perhaps, for him, it was certainly not a good outcome for Bernice.

"Ruby, I'm here to ask you to go with me over to North Mountain to help them. I can sit in the back seat and we'll keep the windows open so we're both safe. I have to help Bernice through whatever is going to happen."

She imagined Bernice cradling her once brutal husband in her arms.

"Please!" she said.

Five minutes later they were heading toward North Mountain.

"I can get us there in about thirty minutes," RubyStarr promised, checking her GPS. "We should roll down all the windows and keep our masks on, OK?"

"On our way!" Alice texted Bernice, once the van began to move. "Ruby is with me!"

She texted again a minute later, prompting Bernice to call 911.

Despite the mask muffling her words, Alice tried to give Ruby some information. "I believe she said that he did not wish to be kept alive through invasive medical procedures," she said. "Now they're in the backyard because she can't find the key, so Bernice was going to try to climb in a window or something, I think. We'll find out more when we get there. I know Bernice is not your favorite person, but will you please talk to her if she calls back?"

RubyStarr slowly nodded her willingness.

As they drove north, Alice decided to catch up with Ruby while they had the chance. "How's work going for you?" she asked.

RubyStarr shrugged."Well, like, I've been working, like, a million hours! It's like, really nuts but I'm glad to have the work. I know everyone's really scared to have their loved ones in nursing homes these days, and I don't blame them. So even though I'm crazy busy, I feel like I really am, like, an essential worker."

They hit a bump in the twisting country road, and Alice winced. She wanted to get to Bernice as fast as possible, but she also wanted her back to survive the journey. She tried not to look at how fast the trees were whipping by the car windows as Ruby accelerated. She hoped this meant they were on the home stretch.

"I worry a lot," Ruby continued. "I'm likely to get exposed to the virus, so Warp could get it from me, and, like, you know, we might not even know if one of us has been, like, contaminated? So, yeah, it's hard not to get, like, super stressed."

They drove in silence for a minute before RubyStarr turned toward Alice.

"Look, I've agreed to help you with Bernice, but we don't know if the police have been called, right?"

"No, we do not," Alice agreed.

"Then you should call the police. We may need their help."

"You're right!" Alice said, "but I feel funny doing it. I don't have Bernice's permission to tell anyone about, well, the abduction from the care facility."

RubyStarr was struggling to read the small country street signs. "I sure hope this is right. Doesn't look at all like my GPS map."

"I could call 911. Should I just give the address Bernice gave me and just say that a man may be dying there?" Alice asked.

"Well," Ruby said cheerfully, "We don't have to make the decision yet. I think we're here."

Chapter Eleven
Southern Vermont

Alice was surprised by the house Bernice had once lived in with Donald. It wasn't what she had imagined.

The house was large, and set far back from the road, a long driveway leading up to a three-car garage. The front lawn was immaculately trimmed, designed to showcase the flower beds along the side. The early flowers of May, tulips, daffodils and clumps of delicate purple crocuses were bright in the afternoon sun. Bernice's husband Donald must have a passion for gardening, or enough money to pay for professional lawn care, she thought.

Alice recognized Bernice's small compact Ford parked in the driveway. There were no other vehicles in sight.

"I guess we should park out here on the street to leave space for an ambulance and possibly a cruiser," Ruby said. "Alice, please do not get within ten feet of either the husband or Bernice! You cannot take the risk I'm about to."

Alice opened the door and began her shuffling trip across the yard while Ruby prepared for work. RubyStarr pulled on a protective shield over her mask and pulled scrubs over her clothes. She caught up with Alice as they rounded the corner of the house.

Alice was galvanized by a surge of anxiety. For whatever reason, she had been imagining trained helpers already on the scene. Now it was all on Ruby's shoulders.

"Uh oh!" Ruby exclaimed. She began to run across the grass, toward Bernice and Donald.

Alice stopped in her tracks, staring in horror. Even from fifteen feet away, the scene made her queasy.

Bernice was seated next to a large tree stump, her husband's body sprawled on the grass beside her. His head was cradled in her lap in an unmistakable pool of blood.

Ruby, wearing her medical mask and her protective shield, knelt down and began checking Donald's vitals. Bernice was a horrible shade of white. She stared at them, speechless.

"He fell!" she finally croaked, continuing to focus on Alice. "He fell," she whimpered. "He hit his head on the stump. He isn't dead, is he?"

Both Alice and Bernice looked to Ruby for the answer. She was still examining him.

"Have you called 911?" Alice asked Bernice.

Bernice shook her head. She began to rock back and forth, causing small rivulets of blood to trickle down from Donald's head and dribble onto the grass.

Alice felt extremely faint.

RubyStarr glanced at Bernice. "You must call 911," she told her. "Or do you want Alice to make the call?"

"They're going to say I killed him!" Bernice gasped, a rough sob punctuating this declaration.

No one spoke or moved for a moment. Then Alice punched in the emergency number on her cell.

Once she was sure that help was on the way, she sat quietly. She tried to think what would be most helpful to Bernice at this moment. She was glad she had brought RubyStarr along, but it might be too late to save Donald's life.

"Ruby dear," she said, after a respectful pause, "can you give us more information about Donald's condition?" Bernice was prone to paranoia, and the traumatic nature of her rescue attempt might push her to fear the worst. Alice needed more information.

After continuing to take his pulse, and listening to his heart, RubyStarr looked at Bernice. "You know I'm not, like, totally expert in medical trauma, but let's hope the EMT's will show up soon. The situation doesn't look good."

She crouched down, looking closely at Donald's head and the wet blood. "How did the head wound happen?" she asked Bernice, her tone suddenly gentle as if she were speaking to a child.

Bernice shook her head. "He fell. I couldn't hold onto him anymore. He just fell. It's my fault. I killed him, that's what everyone will say. I killed him, I killed him!" She was beginning to shake and hyperventilate.

"Look at me, Bernice," RubyStarr said. "Look at me! We don't know exactly what's happening right this minute. The EMT's will come very soon, and they'll take him to the hospital, and then we'll see. Now listen to me, Bernice! You have to stop saying you killed him. It's possible he can still hear you. Your job is to tell him he's going to make it, OK?"

Bernice nodded her head, shivering and rocking. Although she was quiet, she made no effort to follow RubyStarr's directive.

Alice felt helpless, not being able to comfort Bernice with a hand on her back or a hug. She could at least help talk Bernice out of her panic.

She walked a little closer, still trying to keep the mandatory six feet of distance from Bernice. "They'll be here within twenty minutes," she said. "Maybe sooner."

"I'm going back to the car," RubyStarr told Alice, "to see if there's a blanket or old coat or anything at all that I put over Donald to keep him warm.".

Time seemed to drag on forever and Alice couldn't contain her curiosity. "Bernice," she asked, "why were you over here next to the tree stump instead of just waiting for us on the back porch?"

Bernice began to cry softly. "It was our special tree," she said. "We got engaged under this tree."

Alice was dumbstruck. She had never heard Bernice sound the slightest bit sentimental about her marriage. She was relieved to hear a siren and then radio static of a police car or ambulance.

A woman's voice began calling from the direction of the driveway. "Hello? Hello? Anybody home?"

"We're back here!" RubyStarr called, and trotted off to direct them to the backyard.

Just as Ruby disappeared around one side of the house, an older woman came around from the other side. "Holy Mary! What the hell is going on back here?" she screamed, her voice rising with each word.

She stopped in her tracks when she saw Donald's body and all the blood. "Oh dear God, what have you done, Bernice? Have you killed the poor man? God in Heaven, what kind of devil's work have you been up to? I'm calling the police. Don't either of you move, you hear me! I'll get my husband out here with his gun and if either of you moves, you're dead meat! I mean it!"

"The police are already on their way,'" Alice told her. "And the ambulance is here to take Donald to the hospital. It would be better for everyone if you could stay calm. If you want to be helpful, you could go back to the front of the house and let the neighbors know that Donald will be getting help at the hospital."

"Who the hell are you?" the woman asked, scowling at Alice before she turned her attention back to Donald. She stepped a few feet closer to peer at him. "Why's all that blood coming out of his head?" she asked, glaring at Bernice. "What do you think you're doing, coming back here? Haven't you already done enough harm? Now look at what you've done! I hope they lock you up for life!"

Alice was relieved to see the EMT's coming across the yard with a stretcher.

Chapter Twelve
Central Florida

"There's some good news about Kori!" Nancy Warren told her husband Steve. "Flo wants to come over and talk to us tonight. All she would say on the phone was that Kori's been found and she's alive. We'll get the rest of the story in a little while."

An hour later, Flo was sitting on their screened porch, beaming at Nancy and Steve. "OK, let's start with giving thanks that Kori has been found and that she's alive!" she said.

Nancy wondered how many of the campaign workers Flo was visiting personally today, group by group, person by person, sharing the news face to face rather than calling or sending a group email.

"So this is what I can tell you," Flo said. "Kori was found over on the West Side. There's a lady named Ruthie who sleeps rough over there. She was the one who alerted the police, but she claims not to know anything about Kori or how she got there."

Flo's voice got quieter and very sad. "There's a lot to worry about. Kori is in pretty bad shape. She got beat up bad. So far, she hasn't been able to speak. I went over to see her at Advent Hospital this morning as soon as the cops had finished questioning me. Kori had a flyer for the campaign in her pocket, with a handwritten note on the back. It was a threat to kill her. I was the only link they had to help them identify her.

"When I got there, she definitely recognized me but, like I told you, she can't talk. Her jaw is broken.

"The hospital staff asked me if she has any next of kin, and I told them about her grandmother over at Sunset Village. Of course, the grandmother has serious dementia so she can't help. As of now, no one at the hospital can understand what Kori might be trying to communicate.

"The charge nurse said when they get her stabilized medically, then they'll get her started with some speech specialists, but because of the broken jaw, it's hard to say when she'll be able to speak.

"So, here's the thing we have to focus on now. If Kori seems stable medically, they could discharge her as early as tomorrow.

"I've been trying to figure out where she could go to convalesce. She may have insurance to cover rehab for a week or so, but the nurse didn't seem optimistic about that option. There are very few beds available because so many facilities are on lockdown due to COVID. Kori would do better if someone she knows could house her and do some caretaking, at least for a while. So you two came to mind."

Flo looked thoughtfully at Nancy and Steve.

"So I have a big ask. I need to know if you would be willing and able to take care of Kori in your home. You two will possibly be in some danger if she's staying with you. Hopefully, this will be short term. The speech specialists and other PTs will continue to work with her on an outpatient basis.

"I know this is a lot to ask," she continued. "Please think it over before you give me your response. Then call me, and we'll talk through as many questions as we can tonight.

"And please do not think I'll think any less of you if you can't take this on. There will be plenty of chances for all of us to help Kori during this very difficult time."

"Can she walk without help?" Steve asked.

Flo nodded. "I believe so," she said. "I'm assuming that she'll need some help - probably from you, Nancy - with the toilet and dressing and that kind of thing. But the good news is, Kori's young and strong. From everything they told me, the rest of her body has not been too badly damaged. The really bad blows were to her head. Don't know if someone was trying to kill her, but they sure didn't want her to be able to talk."

"Can you tell us why you've asked the two of us?" Nancy asked. Her head was spinning with questions, but she needed to know the answer to this particular question.

Flo smiled, the first real smile Nancy had seen since she sat down on their porch. "Two reasons. First, I know for a fact that Kori really likes you two! She always lights up when she's talking about you.

"The second reason is more strategic. You're snowbirds, and that means you're not well-known locally. We don't know if Kori's attack was something random or not, but if it was a planned attack, we want her with someone who's pretty much unknown locally."

Late that night, hours after they had called Flo to tell her they would love to offer their home to Kori, Nancy came into the bedroom. Steve was already in bed, but was staring at the ceiling, his eyes open wide. She sat down next to him on the bed and reached over to hold his hand.

"We're white," Steve said, hearing her unspoken question. "Kori is one of the most gracious human beings I've ever met, but she may not feel comfortable being cared for by white folks."

"I hadn't thought about that. You're right, of course. I'm still so oblivious sometimes!"

Steve put his arm around his wife. "We can check in again with Flo but she probably wouldn't have asked us if she thought it would be a major barrier. Hopefully, Kori will be able to speak for herself soon, so she can tell us or Flo if she is uncomfortable with us.

"I do know one thing that's a real plus," he added. "Kori really loves you! I can see it when you two are working together or when you're just joking around. So if she rejects our offer, it won't be because she doesn't care about you, I know that."

"I thought you'd say you were worried about the danger of having someone else living with us while COVID's still running rampant," Nancy said.

"Well, I am worried. It's possible that Kori may have been exposed to the virus during the attack on her or in the hospital. But someone has to take this on."

Chapter Thirteen
Western Massachusetts

Alice finished the last sip of her large cup of coffee, and carried the cup into Gerard's kitchen. She carefully rinsed it, glancing around to see if there was anything else they should bring to Felicia's.

"Well, my dear, do you think you are ready to depart?"

Gerard nodded somewhat reluctantly. He gazed at his apartment sadly. "*Adieu!*" he said, waving goodbye to his kitchen.

Alice gazed down at the river one last time before she began her slow descent to the street. The sound of the water rushing toward the dam gave her a jolt of energy, inspiring her to tackle one more journey at the end of her extremely full day.

Felicia was waiting for them on the front porch, waving as enthusiastically as if she hadn't seen them for years. "Welcome to *Chez* Felicia!" She scampered down the front steps, and abandoning caution, attempted through her mask to give Gerard a proper French greeting of a kiss on both cheeks. At least, Alice thought, Felicia and Gerard were both wearing their masks.

They would have to decide tonight what to do about the masks and social distancing now that they were making a home together.

"Now," Felicia said, turning to Alice, "why don't I carry the heavier things? You and Gerard take only what you can manage safely, or it can wait until morning. I don't want our first night together to be marred by anyone's back going out!"

After most of Gerard's things had been deposited in the large bedroom at the back of the house, Alice carried in several cloth bags of her own that she had quickly crammed with overnight necessities. In the morning she would go back on her own to collect Mother Jones and more of her clothes and books and her laptop.

"I've made us a comforting meal," Felicia said sweetly. "Gerard, do you know about American comfort food?"

Gerard looked puzzled, stroking his mustache thoughtfully. "Is this the meal for the, *ah, la personne avec la maladie* while she, ah, she convalesce?" he asked.

Felicia's laughter filled the kitchen where they were seated at her large wooden table. "Such a clever guess!" she trilled. "No, it's not for a recovering hospital patient, but I suppose it could be. It's often some kind of food that reminds you of childhood, something that would make a child feel comforted when they were sick or sad. Mashed potatoes, for example, is a popular American comfort food. Or mac and cheese."

Alice glanced at Gerard. His face was contorted in an expression of distaste.

"The mashing of the potato I do not understand. But maybe the tender new potato, very small, roasted with the garlic and much butter? This one, it could be my food of comfort. My *grandmere*, she gives me this when I am still a small boy."

He looked proud of himself as he continued to offer more palatable food choices. She knew he needed to counteract the very thought of mashed potatoes, an American food he found somewhat disgusting. He hadn't yet acknowledged the existence of mac and cheese.

"You will approve of the comfort food I made, at least I hope you will," Felicia said eagerly. "I have created a cheese soufflé with a side of lightly steamed parsley potatoes, and an endive and pear salad with blue cheese dressing!"

Alice thought Felicia deserved three rousing cheers for producing a meal that was not made solely from root vegetables, perhaps even a meal without coconut oil and something pickled in strong vinegar. This veritable banquet was outside Felicia's culinary wheelhouse, and Alice was touched by her friend's thoughtfulness. She told herself to enjoy this inaugural meal, a time to celebrate the unexpected new living arrangements.

"It sounds marvelous!" she said. After this day of heavy emotional and physical lifting, she had quite an appetite. Then she thought about Bernice, and her stomach knotted. Why hadn't she called to report on Donald's status?

You must stay in the present moment! Her inner guru was hard at work. She stopped willing her phone to ring. In this case, no news really was likely to be better than the news she was dreading.

Over dinner, she told Gerard and Felicia about the disturbing situation with Bernice and her ex-husband. She was truly afraid for Bernice, given her history with her ex-husband. Who knew what the neighbors had been told when Bernice moved out and started her new life.

She had a sliver of doubt that Donald's fall onto the tree stump was completely accidental but she decided not to share that. She could talk about it later if it was still nagging at her.

After the meal, Felicia insisted on doing the clean-up. Gerard excused himself and disappeared into the bedroom while Alice took a dishtowel out of the wooden cabinet next to the sink, and prepared to dry the dishes.

She noticed that Felicia's dish soap was something local, some blend of fragrant herbal ingredients. She wasn't so sure it was doing much to clean the grease from the dishes, but she was not going to question Felicia's housekeeping this first night of their co-existence.

She couldn't keep her mind from going over and over the scene in Donald's backyard.

"Felicia," she said when their chores were finished. "Could we make some tea and sit at the table for a few minutes?"

"Of course!" Felicia said. "We can talk all night if you want to. It will be like a sleepover!"

"I don't think I have the stamina for that," Alice said, "but I need to tell you more about what happened with Bernice earlier today."

It took at least a half hour to recount the entire saga, but to her credit Felicia listened without one interruption. "I haven't heard back from her since the ambulance crew took over," Alice concluded. "It's been hours, and it's unlike her to leave me hanging when something this dreadful is going on.

"Of course I really don't know what to do for her under these conditions. If Donald died, she must feel so alone right now. And maybe she's afraid about what the authorities may conclude about the cause of death. For all I know, she may have driven to my house and be sitting there waiting for me to show up. You know how she prefers unplanned appearances."

Felicia looked thoughtfully at her friend.

"Alice, please keep in mind that Bernice must not have close physical contact with you or anyone else right now, if her husband has the virus," she said. "You know that no matter what was going on, Bernice would be concerned with your well-being. She wouldn't endanger you by showing up at your house. Why don't you just call her?"

Alice sighed heavily. "I suppose I must," she said. "Do you mind if I call from in here? I don't really want to involve Gerard in any more of this particular drama tonight. I'm hoping he's already fallen asleep."

"Of course!" Felicia said. "Alice, my house is your house right now. If you need privacy for the call, I'm happy to go on to bed. Or I can stay here and keep you company while you talk. If you need me, I can help you figure out what she needs to do next."

"I'd like you to stay."

Felicia nodded, and waved at the living room area adjoining the kitchen. "Why don't you pick out the most comfortable chair and make yourself at home."

Alice chose a soft recliner that was more or less the right size for her. She tapped in Bernice's number, not sure if she hoped to hear a live voice or Bernice's recording.

There was no consolation in getting Bernice's familiar, gruff recording: "'If it's an emergency I'll call back. Otherwise, no guarantees."

"I have to tell you my weird suspicions," Alice began, as soon as Felicia plopped down in the chair across from her. "This is awful," she said, then stopped.

Felicia waited for Alice to continue, her eyes bright with interest.

"She was exhausted, scared, and at her wits end," Alice said. "Maybe she wanted to end his life quickly rather than prolong it, fearing that he would have to face the possible long drawn out ordeal of COVID. Maybe, as she got increasingly weary, she dragged him over to that tree stump where he slipped out of her arms and fell, hitting his head, but maybe she dropped him on purpose."

"Whew!" Felicia said. "That's quite the scenario!"

Felicia and Alice remained in silence as they considered Alice's grim hypothesis.

"Can you think of any reason Bernice would have dragged him out to the stump like that?" Felicia asked Alice.

"Well, she told me that was their special tree, where they got engaged," Alice told her.

"Then what happened when the ambulance arrived? You and Ru-byStarr were there, right?"

"I hovered in the background while the EMTs were moving Donald into the ambulance. I assumed that they were going to the closest hospital, and that Bernice would call me when she could," Alice explained.

Felicia frowned. "What did RubyStarr say about whether the man was dead or not?"

"She wouldn't commit one way or the other. The thing that was really troubling Ruby was that we both might have been exposed to COVID. I have to say she was more distressed about the possibility of contamination than the medical status of Bernice's ex-husband."

Alice stopped talking and checked her oxygen. "Oh dear," she said, her voice heavy with disappointment.

"What is it?" Felicia asked

"I just realized I need to refuel both my portable tanks, I'm afraid. I suppose I have to do it tonight even though I'll admit my energy is running out. I'll have to make some kind of arrangement tomorrow to get the big stationary tank over here." She looked miserable.

Felicia stood up and engaged in an interesting series of stretches and shivers. Then she smiled brightly at Alice.

"Let me go over to your house and fill the tanks right now!" she said briskly. "I'm not tired at all."

"Oh Felicia, you are an angel!" Alice told her.

As soon as Felicia left, Alice tiptoed into the room that she and Gerard were sharing. He was sound asleep on the bed, folders full of notes and articles strewn all around him on the bed. Alice eased herself down next to him to wait for Felicia's return. In less than a minute, she was sound asleep too.

Chapter Fourteen
Western Massachusetts

"Alice you won't believe what just happened!"

Alice opened her eyes to see Felicia standing in the doorway of the bedroom, startling her out of the deep sleep. "What time is it?" she asked irritably. Why on earth was Felicia waking her and Gerard in the middle of the night? If this was a predictor of Felicia's boundaries, the new experiment in sheltering together might have to end prematurely.

Gerard was not any happier than Alice about being unceremoniously yanked from his sleep. He stared at Felicia as if he had never seen her before. "*Pas question!*" he croaked irritably.

Felicia looked as if she had just swooped in from the clouds. Her eyes seemed to glow with a weird light, and her hair was a wild tangle of grey curls. "What did Gerard just say to me?" she asked Alice.

"He told you no way!" Alice said, glaring at her friend.

Felicia giggled, then tried to look slightly contrite. "I'm sorry to wake you both, but I have to tell you what just happened! I went over to your house as planned," she continued, "and guess who was there?"

Alice stared glassily at her. She couldn't deal with one more thing. Maybe she had left the TV on?

"Rachel Maddow?" she asked.

Gerard sat up, staring down at Alice who was still flat on her back.

"Rachel Maddow, she is at your house?" he asked eagerly. "How does this happen?"

Felicia shook her head. "No, nothing like that! I was in your living room, filling your portable tank from the stationary tank when I heard someone opening the back door. I called out a greeting, having no clue about the identity of the person dropping by. It was dark and when there was no answer, I began to feel quite nervous.

"I couldn't really see into the kitchen from where I was, but I heard footsteps, soft tip-toe sounds, then I thought that the person might be leaving again.

"By this time I feared they were up to no good! I could have dialed 911 but my hands were occupied. I had been right in the middle of the process of filling the little oxygen tank, and my phone was in my pocket. Then I decided to call the intruder's bluff!

"'Show yourself or I will shoot!' I called out, making myself sound like a geriatric action figure.

"To my surprise, Bernice walked into the room, her hands up over her head!

"'Don't shoot me, Felicia!' she was whimpering, tears dribbling down her face. 'I can explain.'"

"'Let me finish what I'm doing here, and wait for me on the porch,' I told her firmly. I thought immediately that she'd been exposed to COVID, so my first thought was to get her out of your house and keep her away from me, too."

"Felicia, could you cut to the chase, please," Alice said. "Tell me succinctly exactly what Bernice was doing there."

"Always the school teacher!" Felicia chuckled.

Alice and Gerard glared at her, united in their frustration.

"OK, OK!" Felicia said. "Bernice filled me in. The EMTs worked to revive Donald in the ambulance, and then the emergency room personnel began treating the head wound and trying to stabilize him. She was told to leave and go to the waiting area."

Felicia continued, lowering her voice to a dramatic husky register. Alice was distracted by the thought that Felicia had missed her calling as a mysterious femme fatale of the 1940s.

"Instead of being grateful that Donald might make it, Bernice told me that she was scared to death! Evidently he had regained consciousness momentarily while they were in the ambulance. He opened his eyes, pointed at her, and attempted to speak. He was trying to say either Mother! or Murder!

"She decided to leave the hospital before she was charged with manslaughter or worse if he died. At the very least, she thought she would face charges for taking him out of the nursing home without the approval of the medical staff. So, long story short, she's on the run. Who could blame her?

"I didn't tell her where you were. And strangely enough, she didn't ask. What surprised me more was that she didn't ask me what I was doing in your house. I began to wonder if she might be desperate enough to take me as a hostage or something."

She stopped, looking to see what Alice might think about her fear. Since there was no response, she sat down in one of the rocking chairs in a corner of the spacious guest room. She looked uncharacteristically wrung out.

"I made it back with your portable tank filled, but I didn't even get to feed Mother Jones," she confessed.

Alice was still lost in thought as she contemplated Bernice's complicated situation.

"I'm sorry, Alice," Felicia continued. "I didn't want to risk getting involved with Bernice. I just didn't want to put myself or the two of you at risk. Bernice was wearing a mask, but she was, without a doubt, thoroughly exposed.

"I did take extra precautions when I got home just now, changing my clothes and showering before I came in to tell you my news."

Alice began to get up from the bed, but immediately felt dizzy. "I think I need that oxygen right now," she said. "Would you mind bringing it in here?"

She was in a real quandary. Could she allow herself to turn away from Bernice, knowing she might be charged with manslaughter or even murder? It was a matter of conscience, no matter how overwhelming the whole situation seemed at the moment.

"I'm going to try to call Bernice and tell her she can stay at my house tonight," she announced when Felicia returned with the spare oxygen tank. "The police wouldn't think of looking for her there, and right now, she needs a place to sleep. When we go over to collect the cat, I'll see if she wants me to help her decide what she should do."

Gerard looked bewildered. Alice wondered if this last episode of today's endless adventure had put his already stimulated brain into overdrive. Even Felicia was looking a little ragged.

Alice thought about everything that had happened in just one day, and started laughing.

"I'm sorry," she said, trying to look appropriately serious, "but only this morning, I thought it would take all of our energy to decide where we were going to shelter. Now it seems that we might have to decide about harboring a fugitive! And to think my biggest worry at the beginning of the COVID quarantine was fearing I'd be restless staying at home all the time!"

"Life is an endless mystery," Felicia intoned, and began her tapping ritual. Gerard smiled sweetly at Alice just before he closed his eyes and went back to sleep.

Chapter Fifteen
Central Florida

Two days after Kori moved in with Nancy and Steve, Nancy got a call.

"Nancy, there's a friend of Kori's who called to see if he could visit her," Floriana said. "Charles knows Kori from the nursing home where her grandmother lives. He's the evening shift supervisor and very devoted to the grandmother. I've known him since a few years ago when my mother and then my uncle were residents at Sunset Village."

"OK," Nancy said. "Let me go check with Kori to see if she's up for a visit."

Kori was staring out at the trees, her favorite activity as far as Nancy could tell.

"Flo just called," Nancy told her. "Your friend Charles from Sunset Village would like to stop by and see you. Would that be ok with you?"

Kori looked thoughtfully at Nancy. Then she nodded. She made a sound that Nancy interpreted as "OK."

When Charles called, Nancy warned him that it would have to be a short visit.

"Kori's still wrung out from her ordeal, and she can't yet communicate easily. I assume that Floriana told you that. Kori has very little physical or emotional stamina."

An hour later, Nancy opened the front door, and was immediately dazzled by the handsome man waiting there. His clothes and his mask were beautifully matched, the dark purple mask a striking contrast to his tailored grey shirt and lavender tie.

"I'm Charles, obviously," he said, his eyes smiling at her above his mask."I am grateful to you for letting me visit Kori. I know in times like these, it's complicated to have visitors."

"I'm happy to meet you," Nancy said. "I'll take you to her. We'll just follow this stone path along the side of the house to our Florida room," she told him. "Kori is settled on the couch out there. I'll be in the house."

Nancy hoped that seeing Charles would be a positive thing for Kori. The poor woman seemed to be so agitated that almost nothing calmed her except sleep. And she didn't seem to be sleeping much.

Soon after her arrival, she began restless pacing that could go on for hours. Nancy wondered if she should be trying harder to find out what this was all about. She had been hesitant to push her, though. It was complicated and exhausting for Kori any time they asked questions and she labored to write her answers on a pad she kept near her.

Kori had accepted the pad, the pen and the suggestion that she use this means to communicate. She had written "thank you...good idea."

Nancy could hear their guest pacing during the night. She had wondered if she should call Flo to ask if there was someone at the hospital she could call. Maybe someone should evaluate Kori for anti-anxiety medication.

Maybe Charles would turn out to be a wizard visitor who could help Kori relax and sleep. Their little household of three was starting to need a little magic right about now.

She led Charles to the porch, and then opened the door to peek in at Kori. She was sitting on the small couch. It was a perfect size for the screen porch and surprisingly comfortable.

"Your friend Charles is here," she told Kori gently. "Ring the bell if you need anything, OK?"

Kori nodded to her and gave her what might have been a smile, though Nancy couldn't really tell. She gestured for Charles to go in. It wasn't until after she left him there with Kori that she realized she hadn't offered anything to him to eat or drink.

It felt rude to be in this Southern culture of hospitality, and not offer refreshments.

For now, Nancy told herself, she should stay out of the way, and give Kori space to visit with her friend.

Less than fifteen minutes had passed before Nancy felt compelled to bring a tray out to the porch. She had fixed a pitcher of iced tea, a bottle of homemade lemonade, two glasses and two straws.

"Excuse me," she called to them as she pushed open the slider door to the Florida room with her foot. She carried her tray to the small table next to Kori. Before she could lower the tray, Charles was at her elbow.

"Let me help you," he said, taking the tray out of her hands.

"I should have offered you something to drink when you first came, Charles," Nancy said apologetically. "Do you like iced tea or would you prefer lemonade? I can bring out some sugar for the tea. Or you could mix the two if you would like to try it the way I drink it."

"I love the idea of the lemonade-tea mix!" Charles said. "Do you have a name for it?"

Kori quickly tapped the pen against her notepad to get Nancy's attention. "Boston TEA Party!" she wrote quickly. Both her brain and her hand coordination were working just fine.

Nancy showed the note to Charles, who laughed and gave Kori a big wink. "Nothing wrong with your brain!" he told her.

Kori's eyes were twinkling above her mask.

"Shall I pour?" Nancy offered.

"I got this," Charles told her. "Thanks so much!"

About a half hour later, Nancy thought she could hear Kori crying. It might be none of her business, but she and Steve were supposed to be keeping their guest safe. She decided to check out what was happening, in case Kori needed her.

Charles was squatting beside Kori, awkwardly patting her back as she continued to shake with sobs.

Nancy pulled a chair over and sat as close as she could get to Kori and still be at a semi-safe distance. It was a relief that Charles was keeping his mask on. Kori had pulled her mask off, and was hunched over, her arms wrapped around herself, rocking as she wept.

"Is this about her Gram?" Nancy asked.

He nodded. "I think I just made it worse for her, telling her that Miz Rosabelle doesn't understand where she's at. I wish I hadn't said that. I told her that Kori was a little sick, but she'd be back soon. But Miz Rosabelle, she can't understand all those words. She just knows Kori's not around."

He shook his head. "Usually Miz Rosabelle is the sweetest, most positive little lady you could hope to know. This just isn't like her."

Kori surprised them both by very suddenly picking up her note-pad, and writing a message. The tears were flowing more slowly as she handed it to Charles.

"Tell her I am not sick! I will come to see her very soon," she had written.

Charles nodded, and Kori reached for the pad to continue her message. "Gram never OK after Mom died. Could believe I've got cancer, like Mom?" she wrote.

"Oh I am so sorry!" Charles said, reading it. "I'm sorry, Kori! Last thing I wanted to do was upset her."

Kori nodded vigorously, and reached over to pat his hand.

Nancy noticed that Kori was looking exhausted now. "Maybe we should wind down the visit now," she said, looking at Kori for confirmation.

Nodding slowly, Kori squeezed Charles's hand. She tried to speak but the sound was garbled.

"It's OK," he said. "I'll be back in a few days."

Kori nodded.

"I have an idea," Nancy said. "Maybe you could take a selfie of you and Kori, and show it to Gram. Then she could see for herself that Kori's OK."

Kori held up her hand in the 'stop' signal. "Face looks awful!" she wrote on her pad. "Will scare her, not comfort."

"Well, maybe you're right," Nancy said. "Maybe by the next time Charles comes over, you'll look a little bit more like yourself."

After Charles left, Nancy told Steve about the sadness Kori had expressed. He sighed. "Maybe we need to have a conversation about this with Kori" he suggested. "If we're keeping Kori's investigation a secret, how do we determine who's in the loop? Is Charles just a friendly staff member who loves Kori's grandmother and wants to help, or is he part of the lawsuit?

"Should we ask Kori if Charles knows about her project? Does she trust him or not? And how much do you and I need to know in order to be competent guardians?"

They looked at each other, the silence heavy between them.

"I wish Alice Ott was down here with us," Nancy said. "I'd love to pick her brain!"

Chapter Sixteen
Western Massachusetts

Alice woke up, wide-eyed as she stared at the ceiling. She wondered if she might still be dreaming. Then she remembered that she was here at Felicia's. She had to get back to her house as soon as possible to make sure Bernice was all right.

The phone call to Bernice last night had gone unanswered, so Alice had texted her. "Stay where you are," she wrote. "Will check in tomorrow."

She patted the bed to feel if Gerard was still there next to her. Rather than rolling over to see if he was still in bed, it was easier to reach out to him when she first awakened. At this age, she appreciated conserving energy whenever possible.

The space beside her was empty and she was a bit surprised. It seemed early for Gerard to be up. He was not a morning person. Alice was the opposite. She often woke with plans for the day percolating in her head and a burst of energy to greet the new day.

Today she was not so cheerful. She wished Bernice's drama had only been a dream and that she could just go back to sleep.

The bedroom door opened, and Gerard surprised her by appearing with two large mugs of coffee. "Ahhh!" he exclaimed delightedly. "You wake up! *Voilà!* I have *café au lait* for you!"

Alice retrieved her glasses from the bedside table, and beamed at him. She gestured for him to sit next to her on the bed. After he had safely delivered the coffee to the bedside table, she pulled him close for a long kiss.

"And now I too wake up!" he said, kissing her hand before reaching to get his coffee. "I have news of your friend!" he told her.

"News about Bernice?" Alice asked, feeling a mixture of relief and dread.

Gerard grinned. "She leaves a long message for you on Felicia's phone. I can tell it to you or Felicia, she can play the phone to you."

"Let's keep a few minutes for ourselves first," Alice said, kissing his cheek. "Why don't you tell me."

"Bernice, she says this: 'Do not worry. Mother Jones, she have the answers!'" Gerard looked pleased with himself for delivering this strange message, but Alice wasn't sure she understood. Was it his unique translation or was Bernice being purposely mysterious?

She sipped her coffee, then looked at the clock. It was still early enough to give herself some time to wake up gradually before she listened to the message on Felicia's phone. "Come closer," she told Gerard, and pulled him down next to her on the bed.

An hour later, Alice and Gerard were ready for breakfast. Gerard hummed cheerfully as he whipped up a fresh batch of almond croissants. In her predictable efforts to counter balance the fat and sugar count of the meal, Felicia constructed a protein-rich frittata.

Alice knew that she would have to force herself to leave the comfort of the threesome to drive over to her house to collect Mother Jones. She didn't know whether to expect Bernice to still be at the house. One thing Alice could predict was that Mother Jones would be furious. The cat was not likely to overlook the various surprises inflicted on her, and the absence of her evening meal.

"In addition to the disturbingly late hour when Bernice called, what really surprised me," Felicia told Alice as she got up from the table, "was that she called from your landline."

"What time did she call?" Alice asked.

"It was just after two a.m." Felicia reported disapprovingly. "Fortunately, it didn't wake me, but that's only because I leave everything electronic on the ground floor overnight. I should explain why I do this."

She paused so that both Alice and Gerard could give her their full attention. "I deeply believe that the bedroom, the healing room, and the meditation room should remain untainted by electronic energy. Perhaps you should do the same, Alice!"

Felicia smiled aggressively. She and Alice never agreed on the topic of toxic electronics and what must be done in defense.

"Anyhow, as you know, I am very sensitive to electronic intrusions," she continued, "and despite my precautions, I could easily have been awakened by the phone ringing. In that case, I would have been out of balance for the entire night! I can forgive Bernice for the hour of the call, but only because of her difficult circumstances."

"Maybe she waited to call late, knowing that you wouldn't answer," Alice said sharply. "Right now, I'm feeling very anxious about her. I really don't know what to expect when I go over there. I'm concerned about whatever her plans might be, and I'm wondering about Donald." She hesitated for a moment. "Well, to be precise, I'm curious about Donald's status. But I really am not sure how I could help Bernice right now."

Felicia and Gerard both nodded vigorously.

"I wish I understood more about how she got herself tangled up in all this," Alice continued. "Why did she decide to liberate him from the nursing home in the first place, especially if he was so sick? Bernice is usually such a highly organized person, plotting every detail of how she will achieve her goals. She has the mind of a skilled chess player. I'm baffled by what drove her to undertake this mission."

"Do you think she's still at your house?" Felicia asked. "Maybe we should go over there together. If she's planning to go on the lam, maybe we can help her think things through."

"I'm trying to second guess her strategies," Alice said, carrying her cup and plate over to the sink. "If Donald has survived, Bernice has much less to fear, wouldn't you think? But whether he lives or dies, she may be fearful that certain accusations against her may have been taken seriously by the EMTs."

Felicia looked at Alice, raising her eyebrows.

Gerard was trying to extract a bit of dried rosemary from the fritatta that was lodged between his front teeth, so he missed Felicia's questioning glance. Alice indicated with a quick shake of her head that she had not yet told Gerard about the ambulance. She wasn't comfortable passing along the news that en route to the hospital, Donald might have accused Bernice of attempted murder.

"I think maybe I should go alone," Alice said, after a moment of consideration. "I can easily manage picking up Mother Jones and her paraphernalia. Supposing Bernice is there, I think she might not talk so openly if you two are with me."

"I have the important papers I must study," Gerard said. "I prefer not, as you say, to take the break." He was clearly relieved that he didn't have to participate.

"Are you expecting me to offer her sanctuary?" Felicia asked. "I certainly had not planned on sheltering someone who's been exposed to COVID. I'm not only thinking of my own health, but your safety also."

"I can't imagine that she would want to stay here," Alice said. "She's too much of an introvert to want to join a commune, no matter how temporary! And I would never ask that of you, Felicia."

Felicia frowned as she watched Alice gathering together all her accessories.

"Alice, please be very careful. It's a risk for you to go into the house even if Bernice isn't there. We don't know how many hours she's been holed up in there.

"Make her come outside for your conversation. Ask her to feed Mother Jones for you, and to open all the windows. We can go over together later in the day to bring Mother Jones here. I am assuming the cat will not be transmitting Bernice's exhalations since we know Mother Jones is not a fan of hers."

As she drove, Alice told herself to enjoy the beautiful morning colors. The morning sun shone on miles of beautiful pasture land. She wanted to soak up all the beauty of her surroundings so she could face whatever she was about to encounter.

When she arrived, Bernice's car was nowhere in sight, but she may have hidden it somewhere and walked to the house. Alice hadn't decided if she was going to ask Bernice point blank if she had intentionally dropped Donald. She didn't want to face this moral dilemma.

If Bernice confessed, then what would she do? "I will listen to my conscience," she said aloud, trying to sound confident. Then she carefully secured her mask, and headed for the house.

As she opened the back porch door and stepped into the kitchen, Mother Jones trotted towards her, complaining loudly about the missed meals. "Oh you poor hungry kitty! I am so sorry!" Alice apologized half-heartedly, distracted by the possibility of encountering Bernice.

Retrieving the cat food bag from the pantry, she listened for any sounds of Bernice. Whatever noises she might have heard were drowned out by Mother Jones' bleats of hunger and loud anticipatory purring.

As Alice scooped out the kibble, she felt something inside the cat food bag scrape against her scoop. She put an extra large serving of food down for the cat, then re-opened the bag nervously and peered in.

She spotted a small piece of paper folded into a compact little square. Alice smiled. "Mother Jones has the answers," she said aloud, recalling the bizarre message.

She unfolded the paper and read the note Bernice knew she would find:

"Alice, sorry to leave you this note. I'm really sorry I came into your home without permission. I left windows open & slept only a few hours (on sofa).

"I believe I am in real danger! Heading out now for safe place where I can lay low. Will not contact you again unless it is safe.

"Don't try to contact me! Please, Alice, be safe. Your friend always."

The note was unsigned. Alice scanned her small house for signs of Bernice, but there was no trace. Finally she loaded a contented Mother Jones into the soft cat carrier, loaded the carrier onto her folding cart and wheeled the cat out to the car followed by the case of cat food, and finally the litter pan and litter.

She sat down on the front porch for a few minutes to catch her breath.

By the time she got to Felicia's, Mother Jones had stopped protesting from the back seat, and had fallen asleep. Alice envied the cat's capacity for being at one with the present moment. She longed to be in her own rocking chair on the back porch of her own house.

Chapter Seventeen
Central Florida

Jake Costello loved meeting with clients at JHook, a seafood restaurant on the Intracoastal. The restaurant was spread out so there was ample seating on the decks outside, as well as tables spaced far apart indoors.

There was plenty of space to be out in the fresh air, perfect for COVID times. It was noisy and cheerful, and Jake swore they had the best fish in Central Florida.

Families came to rent kayaks, then have a big meal after paddling on the river. Later in the evening, the clientele was a mix of young single adults, and older people who were enjoying the freedom of retirement. You could eat big platters of local fried fish and shrimp, or you could just go for a few drinks. Everyone loved JHook hushpuppies. Jake would treat his table to an order so everyone could have the celestial taste experience.

Jake had been using the restaurant as his second office since COVID changed the rules of human contact. The dining spaces were seafood shack rough, with picnic tables, high rafters, and nothing enclosed except the kitchen. There was a steady hum of voices coming from the kitchen, the bar, the diners, even the gulls. The place was ideal for legal consultations. It helped clients relax, and they could have a confidential conversation and not fear that someone was listening in.

Jake always made sure he was there early so that the clients would feel confident about his dependability. He got his clients something to nibble on even if they weren't up for a meal, or he bought them a drink if they weren't eating. Even the occasional clients who didn't want either food or drink were happy with the view and the relaxed feeling of the place. He felt good about the meeting he was about to have.

Rufe was someone he thought he could count on, a smart young Puerto Rican quickly promoted from nursing assistant to shift supervisor at Serenity Place, the number one rated nursing home in eastern Volusia County. Recently, Rufe had been promoted again to an office management job at the TouchStone Corporation, the corporation that owned Serenity Place. Perfect placement for someone who had come forward to be one of the primary informants for the lawsuit.

Jake had organized a series of clandestine meetings with Rufe and other nursing home staff to build a case against TouchStone. In just five months, it was becoming apparent that the corporation had skimmed a big pot of money into their administrative pockets. An amount upwards of $100,000 had been diverted from Federal emergency funding. The COVID grant money had been earmarked for protective equipment, medical equipment and overtime pay for frontline workers at Sunset Village and Serenity Place, two of TouchStone's biggest nursing homes.

Meanwhile, COVID spiked in both nursing facilities. No surprise there!

Jake had been hired to put together a major lawsuit by Kori Harris and a few other family members upset about their loved ones in the nursing homes, as well as a handful of the nursing home workers like Rufe. He just about had all his ducks in a row. Rufe was part of the team that was organizing workers at Serenity Place and Sunset Village.

The guy meeting with them tonight, Mitch, was new to Jake. He had recently been recruited for the lawsuit. Mitch worked in the dementia unit at Sunset Village where he was recruited by Charles Dubois, one of the original whistleblowers. Charles was, like Rufe, a solid guy. He was a night supervisor at Sunset Village who happened to be the first employee willing to be a whistleblower for the lawsuit.

Charles had called Jake just before he left the office to tell him he had recruited Mitch, and was sending him over with Rufe for the meeting.

This was the third time Jake was meeting with Rufe. He had first met him with other like-minded workers for a brief orientation. Jake had his drill down to a bare minimum, reassuring them that they would not be billed for his time. Only after they won the lawsuit and got a settlement, would Jake take his cut. The plaintiffs knew they might be asked to testify in court, or sign a statement under oath. They were assured that their identities would be protected to the extent possible. Jake would end the initial meeting by telling them how brave they were.

Next, the waiting game began. He would wait to hear who was in and who was getting cold feet. Some never got back to him, and he had to trust that they wouldn't rat out their fellow workers.

As each person joined the lawsuit, Jake would meet with Kori Harris, the major force behind the case. She was the person the whistleblowers went to first, sometimes whispering in a stairwell what they had observed about lack of PPE, failure to be paid for overtime, and threats of termination if they refused to work a double shift. Sometimes the information came to Kori in the parking garage or at a coffee shop. They told her what they knew and talked with her about the risks of speaking up if they joined the lawsuit.

She was the biggest hero of the story. Kori had started the whole process and she inspired people. She was also skilled at vetting each person who felt moved to join the case. Jake depended on her more than he did anyone in the law office.

But now things were different.

Ever since Kori was attacked, very few new employees were coming forward. The good news was that most among the already committed were not backing out. Jake was moved by their courage, but he worried that there would be another victim like Kori, then another. Maybe it would be him, but more likely it would be someone from among the whistleblowers, someone the bad guys wanted to use to send a message.

"Hey Rufe! Hey Mitch! Glad you could make it!" He stood up to elbow bump.

He quickly got a waitperson to take their orders, noting that neither of the guys ordered an alcoholic beverage. Rufe got a fish sandwich, and Mitch said he had already eaten and just wanted coffee. He seemed pretty nervous, but that was to be expected.

Jake ordered the fried shrimp platter, telling his favorite waitperson, Sienna, to add the usual. Everyone on the wait staff knew what Jake's "usual" meant.

An hour later, Jake was confident that both men were ready for the next step. He wanted to start the legal procedures and finally get things rolling.

As he was leaving the parking lot, he noticed that Rufe's car was pulling out onto the road. He liked seeing what his clients drove. It was satisfying to check out if the car fit the profile he created in his mind when he was assessing a client's style.

Rufe was driving an uninteresting Dodge, a faded red. That wasn't at all what Jake would have put him in. Maybe he had his wife's car tonight. He had thought that Mitch was riding with Rufe, so he was surprised there was no one in the passenger seat. He waited a moment, looked around to see if Mitch was in his own car, whatever make and model that might be, then pulled out onto the road after Rufe.

He glanced in his rearview mirror and freaked out when he saw another vehicle roaring out of nowhere, charging up behind him – some kind of speed-crazed maniac! He moved as far over in his lane as he could to let the jerk pass him. Jackass!

In the next horrible moment, he watched the car pass him, accelerate even more, and then slam into the side of Rufe's car, propelling the Dodge into a rollover. His vision clicked into trauma-triggered slow motion as he watched Rufe's car smash into the trees that lined the side of the road.

"Oh God! Oh Jesus!" Jake whispered as he pulled off the road, his hands shaking. Jumping out of his car, he ran to Rufe's crumpled car. Within seconds, he had called 911 to report the accident. "Send an ambulance!" he shouted at the dispatcher. Seeing a glimpse of Rufe in the wreckage of the car made him almost puke, but he made himself focus on how to get the poor guy out of the car in case it was about to explode. He could already hear a siren in the distance, and then another.

When he hoisted himself up onto the sky-facing side of the car to look through the smashed side window, he got a better look at the angle of Rufe's head and a terrifying amount of blood inside the wreckage of the car.

He hoped he wasn't going to pass out.

The ambulance was almost as fast getting there as the cops. After the officer checked out the car, conferred with the ambulance driver, and radioed the dispatcher, he came over to where Jake leaned against his car. Jake was shivering, and scrolling to see if he had a home number for Rufe.

"Bad scene. Hard to see something like that," the cop said gently.

Jake nodded. "You think he's going to make it?" he asked.

The cop shrugged. "I don't know. Amazing what they can do these days. I've seen my share of bad crashes, and thought plenty of times it was all over. Then sometimes they surprise everyone and they pull through. I always hope for the best."

"I knew the guy," Jake said quietly.

"Geez, that's even worse," Officer Perry said. "You mind telling me a little more? You're the only eyewitness, and you can identify the victim. That's very helpful. You weren't in the car, right?"

Jake looked at him. "What kind of question is that? No, I was driving behind him in this car here, my car." He felt unreasonably angry.

"So what happened?" the officer asked.

"We had just had a meal together at JHook's. Rufe pulled out of the parking lot right ahead of me." Jake stopped. He was having trouble trying to remember details. He felt weirdly blank.

"So you left the restaurant and each of you went to your own car, and then what happened?" Officer Perry asked.

"I saw him waiting to exit the parking lot as I was pulling out of my parking space in the lot," Jake said. "I pulled onto the road behind him, maybe ten seconds or so after he did. I looked in my rearview mirror and saw a vehicle barreling up behind me like we were at the Daytona track, so I quickly moved over to let him pass. Then he swerved around me, accelerated even more, and smashed into the side of Rufe's car."

"And that driver just kept going?"

Jake nodded, stunned as he began to consider the implications of this being a hit and run.

"Can you give me a description of the car?" the cop asked.

Jake stared at him in dismay. "Shit!" he said, horrified that he couldn't remember anything about the vehicle. "What's up with this? I'm a lawyer and I can't even give you a description of the car, let alone the license plate. I don't know why I can't picture any details. It just all happened real fast, I guess."

He could cry with frustration. What an idiot! How could he, of all people, fail to get even the most basic information about a vehicle that might have just killed his friend! The jerk might have intentionally driven into Rufe's car in a cold-blooded attack. Maybe he intended to kill Rufe.

He started shivering even more, taking it in. This was no coincidence!

"Seeing something like this can cause a PTSD response," Officer Perry said reassuringly. "Sir, I'd like to ask you if you'd be willing to follow me to the station? We can get one of our crash specialists to help you try to recall some details. They have hypnotherapy training, and they're good at helping a person retrieve whatever the trauma blocked out.

"First, though, you can help by giving me your friend's name so I can try to locate him in the ER. If he regains consciousness, I'd like to find out if he's able to recall anything."

Jake put his head in his hands. Jesus! This was horrible. He was increasingly sure this was no accident. He tried to think about what he wanted to tell the cops. He hoped the hypnotherapy wouldn't make him spill information about the lawsuit. He wasn't ready to go there without talking to his clients.

"Let's take a minute or two right here," the officer told him. "It'll give you time to recover before you try to drive. Are you ok with that?"

"Sure," Jake said. He gave Officer Perry Rufe's full name, and said they had eaten at J's. "Listen, I don't feel so good. Can you give me a little space?"

The cop walked away to call the hospital and identify the crash victim, then walked back over.

"Good news so far." he said. "Your friend is still alive," he said, "but he's in bad shape. I would like you to come to the station and tell us what you know about the victim, and see what we can do to help you retrieve any memory of the vehicle that hit him. If you're not up to driving, I can drive your car back into the parking lot at JHook's and then we'll bring you back later. What do you want to do?"

The last thing he needed was to have someone see him in the back seat of a police cruiser! "I'll follow you," Jake said. "I'm ok, I think."

Chapter Eighteen
Western Massachusetts

Alice was having trouble trusting that there was a good outcome for the world she was presently inhabiting, yet there was some predictability to her daily life that seemed to come easy to the three of them. Although it had only been four months, sometimes she felt as if she had been sheltering at Felicia's forever.

They had been negotiating the details of daily life with surprising ease. Even the meals were going relatively well, although there had been some fractious debates about the health content versus the tastiness virtues of a dish. Gerard continued to make delicious but high fat meals, and Felicia continued to never whole-heartedly embrace these offerings.

Countering Gerard's risky gastronomic productions, Felicia sometimes responded by concocting strenuously healthy meals, a challenge to her guests' digestive capacities. Most of the time, though, meals and all the other demands of cohabitation moved serenely along.

Alice had been able to protect her individual pursuits, somehow avoiding hurt feelings. It was nothing short of miraculous. It was helpful to be old, she thought. The three of them had, collectively, more than enough practice in negotiating relational complexities.

Today she was relaxing in a lovely old wicker armchair in the yard. It was surprisingly comfortable, and Alice was working her way through a mind-altering study of race and caste by Isabel Wilkerson when her phone buzzed. She was too distracted by the book to even check her caller ID before answering the call.

"Alice, it's Bernice!" a very familiar voice greeted her. "Can you meet me at the Interstate-91 Diner in Whateley?"

"Oh my! What a surprise! I'm so glad to hear from you!" Alice exclaimed.

"Can you meet me? Soon??" Bernice persisted.

Alice hesitated. "Right now?" she asked, still stunned to hear Bernice's voice, and learn that she was nearby.

"It's short notice, I know. But I need to see you, and there isn't much time."

Although there were warning bells ringing in Alice's mind, she very much wanted to see Bernice and find out what was going on.

"I'll be there in twenty minutes or so," she said.

"Meet me in the parking lot," Bernice said. "I'll find your car and then we can talk outdoors."

Today Alice was going to be the risk-taker, very briefly leaving her harmonious sanctuary in order to meet Bernice. It made her feel slightly fluttery.

She could hear Felicia chopping something in the kitchen. Just as she stepped out the front door, she called over her shoulder that she was going over to the diner to meet someone.

"Alice, you be careful!" Felicia called after her. Alice had no doubt that both her housemates would be cautioning her doubly if they knew who she was meeting. Better that she make this a solo mission, she thought, hoping she wouldn't regret the decision.

She was amazed that her friend had finally returned to the Valley. As far as Alice could find out, Bernice had not been charged with anything regarding her ex-husband's near death experience.

She had continued to wonder who else might suspect Bernice of attempted murder. The scene in the backyard still haunted Alice. Hadn't Bernice always portrayed the marriage ending with great rancor and many accusations?

After many long soul-searching conversations with Felicia and Gerard, Alice had finally decided that there was nothing she could do.

The trio at Felicia's was getting used to letting most sleeping dogs lay. Now, apparently, the dog was wide awake.

When Alice drove into the diner parking lot, she looked for Bernice's car even scanning among all the big semis congregated beyond the diner. She wasn't sure where she should park, but decided to go back near the front of the diner.

She didn't have to sit long before a familiar voice spoke from somewhere behind the driver's window.

"Hey Alice," Bernice said calmly, "I'm right back here!"

Alice stuck her neck out the car window and craned her head to look. At the rear of the car, she beheld a whole new version of Bernice.

Bernice's hair was a surprisingly bold blond, and it was styled in a 1950's cut that was evenly trimmed to just above her shoulders. She was wearing a drab grey skirt and a Navy blue blouse, a distinctly retro look. Bernice's cosmetic make-over was so different from her previously no-frills look that Alice gasped in sheer surprise. She couldn't tell if Bernice had gotten tan or if it was a cosmetic illusion.

"Bernice, I am truly delighted to see you again," she finally said, recovering her manners after gawking at Bernice for a full minute. "Where do you suggest we talk?"

"I could sit in your back seat, and we could visit with all the windows open," Bernice suggested.

Alice felt her stomach tighten. "I'm not sure that would be safe," she told Bernice firmly.

Then she had an idea.

"I have two folding chairs in the trunk. We could drive up to the top of the hill in the center of Whately and set up our chairs behind the village church. It's a beautiful view up there, and I doubt anyone else will be around. It's maybe five minutes from here."

"OK, I'll follow you, Alice," Bernice said sweetly.

They drove across the old state road and up the hill, each in her own car. Alice was relieved to see that when she got out of the car, Bernice was finally wearing a mask.

"This is very pretty," Bernice commented. "It feels safe, hidden back here behind the church! Do you ever worship here, Alice?"

Alice looked at Bernice in surprise. Surely her friend knew her well enough to know this would be highly unlikely. When they could, Alice and Gerard spent blissful Sunday mornings staying in bed and reading the New York Times, The Washington Post and the local Gazette. They had the house to themselves since Felicia did something like ancient outdoor dancing on Sunday mornings.

"Now that I'm back home," Bernice said, "I expect to attend Donald's church with him. He's deepened his faith practice considerably since the experience of COVID."

Now Alice was even more startled. "You're back in touch with him?" she asked, confusion and apprehension pushing her voice up so high that she was almost squeaking.

"Not at first," Bernice said calmly. "But then I came to the decision that I needed to know if he was alive, so I wrote him a letter. I was afraid he would be angry with me or else someone else might open it, if - well - if the Lord had taken him home, you know? But I wanted to be in communication with him. I told him I would like him to call me."

"It took almost two weeks before I got the call back I'd been praying for," Bernice continued. "He didn't sound like the tough gruff Donald I married. For a few minutes, I thought someone was impersonating him, trying to find out where I was. It could have been the police, for all I knew!"

"Good heavens!" Alice said softly.

"Can we take our masks off now?" Bernice asked. "I want to see your face. We're outside in the open air, and we must be easily six feet apart!

Alice hesitated. Was it safe to be talking unmasked with Bernice, given her recent history? "Well, you have been traveling," she pointed out.

"Oh I was very careful, you better believe it!" Bernice said quickly. " This hysteria about the virus is just a liberal myth that the socialist intellectuals are trying to use to destroy the American way of life. God will protect us!"

Alice wondered if someone had been holding Bernice hostage, long distance. This language was so not Bernice!

Alice was struck speechless by Bernice's next announcement. "I have asked Donald to remarry me, Alice!" she confided in a breathless teenager's voice.

In the dead silence that followed, Bernice seemed cheerfully oblivious to Alice's lack of congratulatory cheer.

"I'm dreaming of a late summer wedding!" she confided. "We're only waiting for the fuss about the virus to pass, so no one has to even think about mask-wearing."

Alice felt that this simply confirmed that she had ample reason to be flabbergasted. Could her ex-husband's return from death be causing Bernice's conversion? And if she wasn't brainwashed, then what was she up to?

When Bernice had originally left Donald, not long after Alice met her, she had slowly begun to reveal rugged competence, a strong desire for independence, and a fierce distaste for male dominance. Before her emancipation, it was hard to persuade her to stand up to Donald, let alone divorce him. But once she freed herself, she never seemed to look back.

Now she was billing and cooing about Donald as if he was not only brought back from the dead, but glowed with heavenly light. He sounded more like an action figure than a real human being.

"Donald is so grateful to the Lord for bringing him back to life," Bernice told Alice. "He's recommitting his life to serving Him, and he wants us to do this together. We will bring light to the unbelievers! Even you, Alice!

"Now I am ready and willing to give myself to him as his helpmate! We have so much work to do here."

Alice couldn't tolerate another word.

"Bernice, are we talking about the same Donald who used to criticize you and harass you and make you afraid of your own shadow? He sounds like a Ken Doll for Jesus, the way you talk about him!"

"I know you're used to thinking the way you probably have for many years, Alice," Bernice said patiently. She smiled so sweetly that Alice felt compelled to smile back. "If you could try to hear me out, I would so appreciate it! We've been friends long enough that at least you owe me that, don't you think?"

"I suppose you're right," Alice said reluctantly. She would make herself be as open as possible. Although, she was in fact very respectful of Jesus, she wasn't likely to subscribe to the hierarchical religious concepts that Bernice was embracing.

"It's changed the way I think about everything!" Bernice said, ecstasy causing her voice to thrum with the intensity of her conviction. "I have come to understand that the Lord has bigger plans for me than wasting the rest of my life in a jail cell or in the fearful life of a fugitive. Donald has forgiven me, and so has God's only son, Our Savior Jesus Christ himself!"

Alice vowed that she was going to do her best to talk Bernice down from her celestial cloud at some future time. For right now, she would try to ascertain if she was safe.

"Bernice, where are you going to be staying now that you're

back?" she asked.

"I'll be with Donald," Bernice said, seeming surprised by the question.

"Have you two talked over what happened that night?" Alice stared into Bernice's eyes, trying to see if there was a flicker of fear or, at least, confusion.

Bernice's eyes were pools of innocence. "I thought I might have lost him that night," she said, "But the Lord saved us both."

"What does Donald say about that night?" Alice asked.

Bernice remained enveloped in her serenity. "Donald has forgiven everything," she said. "We are about to start a new life together. Please, Alice, at least give me your blessing."

"Well, I will try to be happy for you," Alice said, although she couldn't see how, as a sentient being, she could summon up much happiness for Bernice's choice to be so subservient to a man who had once been her abuser.

Chapter Nineteen
Central Florida

"C'mon in," Jake said, and walked Charles quickly down the hall to his office. "I'll make us some fresh coffee."

He went over to the little coffee-maker tucked in one corner of his office. "Take a seat," he said, waving at the assortment of chairs. Jake always wanted everyone to be comfortable.

Charles collapsed into one of the club chairs facing Jake's desk. He slumped, his hands twisting nervously together between his knees.

"Coffee will be ready in a couple of minutes," Jake said, sitting on the chair nearest to Charles. "Sorry I had to give you the news about Rufe so late last night. It breaks your heart, right? Terrible to lose such a wonderful man."

Jake could only imagine how Charles was absorbing the news, considering Kori's assault only a few weeks earlier. He knew that Charles and Kori were close. The shock Charles was probably feeling around Rufe's death was the message intended for everyone involved in the lawsuit. *You could be next!*

"Thanks for coming in to meet with me," Jake continued. "I called Kori, but I haven't heard from her."

"It's the last thing she needs," Charles said.

He took the cup of coffee Jake handed him, but sat there staring at the coffee as if he didn't recognize what it was. Jake decided to wait him out.

"You said you wanted to ask me about that guy Mitch?" Charles finally said, looking up at Jake and taking a tentative sip of his coffee.

"Yessir, I do," Jake said. "Mitch showed up with Rufe for your meeting at JHook's last night. You arranged for him to get a ride with Rufe, right?"

"Yup," Charles said. "Good thing he wasn't riding with Rufe after all. We might have had two victims."

"Well, tell you the truth, it makes me wonder why he was not in the car with Rufe when Rufe's car got hit," Jake said. "It may not mean anything, but I need to find out more about the guy. I tried to reach him last night after the crash, and then tried again this morning. I used the phone number he gave me at the restaurant. Another red flag: the number didn't work. It's out of service.

"I'm thinking that someone told the killer that Rufe was at JHook's, and maybe even reported when Rufe left the restaurant. So what can you tell me about Mitch?"

Charles' face was covered in a light sheen of sweat. "Not all that much," Charles said. "I only met with Mitch a few times, just work-related stuff. He hadn't been working at Serenity Place very long, so I was surprised when he seemed so determined to meet with me about the lawsuit.

"I put out the word to our underground grapevine that we needed a few more plaintiffs. It might not have been the safest way to go about it, but I've been trying to pick up the work that Kori had been doing, and I was trying to keep everything going without exactly knowing what I was doing. Anyhow, Mitch called and asked to meet with me.

"It was a weird meeting. He wouldn't talk to me unless I met him where he chose."

"So where'd you meet him?" Jake asked.

"At the No Name Saloon over in Edgewater? You know the place?"

Jake shrugged. He knew its reputation, a big favorite during Daytona's infamous Bike Week. "Not much," he answered.

"The place operates mostly outdoors, so there's a lot of room for social distancing. I was OK with that," Charles said. "But it's a biker bar. Not my kind of place. Not a place I would ever think to go."

Charles gave Jake a meaningful look. Jake could imagine that the way Charles dressed, very elegant and upscale, meant he might not feel at home at the No Name Saloon. And it was probably a racial thing. Jake was impressed that Charles had the courage to go there.

"Anyhow, I wasn't crazy about it," Charles continued, "but I told him, 'OK, I'll meet you there.' We didn't have much time. Truth? I was super uncomfortable in that place, so I didn't spend long enough asking Mitch why he wanted to get involved in the suit.

"I should have never put the guy in touch with Rufe without knowing more about him. Kori would have done much more checking out the dude. I didn't take the time to do the kind of prep Kori would've done."

"Hey man, you did the best you could," Jake said. "No one's going to take your inventory on this. So tell me what you can about Mitch."

"He seemed real nervous," Charles said. "He didn't tell me much about his job except he's responsible for inventorying the supplies on the dementia unit over there, does the shift scheduling, and some patient contact too.

"Their memory unit is ultra fancy, by the way, a place rich people can park their elders without feeling guilty. It's way upscale compared to Sunset Villages.

"I was surprised, you know, when it turned out Serenity's getting screwed over too, right? I know some nurses and aides and at least one supervisor from over there: same crap with scarcity of PPE and overtime hours not getting paid out. "

Jake nodded. "Did you tell Mitch what to expect if he agreed to join in the suit?" he asked Charles.

"Well, a little," Charles said. "He was curious about that, like he wanted to know how many people were already on board, who was in charge, stuff like that. I told him your name, and said you'd be explaining more about it.

"When he said he definitely wanted to do it, I told him about the meeting with you and Rufe. I figured you two would fill him in on details I'd missed. I knew I was rushing things a little, but Kori had just told me you were about ready to go ahead and file the suit. I just thought I'd let this guy join before you stopped taking new plaintiffs."

Jake sat in silence.

"I never imagined someone would get killed because I screwed up," Charles finally said. "You think Mitch set up Rufe to get hit last night?"

"He could have," Jake said. "But we don't know that. I'm about to call Serenity Place and see if he came in for work this morning. If he's there, I'll drop by and have a chat with him. We can't jump to conclusions. But listen, man, forget blaming yourself for what happened last night!"

Charles stood up and took a step toward Jake's desk to put his half-finished cup of coffee down. "I need to go see Kori now," he said. "Looks like we don't have much of a safety net."

Jake nodded. "You should also think about your own safety," he said. "Can you take a little time off from work, maybe find some place safe to go for a week?"

Charles shook his head. "Can't afford a vacation right now," he said. "What about you?" he asked Jake. "You're kind of a sitting duck, aren't you?"

Jake grinned. "My law office is pretty impenetrable," he said. "We figured out how best to protect ourselves if a client gets lethally pissed off with us."

He winked at Charles but he was thinking how he couldn't describe the vehicle that came up from behind him and killed Rufe. Standing up, he grabbed one of his cards. "Here," he said, "keep this on you at all times. Call me if anything seems weird to you. Anything!"

He walked Charles to the door of the elevator. "Give my best to Kori and tell her she's got to stay safe, whatever it takes. Tell her to call me and we can talk more. And you take care of yourself, Charles. No heroics. OK?"

Charles gave him a strange look, and Jake was left wondering what Charles would do next. Nothing he could do about anyone else's next move, and he knew it well.

Chapter Twenty
Central Florida

Bernice had invited Alice to come over for tea.

As she drove past the farms on the road to North Mountain, Alice reminisced about strawberry picking with her granddaughter. It had been a few years since she could bend or squat in the early summer warmth to pluck berries from the rows of luscious smelling plants. She wondered if the young woman also sometimes thought fondly of their strawberry picking excursions.

Bernice was waiting on the long side porch when Alice arrived. She was relieved to see that Bernice looked more like herself, still trim in her flowery shorts and a short-sleeved polo shirt. She hoped Bernice's familiar sporty style was a part of the feisty, in-your-face Bernice that Donald's resurrection hadn't completely erased.

"Oh hooray, Alice! You made it!" Bernice called excitedly before Alice could even get out of the car. She waved extravagantly, like a 1950s movie diva waving to her fans.

Alice had pulled in next to Bernice's familiar little car. She wondered if Donald still drove, or if he had become a helpless invalid.

This thought gave her a sudden new insight into Bernice's total devotion to her once despised ex-husband. Bernice the Protector had been given the task of rescuing an aging, fragile man who had survived a close encounter with death.

Bernice loved nothing more than the role of protector. How silly of her, Alice told herself, not to grasp this sooner. But there were still warning beeps going off in her mind, louder than a truck backing up. She carefully donned her mask before stepping out of the car.

"Alice, you were so kind to make this long journey over the mountain to see me," Bernice said.

She offered numerous choices of tea, cold beverages, and snack options and went back into the house, returning with a giant decorative tray filled with edibles, both savory and sweet, a teapot with two cups, cream and sugar, along with two glasses and a pitcher of what looked like Kool Aid.

"Good gracious! How did you manage all this so quickly?"
Bernice winked at her. "I think you may have taken a quick nap,"
she said. "Don't worry, though. I'm used to it. He -" she looked
over her shoulder at the house – "he drops off all the time, then
wakes up and claims he hasn't been asleep! I think it's sweet,
really."

Alice stared at her in surprise. "You never used to think that a
lapse in attention was sweet," she reminded Bernice. "You've
scolded both Felicia and me more than once about the importance
of staying alert. You've been my go-to person for absolute vigilance! And," she added, "speaking of vigilance, why aren't you
wearing a mask?"

Bernice looked chagrined. "Oh, Alice, I'm really sorry! Of
course I should have remembered that you would feel more comfortable if I had a mask on. I'll go see where I put that thing. Perhaps it's with my car keys." She scurried back into the house.

Alice glanced at her watch. She couldn't stay with Bernice too
long or her oxygen would run out before she made it back to Felicia's.

Bernice came back wearing a cloth mask. "Now let's start catching up! Have I told you that Donald and I are getting married very
soon?" she asked, smiling demurely.

Alice had just lowered her own mask so that she could take a sip
of iced tea. She gulped, glad that she wasn't mid-swallow when the
announcement was made.

"I knew you were thinking along that line," she said cautiously,
"but I had no idea when. May I ask you, Bernice, why the act of
getting re-married seems so compelling? You've just recently
gotten back together."

She hesitated, but decided to plough on. "Bernice, I must tell you
quite honestly, I don't see the point."

Bernice laughed merrily, and thrust the plate of freshly baked
cookies toward Alice.

"Have one!" she urged rather aggressively. "I bet Felicia's not
letting you or Gerard have anything made with sugar! Just one little cookie won't do you any harm, you know. Don't let yourself
turn into one of those fearful Sheep People who worry about every
little thing."

"Bernice, you know me better than that!" Alice said, frowning. She needed to regain her social balance. She reached out and grabbed two of the biggest cookies on the plate.

"Gerard and I are not letting Felicia turn us into total health nuts, even though she may have secret hopes of that."

"I'm sure you want to know more about my wedding plans," Bernice said. "The little Baptist church over in Brookville seems like it may be the best location for the wedding. I've been meeting with the pastor, and he's all for it. I certainly hope you and Gerard will attend!"

Alice stared at her in consternation.

What on earth had happened? Was Bernice assuaging her guilt for Donald's close encounter with death? If she had experienced a homicidal impulse in the midst of her rescue mission, her conversion could be driven by fear plus guilt.

Alice remembered her first impression of Bernice, a timid woman in a flowered dress. That woman was frightened that her husband would see her in the hospital cafeteria simply talking to Alice, fearful of Alice's reputation as a notorious social activist.

She would never forget how terrified Bernice had been when they started the action group in North Mountain. Donald had showed up at one of the women's secret meetings, and Alice had witnessed him bellowing at Bernice to leave the meeting and come home with him. Bernice had curled into a ball of fear at the sound of his voice.

But the other women had helped her gather the courage to defy and resist Donald's bullying. Not long after embracing this new-found bravery, Bernice had left her husband and become involved with the activists.

Bernice never seemed to lack courage from that time on. She was something of a loner, not easily trusting others, but she excelled at showing up to protect Alice and her friends.

"Bernice," she said thoughtfully, "I would never have predicted that you would want to be Donald's wife again, and I'm surprised by your new religious convictions. But I want you to try to explain it to me."

She picked up another cookie and began to munch, showing as much enthusiasm as she could without spewing cookie crumbs all over.

"Mmmm! This is another of your surprises, Bernice. I never remembered you being a star baker!"

There was a sudden shout from somewhere inside the house. Alice looked at Bernice apprehensively. "Is that Donald?" she asked.

"He gets these fits sometimes,'" Bernice said, lowering her voice. "He gets mad as a hornet, sometimes right out of the blue. He's probably having a fit about something he doesn't like on TV. He gets all worked up when he sees people talking about COVID restrictions. "We'd be better off living in Florida where they're not Sheep People."

They could hear Donald shouting at the television from inside the house. Bernice stared at something above the trees for a long minute. Finally she took a deep breath, and looked Alice in the eye.

"Alice you know about my life before Donald. You remember how I told you about Eunice. She was in the military service with me, and we fell in love? You remember about Eunice? The sinful relationship?"

Alice couldn't refrain from speaking her truth. "It was not sinful," she stated calmly.

"Well of course you would say that," Bernice said, shrugging.

Alice nodded. Bernice's relationship with The Holy seemed to have a back story that she hadn't expected.

"When I lost Eunice while we were still in the service, I thought I couldn't survive," Bernice continued. "But anyhow, it all came around again when my dear Haley was killed by her husband. I just kept thinking how I never am able to protect the people I love. I made a vow that I must commit myself to protecting everyone I possibly could.

"But my relationship with Donald was different. I just didn't think about trying to protect him. It was really the other way around. I was afraid a lot of the time around him, and so I had to think about protecting myself. He was always keeping me on the alert.

"Then you and your friends came along. You were like some kind of guardian angels or something. You rescued me, and I was so grateful." Bernice stopped, her eyes filling with tears.

Alice wanted to touch her hand to comfort her, but from six feet away she could only nod. She realized sadly that Bernice couldn't even see her smile behind her mask.

"But my life was lonely after I left Donald," Bernice continued. "I wasn't needed by anyone, although it was kind of a relief that I didn't have to keep on the alert, protecting myself. I didn't know how to fit in with you and the other ladies. At least I could be useful to you, and I kept watch over you the best I could."

Bernice stopped briefly, wiping a few tears away with the back of her hand.

"When the hospital called me about Donald," she continued, "I went over there out of duty. I was his medical proxy only because he was too cheap to get the documents changed after the divorce.

"But then something really woke up in me when I saw how helpless he was. Alice, I knew I had to protect him. I could rescue him from a horrible painful death. I believed that he would have died if they intubated him. That night, dragging him to the back of his house, thinking he was going to die there, I was afraid I'd be arrested and charged with his death. But in my darkest hour, a miracle happened!"

Alice sat in silence, her eyes holding Bernice's gaze. Bernice was retelling a transformative moment of biblical proportions.

"God brought the ambulance," Bernice said, radiant with the memory, "and, well, you know the rest of the story. Donald came back to life! Now when I look at Donald, I know he's the one I was meant to save. It's that simple," she concluded, smiling serenely.

Alice was moved even though Bernice was speaking about a parallel universe that she herself might never understand.

"I think I'll have another cookie," she finally murmured.

Bernice smiled as she passed her the cookie plate.

"You know, I think I'll have one myself," she said.

Looking at her watch, Alice stood up and straightened out her back.

"You know that I'd love to stay longer," she told Bernice, "but

my air will run out within an hour, so I have to be on my way.
We'll have to talk about this more very soon!"

Bernice waved goodbye as vigorously as she had welcomed
Alice earlier. Her radiant smile almost began to convince Alice
that at least for now, there was not much trouble in paradise.

Chapter Twenty-one
Western Massachusetts

Gerard was waiting for Alice when she got home. "You have had the important conversation?" he asked, studying her face thoughtfully.

"Yes, I think so. But it wasn't what I expected. I think I understand some things I didn't before. I'll tell you and Felicia all about it over dinner."

Gerard smiled. "I will hear of your visit with Bernice while we eat Felicia's barley-and-root surprise." He looked mischievous. "I have made the fresh apple and *fromage tarte*! This will give your tasting buds a good dream after we eat Felicia's gift for our health," he said, with the flourish of a proud chef.

Alice went back to her small computer table in the corner of their large bedroom, and tried to type some of her post-Bernice thoughts.

"You know about my passion to uncover injustice," she typed. "You understand how it energizes me when we fight for change."

This sounded like a bad after-dinner speech at an ACLU fundraiser.

"Anyone ready for supper?" Felicia called from the kitchen.

The meal began with Felicia's apologies for the main dish, the barley and root concoction Gerard had mentioned. "I'm afraid I was heavy-handed with the vinegar," she told them. "Then I thought I'd add a few spoonfuls of honey to counteract my mistake."

"*Ah non, non!*" Gerard reassured her. "*Ç'est délicieux!*"

Alice was too distracted by what she wanted to tell them to comment. After she had silently eaten enough to convince both cooks of her gratitude, she tried to summarize her visit with Bernice.

When she finished, Felicia shook her head. "I don't get it! It seems so peculiar to me. Not only is it not like Bernice to say all these pious things, but it doesn't seem in character for Donald to be forgiving."

Alice sighed. She hadn't thought much about Donald's part in the story. That wasn't where she was heading with the story.

Gerard cleared his throat, "Perhaps this Donald, as you say, he goes along with the story that Bernice tells. Maybe he is so damaged by the illness and the blow to the head, he doesn't know what is happening. Maybe this Donald, he is the victim of a trap that Bernice, she makes for him?"

Alice stared at Gerard.

"What do you mean?" she asked sharply. Was Gerard actually sympathetic to this man who was known as a wife abuser? It was hard enough to hear Bernice's version of Donald, but was Gerard now championing the man?

"Maybe Bernice, she has the plan to take the revenge?" Gerard speculated. "Perhaps she pretend the marriage, it is for love. But *non*! It is to acquire this Donald's money? Perhaps Bernice, she use the marriage to make the guarantee that she is not charged with the crime of intended murder!"

There was a silence at the table. Alice studied Gerard thoughtfully. Suddenly she had no more energy for the Bernice and Donald saga.

"I'm too tired to explain this. I'll try again tomorrow after a good night's sleep"

Three hours later, Alice was still wide awake. She headed upstairs to Felicia's meditation room.

"I have to talk to you!" she said.

Felicia looked at her in disbelief while holding the complicated yoga pose Alice had interrupted when she flung open the door. "This is a first!" Felicia added. "I'm always the one who violates your no phone calls after nine p.m. rule! It must be important since you're bursting in here in the middle of my yoga practice, another thing you never, ever do! What on earth is going on?"

Alice suddenly felt hesitant. But if she didn't explain herself right this minute, she wasn't sure she could hold onto her resolve. It was like going into cold water. You had to just push yourself on in, even when the first minute or two made you think it was just too cold for swimming. She had spent her whole life going ahead and pushing on into the hard things.

"I have to tell you some things you're not going to like hearing," she said. "but I absolutely need you to listen with an open mind."

"You and Gerard don't like my cooking!" Felicia said, looking sorrowful. "I'm just trying to do my part to keep us all healthy. If it were not for the threat of COVID looming over us, I'd just wallow in the blissful pools of butter fat that Gerard's pastries and soufflés offer. But, Alice, all the fresh produce provides a balance. Surely you know that!"

"No, no! That's not what I came in here to talk about," Alice reassured her. "Gerard and I love what you bring to our meals. We are grateful," she offered as a conciliatory segue to what was on her mind.

She looked around Felicia's meditation room to see if there was anything above knee level where she could sit down. She knew better than to try to lower herself onto any of the little prayer pillows. She would only be able to get back up if someone else hauled her onto her feet.

"I know, I know,' Felicia said. "I know you can't sit comfortably in here. Let's move to my healing room. I have that lovely old rocking chair, or of course you could lie down on the massage table. Or I will stretch out my spine as I recline there, and you can sit and tell me what has you so agitated."

They moved to the healing room. It smelled wonderful, a predominant lavender overlay with cloves, lemon verbena, and other herbs that Alice couldn't quite identify. She settled herself in the rocking chair and leaned back into the soft headrest. Felicia lay prone on her massage table, her hands folded over her belly, a small smile welcoming Alice's presence.

"I need to make some big changes," Alice told Felicia, after pausing for a minute to gather her thoughts. She couldn't stop her voice from trembling slightly.

"I've been thinking that I need to be doing something more active," she said. "Even though Bernice's sudden conversion makes me anxious, at least she's passionate about the changes she's making, and the commitments. I don't feel passionate anymore, Felicia. I feel old. I'm not out in the world, showing up for justice. I just don't feel like myself."

Felicia remained very still. Alice looked carefully at her to see if she had fallen asleep. "I'm listening," Felicia told her. "I'm just keeping my eyes closed so this will seem like a dream. You're making me anxious! I know how you sound when you're seized by some new idea. Nothing will stop you, not even the risk of death, apparently."

She continued to lie still on the massage table, but began her tapping exercises to decrease her stress levels.

Some things never changed, Alice thought. She couldn't help but smile at Felicia's response. They were each just being themselves.

Felicia hummed softly to herself as she continued to tap various energy points on her face, her arms and under her armpits.

Alice sighed. "I'm sorry," she said. "I should wait until morning to have this conversation with you."

"I'm not the one who's tired," Felicia said pointedly. "I can talk all night if you have the stamina. But I know you don't. That's part of this, Alice. We are all old! We can't go on doing all the things we did before. It's not just the COVID stopping us."

Alice was struggling to formulate a rejoinder when the door swung open slightly and Mother Jones stalked in. "Oops!" Alice said, glad for the reprieve, "Mother Jones seems determined to enforce her rigid schedule. It's her bedtime, and we know she won't let any of us rest unless I take her down to the bedroom with me. We can talk more in the morning."

Felicia stopped tapping, and gracefully ascended from her massage table.

"You might want to ask the Dream Goddess for guidance during your sleep tonight," she said cheerfully. "See you in the morning!"

Gerard was deep asleep in their bed. Alice got ready for bed, and crawled under the covers, gratefully snuggling up to Gerard as she fell asleep.

Mother Jones waited until all was still, then jumped onto the bed. She purred as she heard the human snores begin. She had accomplished her mission, and all was well.

Chapter Twenty-two
Western Massachusetts

Felicia was standing over Alice, thrusting the phone toward her as Alice struggled to open her eyes.

"Nancy Warren is on the phone," she told Alice. "She says it's urgent!" Handing the phone to Alice, she scurried out of the room.

"Good morning, Nancy," Alice said, her voice hoarse from sleep. She was worried and feeling disoriented. "Why are you calling me on Felicia's phone?"

"You weren't answering yours and I really need to talk, Alice! I'm sorry if I woke you up. I remember you as more of an early morning person than I guess you are these days."

"It's all right, Nancy, go ahead! Tell me why you're calling."

"Remember when I emailed you about the election and the lawsuit? Now things have escalated down here."

Alice thought quickly. Nancy Warren had written her a few weeks earlier about the very disturbing incident involving a young Black woman who had been working on a lawsuit against a big healthcare corporation and had been badly beaten up.

"Yes, Nancy, what has happened?"

"A man who was involved in Kori's project, a whistleblower?" Nancy's voice was tight with tension. "He was run off the road right after a meeting with the lawyer who's representing the law-suit. He died in the car wreck! And, Alice, it was a hit and run! We're sure this was cold-blooded murder!"

Chills were electrifying Alice's spine as she considered what she had just heard.

After a brief pause, Nancy continued. "Kori is recovering from her assault, and she's physically able to talk now, but this thing has thrown her into a terrible state of mind. The lawyer wants to push forward with the lawsuit immediately because he says the murder of a person of color has created a martyr for the cause! Jake says if they move quickly, and go public with the suit, the public will be much more sympathetic now."

"How do you know for sure that the man was killed because of the lawsuit?" Alice asked.

"Oh there's not much doubt, given the circumstances. He had just met with the lawyer, then started the drive home and was immediately broadsided. It was lethal, an intentional hit-and-run, witnessed by the lawyer who he had just finished meeting with.

"But, back to Kori. The lawyer also wants to go public about the attack on her. He's urging Kori to be interviewed for a human interest story on her relationship with her grandmother."

"Remind me about Kori and her grandmother."

"Well, Kori moved down here to be near her grandmother who's in a nursing home, one of the two nursing care facilities owned by the TouchStone Corporation that I've told you about. So because she was there every day with Gram, Kori got really friendly with various staff at the nursing home, and she found out about a big COVID grant that they were supposed to be using for protective equipment and overtime pay. It seemed to be disappearing! They weren't seeing any of that money made available to the nursing home staff. So Kori started organizing for the lawsuit."

"Does Kori want to do the article?" Alice asked.

"She's very upset," Nancy said. "I don't think she's decided what she wants. This is not the way she wanted the public to get behind the lawsuit. She never wanted it to be about her.

"And she's also worried about the group filing the lawsuit. There's still so much work to be done to get the plaintiffs ready to launch the first legal steps. Everyone's unraveled by this latest attack. No one can feel safe when a courageous employee speaks out about corporate wrong-doing and then gets killed."

"What does your friend, that brilliant woman whose campaign you're involved in, what does she think?" Why couldn't she remember the woman's name? She sat up in bed and put on her glasses. It helped her think better.

"Flo's hoping they still have a pretty solid case. I think she agrees with the lawyer that they should go forward with the suit. Meanwhile, she's considering a separate lawsuit against the police for failing to pursue an investigation into Kori's attack. She wants their commitment to investigate both attacks."

Alice wondered what Nancy hoped to hear from her. It was hard to jump in and have opinions, let alone answers, about a situation that she knew so little about. She had questions, but it seemed better to let Nancy tell her as much as she needed to before Alice tried to respond.

"Flo wants the attacks to be named as lethal tactics to stop the lawsuit against the TouchStone Corporation," Nancy continued, "and she wants the police to be held accountable. She's ready to declare both Kori's attack and Rufe's murder for what they are: two hate crimes ordered by whoever it is who has the most to lose if the lawsuit goes forward. Wow! Right?"

Alice wondered if this promising political campaign could be helped or hindered by Floriana's strong message about the treacherous corporation.

"Are you afraid for Floriana's life?" she asked Nancy.

"Well, yes, I think everyone is worried. But Flo's amazingly resourceful," Nancy said. "She's got huge support on the West Side - that's the Black neighborhood. Plus the city and state leaders don't want harm to befall her. They obviously want to preserve the image of being a peaceful part of Florida where tourists and snowbirds come. She wants this story to get picked up by national media.

"Would any campaign workers be tempted to quit if the campaign and the lawsuit are publicly linked?" Alice asked. "I can imagine that some want to work for a Black female candidate, but they might not want the campaign to make accusations against this big corporation. Doesn't the corporation provide a sizable number of jobs in the area?"

Nancy sighed loudly. "Your question gets to the heart of a major dilemma for Flo."

There was a pause and Alice considered asking Nancy to give her a few minutes to have coffee and wake up before continuing their conversation.

"Alice, I wish you'd consider coming down here to help." Nancy said. "We need your ability to look at the big picture and to ask those very useful questions.

"You've had a lifetime of making decisions like this, when to turn away and when to press on. I always felt so secure when we worked together. I know it would be a long trip for you, and I know it's no longer a really safe one. But will you at least consider it?"

Alice felt a sudden surge of energy. Maybe this was exactly what she should do!

Chapter Twenty-three
Western Massachusetts

Alice loved the view from the rocking chair on Felicia's front porch. From the top of the mountain, you could see as far as Mount Monadnock, a good fifty miles away in New Hampshire. It was a truly magical location.

She allowed herself a fleeting moment of envy for her friend's good fortune to have this wonderful old farmhouse. She had to admit she was getting spoiled by life in this spacious and beautiful place. Leaving both the safety and luxury of her life at Felicia's would be difficult.

But how could she resist the call to get back into the ever-expanding fight for justice? Nancy's story had opened a door that she didn't think she could walk past.

She rocked thoughtfully for a while, considering her options.

Thirty minutes later, she was back in the bedroom, busy at her computer. She found several inexpensive flights to Orlando. Then she should rent a car.

She felt her stomach clench at the thought! Finding her way out of a big international airport, and driving on unfamiliar highways in a rental car seemed beyond overwhelming.

There was also the consideration of how dangerous flying remained. Air travel offered perfect conditions for contamination: no fresh air, travelers coming from places where people might or might not wear masks, being too close together. Both the airports and the planes were a real risk.

Alice shuddered. Felicia would have an all-out fit!

Another worry about her new venture was that Gerard might revive the pursuit of his own quest. Her trip to Florida could present a golden opportunity to argue his own need to travel. Could he get himself to Fort Detrick, Maryland without her? If flying was dangerous for her, it was doubly so for him. She couldn't let him head into a precarious journey on his own.

She shook her head, wondering if she could possibly persuade Felicia and Gerard to consider going on a car trip together. The three of them could help each other manage the rigors of such a journey. She needed to think about what a COVID-safe trip would look like.

They could travel slowly, and even stop for a day in Maryland to help Gerard locate his old colleagues. She had a friend in the D.C. area, an activist with a separate guest house on her property. She was sure Katherine would host them for one night.

Even if she managed to talk Felicia into the trip itself, she winced as she anticipated her friend's feelings about their destination. The state of Florida was not known for safety regulation. Felicia would probably see this venture just a little less dangerous than swimming in Boston Harbor!

But Felicia might contain her anxiety if she became committed to keeping the three of them healthy. Alice would lean into their need for Felicia's herbal magic, her healthy cooking and her other superpowers. Felicia would become the one with the magic fairy dust to keep them alive!

Then she started to wonder where they would stay once they got to Florida.

Maybe this was the time to put the need out to the Universe, and then see what came their way. It sounded much more like Felicia to think this way, but it had worked for her many times. Alice told herself to give it a try and make a random appeal to the Great Whoever! If Bernice could throw herself into the arms of an invisible deity, Alice could at least let herself be buoyed by hope. And she already held a deep-seated belief in the random kindness of strangers.

For now, she told herself, she would simply enjoy the new energy coursing through her. She felt more like herself than she had for months.

She needed to be very precise in her strategizing. She needed to fine-tune how persuasive she could be, outlining the details of her plan for Florida. She went out to the front of the wrap-around porch and made her way around to the back. Finally she spotted Gerard and Felicia in the backyard, looking at something in the big crabapple tree.

Felicia was using her binoculars while pointing upwards. Should she tiptoe across the grass so that she didn't disturb their bird-watching, or just wait until one or the other turned back toward the house?

She decided to wait.

After making her way down the back steps to the picnic table, she settled herself and sighed happily. The weather was perfect for her purposes, and now that all three of them had enjoyed a good night's sleep, she hoped that her ideas would be met with more welcome than she had received last night.

Felicia came trotting across the yard to report on her sighting. "Oh you won't ever guess what's in the tree back there!" she exclaimed. "It's an immature eagle, perhaps a year or so old! I must look up the meaning of this sighting. Go take a look, Alice!" She handed her binoculars to Alice and skipped up the steps to the back door.

"The sighting of this bird is *très*, ah, you would say, raw? Because it is *le bebe* and it sit in the tree *comme ça*." Gerard explained to Alice.

"We would say 'rare,' not 'raw,' unless we were cooking the bird," Alice said. She reached over to give Gerard's hand a squeeze. "I have something to tell you," she said primly.

Just as she was getting ready to launch her plan, her cell phone buzzed. It was RubyStarr and Alice could not ignore the call. She owed her young friend for Bernice's rescue.

"Alice, I'm, like, so stressed! If I get any worse, I won't, like, be able to keep doing my work and then we wouldn't have any income at all. Warp's driving me nuts. Without his regular job, he's kind of rattling around and I'm so busy, and I'm at the end of my rope. Right now I'm, like, seriously getting into total rage!

"Couldn't you ask Monsieur Gerard to get Warp involved in some kind of mission kind of thing? I know they've been talking every day about some conspiracy about the virus? Something Gerard wants to track down with one of his former work buddies or something? Could you ask him to invite Warp to take him somewhere or something? Like Batman and Robin?"

Alice stared at her phone. "I'm starting to have a really good idea," she said with a cat-swallowed-the-canary smile.

"I might be able to offer Warp a temporary job," she told RubyStarr, trying to sound more confident than she felt. "It would involve driving a long distance, all the way to Central Florida, actually. And he would be driving Gerard and Felicia and me, stopping for several nights along the way. His expenses would be covered, both for the trip to Florida and the return trip, and he would be well-compensated for his time.

"I think I can safely promise he would be gone for at least a week. If I can make the arrangements, and if he agrees, would that be helpful to you, dear?"

"Florida?" RubyStarr said disapprovingly. "That sounds kind of, like, dangerous? I heard that they are resisting wearing masks and social distancing in Florida?"

"I don't actually know, but Warp should be able to take reasonable precautions, and he wouldn't be in Florida for more than a few nights."

Alice wondered if the thought of Warp's vulnerability would counter-balance Ruby's frustration with her partner.

Warp and RubyStarr had been through many challenges since Alice first became acquainted with them nine years earlier. She had watched them in their late teens and seen them become the grown-ups they were now, a well-matched couple. She considered them honorary grandchildren, and very good friends.

"What's Warp supposed to drive on this big trip? Is it a bus driver job?" RubyStarr asked, looking as if she might be warming up to Alice's scheme.

"I have an idea for that. I just need to put some things together," Alice reassured her.

She needed to defuse the young woman's stress level right now. She would explain the details of her newly-hatched plan later.

"You want me to have Warp call you when he gets back?" RubyStarr asked, yawning suddenly. Alice could see that her tension was beginning to ebb. Good! She had launched Step One of her plan, and it was off to a good start.

"I have to be on my way now, I'm afraid," Alice said. "But I do wish to speak with Warp ASAP. I'll keep my cell on so he can reach me whenever he gets back. Or I may try him myself, unless you think I'd be interrupting a counseling exchange?"

"He won't pick up if he's doing his counseling thing," Ruby told her, "but most of the time he's available."

As soon as Alice turned off the phone, Gerard began his interrogation. "What is it, this plan you speak about?" he asked. "I am filled with joy that you can make our friend Warp to have a job! But you say nothing about this job to me and I am surprised."

By the time Alice finished disclosing her new scheme to Gerard, he had become her willing accomplice. He was predictably enthusiastic about the idea of taking a road trip south, with the first stop being in Maryland. Once he made contact with a biologist there, a former work colleague, he seemed willing to continue on to Florida.

He agreed with Alice that Felicia was going to be harder to convince. Maybe it would be enough simply to ask her if she would be willing to help Alice raise the money to buy a used van for Warp. Gerard was doubtful that Felicia would take the health risks involved in a trip, and Alice wondered if it was even fair to ask her to do so.

There was also the matter of persuading Warp to drive them to Florida.

"I am counting on Warp to see that our investment in a van of his own is not only to help us get to Florida, but a genuine vote of confidence in his capacity to create a self-employment niche for himself," Alice told Gerard. "With our gift of the van," she continued, "I really believe Warp can become self-employed. I am very hopeful that he could keep doing the wonderful work he was doing for the sheriff's department. Maybe he could get a grant, as a sort of start-up fund, but that would come after our trip to Florida."

Alice hoped she wasn't completely off track. She worried that she was spinning out too many ideas. There were many unknowns and more than enough assumptions. Something told her that she should consult with Felicia before she laid out her plan to Warp.

She hoped if they all actually made it to Florida, Nancy would still be glad she had invited them.

Chapter Twenty-four
Western Massachusetts

Felicia was very open to having some time with Alice to follow up on the conversation they had begun the night before. Gerard was occupied with what Alice hoped would be a lengthy phone call.

Alice suggested that since it was such a beautiful day, they should go to the apple orchard off Route Two where there was a spectacular view of the valley and the mountains. It rivaled the view from Felicia's porch.

They rode in Felicia's Cadillac with the top down. "The colors will be turning soon!" Felicia said cheerfully.

They got coffee and cider doughnuts, and found a picnic table where they could sit side by side and look out at the glorious mountains and valleys.

Alice was glad that she had already tried out some of the details with Gerard and RubyStarr.

"You know how I was talking last night about how useless I had been feeling since COVID forced us all into staying home?" she began.

Felicia nodded, smiling. Alice wondered if it was the deliciousness of the doughnut or if Felicia had changed her attitude after a good night's sleep.

"Felicia, I started to recover my feelings of political passion when Nancy Warren called me this morning. She asked if I would consider getting involved in their Florida project! They need help digging in to uncover the assaults against the two whistleblowers who are part of a lawsuit against a big multinational corporation."

Alice went on to summarize the Florida situation and her new ideas about getting involved. She bravely included the plan to help Warp by giving him a short-term job and the van.

Felicia stopped smiling and put her half-eaten doughnut and her cup of coffee down in front of her on the picnic table.

Alice decided to ignore her friend's change of mood and press on. "You and Gerard could come with me! We could be outdoors so much more down there than we can in the winter cold up here.

You know how cooped up we're going to feel then! Imagine being useful and being able to sit on the beach and read outdoors in December! Can I tell you a little about what I'm thinking our role down there might be? We would settle in and then we could ..."

Felicia cut her off before she could get to a single detail of the plan.

"Alice, dear, of course this current shutdown is hard," she said soothingly. "But it's not forever. The vaccine is getting developed, and soon enough we'll begin to see the numbers go down and we'll be starting to do more and more of the things that we miss, right here in New England."

"But I need to do something now!" Alice said quickly. "Gerard has already embraced this new plan, and I've been waiting to share it with you. I think I have figured out a way ..."

Before she could finish her sentence, Felicia challenged her again.

"Well, Alice, of course we all miss those things we can't do now. But honestly I'm really surprised! I'd thought you were adjusting well to this quieter life. Have I been missing something?"

Felicia sounded annoyed, and she certainly didn't sound the slightest bit interested in the vision Alice had tried to share.

Alice regrouped and shook her head. Maybe she should try a more personal approach.

"This just started, this need I'm feeling to get out there and make a difference. Maybe it was hearing how excited Bernice was about her new-found path. It was her passion, I think, that stirred up something in me."

"Don't tell me we could just hop in the car and travel down to Florida and jump into Nancy Warren's project! It doesn't seem as if you're thinking sensibly at all!" Felicia's voice was vibrating with anxiety. "And I don't see how this connects to Bernice's new passion for re-marrying Donald and following Jesus!"

"Well," Alice said meekly, "I believe it is connected. I've been missing dedicating myself to something that I feel strongly about. I feel like myself again when I think about going down there to help with the campaign, and the lawsuit, doing something that could be useful to the Black community Nancy's been working with."

Felicia was silent, although Alice wasn't sure she was actually listening.

"Nancy is so sure we could really help with the murder investigation down there!" Alice continued doggedly. "I want to interview people and do some surveillance. I believe with our history, we really could help figure out who's behind the attack against this wonderful young organizer and maybe even help them discover who masterminded the killing of a young Black man. He gave his life working to uncover the corruption in that healthcare system, Felicia! Don't you want to be involved in something this compelling?"

Felicia eyed her warily. "You have cabin fever. We cannot afford to forget why we have to keep our quarantine practices, and our social distancing!" She gave Alice a fierce look. "No one among us should take unnecessary risks! Why hasn't it been enough for you to make those calls, and write all those postcards, and get everyone to increase our collective donations to the election in Georgia and the other groups we've been sending checks to?"

Alice was surprised that Felicia was so adamant in opposing her ideas. Well, she knew she was stirring up trouble, and maybe not such good trouble. But that had never been a deterrent to Felicia before. She needed to think more about how this new adventure might feel more appealing to Felicia.

It hit her like a lightning bolt that she was hurting Felicia's feelings!

"My restlessness isn't because I'm unhappy here, Felicia. I love the peacefulness and the good food and the priceless companionship you've been providing for these months we've been sheltering together.

"I am so sorry!" she said, reaching over and taking Felicia's hand. "I think I haven't really acknowledged what good care you've been taking of Gerard and me! You are a wonderful friend and a superb host! You make me feel as if I'm living in a five star B & B every single day! I thought you knew this."

Felicia looked at her in surprise. Apologies between them were rare. She was silent for a few moments but at least she didn't take her hand away. Finally she took a deep breath and squeezed Alice's hand in response.

"You might be a little bit right. I do have some bruised feelings, I suppose."

Alice thought about what it would take to reassure Felicia that she was, truly, such a valued part of Alice's inner circle.

"Felicia, I can say quite honestly that I don't think I can do this trip, this mission, without you as my trusted sounding board. If you could be part of it all, I think I could actually trust that we can do it. Without you, I don't think I will be able to come up with the wisdom and strategies to pull this off."

Felicia's mouth actually fell open in surprise! Alice thought that happened only in cartoons and children's books, but she wisely kept that thought to herself.

After a few minutes of deep and unfamiliar silence, Felicia cleared her throat.

"If you persist in this clearly nutty scheme of yours, maybe I will have to accompany you."

Alice grinned, ear to ear. She didn't dare say a word for fear of disrupting this unexpected truce.

"I am not saying that I think this is a good idea," Felicia said sternly. "But I know you when you get going on a new project. I don't think you're going to back off of this one. May I ask if you have a timeline?"

Alice took a deep breath, then repositioned herself so that she could hug Felicia.

After a few seconds, Felicia slid away and shook her finger playfully at Alice. "Not enough social distancing!"

"No timeline," Alice said meekly, "I haven't figured out the dates. I still have to figure out quite a few things, but let me fill you in on everything I've come up with."

An hour later, Alice and Felicia had worked out a substantial number of details about the trip, focusing on the parts that involved Warp, the food and restroom challenges, and even the travel itinerary.

Alice decided to keep any stray worries to herself for the time being. There was enough to think about as they prepared for a long and somewhat risky road trip, and a clearly dangerous situation awaiting them in Florida.

At least, she comforted herself, she was back in the action!

Chapter Twenty-five
Central Florida

Jake called Charles first thing that morning."Hey man, how're you doing? Hope this isn't too early for me to call?"

Charles cleared his throat, and took a moment before he answered. "No, it's OK," he said, "but can you give me five minutes? I'll call you back."

"Sure, that's fine," Jake told him, glancing at the clock. He'd waited until nine to call, but Charles worked the night shift. He was sorry if he'd gotten the poor guy out of bed, but he had some important information he thought Charles ought to have ASAP.

Charles called back in precisely five minutes. "OK, what's up?" he asked. He still sounded half asleep.

"Well, I got some interesting info on Mitch. Seems that our man has some skeletons in his closet, including a serious criminal record. I'm kind of surprised that Serenity hired him, actually."

"What did he do?" Charles asked.

"He had some charges against him for domestic abuse nine years ago that eventually got dropped. But here's the big one: Mitch got a conviction for petty embezzling from his workplace seven years ago, some kind of security business in Alabama! The guy's got a record I wouldn't ignore if I were hiring for a nursing facility. With a history like this, he could do some real harm to vulnerable folks in that setting, wouldn't you think?"

Charles was quiet, and Jake was surprised by his silence. What was up with that? Jake had expected Charles to get really worked up when he heard the news.

Finally Charles exhaled a long breath, and cleared his throat several times. "Well, I sure made a terrible mistake inviting Mitch to meet with you and Rufe," he said, his voice heavy. He sounded so contrite that Jake could've kicked himself! Why hadn't he anticipated this?

"No way, man!" Jake said. "You couldn't have known! Mitch was hired to work at a reputable nursing facility! Why would you ever guess he had a criminal record? Somebody knows somebody, that's what this tells me. This guy Mitch got hired for a job he never should have been able to get. And then quickly promoted. Something tells me he was given the job for reasons that had nothing to do with elder care!"

"Should we even be having this conversation on the phone?" Charles asked. He sounded seriously nervous.

"My phone is secure," Jake said. "You worried about yours?"

Charles was silent and Jake decided he could guess the answer. "What's your day look like?" he asked Charles. "Any time before you go to work today when we could meet for coffee?"

"Sure, I guess," Charles said. "Be better for me if I can meet you this afternoon, outdoors of course. And preferably somewhere that's close to my work so I'm near enough to talk with you and still be on time."

Jake thought for a while. "You know the Wake Up Cafe over near the Beall's outlet on Third? It's in the shopping mall with the giant ice cream cone thing? That's not far from Sunset, right? Could you meet around two? I think the cafe has some tables outside on the sidewalk."

"Sure. I'll meet you there."

At noon, Charles went over to the Warren's house to spend some time with Kori. He thought he should tell her what was happening, but he was worried. He didn't want her feeling like she had to get back into this thing too soon. For all he knew, she might never want to get involved again. She still didn't look too good from the beating she had endured, and her speech had really been impacted by the injuries.

Kori had told him repeatedly that she felt bad about leaving him with all her responsibilities, and he kept on reassuring her that it was fine. No big deal. But it wasn't really OK. He was a nervous wreck. The project needed her, and her Gram needed her. But how could he ask her to come back to Sunset if she wasn't ready?

The only thing Kori would admit to worrying about was when she came back to visit her Gram, she was afraid the poor lady would be frightened by how she looked and sounded. And how would she explain to a ninety-year-old with dementia why she had disappeared for so long?

"Don't you worry about that," Charles told her. "Your Gram is going to see the love in your eyes and that's all that's going to matter to her. Most of the patients in the Memory Unit have trouble with words, but they're right in the groove with emotion. They can feel love coming at them, just like they can feel fear or disgust. Someone goes in with a heart full of love, most of those folks will open right up and feel wonderful."

He didn't want to rush her. But he couldn't put off much longer telling her that her Gram was suffering the effects of not seeing her. It had been almost a month. The old woman was listless, not eating well. She was plagued by restless sleep and night terrors followed by bouts of loud weeping.

Charles had to work hard with folks on his staff complaining that they just couldn't cope with how Miz Rosabelle had changed. They either avoided interacting with her, or they tried to comfort her and then took it personally when she didn't respond to their efforts.

"You go in there and talk to Miz Rosabelle just like you always have talked to her," Charles told Veronica, one of the loudest complainers. "She is hearing you even if she's not responding. And you'd best think again before you tell me that she's gotten disruptive!" He added air quotes to emphasize her complaints. "I don't want to hear any more how she's a disturbance to the whole unit.

"Think about it! You'd be crying too if you had only one person in the world you knew, and then, out of the blue, that person disappears! Miz Rosabelle doesn't know what happened to her granddaughter! She's scared and lonely. You know she's got to feel abandoned. Of course she's weeping and wailing! We can sedate her, but not 24/7.

"So here's what I want you to do, Miss Veronica. Get yourself together and make your heart awareness work for you. Remember that training? You can help the rest of the floor to settle down when they see you take a different approach with her. You're a professional, Vee! You know you make things worse when you're all up in your anger and attitude like this."

Veronica was unmoved. She had threatened to quit on the spot, and Charles secretly hoped she would. What a whiner! Fortunately, most of the staff were doing their best to work with Charles' directives. When the wailing escalated, sweet young Briana would go right over to sit down and hold the old woman's hand. But Miz Rosabelle wasn't fooled. She knew it wasn't her grandbaby, and usually she kept right on crying.

Before he got the call from Jake, Charles had been planning to ask Kori to come back as soon as possible to resume visiting her grandmother. Now he was thinking that maybe he should hold off. He even wondered if he should tell her about Mitch. When he told her about Rufe's death, she had been overwhelmed. "I feel so guilty for getting him involved," she had said over and over. Charles had just sat there next to her, helpless, rubbing her back and offering her tissues. He had repeated the same words Jake had used to reassure him: this was not her fault, no one but the driver of the car killed Rufe.

What should he tell her today?

"Are the other people who were working with Rufe doing OK?" Kori asked him almost the second he sat down on the porch glider. "Do they know Rufe's accident was most likely an intentional hit?"

He shrugged. "I don't know anything about what people who worked with him are thinking. No one I know who's involved in the lawsuit ever talks at work, not even outdoors on breaks. It's too dangerous. I'm supposed to meet with Jake later this afternoon before work. I guess I'll know more then."

Nancy came out onto the porch to take drink orders, just like always. Charles thought it was sweet how Nancy was like Kori's mom, always making sure her friends felt welcome.

He wondered if Kori had told the Warrens that he was gay? He thought she probably wouldn't have outed him without his permission. He wondered if Nancy thought he wanted to date Kori or something like that? Well, he told himself, at this moment, that issue was totally irrelevant.

"I was just saying to Kori that we'd love to give her a ride over to see her grandmother sometime soon," Nancy said, as she turned to go back to the kitchen.

"That would be fantastic!" Charles said, then regretted his overly enthusiastic response. He didn't want Kori to feel pressured. "If you feel ready," he added, looking at Kori.

"Maybe soon," Kori said. She still sounded hesitant.

"Tomorrow's ice cream sundae afternoon," Charles told her.

"Your Gram would be so happy to see you, plus her hot fudge sundae!" Shut up, Charles! Back off! Why couldn't he let it go? She'd visit Miz Rosabelle when she was ready.

"I'm happy to drive you over tomorrow," Nancy said, "but it's up to you, of course. I'll be back in a minute with your drinks."

Charles launched into a distracting anecdote about a resident Kori had encountered often during her visits on the unit. A familiar voice coming from the front of the house interrupted his story.

"That's Flo!" Kori said, her face lighting up.

Charles started to worry. Did Flo know how he had screwed up, inviting a guy with a past like Mitch's to walk right into the heart of the lawsuit? He didn't know how much Jake and Flo talked, but she seemed like she was right on top of everything. She seemed super-human to him, working 24/7 on her political campaign, taking care of the kids, and still keeping track of who was doing what for the lawsuit.

A few seconds later, Flo appeared on the porch. She pantomimed a giant hug for Kori, and blew an air kiss to Charles through her mask. "How're y'all doing?" she asked, looking from one to the other. If he was a straight guy, Charles thought, he'd be in love with Flo! He imagined she didn't have time for a relationship, though. Not only was she running a political campaign but she was an artist. And she was raising two of her own kids, and three more who'd lost their mother.

"You heard the terrible news about Rufe?" Flo asked Kori.

Kori nodded. "Well, now we know how much someone doesn't want the lawsuit to happen! It's getting more dangerous than I ever expected."

"Amen to that!" Flo exclaimed.

"Can I ask if you feel safe, Flo?" Kori asked. "You made a pretty direct hit in your last press release, calling out corruption in a healthcare system right here in Volusia County! Are you doing anything to protect yourself?"

"Just what I wanted to ask," Nancy Warren said, appearing magically with three glasses of iced tea. "Please make yourself comfortable, Flo. I have some fresh muffins coming out of the oven in five minutes. Cranberry nut. Would you like yours buttered? Charles and Kori usually prefer them with butter."

"Bless your heart, I'll have whatever they're having!" Flo said, plunking down on the glider next to Charles. "How's the world's most gorgeous man today?" she asked.

Charles shrugged. "Don't know who you're talking to," he said. Flo was doing a good job of changing the subject.

Flo theatrically widened her eyes at Kori.

"You are such a liar!" Kori said to Charles. "You see that handsome face every morning in the mirror. I know you do!"

"Anyhow," Flo said, "I didn't come over here to harass Mr. Dreamy! Sorry, Charles! So you asked about my safety? I've got some brothers who look out for me. Truth? They enjoy feeling useful!" She looked thoughtfully at Kori. "You want me to send a couple of them over here to keep an eye on this house? They'll do it if I ask."

"You don't think there would be phone calls to the cops from the neighbors, complaining about the brothers hanging around in this white neighborhood?!" Kori challenged her.

"What makes you think my guys are Black?" Flo said with a wink. "One is a good lookin' blonde dude and the other's Greek or Italian or something. Aside from being a little heavy on the tats, they look like your regular white neighborhood guys. So there's nothing much to notice about them. They could get all busy grilling in Miz Warren's backyard looking like neighborhood dads, and you could even get a great meal or two out of it!"

Flo was a total genius at making connections with every shade of human being.

"So tell me how you're both doing?" Flo continued. "Charles, shouldn't you be hiding out somewhere? I heard Jake told you to take a week off. Go as far from Volusia County as you can get and enjoy some R & R, you hear?"

"I can't just pick up and leave my job for a week," Charles said. He couldn't tell Flo that he was sticking around for Kori's sake, keeping watch over her Gram.

Kori's eyes were getting big. "If Charles is in danger, we probably should get your help in protecting the Warrens, you know, with me staying here and all?" she said. "Has Jake said anything to you about their safety? I'd hate it if someone comes looking for me again, and does something stupid to hurt them or their house!

"But," she added, hesitating a moment, "Flo, don't you need those guys for your own security? Especially after your press conference!"

"They are protecting me all the time, as of lately," Flo said. "I'm not taking chances. I know they got my back. But I have more protection than I need. Happy to share if you or Nancy say the word."

Nancy reappeared with a plate of hot buttered muffins, and passed them all around. "Did I hear my name?"

Charles made a quick decision. He should tell them about Mitch. They needed to know for their own personal safety, and possibly for Flo's campaign.

"Stay here with us, Mrs. Warren, if you have a minute," he said. "I need to tell you all about some new developments."

He filled them in on what Jake had told him. When he finished the report on Mitch and his possible role in Rufe's murder, he stopped abruptly. Kori's eyes were huge, the realization of danger literally dilating her pupils. "So you're saying that Mitch could have been hired into that job at Serenity as an informant?" she asked.

"Sure," Charles said, "he could have been paid to report anything that might relate to the lawsuit, like who's running it, which employees may be volunteering to become plaintiffs, that kind of stuff."

He stopped, glancing at Flo. He couldn't read her at all.

"Are you thinking that Mitch tipped someone off to Rufe's location that night? Like he was part of the setup to run Rufe off the road after he left the restaurant?" Kori asked.

Charles nodded, and Flo bowed her head."Holy Jesus, bless and keep him," she said softly.

Nancy took a deep breath, and Charles could hardly look at her somber face.

By the time Charles left, he was still feeling guilty about Mitch, but at least they had all agreed that Flo's guys would be doing drive-by security at the Warren's, plus a few overnight guard shifts.

Despite the new degree of danger dogging them all, Kori sounded as if she was about ready to see her Gram. Charles almost smiled as he drove toward work, picturing Miz Rosabelle's face when she finally laid eyes on Kori.

At two o'clock, Charles sat waiting outside the Wake Up Cafe for Jake. He didn't feel less guilt about his role in the Mitch situation, but he was more determined to keep going with the lawsuit. If Kori, and Flo, and Nancy Warren could stay strong, so could he!

He was getting a little impatient with Jake. It was almost 2:15 and the lawyer wasn't anywhere in sight. He had just about finished his coffee, and was thinking about ordering one of their super delicious omeletts when a deep voice called out to him.

"Charles? Hey, is that really you?"

Charles turned to look at a slick little sports car idling directly across from him in the lane leading into the parking lot. The driver was grinning big time. "I couldn't be sure because of the mask, but when you took it off, I was sure it was you! How've you been?" the guy said.

It took Charles almost a full sixty seconds to place him, and even then he couldn't remember his name. "Hey!" he called back, "How're things with you?"

"Don't tell me you don't remember me!" the guy said.

"I remember you, but I can't pull up the name right this second," Charles said. He thought he remembered liking this man, yet he felt a rush of fear. Everything and anyone could be connected to the lawsuit.

"We worked together?" he asked tentatively.

"Oh you're breaking my heart now!" Sports Car Guy said, with a deep warm chuckle that made Charles feel the edge of a sweet memory. "We met in Orlando. It's been a few years, but I've certainly remembered your name!"

At that moment, Jake appeared at Charles' shoulder. "Sorry I'm late," he said. "I'll just step inside and get a coffee and be right with you." He was inside the cafe before Charles could apologize for not introducing him to the mysterious man.

"Is he someone special?" the man asked, watching Jake enter the cafe, "or is this just a buddy lunch? Or should I mind my own business?"

"Daniel!" Charles said, the name coming to him suddenly. He made a quick decision to ignore the questions. "Sure, I remember now. Been three years at least though, am I right? You still over in Orlando?"

He suddenly remembered dinner at a Moroccan diner and a boat ride somewhere. Good memories, but obviously not something that had gone anywhere. He couldn't remember why.

"I moved over here almost six months ago," Daniel told him. "I'm working with a start-up magazine that was supposed to take off like a rocket but COVID kind of lowered the boom on us. I've been hoping you were still over this way, but I didn't really expect to find you. Guess this is my lucky day!"

A truck came up the lane behind the sports car, horn blaring belligerently. "I'll move to let this dude go on his way, but when I come back around in a second, I'll give you my card, OK?"

Charles nodded, then sighed. He'd take the card but he couldn't see himself following through, the way things were going. Was it really a coincidence that this Daniel guy happened to appear right now? He felt danger circling around him, but he couldn't be sure of anything.

Daniel's car pulled up near him again. Daniel hopped out to hand Charles his card, just as Jake came out of the cafe with coffee and a plate full of small delicious-smelling appetizers. They looked like a cross between a doughnut and a taco.

"Help yourself!" he said cheerfully, offering both Charles and Daniel the plate.

"Thanks, man!" Daniel said, and took one. Then he stepped back into his gleaming car and zoomed away.

Chapter Twenty-six
On the Road

Alice peered unhappily out the window of the new van, wondering what she had gotten them into.

The landscape was so flat and bleak, nothing for miles and miles but a sparse tree line fifteen feet from the highway, and the lingering smell of smoke from recent wildfires. Not only was their mission carrying them through this drastic change of climate, but they were about to enter a culture she might never understand.

As if reading her thoughts, Gerard opened his eyes and blinked in surprise. He turned to stare at her.

"Where is this place?" he asked, bewildered. He had been sleeping for hours each day on their journey. Alice thought he probably would sleep for days to come once they landed in their new Florida home-away-from-home. Even she could barely keep her eyes open.

"We're about seven hours away from New Smyrna Beach," she told him. "We're not even in Florida yet. It will probably be bedtime by the time we get to the house."

Warp turned his head slightly so she could hear him from the driver's seat. He had been a rock, patiently chauffeuring them for more hours than she could stand to count.

"GPS says we'll arrive at our destination by 8:30 tonight," he told her. "We're making pretty good time. You guys good to keep driving or should I look for a rest stop?"

"I'm enduring," Alice told him. She glanced at Gerard. His bladder might be in more trouble than hers, but she didn't want to risk more exposure than necessary. Every bathroom stop was perilous. The COVID numbers were still very high in Florida, and she imagined they were just as bad in Georgia.

"You know you can always use my travel E-E-Z-P-Z device," Felicia suggested from the navigator's seat. She was in the car seat behind the driver, six feet between her and Warp. She was also almost six feet from the third car seat in the back of the van where Alice and Gerard sat.

Alice had no intention of using Felicia's awkward and weird system of cutting down on restroom stops, not unless it became absolutely an emergency kind of necessary.

Still, she was impressed as always, by Felicia's good spirits. They'd been on the road many hours since leaving Maryland, yet Felicia remained as resilient as Warp.

Warp was only twenty-five, but Felicia who qualified as a bona-fide elder, was apparently still enjoying their trip. Alice felt as if she had mistakenly set them up for an Outward Bound road trip for Seniors. She was ready to drop!

"Why do we drive and drive, and it is not *le* destination?" Gerard demanded like an overtired child. Alice could hardly blame him for sounding cranky. She wondered the same thing, even though this trip had been her idea. "My back, it is *très mal*," he continued, "Also, why it is that we do not stop for *le repas*?"

He glared at Alice, and she was shocked.

Gerard was occasionally annoyed with her, but this malevolent look came as a surprise.

"I'm sorry, Gerard," she said gently. "I know all this time in the car gets very uncomfortable. You are right, it is a very long trip, But, *mon chèri*, we really have enjoyed a number of meals. Maybe because we've eaten our food in the car, it doesn't seem like a meal?"

Felicia beamed over her shoulder at Gerard. "When we get to Florida, we'll get real key lime pie," she told him. "And lovely fish: red snapper, grouper, catfish! We'll probably even eat hush-puppies."

Gerard scowled. "I do not eat *le chien*," he said stiffly.

Alice took his hand and stroked it. "She's not talking about eating dogs," she explained. "Hushpuppies are a fried food, like French fries or fried onion rings. But we will eat healthier foods too, just as we do at home."

"But how can it be so unpleasant? So long the distance?" Gerard complained. "We continue to drive and to drive in this place of no water, no mountains, no beauty!"

Alice looked at him thoughtfully. His mood did not allow for a pep talk on behalf of their current adventure. She was surprised that he seemed so disoriented, but he was, after all, eighty years old, and ever since the first outbreak of the virus, he had been

faced with frequent stress and uncertainty. She was probably asking too much of him.

Warp cleared his throat loudly. "Hey," he said, "I'm thinking
maybe we need to stop somewhere and get a fresh cooked meal? I
think there might be more restaurants open around here than back
home. Let's see if there's a place we could order take-out from a
menu? We could even find a picnic table. It would be good to take
a break from the car. I know I could use a little stretch."

Gerard seemed to cheer up at the mention of a restaurant. Alice
realized they all needed a travel break. She nodded as she met
Warp's eyes in the rearview mirror.

"What a good idea!" she said. "Let's start looking for signs."

Less than thirty minutes later, Felicia called out excitedly. She
pointed at a large billboard, Real Down Home Experience! Country Cookin' like Mama's!

"Want to try it?" Warp asked.

Alice was vaguely worried. She pictured images of large bearded
white men gnawing ribs and chugging beer, but Gerard was beaming happily.

"*Ahhh oui!*" he exclaimed, his voice a mix of purr and growl,
"*La cuisine chez Mama!* This is good, *oui?*"

"Here's the exit," Warp said. "Let's do it!"

Ten minutes off the highway, they pulled into the parking lot of a
big low-roofed stucco building. There was a cartoon cut-out sign
mounted on the flat tar paper roof, a portrait of a huge pig in a
white suit and country style straw hat, holding what looked like a
pork chop in one trotter and bottle of Old Dixie beer in the other.
Completing the painting was a catfish in a sort of mermaid cos-
tume, large red lips curled in a welcoming smile.

"Oh my!" Alice said, trying to catch her breath. What did Felicia
sense about the aura of the place? For once, she would really like
to know.

Whatever Felicia's psychic guides might be saying, Warp and
Gerard were grinning like happy children. Gerard leaned forward
abruptly and tugged at the door of the van. Warp jumped out
quickly to give the older man a hand as he lurched out of the side
door of the vehicle.

Alice sat for a few seconds before she decided that her bladder was ready for this stop despite her hesitations. You never know what might show up out of the blue, she told herself. She eased her stiff body out of the treacherously high van, managing to make it safely onto the pavement. She headed toward the door, the other three passengers already moving on ahead of her.

"Masks!" Felicia reminded the group just as they reached the door. Warp and Alice stopped in their tracks, but Gerard was not going to delay his joy as he approached the first restaurant they had entered in many months. He reached for the door handle just as Alice called for him to stop.

"Gerard, we must observe safety precautions!" she told him firmly, even though she too had forgotten about the need for her mask. She dug her mask out of her bag and started to hook it on. Warp trotted back to the van and pulled his mask from the array of things he had stowed next to the driver's seat.

"Where's your mask?" he called to Gerard. "I'll get it for you."

"*Non! absolutement, non!*" Gerard said. "We insult *le chef* if we wear the mask to *le repas!*"

Alice glared at him. "If you won't wear your mask, then I will sit in the car while you go in and order yourself a big helping of the virus."

Gerard looked as if he might ignore her. Finally, with a mournful groan, he stalked back to the van to retrieve his mask. When they were all finally masked and ready to make their entrance, Gerard opened the door with a flourish.

They stared into the darkened room. Alice recoiled slightly from the smell of cigarettes and beer and the very loud country western radio.

"Y'all come on in!" a man's voice greeted them. After another moment of blinking as their eyes adjusted to the darkness, they saw a small bar with a handful of patrons seated on the barstools.

"*Bon jour!*" Gerard called out, waving his hand at the group.

"Y'all be wantin' a table?" the man behind the bar asked.

"We'd love one of those tables we saw outdoors," Felicia responded in her most husky and seductive voice.

The man behind the bar grinned. "You take whichever one y'all want," he said. "We don't have much of a crowd right now, as you can see!"

He handed them their menus. "I'll give y'all a few minutes to figger out what ya want."

As they gathered at the picnic table outside, Felicia's frown signaled to Alice that there were no viable vegetarian choices for her. Alice prayed that Felicia would be willing to settle for whatever was the least objectionable. Under the circumstances, she did not look forward to Felicia ordering something that wasn't on the menu.

Gerard studied the menu selections, and then finally smiled at Alice. She wondered what was making him so cheerful. "I will explore the fried gator steak!" he announced. "This is the meat of the alligator, *oui*?"

Alice and Warp nodded. Warp looked more relaxed, clearly relieved that at least some of them would order from the menu. He grinned at Gerard. "I'm getting the fried catfish with hushpuppies and deep fried okra," he said, "and now I've gotta use the little Bulls' room!"

Gerard watched Warp thoughtfully as he made his way to the Bulls' restroom. Alice wondered if Warp might have to translate.

"Well, I don't know what I should order," Felicia said hesitantly. "Maybe just a small house salad and a piece of their peach pie with ice cream. Georgia's known for their peaches, right?"

"I'm getting whatever fish our host recommends," Alice said, "and a baked potato and a salad. If your peach pie is really good, I'll get a piece to share with Gerard and Warp."

Their host came out to the picnic table to bring them ice waters, and smiled slowly as he studied each one of them. His arms were covered with tattoos, and Alice thought about how RubyStarr would have admired the variety of colors and symbols he displayed.

"You folks ready?" he asked. "We've got some specials today. The pepper fried catfish is good, and so's the boiled shrimp. You mind my askin' if y'all are kin?"

"What?" Warp asked, as Felicia nodded and Alice shook her head. Gerard looked at his companions for explanation.

"Y'all are family, right?" the man continued. "You two ladies, you probably sisters, am I right? And you, sir, are the husband, 'tho I don't know which all of these lovely ladies might be your wife.

And you got to be the grandson!" He smiled warmly at Warp. Alice wondered if he was picturing one day in the future when his own grandson, finally a grown young man, would take a road trip with his grandparents and great aunt.

"You basically got it right," Warp told him quickly before anyone else could explain. He looked back at his menu. "Uh, Grandma Alice was wondering if there was something – maybe fish – that you would especially recommend?"

"Like I said," their server repeated, "the catfish or the boiled shrimp. That's the only seafood on the menu. Gator is good. Very fresh."

"I was thinking about the peach pie with ice cream," Felicia. "I'll just have a little house salad so I don't spoil my appetite." She winked at the man, and he gave her a thoughtful look.

"You must be the auntie," he said. "Mmm-hmm. A woman who knows what she wants! And you, Ma'am, what's your preference?" He smiled very politely at Alice before his eyes slid back to Felicia who was now staring suspiciously at the Confederate flag tattooed on his forearm.

"Could I get the catfish without the pepper?" Alice asked meekly.

"Don't know about that," he said. "Chef doesn't like his cookin' to be challenged, if you know what I mean?"

Alice smiled at him, now inspired to change the direction their conversation might be going. "I'm sorry," she said. "How rude we've been! My name is Alice. How thoughtless of us not to introduce ourselves sooner. This is Gerard, and this is our grandson Warp, and Felicia is, well, most of the time we're sisterly. And you are ...?"

He beamed at her. "They call me Duby. That's for Durbin, Durbin Junior," he said, "and my brother John is the guy in the kitchen. He don't like to alter his recipes. Think you might like the boiled shrimp, Miz Alice. Mighty fresh."

"I wish to enjoy the gator steak, *Monsieur* Durbin," Gerard said, surprising Alice by his sudden entry into the conversation. "I am sure it is *très, très*, as you say, fresh!"

Mr. Duby stared at Gerard for an uncomfortable minute, then suddenly hit his head as if a light bulb had gone off.

"You got to be French! You sound just like Jacque Pepin, just like him! You some famous chef who's gonna surprise me now and tell me you all are lookin' for some genuine Georgia cookin'? You goin' to make me famous, me and John?"

Gerard shook his head sadly. "*Monsieur* Duby, I am not famous. I am only *le chef* in my own kitchen. I am sorry I disappoint you!"

Duby shook his head, but smiled broadly. "I still keep believin' it's gonna happen one day!" he said cheerfully. "Some TV guy's gonna show up and make this place a national landmark. Guess it's just not happenin' today. And what can I get for you, son?" he asked Warp.

"I'm down for the catfish, and also the fried okra and an order of hushpuppies?" Warp asked hopefully.

"You got it!" Duby said. "Can I bring y'all some beverages while you wait? I'll bring a basket of hot biscuits, too."

"I'd love some iced tea," Alice said, "assuming your restroom is open to the public?"

"Why wouldn't it be?" Duby asked in surprise.

"I'll have iced tea, sweetened," Warp said quickly.

Alice guessed that he was trying to prevent a discussion of social distancing and the virus. She had noticed that no one at the bar was wearing a mask, although Duby had remained masked as he took their order. Still, he stood much closer than six feet from them. "Iced tea for me, too," Felicia said, "and even though I'd just love that sugar, I'm going to go for the unsweetened."

"And you, sir?" Duby asked Gerard.

Gerard sighed. "I will drink the water only," he said. Alice knew that what he really wanted was a big glass of iced coffee. She had explained to him that they would probably only be able to get iced coffee after they got settled in Florida where there were enough snowbirds to make it a viable beverage.

When Duby left the table with their orders, Alice turned to Felicia. "Shall we investigate the Heifer's room together?" she asked. "I could use a little help getting there. I'm afraid my legs are a bit wobbly from sitting so long."

Felicia bounced up and came around the table to offer Alice her arm. "I have the sanitizer wipes in my bag," she told Alice. "Why don't I go in and do a little wiping down first, then you can brave it after I'm through."

By the time the two women had returned, the food was already on the table. Duby had just delivered Alice's plate of boiled shrimp, then quickly moved the chair back to the table to seat her.

Alice smiled up at him gratefully, but he was moving around the table to seat Felicia. "Y'all enjoy your food," he said, "and just give me a holler if you need anything."

Gerard inspected his gator steak before taking the first bite. He chewed thoughtfully, and Alice wondered what he was thinking. His slowness to comment began to worry her. What if the food was inedible? She hated to think that any one of them might not enjoy their unusual culinary experience, but it would be the worst if Gerard was the one to be disappointed.

"Ahhh!" he exclaimed finally, "*très delicieux!*"

For a few minutes, all of them became completely absorbed in their meals. Alice wasn't sure how the spices of the boiled shrimp would settle in her digestive system, but her taste buds were humming with pleasure. Even Felicia was happy to discover that her salad was large and very fresh, the tomatoes as perfect as if she had just picked them out of her own garden. And she sighed so loudly after her first bite of peach pie that Alice knew she should order two more slices, one to share with Gerard and the other for Warp.

Duby appeared like a magic genie to answer her summons. After he took the order, he hesitated a minute, then cleared his throat. "The boys and I were just wonderin' if you'll are down here to help prepare for the big rally?" he said. "None of my business, but we just thought we'd ask."

"The rally?" Alice asked, puzzled. She felt Felicia kick her gently under the table.

"Thought you might be travelin' all the way down here from Massachusetts with that fancy new van so's you could help with the big rally in Jacksonville," Duby said. "Gonna be a pile of work to do, getting the city ready for that. They probably gonna have to put the overflow into one of those big ass cruise ships they bring in to accommodate the guests they can't fit in the hotels."

Alice and Felicia glanced at each other. What was their host referring to? Warp looked completely clueless, while Gerard chose this moment to excuse himself to go to the restroom.

"No, I can't say that we're headed for Jacksonville," Alice said politely. "We're on our way to New Smyrna Beach. Have you ever been there?"

Duby shook his head, looking disappointed. "Can't place the town," he said. "Is it on the coast?"

Felicia produced an award winning smile. "It's just south of Daytona Beach. The city stretches from the mainland along the Intracoastal Waterway over to the barrier island and its beaches right on the Atlantic. I've heard that the beaches around there are just beautiful. We're birders," she added. "There's nowhere better than that area for birds. We've heard such exciting stories about Merritt Island! Maybe you've heard of it? It's a wildlife refuge."

Duby leaned in a little closer and dropped his voice. "The boys believe y'all are on some kind of mission. They were guessing either the state convention or maybe you're on a church mission or somethin'? Otherwise they can't figure out what you're doing here, off the beaten path, so to speak. It's unusual to see a group such as yourselves drive a van like that to Florida. I told them you weren't here for a cooking show, even though that had been my first guess. Birds! That's just somethin', driving all the way down here in the September heat to see birds!"

"Well, speaking of those birds," she said, before anyone else could enter the conversation, "we'd better be getting back on the road. It's a long way to New Smyrna Beach."

"Mind if I ask y'all just one more question?" Duby said, with a big smile.

Felicia and Gerard nodded just as Alice shook her head and Warp got up from the table looking as if he was ready to bolt for the van.

"I'll take that as a maybe," Duby said, grinning at them. "Since y'all are from Massachusetts, I was wondering if y'all know that firecracker senator personally, you know, that Elizabeth Warren?"

Everyone shook their heads to indicate the answer was no. Alice braced herself for what might be coming next.

"Too bad," Duby said, looking disappointed. "My wife's a big fan! She would've high-tailed it right up to Washington if that lady had been nominated president. She'd follow that lady anywhere! But she'll be tickled to know I met folks from Miz Warren's home state!"

Chapter Twenty-seven
Central Florida

They finally found Nancy and Steve's house just a block back from the ocean. Being so close to the sea was a special thrill for Gerard. He still missed the Pacific Ocean from his years in California.

Alice was embarrassed when the street number she had for the Warrens turned out to be wrong. The phone number was correct, but she got the recorded announcement in Nancy Warren's cheerful voice, promising to call back within twenty-four hours.

A neighbor had spotted Warp and Felicia wandering around the house where they had mistakenly thought the Warrens lived. She was able to tell them not only that those owners were still up in Wisconsin, but that the Warrens lived near her daughter's best friends' parents, two blocks down from the beach.

Nancy was at the door, watching for them as they pulled up in front of the house.

"Welcome to Florida!" she called, rushing out to greet them. She was gaining speed, but just as Alice was about to call out a warning about distance and masks, she remembered.

"I'm so, so sorry!" she said, covering her mouth by pulling up her T-shirt. "I'll run back in and get my mask! Steve will be home soon, and he'll help you bring in anything you need right now. You can leave all your luggage in the van. It's very safe around here!"

She rushed back toward the house as they began once again to climb stiffly out of the van.

"I'm sorry we aren't completely prepared for you," Nancy shouted back over her shoulder. "We're just back from a late dinner after birding up at Dune's Park! Very exciting birding on the beaches up there! White pelicans, skimmers, royal terns, plovers and ruddy turnstones!"

Alice could picture Nancy striding along a beach, her binoculars trained on a flock of royal terns. She could almost hear the surf now as she stood on the sidewalk, stretching out the kinks in her back and legs.

Nancy ushered them into her house, Alice in the lead with Felicia close behind, then Gerard, limping from so many days of spinal distress in the van. Warp came last, carrying an odd assortment of things. He had Felicia's large cloth bag, a very big cooler with the remains of the food they had packed for the trip, Gerard's cane for the occasional times he needed it, and Alice's portable oxygen tank.

"This is the most hopeful thing that's happened for the longest time!" Nancy declared as she closed the door after her guests. "Come! Follow me right straight through the house to our porch. Once you're out there, you'll really know you've arrived! Everyone calls the screened porch the Florida room. Steve and I eat every meal we can out here, and our cats savor the illusion of living outdoors. Kori's been staying with us and she's out here a good deal of the time too. I'm so glad you can all meet each other finally!"

Alice would have called the space a screened porch, but by whatever the name, it was magical. Glossy green bushes grew all along the back of the house only a few feet from the porch, and there were a variety of multi-colored bird feeders and a birdbath back there too.

"Did I see a magnolia tree?" Felicia asked excitedly. "I looked up when we first got out of the car and spotted what I think were magnolia blossoms right behind your house!"

Nancy beamed with pleasure. "Oh yes! It was one of the selling points when we bought the house. You'll see that it's a very simple house, just right for Steve and me. But this porch and the foliage make it so much more than what we thought when we first saw it. It's just a simple two bedroom house with a kitchen that only one cook can occupy at a time, and a living room that can scarcely accommodate more than four people. But, oh my, when we saw the porch and the birds and the huge live oak trees and the magnolia out back, we fell in love with it! It's a little treasure!"

Standing at one side of the porch glider, waiting to greet them, was an African American woman with very short hair, freckles, and smiling eyes above her mask. She stepped forward very slightly to introduce herself, keeping the six-foot distance but crossing her arms across her chest in a gesture of hugging.

"I'm Kori, and you're Alice Ott, of course! I've heard so much about you!"

Alice returned the hug sign. Then she slipped her mask down for just a second so she could smile at Kori before she put it back up. "I've heard so much about you too!"

Gerard also pulled his mask down briefly to smile at Kori before he remasked and introduced himself. Felicia followed suit.

Warp gestured something like a peace sign followed by a solidarity fist. "Hey Kori! I'm Warp, the chauffeur!"

Kori's eyes widened, then crinkled in silent laughter. "For real?"

Warp nodded. "They needed help with the long drive. And I'm a friend of these three," nodding at Alice, Gerard and Felicia. "We've been hanging together for years!"

"Wow! Years? Really?" Kori looked as if she was holding in a laugh.

"Truth! Since I was a teenage kid."

"Who would like some iced tea and cookies fresh out of the oven?" Nancy asked. "Or can I fix you all some supper? I know you've been on the road all day. By the way, let's move the party outside now. We have a patio that's big enough to maintain enough social distance to be safe. And we even have a portable fire pit that will keep everyone warm now that we're getting into the cool of the evening."

"We ate the last of our healthy snacks for supper" Alice said, "but I'd love tea and cookies, thank you."

Nancy looked at the other three. "Can I make anyone a sandwich?" she asked.

Warp and Gerard nodded in unison at the word sandwich, Warp adding that anything Nancy served would be most welcome.

Felicia had collapsed onto the nearest porch chair, sighing happily. "Just tea for me," she said, "unless you happen to have some sort of fruit, or carrot sticks or celery stalks?"

"You and I are going to enjoy each other's company more than ever, Felicia!" Nancy said. "I love it when someone tells me exactly what she wants!"

Kori offered to guide the group out to the patio, and everyone but Alice followed her. Alice chose to stay with Nancy in the kitchen.

"I'm sorry we seem to have landed on you at this hour,'" she said. "The two men are always hungry, and Felicia is, as you may remember, particular about her food! Tell me what I can do to help."

"Oh it's all good!" Nancy assured her. "I'll give you an apple and some celery to cut up for Felicia's grazing pleasure, and I can handle sandwich production. Kori and Steve and I already ate. Steve baked the cookies for you before he went to the store for more coffee, so he gets credit for the cookies and a few additional staples for your household.

"Alice, you must be exhausted! We'll get you all settled within the hour, I promise. How much have I already told you about the house where you'll be staying?"

"I forget so much these days that you can start from the beginning." Alice said. "I only care that your report includes beds and a coffee maker for morning!"

"I actually have very good accommodations for you. We can provide housing for as long as you want to stay! You'll be living in a sweet little house back on the mainland, in a little town called Edgewater. It's like a sister community to New Smyrna, but the only way to the beach from there is to come to New Smyrna. It's less than 10 minutes away.

"The neighborhood is small and sits right on the Intracoastal. So the Indian River and Mosquito Lagoon are practically in your backyard! Two of our snowbird friends, Anna and Dorie, own the house. It's very much like ours. They bought it not too long after we moved in here. This year they're staying up North, partly because of COVID, but also Dorie's sister isn't well so they're staying up there to help. We've gotten close to them because of the voter registration work we've been doing down here over the past couple of years. They have been working on Flo's campaign since it first started.

"We were so disappointed that they wouldn't be down this winter. When you said you all were coming, I called them right away and they were just thrilled to offer you their house! Even though they couldn't be here this winter, they wanted to do whatever they could to help with the campaign. Lending you their house helps them feel like they're helping.

"You'll be very comfortable there, I think."

Alice was working hard at her sous chef tasks, but she looked over at Nancy, a question forming as she momentarily stopped her chopping and slicing.

"We will be glad to pay them some rent, but I can't promise that we can meet the full rent for an entire house in a nice neighborhood on the Intracoastal Waterway.

"I've already extracted a hefty donation from Gerard and Felicia to help me buy the van for Warp, and to pay him for driving us down here. But we certainly don't want to take advantage of your friends. We'll pay as much as we can for the time we're here."

"Don't be silly! They're thrilled to have you use it! Later in the season, if they get an unbearable yearning to come down here for a few weeks to escape the February snow, we'll figure out something else temporarily. But don't worry, the odds of that are small. Really, they didn't want to rent it. Too complicated to explain now, but trust me, this is making them happy!"

Alice couldn't make herself think forward to February. Would she and Gerard and Felicia still be here? She somehow doubted it.

One day at a time was the best schedule for her, she reminded herself. And suddenly she was so tired that she was afraid she was going to fall asleep on her feet, paring knife in hand! She knew she must not allow such a thing to happen in Nancy's lovely remodeled kitchen. "I'm afraid I have to sit down for a minute," she apologized.

Nancy helped her to the closest chair, and shook her head.

"I am so sorry I let you help! Of course you need to sit down, and then very soon put your head on your pillow and get some sleep. Why don't I take you over to the house right now, then zip back and feed the others."

"Oh my word! Don't you dare! You'll set off a chain reaction! Gerard will insist on tending to me, and Felicia will think he doesn't know what he's doing so she'll insist on coming too so she can grind up some sort of roots and berries potion thing for her bedtime snack, and then Warp will fall asleep in his chair right on your porch! Steve will come home to find a tattooed, long-haired young man zonked out in the Florida room, and call the police!"

Nancy chortled. "You haven't changed at all! Ok, let's join the others on the patio. I'll revive you with ginger tea and the best cinnamon oatmeal chocolate chip cookies you've ever tasted!"

The patio felt slightly crowded when the four travelers settled down with Nancy and Kori. When Steve Warren arrived, he brought out a folding chair from the porch and wedged it in next to his wife. The New England group sat close together while the Warrens and Kori sat knee to knee on the other side of the patio. The evening was cooler than Alice had expected in Florida, so she was grateful for the fire pit's warmth. Despite feeling very sleepy, there was a cheerful hum of conversation that was comforting. Being outdoors in the fresh evening air was delicious!

She tried to stay with her gratitude for the present moment, but she quickly became eager to hear what was planned for the next day.

Gerard leaned closer to whisper a question. "Alice, where do we sleep tonight?"

"We'll be staying in a house not too far from here. I think they will take us there very soon." She could see how tired he was. Even Felicia seemed to be slowing down.

Warp was seated on Alice's left, and he leaned in to speak quietly to Alice and Gerard. "You think we can get ourselves settled for the night pretty soon?" he asked very softly, just as Felicia began to report on their adventurous meal in Georgia.

"Don't tell me you're tired!" Alice whispered to him, winking so he knew she was teasing.

"I'm totally wiped!" he told her softly, "and I need to spend a little time on the phone with RubyStarr."

Alice waited for a good place in Felicia's saga to interject her request. "I hate to interrupt this delightful story, but I'm really quite tired. I'm wondering if we could go to our new home soon? Otherwise, I may just ask for a sleeping bag and camp out here beside your lovely little fire!"

"But I haven't gotten to the part about Elizabeth Warren!" Felicia protested loudly.

Kori sat forward, her eyes sparkling. "Elizabeth Warren was at that restaurant in Georgia?" she asked excitedly.

"That would have been too much to ask! But it will have to be part of our trip recollections to share with you tomorrow. I can see that our dear elders are exhausted!"

"You don't look all that perky yourself, Miss Spring Chicken!" Alice said crisply.

"Oh, of course you're all worn out, all of you!" Nancy exclaimed. "What a long journey you've had! We'll take you over to the house and help you get everything in from the car. The beds are made, and we've tried to stock the fridge and pantry with whatever you might need for breakfast tomorrow morning. There's a coffee pot and a tea kettle, and anything else I could think of."

"And since we know you'll have to quarantine over the next ten days," Steve said helpfully, "we'll be at your service to do shopping and help you with meals and so on."

"Quarantine for ten days?" Alice said. She was shocked that she hadn't thought of that. Felicia looked a little surprised, but Gerard smiled happily. Of course he would be thrilled to be holed up for ten days with his computer! She just hoped the house had strong wifi service and decent phone reception.

She was grateful she had been more focused on the books she packed than her clothes. She expected to do quite a bit of her sleuthing online at first, so the idea of the quarantine didn't bother her all that much, the more she thought about it. If Felicia got restless, Warp could drive her to the beach. Alice imagined that Felicia would walk alone and read for hours as she basked in the Florida sun. She thought that Warp might choose to rest a few days before driving back to Massachusetts.

Their Florida adventure had finally begun!

Chapter Twenty-eight
Central Florida

Jake leaned closer to Charles. "We're going to have to find some way to get more inside information from TouchStone. Losing Rufe has been not only a human tragedy, but he had access to critical information that we need. Now we're operating without his eyes and ears. The other problem is we don't know if there's another 'Mitch' planted inside the corporation, gathering information about who's still involved in the suit and what we're up to."

"Couldn't we just go with what we've got? I thought you said that we had all the plaintiffs we needed to go public with the lawsuit."

"Yeah, I did say that, but I was hoping we'd have more actual documentation about the identity of the person, or persons, inside the TouchStone Corporation who are diverting the grant money. I wanted some solid proof of whose pockets are getting lined, maybe even how much is going directly into their personal bank accounts, any unexplained big expenditures, that kind of real proof that we can nail them with.

"Rufe was closing in on getting documentation," he continued, "some important paperwork: emails, budgets, bank transfers, checks paid out to specific individuals within the corporation. He was close to persuading a couple of office workers he trusted to copy or transmit important documents. But since his murder, both of those office workers have contacted me to say they have to withdraw from the suit. They're scared. I can't blame them, to tell you the truth."

"So we can't just use the basic information we already have?" Charles asked. "We know the amount of the grant and what it was supposed to be used for at Sunset Villages and Serenity Place. And now that funding has mysteriously disappeared. Isn't that enough to go public with?"

Jake shook his head.

Charles wasn't ready to back off. "What about the overtime pay that was budgeted in the grant that suddenly wasn't there to pay those employees for their eighteen-hour shifts? What about the thousands of dollars of PPE that was promised by the grant but somehow never materialized?" He could feel himself start to sweat as he tried to control the anger that was building in him.

"Wish it were that easy. But it's just not. We can go public with what was promised and what hasn't been delivered. We can call press conferences, and/or we can see if Flo is ready to get her campaign to call for a big public investigation. But the insider info I was counting on? It still isn't accessible." He was now speaking so softly that Charles could barely hear him.

Charles looked around, wondering if anyone was close enough to eavesdrop.

"And if we don't get our hands on some actual evidence soon, anything we might have been able to use will vanish quickly," Jake continued. "We have to believe that Mitch was reporting to the bad guys. They're going to be looking to cover their tracks. Without proof of who specifically is making the funds disappear, and whose pockets are getting filled, all we have is a barrage of accusations and a great big puff of righteous indignation!"

Charles felt like the air had just gotten knocked out of him. Was it going to turn out that Kori's brutal assault and Rufe's murder were for nothing? He wished he could think of a new way to help Jake get what they needed.

He sat very still, staring at the uneaten lunch in front of him. Then he remembered something Jake might not have heard about.

"Did Kori or the Warrens tell you about the lady and her friends coming down from New England to help us?"

Jake looked surprised. "No, don't think so. Who is she?"

"She's some kind of investigator, I think. She's pretty old, but she's exposed other corporate fraud, something like that. Nancy Warren knew her when she lived in Massachusetts and she invited her to come down to help us with our investigation. She told Kori and me that this lady has a knack for finding and encouraging whistleblowers. She and the other two are, like, uh, activist missionaries or something, keeping the public informed and involved. That's what she told me."

"Hey," Jake said, grinning for the first time since they had begun their conversation, "we can always use Miss Marple's help, right?"

Charles shrugged. "All I know is, we've got to protect the workers who are already vulnerable, but we've also got to protect the residents at Sunset and Serenity who have no idea what's going on and no power to protect themselves."

"And what's your priority right now?" Jake asked Charles, staring so hard at him that Charles felt like he was being scanned, like Jakes' eyes were the scanner before you board a plane.

"My top personal goal, at this point, is to keep Kori's grandmother alive and safe." It sounded weird, but it was true.

"And what about keeping yourself alive too, man?" Jake asked, studying him thoughtfully. "Will you tell me if you need a break, and/or some protection for yourself? I'm worried for you."

"I'll be fine." Charles said. "Anyway, about Nancy Warren's friends? I can set up a meeting if you want."

Jake looked somewhat doubtful. "Can you find out if they're lawyers or licensed private investigators, at least? I don't want to spend too much time getting advice from a handful of amateur sleuths from up North who don't know a hushpuppy from a hound dog!"

Charles squinted at him. "Sure. If you want, I can meet with them first. And I'll get more background from Nancy and her husband."

Jake sighed. "Good," flashing Charles a quick grin. He pulled out his wallet to pay the check, brushing aside Charles's efforts to pay his share. "Let me know what you find out," he said as he turned to walk away. "And watch your back, buddy."

While Charles was taking his first break at work that night, he decided to give Daniel a call. It would be nice to have coffee or an outdoor meal with someone who wasn't in the middle of all the drama. He was curious about how Daniel had ended up in New Smyrna Beach, and how long the guy had been looking to run into him.

"It's Charles," he said when Daniel answered. What a pleasant surprise to get an actual person answering the phone on the first try! "Thought it would be fun to get together and catch up a little."

"It's a little late for me,'" Daniel said, coughing and sounding slightly annoyed. "My days of spontaneously meeting up for coffee after 10 p.m. are memories now. Could we get together tomorrow?"

Charles went red hot with embarrassment. "Oh no, I didn't mean right now! Hope I didn't wake you up or something! I work the evening shift, so I'm only halfway through my eight hours. No, I totally meant some time during the daylight hours, sometime over the next week or two."

"Let's get together tomorrow. You want to meet me for lunch somewhere? You know the area better than I do, so just name the time and the place and I'll be there."

"OK if we meet on the late side of lunch, like around twoish?" Charles suggested even though he was getting cold feet. Why had he called this guy? But he had to continue with a plan now that he started this thing. "We can avoid the lunch crowd. Norwood's on Third Avenue has outdoor seating, and lots of it. Have you been there yet?"

"Oh yes, sure! Good choice."

He didn't answer Charles about whether he had been there before. Everyone wanted to go to Norwood's. It was where you took someone visiting the area for the first time because of the giant treehouse dining experience. It was a favorite with residents too, so Charles felt safe suggesting it.

"So is two good for you?" Charles asked. He was feeling crazy nervous, second-guessing himself, wishing he hadn't gotten into some new social thing. At least he had Daniel's card so he could call and cancel tomorrow if he changed his mind.

"So before you go, do you have a minute?" Daniel asked.

"Just about exactly a minute," Charles checked his watch. He had at least ten more minutes before he needed to be back on the floor, but he wanted to get off the phone.

"Just wondered what you're doing these days? You had just gotten your nursing degree when we were in Orlando, if I remember right?"

Charles didn't feel like telling Daniel about his work. In fact, he wondered why his nursing degree was the first thing the guy mentioned. He felt a chill of paranoia. Was it possible that Daniel had really just happened to drive by and spot him at lunch with Jake earlier today? Anybody could be part of the TouchStone scam. Daniel could be the next Mitch.

"Listen, I'm happy to tell you more about my life when I see you tomorrow," he told Daniel, purposely speeding up his answer, "but I got something going on here I have to deal with. See you tomorrow!"

He hung up, and realized he was sweating. Maybe it was that he was dipping his toe back into the pool, trying out the dating scene after a few years off. Or maybe his sonar was signaling that something was off about Daniel showing up just now.

It was a relief to be too busy to think more about any of it during the remainder of his shift. There had been a new outbreak of COVID at another nursing facility in the area, and he was getting pressured from one of the managers at Serenity Place to make space at Sunset for one or maybe even two of their residents.

The two they wanted him to take were no longer financially profitable for the TouchStone Corporation, but they couldn't just be dumped out onto the street. Serenity made a chunk more money per resident than Sunset, and the corporation wanted to free up two beds at the high-end facility for elders whose affluent families were trying to get them in before there was another COVID outbreak there. Because of COVID, there was an urgency and way more pressure than Charles had felt in the past. Plus, now his eyes were open to the corruption undermining all the good care that the staff was trying to provide in the nursing facilities.

At 2:30 in the morning he finally locked the door to his office, and said goodnight to the charge nurse. He was thinking about where he might pick up a cup of coffee just to get him through the drive home when he suddenly became aware of footsteps.

Someone was entering the parking garage not too far behind him. It was unusual for anyone else to be leaving right when he did in the early hours of the morning. He felt a chill of fear.

He turned to see who it was, and caught the barest glimpse of someone in motion. It was like a shadow, a tiny glimpse of someone moving quickly behind one of the pillars. Maybe he was mistaken, he told himself, but sweat was breaking out all over his body. He wished he was the kind of man who carried a gun.

He wasn't parked all that far away from the door to the garage.

He could try to make a run for the car and hope he got in before the other guy caught up, or he could rush back through the door, taking the guy by surprise, and hoping to make it safely back onto the floor.

He was frozen as he considered his choices. Maybe heading back to face his assailant would shake the guy up. Of course, whoever was behind the pillar could also just shoot him in cold blood as he approached.

Or maybe there was no attacker. Maybe he was losing it.

"Hey!" Charles shouted. "Yo! Who's there? Could you come out from behind that pillar. I don't like surprises this time of night." He hoped the other person couldn't hear the slight quaver in his voice.

No one moved and no one spoke. Charles decided to head toward the door. He was sweating heavily and he had his keys fixed between his fingers, curled in a fist so he could get a good punch in. At least he could if the other guy didn't shoot him.

Just as he reached the pillar, he heard a small gasp. He stepped to the side, hoping to get a glimpse of his opponent. Hiding behind the pillar, he saw a small dark-skinned man shivering with fear.

"*No Senor! por favor!*" the man whispered. He held up his hands in a gesture of surrender. "I give you, I give you!" the man pleaded with him.

Charles was so surprised that he could barely understand what the smaller man was saying.

"Who are you? What are you doing here?"

"I am Raphael. I clean," the man answered. "*Por favor,* no fight! I give you!"

Was this guy for real or was he the best actor Charles had ever seen?

"Why are you here?"

"I clean," Raphael told him again. He pointed over his shoulder at the door Charles had walked through a minute earlier.

Charles studied him. He knew the regular maintenance staff, but sometimes there were substitutes. He didn't remember anything unusual during his shift, but he'd had so much on his mind that he certainly could have missed a sub joining the regular maintenance crew. Still, he couldn't be sure about anything.

"Where's your car?" He decided he would walk this Raphael to his car and watch him drive away before he went to his own car.

"No car," Raphael said, shrugging.

"Then what are you doing in the parking garage?" Charles asked. He was starting to get angry.

"My wife, she got car." Raphael still looked terrified.

"Where is she?" Charles wondered what kind of weird setup was this. If Raphael was supposed to be taking him out, this was a strange beginning. Why didn't his wife pick him up in front of the building when he got out of work? "Don't you be messing with me, you hear!" he said sternly to Raphael.

"I give you!" Raphael said again, even more urgently than before. Then he started to reach into his pocket.

"No! Don't move! Keep your hands where I can see them!"

Raphael was shaking even harder. This couldn't possibly be an act, Charles told himself.

Maybe he should just go back into the building and give this guy some space to disappear.

Just then, the door to the parking garage opened and a small woman walked out. She stopped in her tracks when she saw Charles with Raphael. Now she, too, looked terrified.

"Hola!" she greeted them tentatively.

Raphael began telling her something in Spanish, both of them keeping their eyes fixed on Charles. He really had to learn some Spanish, he told himself for the millionth time. He hadn't a clue what was going on.

"He say you want car?" she asked Charles, her eyes filling with tears. "I show you car. Car is old, no good! Brakes bad! Engine bad! You not want car!"

Charles felt a wave of despair roll through him as he realized what they thought. To them, he was menacing. He was Black. He wanted to steal something. Welcome to America!

"No, I do not want your car," he said. "My car is over there. I got surprised by your husband. I was afraid. I'm going now. I am sorry I scared you. My bad."

He turned away and walked as quickly as he could to his car. As he backed out of his space and started driving away, he looked in his rearview mirror. He saw the two small brown people standing right where he left them, staring at him. He couldn't tell if they were relieved or still scared out of their minds.

Maybe he did need to get away from all this for a week or so. He would call Jake in the morning and see if the lawyer had any thoughts about how he could protect himself.

Then he remembered that he had a lunch date tomorrow. He'd keep the date, then leave town.

Charles slept in the next morning, sleeping through the alarm and waking only when the phone rang. He picked up sleepily, glancing at the clock. Whoa! He was going to have to hustle to get in his workout and walk and still be at the restaurant at two to meet Daniel.

The call was from Kori. "'I didn't wake you up, did I?" she asked. "Silly me! I forgot your work schedule. Want me to call back in an hour?"

"No," Charles said quickly. "No, no problem. What's up?" He could feel himself getting all tight with anxiety.

"Just wanted you to know that Alice Ott and her gang arrived last night! I think you're going to really like them, especially Alice! They're cool. Even the kid who drove them here is kind of sweet. Looks like some rocker punk from a garage band, all skinny and tats on every square inch but he's got some style going on."

"Great!" Charles said. He was distracted by the disruptions in his schedule. Maybe he should call and cancel with Daniel.

"You have time to stop by and say hello on your way to work?" Kori asked. "They're staying in Edgewater, in a small community off U.S.1 called Pelican Cove East. It's on the river. I don't think they're going anywhere because they have to quarantine. I bet they'd like to meet you. We could even start filling them in more on what's going on with the lawsuit. Tell them about Rufe and all that."

"Uh, I'm not sure," Charles said, trying to think about this. He now had a real reason to cancel with Daniel. No point in rushing into something with him. Plus he might be dangerous. "Can I call you back after I figure out if I can juggle some stuff?"

"Listen," Kori said, "There's no rush. Let's just make it tomorrow. They won't care. Oh, and I really think you're going to love Felicia! She's Alice's friend, and I don't know how old she is but she's kind of like those ladies in the British TV mysteries, an aging but still gorgeous lady who flirts with everyone and is super dramatic? Nancy told me that she's actually just as smart and passionate about political issues as Alice, but she's, like, playing this over the top kind of diva!

"And then there's Alice's French lover, Gerard! He's old too but super good-looking, has perfect manners and a sexy French accent. He was tired when they arrived last night, but still very gentlemanly. Kind of like you, Mister Dreamy!"

Kori loved teasing Charles about Flo's name for him!

"Well, maybe tomorrow would be better," Charles surprised himself by agreeing to meet tomorrow. "Hey, here's the thing. I have kind of, like, a date today before work?"

"Oooh! Look at you! Juggling this whole crazy thing, keeping your job and still having time for a date? How come I didn't hear about this before? Who's the lucky guy?"

"He's someone I met a few years ago, back when we were both living in Orlando. We went out some, but no big thing. I just ran into him yesterday when I was waiting for Jake. I don't even know why I said I'd meet him."

"Is he hot?"

"I guess so. It's been awhile. I don't remember too much about him except I think he had a boat. Or borrowed one or something."

"I hate to be shallow, but is he cute?"

"He's ok for a white guy. I think I kind of liked him, but I was seeing a few different guys back then, keeping things light, you know? Anyhow, he's a little bit of a distraction, I guess."

"So he called you or you called him, and you decided to get together. Good on you, Charles! You need to have a little fun, right?"

Charles sighed heavily. He hoped he wasn't about to be murdered and dumped into the river by Daniel. He was an idiot to go out with him at a time like this! No one was safe.

"You been out of the loop for too long! Go for it, brother! Just don't forget you have to go to work later today! And give my Gram a big kiss from me!"

"You know I have to keep my mask on!"

"You got that right!" Kori said. "You keep your mask and your pants on, you hear?!" She hung up before he could say anything.

Chapter Twenty-nine

Alice was surprised when she woke up and saw sunlight pouring into the bedroom.

She never slept much beyond dawn and she was unaccustomed to seeing bright sunshine lighting up a room when she first opened her eyes. She heard no sounds from Gerard, and she reached over beside her to see if he was still in bed. Sometimes in the early morning he lay quietly awake, scarcely moving until she woke up. No, it seemed that Gerard was already up and about. She sniffed the air hopefully. Perhaps he was about to appear with the morning cup of fresh brewed coffee.

There was no odor of coffee that she could detect, but she could hear faint sounds of conversation from somewhere in the house. They had all been so exhausted by the time Nancy and Steve brought them over to the house that Alice remembered very little about how the house was configured. She did remember the sound of owls hooting somewhere nearby in the night, but she had stayed awake only for a minute or two to listen.

She reached over to the bedside table and was relieved to find her glasses neatly folded there. She had fallen asleep so quickly that she was afraid both the glasses and her book would be on the floor if she had dropped them as she fell asleep. She put her glasses on so she could take a look at the details of their new bedroom.

She liked the bedroom. It was oddly decorated, and Alice wondered how old Dorie and Anna, the owners, might be. On the wall directly across from the bed, there was a big tie-dyed colored cloth print of Janis Joplin smiling cheerfully. Next to the bed, lined up against the wall there were four carved wooden giraffes of various heights. They looked as if they came from Africa, although the tallest giraffe was wearing a tiny pink sparkly hat decorated with an elegant black lace ribbon and black feather. There was also a framed collage portrait on the dresser of Ruth Bader Ginsburg with a sort of halo effect around her head and the word "Dissent" written across her robe.

Alice felt at home immediately.

Felicia appeared in the doorway, peering in cautiously to see if she would disturb Alice.

"Oh goody!" she exclaimed, clapping her hands together like a five-year-old. "You're finally awake!"

Alice made herself sit up in bed so she could put in her hearing aids before Felicia began the story she was clearly bursting to tell. "Where is Gerard?"

"Oh, he's busy in the kitchen, trying to figure out how to make the coffee pot work. We're probably going to have to ask Nancy to buy us the kind of coffee maker that's just a simple carafe with a drip cone. I remember when you coffee drinkers used to make simple drip coffee in our hippy days. Do they even make that kind anymore?"

She seemed to expect no response from Alice, and moved on cheerfully with an in-depth report on the coffee situation.

"Gerard's struggling with something quite frustrating," she said. "It involves putting little pre-packaged plastic containers of coffee into a machine that heats up water and drips it into the little plastic container. The little container thing presumably drips coffee into the coffee pot. Gerard is cursing in French so I decided to come and see if I could rouse you.

"I think we have to make a trip to the nearest Dunkin' Donuts. I was about to wake up Warp to see if he could drive over with one of us to get the coffee."

"Where is Warp sleeping?" Alice asked. "I'm embarrassed to admit that I was so tired when we got here last night that I got ready for bed, and fell deep asleep. Did you find your comfortable guest room that Nancy was talking about? Was there a bed somewhere for Warp or is he on the living room couch?"

She felt remorseful. After dragging the four of them all the way to Florida, last night she had paid no attention to anyone's creature comforts besides her own.

When she found Gerard in the kitchen, he was clearly getting very worked up. "*Le café!*" he growled, "it is coffee dust. It does not smell of *le café*, and the taste is water! American garbage!"

Alice nodded sympathetically. Many people had these coffee makers but she was in full agreement with Gerard's complaints.

"Let me look around and see what I can figure out," she said resolutely.

She began opening cupboards and drawers in the small kitchen. She could heat water in the electric tea kettle, but she needed something cone-shaped and some paper towels to use as a makeshift container to hold the coffee that she would then drip the hot water into. She found a large strainer, and decided it would do even if it was round and wouldn't drip the water quite as effectively. She could hold it over a ceramic pitcher that would hold about two cups of coffee, and she would wait patiently as it dripped.

The next step was to find some ground coffee in one of the cabinets. She sighed. She supposed that if there was absolutely no alternative, she could dump four or five of the little coffee containers – the "coffee dust" – into the strainer. At least that would change the proportions of coffee to water so they could have stronger coffee.

Like the appearance of an angel, they heard a knock on the door and Nancy Warren's cheerful voice.

"I'm here with four cups of Starbucks dark roast coffee!" she called through the screen. "I'm fully masked but I don't think it's safe for me to come into the house. Can someone meet me out back and open the door to the Florida room?"

Felicia glided to the front door. "We'll come outside!" she said. "Warp's still asleep back there."

Five minutes later they were all seated outside on the lawn chairs. Alice and Gerard were gratefully drinking their strong dark roast coffee, Felicia was happily sipping herbal tea, and Nancy was giving them a thumbnail sketch of their new neighborhood.

Once Alice and Gerard had each finished their large cups of coffee, they eyed the remaining two cups. "We must save one for Warp," Alice said conscientiously, "but perhaps we could share the other cup, while it's still hot?"

Nancy raised an eyebrow. "You two certainly love your coffee! I guess you didn't find the coffee maker that Dorie and Anna use? I decided you shouldn't have to lift a finger to do a single thing today, so I just took a chance on bringing you coffee. Steve tried to stock your kitchen pantry and refrigerator with whatever you might like over the next day or two. When you feel rested enough to think about your needs, I'll show you how to order your items. It's a very efficient system and keeps you safe from going inside the grocery store. After you make your order online, they'll tell you when it will be ready, and Steve or I will drive over to pick it up for you and bring it right to your door."

Alice was the only one smiling at Nancy's plan. Both Felicia and Gerard looked quite unhappy.

Felicia shook her head. "Surely there are places where I can purchase organic fruits and vegetables, and a health food store for my proteins and my staples?" Her eyebrows raised to accentuate the importance of her question.

Gerard looked mournful. "I see, I touch, I smell the fresh food before I buy! It make me know it is good or not good! How do I know it is OK if I do not do this?"

"How did you shop for groceries back in Massachusetts?" Nancy asked them, looking somewhat dismayed by Gerard's level of distress.

"Well, one of us, usually Gerard and sometimes Felicia, went to the market early in the morning," Alice reported, "when only seniors were allowed into the store. Everyone was double-masked and the store regulated social distance very strictly. Or we shopped at the Farmers Market on Saturdays, or my son Ben or his wife Molly shopped for us."

She herself was happy enough to have Nancy help her order online, and grateful that Nancy or Steve would be willing to do the pick-ups. But she knew her companions were not so easily satisfied, and they were the cooks. She would see what she could negotiate.

Nancy smiled, although she looked somewhat impatient. Alice could see that they were at the very beginning of learning to negotiate cultural differences.

"Florida does not regulate the way most New England states do," Nancy said. "You'll find that most of the stores are open, but not everyone inside the stores are masked. It's the same on the sidewalks and at the beach. You have to be watchful and learn to protect yourselves. Probably most of your neighbors won't be wearing masks when they're out for a walk. And you'll have to figure out how to stop people from coming right into your house without masking. You're truly in a different world down here."

Just as she finished speaking, a tall older woman from the house next door walked across the lawn toward them.

"Hi, I'm Betty," she said, smiling warmly, hand outstretched for a shake. She was not wearing a mask. "I live over there right next to you. You must be renting from Dorie and Anna."

Alice noticed that even on this cool morning, their neighbor was barefoot and she was also wearing a sleeveless blouse. She looked to be somewhere around the same age as Felicia. Not only did she seem comfortable, despite the slight morning chill, but her smile was warm and inviting. Alice was sorry to do it, but she quickly put on her own mask, followed by Gerard and Felicia doing the same.

Because of COVID, Alice was not about to shake Betty's hand, so she began to cough into her mask to cover her social discomfort. Gerard eased himself up out of his chair and bowed deeply, although he too did not shake Betty's hand. "*Bonjour!*" he said, beaming at her from behind his mask.

"Oooh!" Betty said, putting her hand over her mouth to hide her giggle. "You have such a pretty accent! You're from Canada, right?"

"*Non!*" Gerard said stiffly. "I am from France!"

"Well, that's wonderful!" Betty said. "Are you all from France? I don't think I ever met people from France! How did y'all get all the way down here and end up in Pelican Cove?"

Felicia also got to her feet, her eyes bright with enthusiasm.

"Oh no, Gerard is the only one who's French. Alice and I come from Massachusetts, and we just got here. I love all the trees and the owls hooting last night! What a charming place!"

Betty nodded. "We like it!" she said. "Wait until you see the painted buntings! They're back there at my feeder just about every day right now. If you put some seeds in those feeders behind your house, you'll get them too.

"And we're hoping the owls are going to be having a baby or two in a few months. She'll start sitting on the nest up there in January, up in the big old live oak tree at Chuck and Susan's house, just the other side of me! They're so cute you can't believe it! Hope the hooting doesn't keep you awake at night!"

She turned and started back to her house. "You let me know if you need anything, you hear," she called over her shoulder. "Welcome to the neighborhood!"

"We look forward to getting to know you better," Alice called after her, "but we have to quarantine for at least ten days first. Then we'll be more hospitable."

"That's OK," Betty called back, stopping to turn and wave at them before she went back into her house. "Don't worry about anything. You'll be safe here!"

The newly arrived little group sat in silence, sipping their hot drinks and basking in the warm sun – the morning chill had gone.

Nancy beamed at them. "I can see you're already relaxing into Florida's pace," she said. "I've heard wonderful things from Dorie and Anna about how friendly this neighborhood is. As long as you can handle the sun, sitting out here is a good way to meet people. Just keep reminding yourself to put your masks on when anyone starts to approach. Oh, and feel free to warn them to stay a six-foot distance away. They'll understand, especially right now if you tell them you're quarantining after your car trip down the whole length of the Eastern seaboard. Some people down here, like many other parts of the country, don't seem to believe in the need for masks. Yet most of them want to get their vaccines, and I'd bet anything they all know at least one person who has died of COVID! Go figure!"

Felicia looked over at Alice. "Is this a good time to tell Nancy the plan we were working on during the trip down?"

"The sooner the better. Go ahead! Gerard and I will fill in as needed."

"You told us about how your friends Kori and Charles, and maybe Flo, too, are involved in that lawsuit," Felicia began. "So we hope we can help with that, and we have an angle that might work to further uncover some of the toxic activities the corporation is up to.

"We can take advantage of our collective age and use some of our sleuthing skills. We'll do a little undercover investigating. Being from the North may help too, so we can ask questions that locals might not ask."

As Felicia stopped to take another bite of the coffee roll she hadn't yet finished, Alice decided to step in.

"We thought perhaps we'd make appointments to visit some of these nursing facilities owned by the TouchStone Corporation. As soon as we're through our quarantine, we can go to some of these places and ask to see for ourselves whatever we're allowed access to. In the meantime, we can do some of our investigating online and by phone."

Felicia jumped back in. "Here's the story we're thinking of using to help us gain more access. We'll tell everyone Alice is the wife and I'm her sister, trying to find a place for Alice's husband Gerard to be admitted as a resident. Also part of the story is that Gerard has – air quotes – 'some dementia' so his English is slipping away. Alice and I can go together to the meetings with the admissions people to gather information."

Nancy was looking puzzled. "May I ask a question before you go ahead with the plan?"

"Of course!" Felicia said, and Alice vigorously nodded.

"Alice, are you ok with pretending that you and Gerard are married? I thought you were opposed to marriage because it represents patriarchal male privilege!"

Alice smiled meekly. "That's our plan, but the real issue is whether or not they'll start checking out my financial status, making sure I am financially suited to their facilities. If so, they could find out that we're not married, and/or discover my political activism arrest record. That would make it hard for us to do our surveillance.

"The alternative would be for Gerard and Felicia to agree to act the part of the poor old couple," Alice continued, "though I'm not wild about doing it that way."

"And if we can get as far as getting Gerard admitted, I will even play the doting wife who comes to visit him every day," Felicia added. She had a little twinkle in her eye.

"Not too doting, please!" Alice said, with a warning glance.

"Perhaps they'll allow me to bring my 'sister' and then you can chaperone!"

Gerard was eyeing the two women thoughtfully, and Nancy wondered what he was feeling about being the sacrificial lamb.

"Goodness! You all have been doing some serious planning! I'm not sure any of the nursing facilities are taking new patients since the spikes in COVID numbers began, but you'll find out. The bigger question, is whether the places we want to infiltrate will be on lockdown in regard to visitors. Sunset Villages, that's the place where Kori's grandmother is a resident, hasn't locked down recently. They did a few months ago, and they may well go into lockdown again if the COVID numbers spike, or, obviously, if there's a visitor who turns out to have COVID, or an employee who gets exposed to COVID.

"Right now we still have Charles working there, and he's our invaluable inside informant. But we're all worried that if he stays involved in the lawsuit, he'll be another target soon."

Alice was trying to remember who Charles was, when another neighbor came sauntering across the grass to greet them. She had one of those superzoom cameras slung around her neck.

"Welcome to the Cove!" she said, flashing them a brief smile.

She looked like a professional athlete, Alice thought, very strong in her trim athletic shorts and short-sleeved shirt.

"So you're the new folks from Massachusetts?" their visitor said. "How was your trip down here? Any trouble on the road?"

She abruptly walked over to inspect the van. "You folks have a good model there! I had one of these,'" she said. "Ran well until it died suddenly. Hope that doesn't happen to you."

"Good morning, I'm Alice, and this is Gerard, and my sister Felicia. And Nancy's an old friend from home who lives nearby."

Their visitor hopped up from where she been squatting to examine the left rear tire of the van.

"You have a soft tire there. I'll give you directions to Coastal Tire so they can check it out for you and make sure you don't have a slow leak." Barely stopping for a breath, she continued, "So how did you end up choosing to be here in Edgewater? Friends of Dorie and Anna? Or have they turned their place into an Airbnb? No one's heard from them, and I thought they'd be showing up any day now. They doing ok, as far as you know?"

"*Bonjour!*" Girard said, his enthusiasm startling Alice. "May I see your camera?"

As the woman knelt down next to him to remove the camera from her neck and hand it to him, Alice realized she was, in COVID time, too close to him.

"Excuse me, but you must move six feet away from him!" Alice's voice became unusually high-pitched in her urgency to protect Gerard.

Their visitor quickly stepped back, simultaneously pulling a mask out of her pocket and putting it on.

"I'm sorry! I forget that you all are from the North! My mistake. Around here, we are all so used to being outside when we see each other that hardly anyone wears a mask."

Felicia smiled as though nothing significant had happened. "Don't worry! It's just that we have to be very careful. We're quarantining because we just drove through eleven states to get here. And with COVID, you just can't be careful enough! Perhaps we should wait until we get through our ten days before Gerard looks at your camera. You don't mind, do you darling?" she added, her voice changing to a purr as she spoke to Gerard. Clearly she was practicing her role in case they decided that she was to be Gerard's wife when they did their nursing home surveillance.

Alice glared at Felicia for a second, then turned her attention to their guest. "I don't think I caught your name. I'm Alice, this is Felicia, that's Gerard, and also we've just been treated to coffee and pastries from Starbucks by our friend Nancy, who lives beachside in New Smyrna."

"I'm Sue," the woman said. "Sorry I scared you all. Just wanted to welcome you. If you need anything, let me know." She handed them a card with a pelican on it and her contact information. "As you can tell from my cell number, I still spend part of the year up in New York state. There's quite a population of snowbirds here, but lots of hardcore Floridians too. Everyone's friendly, so don't hesitate to ask if you need anything."

She started to walk away, then turned back. "Oh," she said, "I almost forgot our main attraction. You see the huge old live oak tree right over there in front of Chuck and Susan's house? If you look at all those thick green vines crawling up that tree, right where the main trunk splits into two huge branches and the vines are a tangled mess? There's a great-horned owl's nest there, and we're hoping the male and female pair hanging around the neighborhood get together soon! We're hoping for owlets around February or March."

"We heard about that from Betty, our new next door neighbor,"

Felicia said. "How exciting!"

"Once the babies hatch," their neighbor said, "there'll be a real crowd at the foot of the tree most of the time, especially in the late afternoon, and they'll be hanging around until the sun goes down. Hope you folks didn't come here expecting it to be all quiet and secluded."

"No, we're just here to get away from the cold," Alice said, "and also to explore the nursing homes and assisted living facilities in the area."

"Well, we have quite a few folks here in the neighborhood you'll want to talk to," Sue told them. "You'll hear good stories and bad ones about the local nursing homes. And there are a couple of ladies who work for one of the big healthcare corporations that owns some nursing facilities right here in Volusia County. You should definitely talk to them. If you want, I can send Pearl over to meet with you, with the brochures and video links and all that.

"Or maybe you want a few days to just rest and get acclimated? You let me know next time I see you when you feel ready to talk with Pearl and anyone else who has info about the places you're looking into."

After she was safely out of earshot, Felicia smiled with delight at her companions. "I think we just got lucky!" she said."Is it too much to hope that the neighbor works for the notorious Touch-Stone Corporation?"

Chapter Thirty

Charles was only a few minutes late for lunch.

As he walked toward the entrance, he felt nervous about what Daniel might be thinking about this lunch date. Charles had no problem being with white men, but some of the white guys he dated tried too hard to impress him with their cool clothes, cool moves, cool language.

There was also the little warning voice reminding him that he couldn't be sure he was really on a date. This could be a set up, a carefully devised scheme to find out what he knew and didn't know about the lawsuit.

He could feel his shoulders relax a little when he spotted Daniel. This man was looking sharp, his jeans and soft blue shirt a compliment to his blue eyes. He appreciated that Daniel looked like a regular guy out for lunch with a friend. Maybe this was for real.

"I'm trying to stand six feet away from you while we order our take-out," Daniel said, "but I'm not sure I can hear much at this distance. I'll be glad when we get to the beach." He kept his mask on, and Charles was impressed that it was one of the medically sanctioned N95 masks.

"You're fine. Did you have a chance to look over the menu?"

"Not yet," Daniel said. "Do you have favorites here?"

"I wish!" Charles told him. "I don't eat out much. My work schedule makes it hard to have much play time. Meeting you today is a real treat!"

Daniel gave him a big smile. "For me too. Not a whole lot going on for me, even though I don't have a job to limit my play time. Until we get the magazine really up and running, I'm pretty much making every day up as I go along. It's fun but it's stressful too. Lunch with you is definitely an unexpected pleasure."

They discussed the food choices before ordering, Charles trying to decide what would be light enough for him given the state of his nervous system. Once they finally got their orders in, Charles suggested that they go upstairs and wait at the bar. The restaurant was built around a giant tree and the upstairs open air bar was a big attraction.

Daniel smiled at Charles and cleared his throat. "Hey, great choice," he said and offered Charles his elbow in what had become the COVID handshake. "I've passed this place countless times, but never ventured up here. This is really cool!"

"I haven't been up here much in six months since COVID shut things down. But all the restaurants are trying to stay afloat with a take-out business. Norwood's built this treehouse a few years back so it had ready-made outdoor seating."

Daniel seemed impressed as he looked around. "I'd say that was a great business decision. Hey, when we get our orders, we'll either need to take two cars or we can ride in mine since it's a convertible – a perfect chariot for this beautiful day."

Charles wasn't sure and simply offered a non-committal shrug.

"I hope you don't mind if I ask you a sort of professional question for starters?" Daniel said. "I don't know if you're still in the nursing profession, but I've been thinking of doing an article on nursing homes during COVID, trying to get a human interest angle since it would be featured in a lifestyle magazine rather than a newspaper. COVID outbreaks in the nursing homes is a big topic these days, and I don't see any in-depth local coverage. I've been talking with my business partner and she thinks it's a good idea. What's your reaction?"

Charles felt increasingly anxious. He wondered if he would actually hyperventilate. What was this guy after? Daniel's sudden appearance in his life might not be a coincidence, and, even worse, it could be malevolent. WTF?

He had to find something that might put him back in the driver's seat. "Did you do a search for me online or something?" he asked Daniel. "Seems like maybe my being a nurse was an important motivation for wanting to get together with me."

Daniel blushed, and then coughed. He took a sip of water before he answered. "Um, something like that," he said, his voice suddenly getting hoarse. He took another sip of water. "I know you're surprised that I checked you out," he said. "When I saw you yesterday, it was clear that I remembered you much better than you remembered me. It's not so surprising, though."

Charles squinted at Daniel as he was telling his story. Something about him that he must be half remembering from Orlando tugged at his memory.

"When I moved here, I didn't know how to find the gay community or if there was anything like that. So, yes, I thought I remembered you were moving over here, and I googled you. Sure enough, I found a few Facebook posts that mentioned you. And you were also quoted in an article in *The Daytona Beach News-Journal* a month or so ago. I thought my idea of the magazine feature would be right up your alley."

"Of course," Charles said. "I get it." He was feeling worse by the minute. He had an unpleasant flashback moment, remembering the TouchStone personnel manager who had called him to the corporate building and formally reprimanded him for letting himself be quoted in that news story. He could have been fired for confirming the rumor that the PPE equipment had yet to be seen by staff at Sunset Village.

He should've gotten out of the whole lawsuit thing back then, he thought miserably. Now here he was with Daniel, maybe about to find out that the guy was only pretending to date him but really was hired to protect the reputation of the biggest healthcare corporation in the county.

Daniel grinned, clueless that Charles was at the edge of an anxiety attack. "Yeah, I liked how you said it in that article, when you and other staff learned about the big COVID grant to the TouchStone nursing home chain four months earlier, you all were puzzled about the missing PPE stuff. Puzzled! You said it so politely! Did you get flak for that?"

How could he be sure who Daniel was? This conversation could be designed to draw him into Daniel's confidence so that he could take Charles down later. It seemed more and more possible that Daniel was working for TouchStone.

But wasn't it just as possible that this was truly a coincidence, running into each other yesterday and deciding to get together?

He could be getting really paranoid.

Maybe Daniel genuinely wanted to reconnect. Even the story about googling him so they'd have something to talk about when they met for lunch, could just be wanting to get off to a good start by knowing something about Charles' work and interests. It was pretty common practice now, really, since you could check out just about anyone online.

But it seemed like Daniel was closing in on him too quickly, claiming he wanted to do some article on COVID and the nursing homes. This disturbingly familiar man could be gathering evidence to be used against him. Or Daniel could just be bored, even lonely, being new in town.

Maybe he just wanted to impress Charles. Maybe it was normal to bring up the magazine. He could be trying to make Charles think he had something to offer, like he could put Charles into the public eye. As if he would ever want that, Charles thought angrily!

Their food arrived, and Charles took the opportunity to dial himself back before his head exploded. He had to settle down and figure out what he was doing.

He stalled for time. He painstakingly examined his salad. Then he complained to the young woman who had taken their take-out orders that he had expressly requested no onions. He sent the salad back to the kitchen to have the onions removed. Next, he fiddled with the container of rolls, rambling on about whether he wanted a dinner roll or a corn muffin. When he ran out of evasive chatter, he went to look for whoever had disappeared with his salad, telling Daniel he needed to order salad oil and vinegar on the side so he could mix his own dressing.

By the time he returned to the table, Daniel was checking messages on his cell phone. He smiled at Charles, but he was looking a little annoyed.

"I'm so sorry," Charles said. "What were we talking about?"

Daniel scrutinized him, probably assessing whether he would ever want to get together with him again. Charles wouldn't blame him if he decided against it.

"I was interested in your opinion about how the nursing homes and assisted living facilities are coping with COVID," Daniel reminded him. "As I said, our new magazine could do a good feature article on the topic, and I thought you were kind of an expert on this whole thing."

Charles tried to think of another way to test the underlying intent of this conversation. "Before we go into all that," he finally said, "tell me more about the magazine."

Daniel sighed, looking unsure of himself. Charles congratulated himself on getting some kind of upper hand. Maybe the magazine was a total fake, a smokescreen to lure Charles into his confidence. "It's only about four months old, and we've only put out one issue so far," Daniel told him. "I've got a super smart business partner, young and very geeky. Until a couple of weeks ago, we also had a fantastic reporter/editor. She was the reason I came here to work on this new venture. It was her brain child, she had all the contacts, and she recruited me. Her plans were really enticing. And I wanted to get out of Orlando."

"Well now, which door do I open?" Charles said, forcing a small laugh. "Do I pursue the mystery of the missing editor or your reasons for leaving Orlando? I'll go for Door Number Two, I guess!"

"That's at least an hour's worth of stories," Daniel said. "Mostly it's a sad little slice of life. But if you're interested, I don't mind telling you once we get to the beach and are enjoying this picnic. Do you have enough time?"

When Charles looked unhappily at his watch, Daniel winked at him. "Door Number One is easy. I can tell you the whole thing even before the kitchen brings your salad back. My wonderful writer/editor, Serena, got really sick. She went into the hospital for a relatively routine surgery, got COVID, and is still recovering. I don't think she's going to be ready to work again anytime soon.

"So I'm kind of stuck in regard to the magazine. I need to get another issue out soon or we lose whatever momentum started with the first issue, but I'm really just a photographer. I don't have the skill set for the interviews and the writing. But the big problem is, I don't want to replace Serena, so I'm not ready to hire someone else."

It sounded like Daniel was feeling genuinely discouraged about his new venture. Charles felt slightly trusting. Suddenly he wanted to know more about Daniel's life.

Anyone or anything could freak him out right now, he reminded himself. He was probably being paranoid.

"What's the name of your magazine?" he asked, buying a little time while he tried to figure out how to get to the root of Daniel's interest in the nursing home story.

Daniel hesitated. "*Splash!*" he said, blushing slightly. "With an exclamation point. *The Volusia Splash!* What do you think?"

"It's cute," Charles said. "Seems like you could get people interested with a name like that! It could be an outdoor sport and adventure type of publication, or a 'who's hot in Volusia County,' or even a magazine for kids. How did you come up with the name?"

"The three of us brainstormed, and finally chose the name that raised the fewest objections among us. My business partner, Ashford, wanted to call it either the Volusia Vault or Smash! The Millennial generation casts a vote! And Serena wanted it to be The Volusia Vine, as in 'grapevine' which she said might make women readers think of wine and gossip."

"Who thought up *Splash?*" Charles asked.

"I think I did, but I had other even clunkier ideas. Southern Exposure was my favorite, but that didn't get much of a wow from either Ashford or Serena."

"Is Ashford female or male?" Charles asked.

"Female, more or less. Kind of gender non-specific, really. She/they are in their early thirties and really good at money and marketing. So far I get the impression that they don't have much of a social life, so they have plenty of time and energy to get the magazine out there. But I'm really at a loss without Serena."

When Charles' lunch finally reappeared, Daniel scooped up the check. "I got this," he said. "And yes, I guess I can give you the short version while we eat."

"I'll drive my own car. Meet you there."

Charles could see Daniel's disappointment that he wasn't going to be able to give him the thrill of riding in his sleek convertible.

"Maybe we can take a ride in your undeniably hot car next time," Charles told him. If there was a next time, he thought gloomily.

They were lucky to arrive at the beach during a moderately low tide, a perfect time to walk on the beach if they had time.

"So why did you leave Orlando?" Charles asked, worrying that he was running out of time before he had to leave for work and still might not know enough about Daniel.

Daniel shook his head. "You know, I don't think I want to spoil a great meal for myself. I hate hearing sad stories while I'm eating!"

They ate in silence, the sounds and beauty of the beach filling the space. "If you still feel like talking, we could still take a quick walk by the ocean before I have to go to work," Charles offered when they finished eating.

As they walked along together, Charles felt his lungs beginning to open up. He glanced at Daniel for a moment, and felt something softening up his heart, too. He was remembering a little more why he liked this man. He hoped his extreme nervousness didn't make him seem like a total idiot to Daniel.

"So, long story short," Daniel said. "When you knew me in Orlando, I was still drinking and drugging and keeping myself tough and kind of untouchable, I guess. Then I met another guy a lot like me.

"We had both served in the Marines, we were both trying to act super macho all the time, and we were both working hard, in and around weekend partying, to make a bunch of money. He was a broker, I was selling high-end art and other expensive stuff.

"We ended up falling in love, and we decided we wanted something very different. No more big partying, no more rat race to see how much money we could make. But there was trouble in paradise, of course. He really wanted kids, and that was one part of the dream I couldn't share.

"Finally, when it came down to it, he had found a little baby girl available for adoption, and I just couldn't do it. I walked out on him, and after a few months, I decided to leave Orlando. So here I am, still a little bit heartbroken, and looking to put my life back together."

He stopped and looked at Charles. "Can you relate to any of that?" he asked.

Charles wasn't sure what to say. He had his own heartbreaks, but at the present he wasn't nursing old wounds. But he was remembering something and he had to ask. "Do you have a tattoo on your shoulder that says Semper Fi?" he asked.

Daniel grinned. "Yes, and that's why I remember you," he said. "You don't remember because the night we were partying together and I went home with you, you were flying pretty high. You often were back then, but we were only together as part of a group that hung out at the same bars. Anyway, you saw my tat and you said that you couldn't believe I had been a Marine.

"So I told you about how I had tried so hard to not be gay and to be tough, and joining the Marines was my worst effort at achieving my goal. And then you told me a story that was your own version of having to pretend to be all this macho stuff that wasn't you. And then we cried together."

Charles looked at him. "I don't really remember," he said, but his body felt a memory of something hurting and then feeling very safe with Daniel. His story felt true. It troubled him that he hadn't remembered such a significant event.

"That's OK," Daniel said. "I don't know why I remember, except that maybe I had been getting to that place for awhile, you know, the place where you want to quit trying to be something you're not? That might have been the moment I really got it."

They were back at their cars, and Charles checked his watch. He had to leave right away or he'd be late for work. He felt his phone vibrate, and he glanced at it. Instantly, his gut clenched and he could feel sweat breaking out all over his body even though he felt an unpleasant chill run down his spine. He couldn't believe the caller ID!

The call was from Mitch.

His gut did a series of flips, pure sickening fear. What could Mitch want from him?

Daniel studied him thoughtfully. "You look like something just went way wrong." After a moment of silence, he could feel his face change as an angry feeling began to bubble up for the pit of his stomach. "Is there someone in the picture you haven't told me about? I'm not up for any melodrama, Charles. I'm open to friend-ship or maybe more with you, but not if you've got some jealous husband or boyfriend keeping tabs on you. And, also, just to be clear, I don't really hang out with friends who use drugs a lot."

Charles stared at him. How could he explain this call? He didn't want to reveal anything about the lawsuit. But he also realized that he didn't want to lose this really nice feeling he had about the man.

"It's nothing to do with a relationship," he said. "I'm not in one and I'm not getting harassed by an ex. My personal life is just hanging with my friends when I can. And I'm no longer a drug user. Mostly, my mind, body and soul are swallowed up by my job.

"Look, I'm so sorry about this call. I really do have to call the person back. I'm just surprised to hear from him. And right now, I have to get to work."

Daniel looked somewhat relieved, but Charles could see that something had shifted between them.

"This had been great, really!" he told Daniel. "Next time I'll be the one taking you to lunch. Oh, and I'd love to take a ride with you in your jazzy car! Ok if I call you when I know how my next day off is looking?"

"Sure, Charles. Looking forward to hearing from you!"

Daniel looked a little shaken, and Charles wondered if he trusted what he had just heard.

Charles pulled out of the parking lot, trying not to look back. He knew he looked pretty sad, and he imagined Daniel wasn't looking too happy either.

Once he was out of the parking lot, he checked his rearview mirror. He half wished he'd see Daniel on his tail.

He looked in the mirror again. No Daniel. Well, he told himself, it could be worse. What would he do if Mitch appeared? Unable to put Rufe's horrible death out of his mind, Charles drove as fast as he could to Sunset Villages. He'd get himself safely off the highway and onto his floor, and then he'd figure out what to do about Mitch.

His work shift kept him so busy that he could block the worrying triggered by Mitch's call. It helped that there were no further calls from him or anyone else.

When it was time to leave, Charles timed it so that he could walk out to the parking garage with one of the male nursing assistants who also was finishing his shift. Tyrell was a big guy, and Charles felt relief when, after wishing Tyrell a good night, he made it into his car and began winding his way down through the parking garage with no one on his tail.

Just as he was slipping his pass into the machine to open the gate at the exit, Mitch appeared. He was standing right in front of him, only about a foot from his car, nothing between them but the exit arm.

Charles watched the exit arm lift up. He inched his car toward

Mitch. Mitch stood there, stubbornly blocking his way. The mechanical arm hesitated above his car, then went back to the upright position. There they were, facing off.

Was he supposed to drive forward until he hit Mitch? There was no way he could do it. He rolled down his window a crack.

"What the hell do you want, man?" he snarled at Mitch in his toughest street voice.

"I need you to help me," Mitch said. The guy looked terrible. He needed a shave, and his eyes were really red. "Please, Charles," he said. "I'm desperate. Just let me talk to you for a couple of minutes, and then I'll get out of your life again, I promise."

Charles could see headlights coming up behind them. It was probably Tyrell leaving the garage. He could ask Tyrell to help him by scaring Mitch enough to make him move out of the way, but then the problem would continue. "Put your hands up where I can see them," he told Mitch sternly.

Mitch complied. Charles wasn't surprised that he was empty-handed. "Now step to the side, and let me drive out of here. Half a block down, I'll pull over at the entrance to the parking lot on the right. I'll wait for you there, and we can talk for a couple of minutes. I'm going to stay in my car, though, and you can talk through the window on the passenger side. And I'm not sticking around for a bunch of crap, so you'll have to make your point fast."

"Please Charles, just please don't take off," Mitch said. "If you do that, I'll have to keep following you until you talk with me."

Charles started moving the car slowly until Mitch stepped aside. In less than thirty seconds, he pulled over at the entrance to the all-night parking lot up ahead. As he waited for Mitch to catch up, he wondered if he was about to be shot or else mowed over by a car that would come from out of nowhere. He was too tired to come up with any alternative plan as he watched Mitch trotting toward him.

Chapter Thirty-one

It was hard to say which one of them was the most restless by the fourth day of quarantine rolled around.

Warp was already making plans to head back north. "I can tell RubyStarr is getting lonely," he said as they sat in the gentle morning sun out in the front yard. The lawn furniture was surprisingly comfortable, and now that they had a decent coffeemaker, they were all enjoying their morning beverages.

"I'm thinking that I might head back pretty soon," he continued. "Of course we have to get you folks a car, but I'm hoping that won't be hard. Sue was telling me there are lots of used cars down here, mostly in super good condition. She says there are so many retired people down here that when one of them can't drive safely anymore, they sell their cars cheap even when the car has a bunch of miles left on it. And of course, there's nothing like the wear and tear we have back home because there's no salt and chemical damage from the winter roads. Even if those cars are kind of dinged up, down here the dings don't go to rust so quickly."

He might have continued, but Felicia cleared her throat and nodded her head in Alice's direction. "We are aware that there are many seniors down here, but there's no reason to imply that there are more than the usual number of dings on those cars they're turning in!"

As Warp turned a deep shade of red, Alice jumped to his defense.

"But we old folks are increasingly likely to be bad drivers, most of us, by the time we turn seventy-five or eighty, not to mention those who are still driving at ninety. Our eyesight is going and our reflexes are slower. Warp is simply stating the simple facts, Felicia. I myself have quite a few friends my age with multiple scrapes and dents on their cars."

"Sue was the one saying it, not me," Warp reminded Felicia, still looking embarrassed.

"Is it necessary for us to have the car?" Gerard asked. He had spent much of his life in Paris, Washington D.C, and, most re-

cently, San Francisco, where he didn't need a car. He was still surprised by all the car travel that was required for Americans living
in less metropolitan areas.

"Oh I can tell you, you have to have a car to live here," Sue said,
as she walked across the lawn to join them, coffee cup in hand.
"You'd get very tired of being stuck here, and there are so many
wonderful places to see. I'll take you car shopping whenever you're
ready. I can fit all four of you in my camper, if everyone wants to
go."

Alice knew this was challenging for Warp. He didn't want to
leave them stranded, but the agreement had always been that the
van was their gift to him. They had promised that he could go back
home as soon as he had rested a bit and they were safely settled in
their Florida home.

"Perhaps Warp, you and Sue could both help us look for a car
sometime today?" she suggested. "I think you should be able to
head home tomorrow. Sue, it would be so kind of you to help us
out. Do you think we can stay outdoors while we buy a car?"

"Oh I'm sure that won't be a problem," Sue said. "The dealers
have their cars outside on their lots. The only time one of you
might have to go inside would be to sign papers to buy the car.
Even that could probably happen outside if you make that request."
She quickly pulled her mask all the way up over her nose instead
of riding below her nostrils, something Alice had observed as a
typical Florida mask-wearing practice.

"And would you be willing to test drive the cars for us to make
sure they handle well?" Alice added. "You know the roads, and we
don't, so it would be much safer for you to be our test driver.

"I don't believe Gerard should have to participate," she added.
Gerard smiled at her gratefully. They had just talked about how
difficult it was for him to pretend to be suffering from dementia
whenever they were around their new neighbors. Once they had
what they needed from his fake institutionalization at Sunset Villages, the plan was for him to have a sudden 'cure.' Then he could
go back to being the still brilliant scientist and researcher, and he
could have any conversations he chose.

They had agreed that, for now, the less time he spent with Sue,
especially, the better. She was very sharp, and also spoke passable

French. Her grandchildren lived in France and she visited them there. Gerard had already forgotten his pretend diagnosis several times while discussing scientific matters with her.

Alice wondered how long it would take to make the inside surveillance part of the plan operational. It was very possible that the high numbers of people still getting COVID would preclude any of the local nursing homes enrolling new residents. In fact, it was quite possible that even a visit to tour one or more of the facilities might not be possible. Lax as the majority of Floridians seemed to be about masking and social distancing, continuing to congregate in bars and restaurants and sports events, the fragility of the nursing home population was taken very seriously and there had been temporary lockdowns.

Sue agreed to go car shopping with them in an hour, and Warp went back into the house to call RubyStarr.

"Alice," Felicia said, the minute Sue was out of earshot, "I've been thinking about our strategies, and I think we need to work out a solid Plan B in case we can't get into the TouchStone nursing homes at all. I have an idea, and I'd like you and Gerard to hear me out."

"Oh good!" Alice said. "We definitely need a Plan B."

Gerard nodded his agreement. He looked relieved that there might be another way to infiltrate the TouchStone enterprises besides him passing as an old man with dementia.

"Do you think maybe we should go back into the house and have this conversation on the screened porch?" Alice suggested. "We could have cold cereal for breakfast, and talk about your new idea while we eat. Then we'll be ready when Sue comes back for our car buying expedition."

Gerard surprised them by not balking at the suggestion of cereal, and this further confirmed Alice's worry that the surveillance from within might seem more overwhelming to him than she had realized. He was obviously very eager to hear the new alternative.

They had just poured cereal and seated themselves at the card table at one corner of the porch, when Alice's phone buzzed. She realized instantly that she had made the mistake of keeping it with her in the pocket of her gym pants, and now she felt compelled to see who was calling. "It's Nancy," she told the others.

Gerard frowned. He was passionately opposed to anyone taking phone calls during a meal.

"I'll call back," she reassured him, and let the phone take a message. When the phone rang again, and once again she saw Nancy's name on the caller I.D., she hesitated. Just before the fourth ring, she pressed the answer button.

"Hi Nancy, we're just starting our breakfast out here on this sweet little porch. Can I call you back?"

"Oh dear, I'm so sorry to interrupt your meal, but something quite important has come up. Can you call me back within a half hour at the most?"

"Of course!" Alice assured her. She firmly clicked the phone off, muting the ringer before another call spoiled Gerard's meal.

"Do you still want to hear my plan?" Felicia asked. She hated being upstaged when someone else threatened to get her audience's attention.

"*Oui!*" Gerard answered firmly. Alice nodded her assent.

"Well, you know that back in the day, I was once a journalist, and a very good one if I do say so myself!" Felicia beamed at them, pausing for effect. She was clearly more comfortable taking a tiny trip down memory lane than either of her companions were, at the moment.

"Where are you going with this, Felicia?" Alice prompted her.

"I've had an idea forming since the minute I woke up!" Felicia exclaimed, "and it just might work! Maybe we could pretend that the three of us are a team of writers traveling to different parts of the country to do interviews with staff and residents of nursing homes. We could say that we're trying to produce an upbeat story – either a feature-length article or perhaps even a book – about nursing home successes! We're looking to portray positive human interest stories in the time of COVID. We're, of course, starting with the administration, interviewing them as to how they've managed so well in the midst of the pandemic."

"Slow down!" Alice said. "How could we prove that we're journalists or prove there's a publication they'd want to give interviews to? Don't you think they'd have to see our credentials?"

"I'll get back to that in a minute,'" Felicia said, "but let me spin out a little more of the plan. We'll fill in the details later, ok?"

"I suppose that's OK," Alice said. She was trying to be open to any ideas any of them could generate, but this was sounding more than a little flakey. She looked at Gerard for support, but he was busy exploring his cereal. He seemed to be willing to let Felicia continue.

"So here's the story," Felicia said resolutely. "We're here in town for a week or more, and we've heard such good things about TouchStone's nursing homes! So we talk our way into an interview, which will lead to more meetings.

"We could start with pitching the idea to key PR people at TouchStone, asking them to put us in contact with staff at the nursing homes. We'd be asking them to hand pick the employees who would give us mini-interviews about themselves, and help us enlist their most photogenic, best adjusted, happiest residents for our project. We'd be on a mission to show that it's not all doom and gloom in nursing homes right now!"

Alice cleared her throat and raised her eyebrows at Felicia. "Really?!" she said skeptically.

"Listen! Here's where the serious action comes in!" Felicia said, undaunted by Alice's wet-blanket response. "At this point, the corporate folks love us and the employees we've been directed to talk to, they love us too. It will seem like we're there to give them great free PR, right?

"So, then, in the course of developing these warm and fuzzy relationships, we would pull off some creative distractions, thus allowing us to get access to financial records, copies of the big federal grant, even manage to do some follow-ups with a few employees we discover who might tell us the real truth of the situation.

"Before we go for the really sensitive stuff, we'll find opportunities to look at records of the boring stuff, you know, like number of admissions per month, number of visitors, how many staff have been hired per year or month, or whatever. We would time our requests for this info at break times, change of shifts, whatever. We could be theatrical, disarming, like saying 'Oh sweetheart, can't I just go ahead and look these stats over, so you don't have to waste your break reading them out to me?' or 'I can just look this over on my own so you don't have to stay late to help me after your shift ends?'

"By then, they have become so used to us that they think we're the best cheerleaders ever, harmless old people who would never have any tricks up their sleeves! That's when we get access to numbers that don't add up, like the number of overtime hours staff had to put in and a corresponding absence of proof that they got paid for this overtime! That kind of thing!"

Felicia stopped to see how they were reacting. "Kind of exciting, don't you think?" she said hopefully.

"Felicia," Alice said, "it's a wonderful fantasy, but how would we ever convince them to let us have access, even at the beginning part of your plan? We don't have any credentials to prove we are those writers or journalists we say we are. We can't produce letters from bonafide publishers asking to publish our interviews. We can't even give them our real phone numbers or websites to contact. Why would anyone believe us?"

"I'm working on that," Felicia said. "Remember, I did have a real career in journalism and I may be able to use some old contacts for backup. And Alice, you should know that anyone can put up a website! Maybe we should say that our publisher is in France. We'll have them call Gerard on his cell. We can create a story that he can give them when they call. We just have to get creative!"

Both Alice and Gerard were looking doubtful. Alice wasn't sure how much Gerard had understood because Felicia tended to talk very fast when she was excited.

"I'm sorry," Alice said, "but I have to call Nancy back now. Maybe we can keep trying to work out how to make your idea more feasible, after I find out what Nancy's calling about."

Nancy answered the phone in the middle of the first ring. "I'm so glad it's you," she told Alice. "Something's going on and I don't quite know what to do next. Maybe you can help me figure this out."

"I can try. I have no other real plans, except we need to buy a car fairly soon."

"Here's what just happened. The phone rang very early this morning. Steve and I were still asleep. It was our landline, and I was surprised since not many people have that number anymore. I was shocked when the caller was, well, someone you've met recently. I couldn't imagine why she was calling me!

"Where are you?" I asked the caller.

"'A friend is in trouble,' the caller said, 'and I'm trying to help. We're going to visit old friends of yours, and I've lost their phone number so would you please call them and say we're on our way over there, if you don't mind?'

"'Sure, no problem,' I told them, but I was really shaken. Alice, I have no idea which of the caller's friends might be in trouble, but the caller hung up before I could ask anything else. So I thought I'd call around to everyone I can think of, just to see if there are any new developments."

Alice was puzzled. Nancy's story was too vague to make sense to her. But she certainly got it that her dear friend was very worried. She thought very carefully before she spoke.

"Well thanks, Nancy," she finally said. "I'll stay alert! Our guard dog will let us know if someone shows up."

Nancy laughed, a weird sound that didn't sound like her. She had to be aware that the New Englanders hadn't brought a dog with them.

Alice's reference to the guard dog was her off-the-cuff effort to communicate something back in Nancy's coded style that could be deciphered to mean they would stay on high alert. Aside from her weird laugh, Nancy had no response to Alice's cryptic communication.

"Ok, then," Alice said, feeling totally inadequate. "Is there anything else?"

"Oh, well yes, Nancy said. "My caller also said that someone inside is in danger. I don't see how I can involve the police with so little to go on. But I don't want to wait for another tragedy to happen if there is anything I can do to prevent it."

"I wish I could help more, Nancy. Whatever does or doesn't happen, let's keep in touch today, all right?"

"Of course," Nancy promised and hung up abruptly.

Alice looked at her watch, wondering if they should cancel their plans to go car shopping..

"Well, well, well! Something very strange is happening," she told Gerard and Felicia. "Nancy just gave me the most peculiar message, clearly her effort to communicate something in code. I don't understand it. And I'm not really sure why she felt she had to speak in such veiled language."

"Perhaps it is her phone, it has the, ah, the tapping?" Gerard suggested.

"Oh I don't think you understand tapping," Felicia said. "It can't really be done well over the phone. You really need to know the physiology of the method. It is a form of hypnotherapy, to be sure, but it doesn't involve garbled communication. And the person has to know the method of tapping on healing points, systematically, actually sequentially, involving progressive areas of the body. It's difficult to do over the phone, and ..."

"He's talking about electronic wiretaps," Alice said impatiently, not at all sorry for interrupting Felicia's lecture on the tapping method. "Like when your phone calls are recorded and monitored by someone spying on you, something usually done by someone with the official power to do that, like the FBI or Homeland Security."

Honestly! Sometimes Felicia could be so off! In Alice's opinion, she spent too much time in woo-woo land.

"Why would anyone tap Nancy and Steve's phone?" Felicia asked. "They're just retired people who are working on an open, honest political campaign. And they've been working on voter registration in the Black community down here for several years. Why is that so secret or threatening?"

Alice thought a minute. "We know that something dangerous or at least frightening is going on with their friend Kori, something related to the lawsuit. Maybe that's what Nancy was trying to tell me, but I'm not sure I understand who she was talking about. Or what she thought I might know or not know."

"Well, come on! What on earth did she tell you?" Felicia asked impatiently.

"Just that someone's friend was in trouble and they needed to visit old friends of Nancy's but the caller didn't have the old friends' phone number and needed Nancy to call to give them the message."

"Well it couldn't be clearer to me!" Felicia said. "Someone will be showing up here to visit us, but we just don't know who's coming, when they're coming, or why."

Alice nodded. "I guess that makes sense. I wasn't thinking about why she would involve me, given that she knows we're still so new to everything happening down here. But maybe that's exactly why she needs us to provide cover or distraction or even shelter."

Gerard studied them both. "I do not understand what things you speak of," he said calmly, "but forever it is this way, that the man, he does not understand what the two women they say to each other. This is not the new surprise for me."

Chapter Thirty-two

Charles rolled down the window two inches on the passenger side of the car.

"What's up?" he asked. "And, Mitch, put on your damned mask!"

"Listen, someone's trying to kill me!" Mitch said softly, after extricating a mask from his pocket, his hands trembling as he put it on. Charles was having trouble hearing him through the mask and the two inches of space he allowed Mitch to speak through.

"Why is it my problem?" Charles asked. "What goes around comes around, right?"

Mitch stared at him, his bloodshot eyes making Charles want to roll the window back up. "What are you talking about?" he asked.

"You set up Rufe!" Charles said, his voice rising. What could this punk possibly think anyone owed him?

"No way, man!" Mitch said. He sounded genuinely indignant.

"You meet with Jake and Rufe, then you three leave the restaurant, then Rufe just happens to leave the parking lot and immediately gets mowed down by a hit and run killer? I don't believe in coincidences, Mitch! You set him up to get killed!"

"Not what happened!" Mitch said stubbornly. "I went back into the restaurant to use the restroom, and when I came out, I drove home. I didn't know Rufe had been hit until the next morning when I heard about it at work. When I heard, I left work and took off, I was so scared! They've been following me, and I'm getting phone calls telling me they're going to kill me too."

"That's a whole lot of crap," Charles said, but he was shaken. He tried to think about his responsibility in all this. It was his fault, for sure, that he hadn't found out more about Mitch when he sent him to that meeting. But how could he know the guy had the history he did? "Why don't you call Jake and tell him about it?"

"I can't get him to call me back. He's the person I want to talk to, believe me. I want him to get me into some Witness Protection program or something. I can't go home. I can't use my credit card for a hotel room because I'm afraid, whoever they are, they'll track me if I use credit. I've withdrawn a bunch of cash to pay for food and gas, but I'm sleeping in my car. Yesterday I figured out they could find me if I keep driving my car. So I kind of abandoned it, and now I've been taking the bus and trying to keep on the move.

"Last night I found a garden shed to sleep in. It's in the backyard of a house in my neighborhood where I don't think anyone's living right now. I'm afraid to go into my apartment to get clean clothes, so I look more and more like the guys at the shelter.

"Listen, man," he said, looking at Charles with desperation deep in his gaze, "all I want from you is to persuade Jake to help me."

Charles thought about it. He didn't want to stay out here at two a.m. on the street. He felt exposed, out in the open talking to this white man he didn't even trust. Any minute he could get told to step out of his car by some cop, if he didn't get shot first. And meanwhile, White Boy Mitch would just walk away.

"I'll call Jake first thing in the morning," he told Mitch. "I'll tell him about our conversation, and that you really need to talk to him. So if you give me until at least eleven o'clock tomorrow morning to reach him, then you go ahead and try him again. With a little luck, he will have gotten my call, and he'll talk with you."

"I sure would appreciate that, bro!" Mitch told him.

"Don't call me that, man!" Charles snapped at him. "I am not your brother!"

"Sorry!" Mitch said. "Wait!" he shouted, grabbing at the window as Charles turned on the car engine. "Um, listen, uh, do you think I could maybe sleep in your car or something tonight? I know where you live. If you leave the car unlocked, I'll just grab a few hours of sleep and I'll leave it just as clean as it is right this minute."

Charles could feel himself waver as he saw how longingly Mitch was looking at his big clean car. Snap out of it! he told himself.

"You try the homeless shelter yet?" he asked Mitch.

"I went there last night before I ended up in the shed, but they make you show ID. The trouble is, I, uh, well, I have some minor legal trouble that comes up on my record. They told me I had to get cleared at the police station before they could let me stay at the shelter. But I didn't go to the station. I don't do so well with cops."

"And there you are, with your white skin and all," Charles said, shaking his head. "Huh! I don't know what to think about that."

Where Mitch slept was not his problem. On the other hand, finding out what else Mitch might know about the TouchStone criminals and their strategies might be helpful. He needed all the help he could get to figure out how much danger he himself was in, and how to keep other co-workers safe, especially Kori.

"Mitch," he said, staring into the frightened eyes of the man clinging to the side of his car, "is there anything you can tell me about whoever is working against the lawsuit? Did the corporation hire some professional thugs to kill Rufe and beat up Kori and threaten you? Or maybe it was somebody who works for Touch-Stone, someone in administration, or maybe even some of our co-workers from the nursing homes? It would make me feel a whole lot more like helping you if you could tell me anything about who the bad guys are."

Mitch shook his head. "I have no clue. I only got involved in this whole thing because I wanted to stop those no good millionaires at TouchStone from stealing the grant money that was supposed to pay for our PPE stuff and our overtime.

"I don't know the guy who called to threaten me, or how they got my cell number, but they've got me scared out of my mind! I thought Jake would protect anyone who signed up to be part of the lawsuit. Now here I am, running for my life! I'm afraid to show up for work, and I'm probably going to have to move, and find another job, and who knows what else. Maybe I'll even have to move out of state. This sucks!"

"Yeah, it does," Charles said.

He wished he knew if he could trust Mitch. The man's history didn't give him much confidence. But he got it that Mitch was terrified, and he felt sorry for him.

"Listen,'" he said, "I'm sorry I'm not comfortable with you sleeping in my car or hanging around my place. You should probably go back to the shed where you slept last night. I can give you a nice soft beach blanket I've got in my trunk. I'll just pop the trunk, and you walk back there and get yourself the blanket. And I've got some gym stuff in the back too, like a pair of sweatpants and a tee shirt and gym shorts. Don't know if they'll fit you, but they're clean, and you're welcome to them. And I promise you, I'll call Jake in the morning and tell him to talk with you."

He watched in his rearview mirror as Mitch scurried away with the blanket and the bag of gym clothes in his arms.

Driving home and looking forward to a good sleep, he checked the mirror repeatedly. The empty streets had never looked so good.

He fell asleep the second his head hit the pillow, but then woke up again. He thought he heard something, but all he could be sure of was the sound of his heart pounding and the hum of the air system. His cat, Jeremiah, began to purr hopefully.

"It's nowhere near morning yet, big guy," he told the cat. "Go back to sleep." Jeremiah obediently rolled over against Charles and was quiet again.

Charles thought over his encounter with Mitch. Why was someone going after this guy if he really was such a minor player? And why was Jake refusing to take Mitch's calls?

When he tried to go back to sleep, his head kept buzzing, going over and over details of the last twenty-four hours. He tried to calm himself down by replaying his lunch date with Daniel. Reconnecting with this man made him feel happy. He could use something good happening in his life right about now.

He thought about Daniel referring to his earlier life as a Marine. A former Marine could be a handy guy to have around, he thought. Too bad they hadn't run into each other sooner. It might take a Marine to get him out of this mess with TouchStone. He wondered what skills Daniel had retained from his Marine training.

No way! He told himself he shouldn't ask Daniel to get involved with this nightmare. It wasn't right. Not after one date, or their not-a-date, or whatever. After running a few more laps on his mental hamster wheel, he finally fell asleep again.

He was awake again at five-thirty a.m., three hours before his alarm was set to go off. Grumbling to himself, he got up to use the bathroom. Jeremiah began purring and rubbing his head against Charles' legs as he tried to walk back to the bed.

"Go back to sleep," he told Jeremiah gently, but the cat had his own plans. In less than a minute, he heard the familiar crash of a chair rolling across the tiles and banging against the dining table. This was no intruder, he reminded himself, even though his heart was pounding.

Jeremiah was almost two years old, but he used his kittenish tricks to keep Charles alert. He was an expert in finding ways to make his human pay attention. If the rolling chair didn't work, a lamp might crash onto the floor, or a pile of magazines, or an empty coffee cup would be swept off a side table. The cat had a mighty spirit and a mean right hook!

Charles decided to get up and feed him and take a shower. He wasn't going to sleep anyhow, not with his mind racing this way.

Chapter Thirty-three

Once it was closer to a normal time for most people to wake up, Charles decided that he had to call Kori and tell her everything that had happened with Mitch.

He didn't want to tell her the story on the phone, and he didn't really want to involve Nancy or Steve. They were already doing enough to help Kori. He didn't want them to know more than they needed to, at least at this point. He would call and ask her to have breakfast with him.

He had to find a new place for Kori, now that he knew how dangerous things still were. He wondered if he should persuade her to leave the state. Maybe they should take off together and find some place to hide out for a month.

As he was driving over to pick her up for their 7 a.m. breakfast visit, he wondered if he should try to contact Tianna. She was an old friend from work who had married a Cuban man and would be willing to have the two of them visit her for a little while. That would involve passports, though, and he thought his might be expired.

The hardest thing for him would be that he would have to request an unusually long leave from work or else take all his remaining vacation days that had accumulated over the past year plus. If he left without adequate time for a sub to be oriented to the tasks and responsibilities of his job, he could end up unemployed.

TouchStone would probably love an excuse to fire him or lay him off, despite his impressive seniority and excellent evaluations.

It felt like being a rat in a maze right now. He could drop dead from exhaustion before he ever figured out how to make it to the end.

Kori was waiting at the back door of the porch when he tiptoed around the side of the house. They walked in silence to the car, and it wasn't until they pulled away from the curb that Kori broke the silence.

"Where can we go to get breakfast and still have a private conversation?"

"I'm thinking we'll get take out from Dunkin' and go to the beach?" he suggested. "Or we can find a Starbucks."

"I was thinking of Hottie Coffee. They could use the business, and we could still do takeout and be near the beach. Just go across the North Causeway and cross over U.S.1. I like to do business on the West Side any time I can, and you know you should too."

Charles sighed. She was right, but it would slow them down. They would have to chat for awhile with whoever was working and with any customers who happened to be there enjoying coffee and the super delicious baked goods you could count on at Hottie Coffee. There would be mandatory conversation with anyone they crossed paths with if they went for breakfast anywhere on the West Side. Lord help them if they ran into someone who knew Kori. They'd be there all morning!

"You don't look convinced," Kori said. "Too down home for you?"

Kori loved giving Charles a hard time whenever they argued over a place for a meal or a drink. She always wanted to patronize Black-owned businesses or at least businesses that employed a meaningful percentage of people f color.

Charles would more likely choose speed and convenience over conscience, and Kori usually didn't let him get away with it. Today she was willing to give him a break. "Never mind. I can see that you're in a hurry. You choose."

They picked up coffee and breakfast to go at the Dunkin'. "Will you give me a gold star if I choose Bethune Beach?" Charles asked. "We're not that far away."

Kori had been impressed when Charles told her the history of Bethune Beach. It was an important part of the Black history in Central Florida, and, in fact, the history of race in the U.S.

Kori reminded herself to tell Alice Ott and the others about it the next time she saw them. Maybe they could go too while they were exploring the area. She wanted everyone to know the impressive history of Mary McLeod Bethune's life, including her successful efforts to secure a beach that was open to her people, Black people. This was back when Jim Crow was blantantly alive in the South.

Charles had a couple of comfortable beach chairs, and they set them up six feet apart on the nearly deserted beach. "OK," Kori said, "what's going on?"

She had noticed Charles looking in his rearview mirror almost constantly ever since they started their journey this morning.

He opened his coffee and took a sip. "Oh excellent! It's still hot!" He took a bite of his SuperCinnamon bun."Mmm mmm mmm! Perfect! But not as good as Hottie Coffee's, of course!"

Kori poked him gently. "Go ahead with your story."

"So, Mitch called me yesterday. I was freaked out and almost late for work and didn't return the call. But when I drove out of the parking garage at the end of my shift, he was waiting for me at two this morning!"

"Mitch? Am I supposed to know who that is?"

"He's the guy who was meeting with Jake and Rufe the evening Rufe got killed, remember? He's been MIA ever since that night."

"Uh oh! Now I remember."

"Jake and I both thought he probably tipped off someone when he and Rufe finished their dinner meeting, probably gave them the exact place and time. He never came back to work at Sunset after that night, so I've been convinced he was working for whoever is trying to break the spine of the lawsuit."

"And there he was waiting for you at two a.m.? Whoa! Oh Charles, how horrible! What happened?"

Charles went through the whole story as quickly as he could, ending with his conversation with Mitch at the parking lot. Finally he stopped, and tried to enjoy his coffee and pastry. Nothing tasted the same.

Kori was staring at him, her eyes wide. "Do you think you could be the next target?"

Charles shrugged. "I don't have a clue. I don't think I'm safe, but neither are you. Evidently even Mitch isn't safe. We're all obstacles to TouchStone's trying to get away with a major crime, I guess, and any one of us could wind up a victim."

He and Kori were quiet for a minute or two. Then she sighed heavily.

"Charles, I have something to tell you too. More bad news, I'm afraid. I got a threatening phone call this morning, and the person called Nancy Warren's phone to deliver the message!"

Charles felt his entire body clench, shock and anger taking over every muscle. "Tell me everything."

"It was early, early enough that it woke Nancy up. She came in to tell me right after she got the call and had talked to Steve.

"The caller was a white man, she thought. He said to give me the message that he knew where I was staying, and if I didn't get out of everyone's business, he'd track me down and take me out. And he'd take down Nancy too. It felt extra horrible, imagining Nancy hearing that.

"I told her I would find somewhere else to stay for a while. She protested, but I know it would be safer for the Warrens if I wasn't at their house. So I guess the writing's really on the wall. We both are in need of a safe house, just like Mitch."

They looked at each other sadly. "Could you hold my hand?" Kori asked. Charles reached out to squeeze her hand, and didn't let go for a good minute.

"Later this morning, when I call Jake to ask him to take Mitch's call," Charles said, after a few moments of silence, "I can try to find out from him what our protective options are. I don't know if there are safe houses or something like that where we could go into hiding, but at this point we need answers from him."

"I'm not going anywhere out of town or anything like that," Kori said, "unless I take Gram with me. I'm not leaving her at Sunset. If I'm not around to make sure she's being taken care of, and you're not there either to keep track of her, I'd go nuts worrying about her. So wherever I go, Gram comes too!"

They sat in silence for a while longer, staring at the waves and the sea birds but not really seeing anything.

Finally Kori broke the silence. "What would happen if I just go in and take Gram out of there? You know, like just make an end run around the meetings and paperwork and whatever else would slow down the process? I don't want anyone calling security or calling the cops on me," she added, "but I don't want to wait around any longer to see what's going to happen next. I'm ready to just grab her and get out."

Charles shook his head. "I don't know what would happen, under the circumstances."

As the danger mounted, whoever was working to silence them was really putting the pressure on. The whole thing made him dizzy, his heart was pounding and he was getting a massive head-ache.

"What's the usual procedure when someone wants their loved one to be discharged?" Kori wasn't letting go of this.

"Normally you'd have a meeting with someone from administration and they'd probably request some kind of written report from the doc who happens to be available, enumerating the symptoms, the things your grandmother can't do for herself, her medical prognosis…that kind of stuff. That's more to cover their asses, you know, to have it on record that, even though the doctor advised against it, you took your grandmother against medical advice. Then you'd be meeting with me or whoever's in charge on the floor at the time she's discharged. We would give you the information you'll need once you're on your own with her."

He watched Kori in silence. She was looking like she was considering a hundred variables at once.

"Kori," he said as calmly as he could, "I don't really see how you're going to be able to take care of her by yourself, especially if you're on the run. Where would you imagine going?"

He was frustrated and scared for both Kori and her grandmother. Miz Rosabelle was a sweet, agreeable lady who could do next to nothing for herself. She couldn't walk without significant assistance, and she certainly couldn't dress or toilet herself or feed herself. If she wasn't where someone could keep an eye on her, she could easily get confused, and try to get up and wander. That meant that in seconds she could crash into something, fall, and get hurt. Without a doubt Kori's grandmother would be seriously injured if she wasn't monitored pretty much 24/7. The time had passed when she could safely live anywhere without trained nursing care.

Kori shook her head. "I'm not leaving her. No way."

"We have to contact Jake. Maybe we have to back off and shut down this whole effort. Or we have to go public immediately so that the TouchStone Corporation might be more nervous about going after us. But you and I and Mitch all need safe places where we can stay for at least a little while."

Two hours later, Charles sat with Kori, Jake and Floriana in

Jake's conference room. It took awhile to tell Flo and Jake what had transpired.

When it was all on the table, Flo shook her head and sighed."You two are real heroes! I'm so sorry all this has happened to you. We surely have to do something so no one else gets hurt or killed. Jake, can we go public now? Do we have enough leverage to force TouchStone to come up with some real answers about where the missing federal money is?"

Jake grinned at her. "We can do anything we want," he said cheerfully, but then the grin faded. "The question right now is whether we have enough documentation to support what we're trying to expose? That depends, in part, on who is willing to come forward and what can be documented in their complaints. If you don't mind, I'll take you, Charles, as an example.

"You're our star witness, at this point. You're a shift supervisor, you've been working at Sunset Villages for over three years, and you have super evaluations. But in the courtroom, what can you stand up and tell us definitively about the missing overtime pay?

"You probably couldn't give more than a ballpark estimate of how much overtime has been performed in the last two or three months. Maybe you have a rough idea of how many of those overtime hours have not been paid out, but you could only base your claims on what you have access to, like how many staff during your shift were working overtime and when, and what individual employees told you about not getting the overtime in their checks. But then you'd have to match the overtime records from the payroll department with the employees' pay stubs to prove how much each of those employees is owed in unpaid overtime.

"To bring that into a court case, or even to confront the Touch-Stone administration with that data, would require each individual employee who didn't get paid for their overtime to be willing to be identified and to go on record as not having gotten that money.

"And what could you testify to pertaining to the missing PPE? You could tell us what you had requested versus what your staff actually received, but you'd have to be able to show records to prove all of it. Mitch was in charge of ordering PPE for the dementia unit at Sunset, right? Now he's gone, so what do you think has happened to those records that he would've been keeping?

"You can give me copies of all the requests you yourself may have signed, requesting PPE, but what you claim you actually received is more of your own estimate than it is hard evidence. The same holds true for salaries. We need the records as hard evidence."

Jake stopped, seeing how discouraged his listeners were looking. "We'll figure out in actual detail what we could go ahead and claim right now," he said, "But with Kori's attack and Rufe's murder still so fresh in people's minds, we're probably going to continue to have employees dropping out, no longer daring to be plaintiffs who testify in court or even in court documents.

"Long story short, we're still at the stage of making our accusations against TouchStone from the position of a relatively small number of disgruntled employees. I don't think we have a strong enough case to get back salaries paid or force the delivery of all that missing PPE equipment.

"What we do have is the potential for making a big public stink. That's worth something."

There was a very long silence. Finally Flo cleared her throat. "We could just start with the concerns that a number of employees have brought to my attention. I can put out a press release to the media and social media, and maybe even try for a press conference where I express my concerns about the growing lack of confidence I'm hearing from a variety of the nursing homes' employees. We could make this into a bigger issue in my campaign without testimony from specific employees. What do you think about that?"

Jake was silent. Charles thought maybe he was holding back, waiting to see what he or Kori might say.

"I'm still trying to think of the big picture," Kori said, "but my personal concerns are getting more urgent. I'm really scared for Gram and me, and also scared for Charles, of course."

Charles was so tired that all he wanted was for the unknown dangers to blow away like a big pollution mass, and give him a chance to breathe again. But there was some information that he was holding back on sharing with the others. What if he mentioned Daniel and the magazine and the possibility of having a local magazine do the story Daniel was hoping to do?

But, then again, what if Daniel was using him? What if he was actually somehow working for TouchStone?

"First things, first," Flo said. "What can we do about safety for Kori and Charles and the others who are still committed to the suit?"

Jake looked uncomfortable. "I was afraid this moment would come," he said, "but I hadn't expected the level of violence they're perpetrating. I'm not quite sure, honestly, what we can do. It's not like my law practice has our own Witness Protection program. There's nothing we can tell the police that we haven't already told them after Kori's attack and Rufe's murder, no way to connect TouchStone to either crime, so far. My best and only suggestion is to advise you two to get out of town for a few weeks or even a month or two."

"I'm thinking of something," Kori said, "even though it's kind of out there. Nancy Warren is friends with this older lady, Alice Ott, an activist from New England, and now she and a couple of friends are actually down here. Nancy's always saying how inspired Alice Ott is when it comes to thinking outside the box. Maybe we should see if they could come up with something?"

Flo and Charles were open to the idea of fresh minds. Alice Ott was about all they had, at this point. Flo had heard Nancy claim that Alice was a force of nature, a person who was not only fearless but very creative when it came to strategies for bringing down corrupt systems.

Charles wasn't ready to lay out the vague possibility that Daniel's magazine story could save them.

Jake looked as if he had some serious doubts, but he wasn't going to argue with them. "Ok, go for it!" he said. "Just don't tell me anything you're planning that would entail breaking the law. Someone needs to get back to me about what y'all end up deciding. I'll give you the phone number for the burner phone I've got on me for the next few days. And, BTW, I'd recommend for you two, Charles and Kori, to get burner phones too, as in immediately and for God's sake, find a safe place to stay!"

Chapter Thirty-four

It was mid-morning when Alice heard someone knocking on their front door.

Gerard was buried in his research at the back of the house. The owners had set up a computer desk and nicely upholstered desk chair in the corner of the bedroom. Gerard was very happy with the whole arrangement. He had an excellent work station, the privacy of being able to retreat to the quiet bedroom, and a large window that gave him a wonderful glimpse of colorful Florida birds visiting the little bird feeders behind the house.

Alice wasn't sure where Felicia had gone. There were no sounds in the house that would give her a clue as to her whereabouts. Maybe she had walked down to the community dock, where, no doubt, she had found people to chat with even behind her double mask. Alice was very sure that Felicia would maintain the correct six foot distance.

When she opened the door, she saw the slender young Black woman, Kori, who was living with the Warrens. Behind her was a very handsome Black man, and a Black woman who could be any age. She was wearing a multi-colored resplendent shirt, and she was beaming at Alice. "I'm Floriana," she said, stepping around Kori and holding out her hand for a shake. 'You must be Alice Ott. We finally meet!"

Because she and the other two were masked, Alice thought they might understand if she was reluctant to shake hands. "We're still under quarantine here," she told Floriana apologetically.

"Mrs. Ott, I understand why you can't invite us inside, but we need privacy. Is there somewhere behind the house where we could sit?" Kori asked, after an uncomfortable pause.

"Oh my, well, if you don't mind that it's not very spacious back there, then follow me to the back yard," Alice said. "I just need to get my cane and my oxygen, if you can wait a few seconds." She moved more quickly than she thought she could, grabbing her cane, her portable, and a mask, all in record time. "Follow me!"

she said cheerfully as she led the little procession alongside the house and to the tiny backyard.

She realized once she got back behind the house that she needed chairs for everyone. There were beach chairs in the garage that she remembered Nancy showing her when they first moved themselves into the little duplex. There was no other way to manage this but to ask for her guests' help, so she apologetically sent Charles and Kori to get the chairs.

"Where are your other friends?" Flo asked when Alice returned to the backyard. "I heard that three of you came down to stay, and that a young friend drove you down in that big van parked out front? Are you all living in this little house?"

"We're figuring it out as we go," Alice said. "Gerard and I share the back bedroom, and Felicia's in the other bedroom, and Warp – the friend who drove us down here – is sleeping on the back porch. We offered him the long couch in the living room, but he says he loves the porch because it reminds him of going camping. He's from Vermont, so he doesn't mind even though it gets cold at night out there."

"Wonder how long y'all are going to last down here." Flo said, studying Alice thoughtfully. "Maybe Nancy and I need to find a bigger place if we're going to hang onto you. How long are you fixing to stay?"

"We really don't know," Alice said. "Warp will leave very soon, maybe as soon as tomorrow, and head on back North. His girl-friend wants him home, and I think he needs a break from us old folks! We three have been a pod at Felicia's house since early spring, because of COVID, so at least we've learned to live to-gether. I'm the one who talked the others into coming down here, and I don't know how long Felicia and Gerard will want to stay."

Charles and Kori reappeared with two small beach chairs and two taller ones. They were giggling. Kori told them that Charles insisted that the short ones were children's chairs and she had to badger him into bringing them around to the back.

"I can sit on one of them," she said, "but I'm not so sure Charles can get down low enough to be in the other or if he could even fit in it. And we certainly don't expect either of you ladies to take the small chair, so is there a chair inside the house that could come outside?"

"Sorry we're so demanding as your uninvited guests," Charles said, smiling so warmly that Alice was instantly charmed.

"It's a pleasure to have company," she said, surprising herself with her burst of enthusiasm. "I'm just sorry I don't have an easier solution for where we're going to sit. Also, I must confess I don't have much to offer for refreshments. I'm happy to get you hot tea or iced water, but that's about all I can serve you this morning." She was not about to start all the complicated business with the coffee pot.

After all three of her guests declined a beverage, she went back into the house to look for another chair. "Gerard," she said, poking her head into the bedroom where he was ensconced with the computer, "would you please join me in entertaining our morning guests? Nancy Warren has sent them to us, I believe."

Where on earth was Felicia?

Finally the three visitors, Alice, and Gerard had all managed to settle themselves in a lopsided semi circle at the back of the house. The need for social distancing made the arrangement challenging, but everyone had agreed that they needed to be as safe as possible. Even visiting on the screen porch seemed too risky, considering the recent car trip Alice and the others had just completed.

Flo took the lead. "We're in a kind of desperate situation," she began. "The dangers surrounding the lawsuit seem to be escalating, and we need some help thinking about our next move. Charles can summarize."

Just as Charles was wrapping up his experience with Mitch, a voice called out from inside the house."Yoo-hoo! Where is everybody? Do we have visitors?"

It was a relief to Alice that Felicia had returned from wherever she had gone.

"We're out behind the house!" Alice called, "and yes, we do have visitors! Come join us, and bring your own chair!"

By the time they had all scooted around to make room for Felicia and the rather bulky chair she dragged off the back porch, Alice was feeling overwhelmed. Felicia was sitting almost in the next door neighbor's yard at her end of the loop, Charles' head was barely an inch below the low branches of the magnolia tree, and Kori was wedged in tight with bushes on either side and a bird feeder hanging just slightly above her right shoulder.

Alice was grateful that there was almost no wind, a rare occurrence in the four days they had been living in Florida. At least nothing was likely to blow down and hit one of them. She was also relieved that her next door neighbor was at work. Indoors, they were only separated by the wall between their two sides of the little stucco duplex, and their yards were more like one continuous stretch of grass, with the bushes forming a boundary only between their yards and the mobile home community on the other side.

"We're here because we need help," Kori said, and briskly summarized for Felicia what Flo and Charles had already said. Her voice was soft, and with the mask and the slight speech impairment that remained from her assault, it was very hard for Alice to hear her. She could clearly discern the word 'help.' She waited for the conversation to become more audible.

Suddenly everyone seemed to be looking at her, waiting for some response that clearly she was not understanding.

"We wish we didn't have to come with this urgent agenda," Flo said. Alice was relieved that she could hear Flo's voice easily. "We know you've just barely settled in and all. But you can blame it on Nancy! She says you're the best, and if anyone can help us figure out what to do, you're the one."

At the moment, Alice felt she was anything but the brilliant strategist Nancy Warren loved to boast about. But they were looking at her so hopefully that she instructed herself to lead with questions. Surely if she explored their answers to her questions, she could come up with something they might not have considered yet.

"Could you tell me again where you think you are right now, at this juncture of the fight – or let's call it the battle, for want of a better word?" Alice asked.

Flo nodded. "It's come down to whether or not we go to the press right now with what we suspect, and put public pressure on Touch-Stone to explain what's happened to all that federal money? The problem is that we don't have enough employees left in our dwindling pool of plaintiffs who could come up with hard evidence. TouchStone's intimidation techniques have been too successful.

"We had hoped to get more proof. We were hoping to find someone who has access to proof that TouchStone received the grant.

Harder still, we need proof that someone – at the top administration level, a CEO or two – suddenly got big bonuses or some unusual payment for something that isn't usually in the budget. Of course, we were still working on recruiting employees from the nursing homes to build up the number of staff who didn't get paid for their overtime and didn't get the PPE they were promised. But since Kori got beat up, and Rufe got killed, and Mitch says they've threatened to kill him, we're thinking we might have to give up getting that kind of employee testimony. Maybe all we can do now is put on a press conference from my campaign where we could launch the accusations."

"I would call out the corporation for stealing the money," Flo continued. "But we had expected to have something solid to back up our accusations. I don't know whose left who would still be willing to testify."

"What does your lawyer advise?" Alice was puzzled about the role of this lawyer. Was he part of a big firm? Was he doing this lawsuit on his own or did he have extra money and power backing him up?

"Jake kind of wishes we could tough it out, keep trying to get some evidence," Charles said. "But he's worried about Kori, and me too, I guess. He recommended that both of us get out of town for a few weeks, let things cool down." He glanced at Flo. Jake hadn't said anything about her being in danger. She certainly couldn't just leave town, not with her kids, and her political campaign in full swing.

"But I can't leave my job," he continued, "without giving adequate prep time for someone to take over. And it's not easy for Kori either," he added. "She doesn't want to leave her grandmother in there without someone to keep an eye out for her well-being."

Kori was very quiet.

"You're surely at that awful juncture between a rock and a hard place, as they say," Alice commented. She looked at Felicia and Gerard. Maybe it was time to share their still forming ideas. "Should we fill them in on our fantasy of infiltrating?"

Gerard shrugged. His part was so unpleasant that he seemed to prefer not to discuss the details lest he make it real.

"I've been working on my own plan," Felicia said, and began

glowing with the enthusiasm generated by her own creations. "I could pose as a journalist doing a big story about nursing homes in the time of COVID. I'm a former journalist, and I know how to pitch this to the PR department at TouchStone. I could bring in Alice and Gerard as the vulnerable old couple considering where Gerard might go now that Alice can no longer care for him at home. It would be a human interest story with these two at the brink of making the decision. All we need, really, are some sort of credentials for me, proof of my affiliation with a newspaper or magazine."

Charles stared at her. How could Felicia and Daniel, two human beings who had never met each other, both come up with the same idea at approximately the same time! Could this possibly be a coincidence? Why was he the link between them? He cleared his throat several times, wanting to share Daniel's potentially valuable piece of the puzzle. Yet something made him hold back.

There were no other plans on the table, Alice thought. Maybe Felicia's plan could work somehow. Their unexpected visitors seemed to be at a breaking point, and she would love to have something to offer them.

Still, she wasn't quite ready to jump on this particular bandwagon, much as she admired Felicia's creativity and boldness. Felicia's approach would take too much time to put into motion. She and Felicia could try to create the missing credentials to get Felicia in the door, but even if they could somehow pull off the interview and get access to records, it would take awhile to find the evidence. Even if Felicia was welcomed in to do a glitzy PR piece on Touch-Stone, it would be a small miracle to get copies of all these records and transactions.

It was, without a doubt, a long shot.

What they really needed was to get more people involved in an organized movement to expose the TouchStone Corporation. They needed more workers to come forward and speak out about the missing grant money, and the failure to produce PPE and overtime pay. Only disgruntled employees willing to lose their jobs, and maybe worse, would have the inside information that could prove the corporation's diversion of the grant money.

How could they find the particular employees who had access to the kinds of financial records they needed, to become whistle-blowers?

Flo's press conference could at least produce more people to ignite the protests against TouchStone. Employees and families with loved ones in the nursing homes would be the most obvious groups to mobilize. But even people with no connection to TouchStone, but who had a conscience, could be moved and mobilized.

The trouble was, by tipping their hand and going public at this juncture, the corporation would find out that there were people attempting to investigate and expose the missing money. All incriminating evidence would no doubt disappear very quickly once that intention was manifest.

She looked at Charles, who seemed to be on the brink of speaking. But there was something holding him back.

"Charles, I'm thinking that we need more people to get involved. Like people who care about how elders are being impacted by COVID. Would it feel safer to you if we try to get our collective foot in the door without you having to be involved? No one down here knows we have any connection to you or to Kori. In fact, no one here, except for Nancy and Steve Warren, have a clue we're here for any other purpose than finding a nice place for my poor Gerard to live out the remainder of his life."

A ringing phone distracted them all. Charles pulled his phone out of his pocket and stared at the caller ID

"I'd better go out to the car to take this. It's important."

"Good morning!" Daniel said, sounding well-rested and cheerful. Charles felt very confused by his rapid shift of emotions. Delight was bouncing around in his head, along with fear and some amount of mistrust.

"How are you this morning?" Daniel asked.

"Oh I'm OK, I guess. Happy to hear from you, that's for sure."

"Are you up for a repeat of yesterday?" Daniel asked. "We could take a ride on old Florida country roads, and maybe have lunch on the beach on the way back. I'm guessing you have to be at work around four?"

"That sounds so good," Charles said, longing for his life to go back to simple and manageable. He wished all he had to worry about was whether or not Daniel was someone he wanted to keep seeing.

"I sense there's a 'but' and a 'not today'," Daniel said. "Would you be up for the same invitation tomorrow maybe? Or sometime soon?"

Charles stood in the driveway of this little house, and wondered what to do. He could disappear for a few hours and forget about all of the mess they were facing. Or he could take a chance on Daniel and tell him what was going on, and see if he'd like to talk with Felicia about being the reporter for the magazine feature he wanted to do.

A flock of white ibises were grazing on the lawn next door, and as he looked up into the live oak tree on the next door neighbor's house, he saw a huge owl landing with something that might be alive in its beak. The owl stared down at him, then disappeared from sight into a tangle of roots and hanging moss.

He heard a series of hoots, and walked down the driveway and out onto the small road that circled its way through the neighborhood. He peered up into the tree to see if he could spot the owl. To his great amazement, there were two of them, and one was feeding some of its catch of the day to the other.

"We think these two might be fixing to start a family," a man's voice spoke from just behind him. Charles spun around to see who had managed to get so close to him without him hearing a thing.

He was face to face with a man with long hair who looked to be an aging hippy. He was smiling warmly at Charles, and then he pointed up at the owls. Charles realized he was wearing a t-shirt that said RESIST in large black letters, with the much smaller letters t-r-u-m-p winding through the bold resist message.

"I've never seen such a big owl," Charles said. "And there are two of them! What did you say about a baby?"

"They're great horned owls. That's the dad and that's mama. She's the bigger one with the food in her mouth. We'll be waiting all winter for the babies to come, then watching them get born and grow up!"

Charles suddenly remembered that Daniel was on the line. He smiled at the friendly neighbor. "Gotta finish a call, but thanks," he said politely, and walked back to the house. "Hey," he said, "Sorry!

I'm at a meeting at someone's house and a neighbor just showed me two giant owls and a nest that he says will have baby owls later in the winter!"

"So is it yes or no for today?" Daniel asked, sounding pretty mellow for someone who'd been waiting for an answer for at least a full minute.

"Yes!" Charles said. "Yes!"

Chapter Thirty-five

Charles went back to the group behind the house. "Kori, could I talk with you for a minute?"

She nodded and walked back to the front of the house with him. "Would you be willing to stay here and ask Warp if he could give you a ride back to the Warren's if you think you could stay there one more night?" he asked. "Or maybe Flo could find a place for you to stay, just for tonight? Tomorrow we'll figure something out but I need to go to work and I need to talk to Daniel first."

She looked at him, a mixture of hurt and understanding in her eyes. "Go ahead. I'll figure out something."

He left to meet Daniel, and fifteen minutes later, Flo rushed off to pick up her youngest child from his half-day program at pre-school.

Alice, Felicia and Kori were left sitting behind the house, quietly engaged in problem-solving after Gerard too left the group to go inside for a stint at his computer.

Alice wondered if Warp could take Kori and her grandmother with him tomorrow on his trip home. There had to be somewhere between Florida and Western Massachusetts where Kori and Ms. Rosabelle could find sanctuary. All they needed, Alice believed, was a few weeks or at the most, maybe a month.

"Do you have any family or friends out of town who would have you and your grandmother stay with them for a few weeks?" Alice asked Kori.

Kori was silent for a while, her head bowed. Then she looked up at Alice, her eyes brimming with tears. "I don't really think so." Her voice was so soft that Alice could barely understand her, but she didn't want to make her feel worse by demanding that she speak up. "I have friends back in Ohio, but there's no one I can think of who has extra space. If it was just me, it would be different. But with Gram's medical needs, I don't think there's anyone who could reasonably accommodate the two of us."

Felicia reached over and patted Kori's knee. "We'll figure out something. So much has been happening that you must feel over-whelmed. I was wondering if you would accept some herbal sup-plements from me, free of charge, of course. You need to boost your chi, which, roughly translated, means boosting your core energies. Your aura is very pale, if you don't mind me saying so."

Kori looked at her in astonishment, then began to laugh. It was a real belly laugh, and it made Alice smile. Just hearing that laugh made her confident that Kori still had some deep energy flowing through her body, even if her aura didn't reflect it.

"That's really funny!" Kori said, wiping tears of laughter away. "I never had anyone describe anything about me as pale! My momma used to tell me she didn't know how she got such a dark little baby! Then she'd laugh and say it was a good thing I looked just like my daddy or she would've had some explaining to do! My momma and my daddy were lighter skinned, and so was most ev-eryone else in both families."

"Oh dear," Felicia said, "I hope I didn't offend you! It's just that auras change color all the time, and your aura looks so pale I was worried. Alice can tell you that I offer everyone advice, solicited or not."

"I am not offended," Kori said. "I know I am really tired, healing from the assault, and worrying so much. I know I'm stressed. Thanks for the offer of the supplements, but I take a multi-vitamin daily, and Vitamin B, E, and D, and Juice Plus capsules."

Felicia looked as if she was about to launch into a major lecture on nutrition, and then, Alice feared, the practice of tapping would come next. Or she would offer to cleanse Kori's chakras or auras or something else that Alice was in no mood to witness.

With no warning, a female voice greeted them from somewhere in the bushes nearby. Sue, their new neighbor, suddenly appeared with her camera. "I hope I'm not intruding," she said, "but Betty next door just told me she'd seen two painted buntings back here. I was just hoping to get some quick pics of them. Have you seen them this morning?"

The three women looked at her, stunned into silence. Alice fi-nally answered. "No, I don't think we have, although I would love to see such a special bird before my life is over." She smiled sweetly, hoping that Sue hadn't been lingering in the bushes, over-hearing their conversation.

It never crossed her mind before now that someone from Touch-Stone might already be keeping the New Englanders under surveillance. However, she was quite sure that, based on what she had observed over the past four days, Sue had been living in the neighborhood for a long time, and she was very unlikely to be a spy for TouchStone.

Felicia looked thoughtful, and Alice was curious about whatever she might be thinking. She raised her eyebrows very slightly, and Felicia caught her quick flicker of curiosity. "I was wondering if you'd happen to know if anyone in the neighborhood has a rental property that's vacant?" she asked Sue.

"Oh, as a matter of fact, I do! There's an Airbnb just a few houses down, Sally's Nest. I was chatting with David, the owner, just this morning, and it's not booked again for three weeks. It's been completely renovated since David's mother Sally died. Everything's very new, and very comfortable, and you can't find a better neighborhood!"

She winked as she delivered the last part of the sentence, and Alice chuckled politely.

"Sounds interesting! Kori, would you like to see it?"

Kori seemed to be caught between relief and dread. "OK. Can I get David's number from you? I'm looking for something temporary for myself and my grandmother. Does David have any minimum number of days required for rental?"

"I doubt it," Sue said. "I can give you his number, but I know he's gone back over to Sanford. I have the code so I can show it to you if you like."

"Let's all go and look," Felicia said. "After quarantine I might want to stay over there with you and help with your grandma for a little while, if there's room for me."

They trooped back to the front of the house and crossed the next door neighbor's yard to look at Sally's Nest. Thirty minutes later, Kori called David, and soon she had secured the place, starting immediately.

"I hate to disappoint you, but I was thinking that maybe Charles should stay with Gram and me," Kori told Felicia. "She'll need nursing care, and he's a nurse, and as you know, he also needs a safe place to stay."

"Not a problem," Felicia said, "I really was just curious, and I also wanted to, well, run interference in case you ran into any trouble securing the reservation. Do you know what I mean?"

Kori looked at her for a minute. "Do you mean because I'm a Black woman?" she asked.

Felicia nodded. "I didn't know what to expect," she said, "but I thought we're in the South, and maybe the owner would rent to me if he wouldn't rent to you. Something like that. Did I make a mistake?"

"No," Kori said, "I'm afraid you were being realistic. There's still plenty of racial discrimination down here. Probably it's in every state in the country, honestly. You were just trying to be helpful. If I get some weird call back that David has changed our agreement or is canceling it, we'll put you on the case immediately and see if you have better luck. Thanks for trying to help!"

Alice had suspected Felicia's offer to share the place with Kori was her friend's semi-conscious wish to get away from Gerard and her for a while. She herself wouldn't mind a little break, a few weeks alone in her own space would feel like a vacation. "Someday," she told herself silently, "I will be back in my own home."

She went back in the house, poured herself a half cup of coffee and tried to decide how best to communicate Kori's safety to Nancy Warren.

Daniel saw Charles waiting for him at the beach and holding a large paper bag that looked like take-out from one of the nearby restaurants. He waved vigorously.

"I have so much to tell you," Charles explained. "I didn't want to lose time ordering and waiting where we couldn't talk. I got a bunch of food so you could choose what you like. And I've got some fancy bottle of sparkling water in my pack that should still be pretty cold."

Daniel smiled the whole time they were walking down to the beach. He gazed at the chairs and a small folding table Charles had already set up on the beach down near the water where it was cooler and the tide was going out. There was even an umbrella in case they got too hot. "How did I get so lucky? You really know how to make a boy feel special!"

"Wait until you hear the surprise I've got for you," Charles said, winking. He carefully arranged containers on the little table between them: pan seared scallops, sweet potato fries, broccoli salad, hot rolls, and cups for the sparkling water. He poured them each a cup of water, and then opened his pack to extricate beautifully decorated little paper plates, bamboo reusable forks and colorful cloth napkins. "Bon appétit!" he said. "And here's to the next edition of *Splash!*"

"You're good! And so optimistic! I like a man who's optimistic."

Before he took a single bite of food, Charles began telling Daniel the story of the lawsuit, including the acts of violence. He was able to summarize and quickly get to the serendipitous moment earlier in the day when he first heard Felicia's idea of infiltrating TouchStone under the guise of writing an upbeat human interest story.

"She began talking about Alice and Gerard who would pose as a couple who came to Florida to look for the best options for nursing care. Then she said that she had figured out a magazine feature to get their foot in the door! Felicia is actually a retired journalist, but she didn't have a bonafide publication committed to doing the story as the feature for the coming month's issue! Totally amazing, right?!"

Charles was so excited about relaying this whole happenstance that he was running out of air.

Daniel took another scallop from the box and popped it into his mouth before he answered. "Are you suggesting that the plan for this next issue of *Splash!* has materialized?"

"It's up to you!" Charles said. "Now you have a retired journalist who can do the interviewing, and Daniel, I'm telling you, she could convince anyone that she's the real deal! I know this is sudden, but now may be the time to take a big leap into complete uncertainty and make this happen, don't you think?"

"Run the infiltration part by me again in a little more detail, please," Daniel said. "I didn't quite get the whole picture."

"OK. There's danger involved, but I figured with your history of being a Marine, you could handle it, right?"

Daniel narrowed his eyes, scrutinizing Charles carefully. "Tell me the whole story, and don't skip anything that's important. I like my comfortable life, and if I'm going to risk bodily harm or being charged with trespassing or misleading the top dogs at this big corporation, I want to know the whole game plan."

Charles used every minute he had before he had to go to work, telling Daniel the whole story of TouchStone, and Kori's grandmother, and the grant and the missing overtime money and PPE.

"And now I have to run, but I'll call you on my break to see what questions you might have. That would be around nine o'clock tonight. Will that work?"

He blew Daniel a kiss as he pulled out of the parking lot. Even though he was still compulsively checking his rearview mirror, he was feeling lighter than he had for a long time. He had a good feeling about this.

Chapter Thirty-six

Charles' phone buzzed as he pulled into the parking garage. It was Kori. He wouldn't get decent reception until he got inside the building so he let her leave a message. When he was safely on the unit, finished with his check-ins, and could finally close the door to his office, he checked his phone. "Got housing lined up," she wrote. "Details to be delivered in person."

He wished they had already gotten the burner phones that Jake had suggested. Kori's vague message reminded him that neither of their phones were secure. He hoped if she was coming here to talk, that she would be able to get past the reception person in the lobby. There was now tighter security since Kori's last visit, due to COVID. If he could get her upstairs for a meeting in his office, maybe he could even sneak her in to see Miz Rosabelle.

His office phone buzzed. "This is James from Security, Mr. Dubois. Got a young lady down here in the lobby wanting to speak to you about a patient. Told her she had to make an appointment, but she says you two already talked and she's expecting to meet with you. You coming down?"

"Sure," Charles said. "I'll be right there. Thanks, James."

As he walked down the hall, he spotted one of his favorite nursing aides. "Hey, Miss Sianna!" he greeted her, "How's my Number One Best Nurse in the Universe?"

She laughed and swatted at him as he passed by her. "What terrible horrible assignment are you about to give me?" she asked. "You know I did the Duke of Earle's bedpan five times yesterday and got called every name in the book for my trouble! What is it you going to ask me to do today?"

Charles smiled at her, suddenly struck with a new idea for how he could get Kori in to see her grandmother. He lowered his voice. "Miz Kori's trying to get upstairs to see Miz Rosabelle right now," he told her, hoping she could still understand his whispery voice through his mask. "I sure would love it if you have an extra set of scrubs in your locker you could let her borrow. You're about her size, and if she was wearing scrubs I might be able to get her past Nurse She-Who-Must-Be-Obeyed."

Sianna looked at him, her gaze steady as she contemplated his request. "Sure, I guess so. How soon you going to get those scrubs back to me, though? I keep the one extra set here, like I'm supposed to for emergencies, but I only got one other clean set at home and I'm on again tomorrow."

"Tomorrow night at the beginning of the shift. I promise!" Charles told her, hoping he'd still be alive and free tomorrow. "And If I don't deliver," he added, "you get a free meal at Uncle Chicken's whenever you want it, and a gift coupon from Beall's to cover two new sets of scrubs."

"You're on! You want to find me when you're ready or you want me to bring them to your office in a few minutes?"

"Bring them to my office in a bag or something, maybe fifteen minutes or so, ok? Thanks, Sianna!"

Charles thought quickly as he rode down to the lobby in the elevator. He thought he remembered James, the employee who had called him from Security.

Kori was looking very nervous as she sat in one of the empty leather club chairs in the large reception area. The security guard was on his cell, paying no attention to Kori although he nodded in her direction when Charles stepped out of the elevator. Charles walked quickly over to her, and greeted her warmly.

"Good to see you, Miz Harris!" he said, radiating enthusiasm. "Come right on upstairs with me. Miz Rosabelle will be so glad to see you on this special birthday!"

Although Kori looked surprised, she scurried right along behind him as they crossed the lobby to the elevator. "Getting to see you on her birthday will be the best gift in the world!" Charles said loudly, hoping that the elevator would come soon and that James would remain engrossed in his phone call.

His wishes were granted.

As they rode up to the tenth floor, Charles explained to Kori how he was planning to get her past an officious nurse who would try to stop any visitor from getting near the patients. This nurse had been known to even block visits from behind the glass window of the day room.

"One of the aides is lending me a clean set of scrubs for you. She's about your size. After you get changed, I'll walk you over to the window where you can see your grandmother close up and she can see you. I'll bring my phone into the room and turn it on for her so you can talk with her using your phone. She'll be able to see you and hear your voice.

"If Nurse Dragon Fire gets to you before I do, just explain that I invited you to come here in person because we've been so worried about your grandmother. Tell her you've heard from staff about Gram's lack of interest in food or socializing since your visiting stopped. The reason I suggested the scrubs, BTW, was hoping no one would pay much attention to you. But don't worry. I'll come right away if I see her approach you, and I'll handle her."

"Do you think Gram will recognize me?" Kori asked

"Of course she will!" Charles told her, hoping he was right. "While we're waiting for Sianna's delivery, could you tell me what your phone message was all about?"

"Good news!" Kori said, "I have rented a little duplex two doors down from where Alice Ott and her friends are staying. There's plenty of room for you to stay there with Gram and me. There's a big bedroom with a queen size bed for you, and another bedroom with twin beds for Gram and me. It's got a living room and a very fancy kitchen, and a beautiful big Florida room out back so we can meet with whoever we want to, and have fresh air, and complete privacy.

"I think it will take awhile before anyone could possibly figure out where we are! I found out about the rental when one of the neighbors dropped by after you left. I was able to contact the landlord right away and give him a deposit for three weeks, starting today!"

"You're unbelievable!" Charles said. He could hardly imagine leaving his own place, but he could no longer trust that he was safe. Then he remembered his cat. "Umm, there's one big question," he said. "Can I bring Jeremiah?"

"Oh oops!" Kori said. "You know, I didn't think about that. I can ask though. But aside from the cat question, what do you think?"

"I think I'm lucky to have a friend like you. We need to have a big conversation about your plan to bring your Gram to live there with us. Let's think about what bare minimum stuff she would need to be able to live outside of a nursing facility. Have you thought about how you're going to get her set up so she's comfortable and safe?"

"I'll go shopping after I leave here," Kori said calmly. "And I'll get us both burner phones while I'm shopping for medical supplies for Gram. And in case you are worried, I've checked and the house is completely wheelchair accessible. The landlord's mother used to live there and after she died, they renovated it to use as an Airbnb."

Sianna knocked on Charles' door and came in with the set of scrubs. "Oh hi!" she said. "It's so good to see you! Miz Rosabelle's been missing you so much! Hope the scrubs fit!"

"Great to see you too!" Kori told her. "And you're an angel to let me borrow these. I'll wash them and get them back to you right away."

Charles left her in his office and went to set up Gram in the day room where Kori could have the best visual access during their phone visit. She slipped into the borrowed scrubs, relieved that they were only slightly too big for her.

In less than a minute, she was at the window, beaming at Gram as she watched Charles hold his phone next to Gram's ear. Kori dialed his number. "Hi Gram! It's Kori! I'm standing right over here so you can see me while we talk. Can you see me?"

Kori waved wildly at Gram until she caught her attention. When Gram spotted Kori, her face lit up in the biggest smile Kori had seen for a very long time. "My baby!" the old woman whispered, her voice faint from lack of use.

Kori's eyes filled with tears. She blew a kiss to Gram, trying to keep from crying. "I'm so happy to see you, Gram! I've missed you! I couldn't come in to visit you because they weren't allowing visitors, but we're going to fix it so I can take you home to live with me now!" She made herself stop talking, knowing that her grandmother's brain could only process a little bit at a time.

"Home!" Gram said softly. "Home, go home."

Charles was so flooded with tears he had to turn away to wipe his eyes. Suddenly he realized that the dragon nurse was heading his way. "What are you doing?" she said, her loud voice causing several people in the day room to turn and stare at her. Many of the residents looked fearful.

"Fire! Fire!" called out one elderly man, and began to rock anxiously in his wheelchair.

Charles moved the phone back from Gram's ear so he could speak briefly to Kori. "Don't worry!" he said. "Just keep talking to Gram and I'll handle this." He moved the phone back into the old woman's hand in time to hear Kori begin to sing to her.

"Miz Greene," he said, taking her elbow gently to move her away from her target, "I'm going to need you to take over the floor for the next half hour. I have a personal problem I must attend to, and you're the only person I can trust at the moment to take over for me. I am so grateful that you're here!"

Flattery worked its magic, and the nurse followed Charles to his office to look over the shift assignments with him. He thanked her profusely and promised to return to his duties in less than thirty minutes.

By the time Kori left, Charles had been able to notify the essential staff involved in discharge planning that Kori was taking Miz Rosabelle home. It was a permanent move, he told them. Kori was removing her grandmother from their facility because she was moving away and taking her grandmother with her.

Afterward, Kori went on a shopping expedition with Warp. They set up the rental so that Gram could move into the little house. Warp would provide the necessary transportation for the move before he went on his way home to New England.

It was much easier getting the wheels in motion for Kori and her grandmother than it was to set up a meeting for Daniel to meet Felicia, Alice, and Gerard. They had to discuss the plan for infiltrating the offices at the TouchStone building. Charles didn't want to call the New Englanders or Daniel too late at night. He left everyone text messages and hoped they would set up a meeting without him.

Even though Kori tried to persuade Charles to come over to the little house in Pelican Cove that night, he felt that he needed to be in his own place for one more night. He did not yet have a plan for Jeremiah, and he needed a night of rest in order to keep everything going smoothly for Kori and her grandmother the next day.

He pulled into the Blue Heron Estates around two-thirty, grateful for once that he worked the night shift and didn't have to be social with his neighbors after a long day of work. Everything looked tranquil, until he was about to turn into his driveway.

There was a flash of light from somewhere along the line of palms growing next to the house, and then another flash from further toward the back of the house. Someone with a flashlight was creeping around his home.

He drove past the house and down the next street, trying to think what to do. He could call the police and report someone was trying to break into his house. But he didn't have very much to go on. He hated the thought of getting the local cops pissed off if they had to come out to check out his house and found nobody there when they arrived. How could he explain that he had good reason to be suspicious of those few flashes of light?

Maybe he should park on the next street and see if he could creep up, and by coming through the neighbor's backyard, take the person by surprise. It was risky. He was a strong relatively young Black man in a middle class, predominantly white neighborhood. He could end up getting shot, or assaulted, or arrested by the police if he got caught sneaking through backyards in his neighborhood.

He could wake up Daniel, and ask if he could spend the night there. He hated that idea! It would give the wrong impression, make Daniel think Charles was coming on too fast and too much. And it could throw off the new plan to get Felicia and Daniel together to do the magazine infiltration.

Maybe he would just go back to his house, use the loud noise of the garage opener as a warning to whoever was creeping around his house, and go on in. Was there any way he could pretend to be armed? He didn't think so, although he did have a nice long very heavy flashlight in the car that he could use to crack over somebody's head if he had to.

Maybe it was Mitch again, wandering around, trying to find a way in so he could sleep in Charles' house. He decided he liked that explanation the best. It made sense and it gave him the courage to head into the house and take on the intruder.

He tried to remember if he had any kind of aerosol spray in the car that he could spray in the intruder's eyes. Maybe that ammonia-based windshield cleaning spray would work.

He headed up the street, coming from the other end of the block this time, and parked a few doors away from home. He saw no more moving lights. He got out of the car and walked quickly toward his house, the spray can hidden under the jacket he had tossed over his arm. He clicked the button on his key chain that unlocked his front door, and power-walked the last minute from the sidewalk into the house.

Jeremiah came out of the dark to rub a greeting against his leg. Charles stood very still, trying to hear any unusual sounds but any small noises were muffled by Jeremiah's loud purr.

He waited for what felt like more than a full minute, then moved toward the kitchen as quietly as he could.

Stopping again to listen for any sounds, he realized that if someone had gotten into the house, he would be at an extreme disadvantage. He was not armed, and if he turned on a light, the intruder would see him much sooner than Charles could see the intruder.

He tried to think if Jeremiah would be acting so relaxed and happy to greet him if someone was in the house. You never knew with cats. They could greet you silently, or purr, or hide, and you wouldn't know what it meant. Why hadn't he gotten a dog? It was like the gun question. He just wasn't a gun-toting kind of guy, and he wasn't into dogs.

Maybe he could silently maneuver himself into a space where he could simultaneously turn on the light and hide behind something. He tried to picture himself reaching for the floor lamp next to his big recliner and diving behind the chair as he switched it on. The intruder could be behind him somewhere, though, or even looking in through the living room window, gun drawn and ready to shoot.

He could think of no good plan. Another minute or two passed, and he still didn't hear any sounds. Maybe he should just trust that all was well, and proceed with his routine.

"Ready for your supper?" he asked Jeremiah, sounding more jovial than he had ever sounded. He still couldn't bring himself to turn on the light.

Jeremiah squealed happily, and Charles could hear him galloping into the kitchen.

Banging into the door jamb, Charles made his way into the

kitchen, and over to the cat's food bowl. Now Jeremiah was singing a feline version of the Hallelujah chorus in anticipation of his meal. Just as Charles bent to pick up the cat's bowl, he heard a slight rustling from the direction of the pantry.

He knew this was serious.

He couldn't let Jeremiah just trot trustingly into the pantry in celebration of the cat food that Charles was about to give him. With a loud shout of aggression he had learned in a mandatory self-defense training, Charles hit the light switch and aimed his window cleaning spray in the direction of the pantry. "Come out with your hands up," he ordered, "or I'll shoot!"

To his complete surprise, out from the pantry emerged the older lady from New England who wasn't Alice Ott. It was Felicia. "Don't squirt me with that cleanser, please," she said calmly. "It isn't a cleaning product that anyone should use, anyhow. Bad for the lungs and nasal passages."

Charles was wordless. How had this lady gotten into his house and what on earth did she want? He felt weak with relief, but that left room for some healthy indignation.

"I assume you're going to tell me what you were up to," he said. "And of course I'm not going to spray this at you. It's not what I use for any cleaning I do in the house, if you want to know. It's just for my windshield."

"Thank you," Felicia said, with a dazzling smile. "I'm sorry if I scared you. It's just that I thought you would be staying over at the little Airbnb with Kori tonight, so I didn't expect you to be home."

"But what are you doing in my house at two-thirty in the morning?" Charles asked.

"I needed to check you out," Felicia said matter-of-factly. "We're about to partner with you and your friend Daniel in some serious espionage, and I wanted to discern if you were really a good guy or if you were setting us up. Surely you can understand my mistrust." She looked thoughtfully at Charles. "You don't seem like a man who would be especially comfortable with the kind of infiltration we're planning. I needed to see if there was anything in your house that would tip me off if you were secretly working for the corporation against the lawsuit, I thought it was possible that you had Kori and the others fooled into thinking you were a good guy."

Charles was wordless with astonishment that someone would risk breaking into a person's house on a mission to see if he was one of the good guys or not. Only a white person would take that kind of risk so lightly.

"I have to feed Jeremiah first, but since you're here, I guess we should talk. Can I offer you a glass of water or some Diet Coke or iced tea or something?" he asked Felicia politely.

He wondered how much longer he could stay awake. He hadn't been sleeping enough over the past few days and it was catching up with him.

Felicia sat down in his little breakfast nook, looking somewhat weary herself. She had to be well over seventy, Charles thought. "I'll say yes to iced tea if it's herbal," she said, "otherwise water is fine."

"So you were able to break into my house," Charles said. "How come you have such special skills?"

"I love knowing about all kinds of things," Felicia said, "and I had a client who came to me for massage and herbal healing. This was after I had retired from journalism and moved into my work as a healer. He was a private investigator, and we bartered. He taught me how to do things like pick locks, and all kinds of surveillance tricks in return for my working with him on his skin problems. We were both very happy with our exchange."

"What were you looking for?" Charles said.

"Well, I wanted to see if you'd received extra checks recently from TouchStone. Or maybe you had notes that would lead to my learning if you were up to something, like memos to someone who was working for the bad guys, a diary, anything I could find on your home computer that would give me any clues about your loyalties."

"Did you have time to check out everything you wanted to?" Charles asked. He was so surprised by Felicia's disclosures that he wanted to congratulate her on her skills rather than threaten to have her arrested for breaking and entering.

"I didn't really have enough time, but I was just returning when you found me in here. I thought I was finished an hour ago, but then I thought of something else and doubled back. Maybe I should just ask you?"

"Be my guest!" Charles said. This woman had seemingly un-shakable confidence. It was probably easy enough if you were her, he thought, old, female and white.

"Are you gay?" she asked. "I just wondered if you and Daniel are involved."

"Would it matter?" Charles asked. He wasn't sure what he wanted to tell her. He didn't have an answer about his involvement with Daniel, and it was none of her business about his sexual orientation.

"What about you?" he asked. "Do you like men or women?"

Felicia smiled very happily. "I like everyone," she said, "and right now, I am sleeping with no one, so it doesn't matter much."

Charles laughed. He had never met anyone quite like this one. He hoped Daniel would be able to work with her, and that she wouldn't break into his house. Even Felicia shouldn't think she could mess with a Marine!

Chapter Thirty-seven

Alice was having a restless night.

The unsettled evening began with Alice worrying that Felicia was ill. Her friend had announced shortly after eight that she was going to bed. This was very unlike Felicia, usually even more of a night owl than she was.

She claimed to be fine when Alice asked if she was feeling sick, but Alice was unconvinced. As far as she knew, Felicia never went to bed before eleven and then often stayed up late reading or listening to podcasts by eccentric herbal healers, psychics, and a broad spectrum of gurus.

Alice was left to worry alone. Gerard retired to the bedroom to continue his voluminous correspondence with other microbiologists, then went to bed and fell asleep reading. Alice removed his glasses and turned out the light at his side of the bed. She was determined to try to fall asleep herself.

She was just getting to the desired state of drowsiness when she was startled by the sound of knocking.

The sound seemed to be coming from the back porch. Alice thought this was something to be slightly alarmed about. Who would knock at the back door at nine o'clock at night when there was a perfectly functioning doorbell at the front? Who would disturb them at this hour, period?

She tried to ignore the knocking, hoping that the person would go away. After listening to the intermittent knocking every sixty seconds or so for several minutes, she decided to find out who it was.

Alice grabbed the large flashlight that the home owner kept by the front door, and tiptoed back through the house to the porch. She shone the light along all three screened walls of the porch, seeing no one. "Who's there?" she asked, trying to sound commanding.

A very quiet voice spoke just outside the porch door. "It's Kori, Mrs. Ott. So sorry to bother you at this hour but I need to ask you something,"

"Oh my word!" Alice exclaimed. "You scared me, Kori! But do come in!"

She opened the door and shuffled back the requisite six feet since she wasn't wearing a mask. Kori slipped quickly inside, her eyes smiling above her mask. "I'm sorry! So very sorry to scare you," she said, "but I wasn't sure it was safe to call you. Anyhow, I decided to just come over here after dark so that no one would see me go into your house in case I'm being spied on. I hope I didn't wake you?"

"No, not at all. Sit down, I'll grab a mask and you can tell me what's on your mind." She was slightly taken aback by Kori's worries, but after all she'd been through, she didn't think that Kori was necessarily being paranoid.

She wondered if hearing their conversation on the porch would bring Felicia out of her bedroom. Felicia had hearing as sharp as a cat's, and she was invariably curious about any human interaction she might be missing out on. Her absence made Alice think that Felicia must be ill.

"I wanted to ask you about something, actually two things," Kori said. "The first is a favor. How do you feel about cats?"

Alice smiled. "I adore cats!" she said. "In fact I'm missing my cat at home. She is a very good companion, and I wish she were a dog so that we could have brought her to Florida with us. Unfortunately, she's a typical cat who doesn't tolerate car trips well."

She looked at Kori thoughtfully. "Are you trying to find a home for a cat?" she asked. "I don't think I could do much to help. We'll be heading back to New England eventually, and I don't think Mother Jones would appreciate a feline roommate at her stage of life."

"It's not my cat," Kori said quickly. "Charles has a cat, and during the time he's hiding out with me over at the Airbnb next door, his cat will need a temporary home. I don't think he'd leave Jeremiah with just anyone. I'm hoping it will just be for a short time. Once we get TouchStone's crimes exposed to the public, I really hope we can go back to our normal lives."

Alice nodded. "I understand. I believe that a short-term arrangement might work. Both Gerard and Felicia have been very kindly cohabiting with my cat, Mother Jones, and me for the past six months, and I doubt they would have a problem with a short-term feline visitor. I don't know how the owners of the house would feel, though. I'll have to ask Nancy to check it out with them. Can I get back to you tomorrow about it?"

"Sure," Kori said, "and thanks! But you'll have to be careful what you say on the phone to Nancy. Her phone might be bugged too. I just don't trust anything right now."

"Was there another question?" Alice asked. She was wondering why this visit about the cat couldn't have waited until morning. She hoped the other matter wouldn't take too long, not at this hour.

"It's hard to know how to say this," Kori said, "but it's about your friend Felicia. I'm worried about this plan Felicia is working on with Charles. Of course we're all desperate, and I appreciate that you all have come all this way to try to help. We all really want to stop this corporation, and uncover the corruption and all. But I'm worried about the new plan."

Kori stopped, studying Alice intently.

Alice decided to listen a little longer without jumping in with her own concerns about the plan.

"Can I ask you, well, uh, is Felicia, is she, you know, grounded?" Kori asked. "Do you believe she can pull off something this dangerous and not get, um, carried away? I worry that she's going to put herself and Charles in serious danger!

"I don't mean to be sounding so critical, but your friend seems so, well, over-the-top dramatic. Maybe kind of impulsive? I need for Felicia to understand that this is not a game! I got beaten up bad enough that I could have died. And Rufe was murdered!"

She stopped, waiting for Alice to react.

Alice smiled. It wouldn't be the first time someone had come to her, worried about one of Felicia's creative efforts at problem-solving. She had learned that most of Felicia's ideas turned out to be quite successful, but she had many years of friendship to solidify her trust.

"You are quite right to want some reassurance," she said. "I've known Felicia long time, and I completely understand how her ideas, generally, would make you wonder how steady she is, and, as you put it so well, grounded. I can promise you that there's no one I'd choose over Felicia when it comes to steadiness and intelligence in a dangerous situation. Believe me, if it wasn't so late, I could tell you many stories about the kinds of situations we've faced together."

Kori sighed audibly, and Alice could see her shoulders begin to relax. "I'm sorry I had to ask," she said, "but Charles has become such an important part of my life just in the year or so that I've known him. So if this plan to infiltrate the offices of TouchStone goes wrong and anything happens to Charles, I'd be, well, I would be devastated!

"Gram could be a victim too. If I can get her out of that place tomorrow, and believe me, I'm going to try, I'll be a little more relaxed. I'm just really worried right now."

Alice understood how anxious Kori was feeling. Her worries were completely understandable. "I am in agreement with you that there's a whole lot to be worried about. But I actually believe that the magazine scheme really does have some merits. Felicia and Charles' friend Daniel each, separately, had the same idea! It must mean something that both of them, never having met each other, came up with the concept of a news article exploring COVID 19 and the plight of nursing homes! And so far, it's the only way anyone's thought of to get us the inside info we need. Having two completely unrelated people come up with the same plan gives it extra weight, or it seems that way to me."

Kori seemed still to be in doubt, but Alice decided to keep going. "Let me ask you this," she added. "Do you trust Daniel?"

"Charles says he trusts him," Kori said, "but I'm worried. He hadn't seen the guy for three years or more, and claims he doesn't really remember him all that well. Then, out of the blue, Daniel just happens to show up? He just happens to bump into Charles? And he just happens to want to do a story on healthcare and nursing homes and COVID? I'm usually suspicious of coincidence. And I'll be honest with you. I definitely don't trust divine intervention, so yes, I'm worried."

"But you do believe that Daniel really does have a local magazine he's trying to keep afloat? I can tell you that, although it seems to be a genuine coincidence, Felicia really does have the background as a journalist. And Daniel needs a journalist for this whole plan to come together.

"I don't know about divine intervention," Alice added, "but I do believe in coincidence. Maybe this apparent confluence of similar plans to go undercover with the magazine as our Trojan horse, maybe it will actually get us inside the belly of the beast, so to speak."

She stopped, realizing that she was not being very sympathetic to Kori's anxieties.

"It's just too loosey-goosey" Kori said, after some hesitation, "that Felicia needs a real magazine to materialize, and Daniel needs a journalist who can pull off the interview, and so we're supposed to believe that these two will be able to get staff at Touch-Stone to trust them enough to let them snoop around, look at sensitive records, and not get caught? It just doesn't seem very realistic to me."

Alice couldn't help but agree that the action part of the plan was a very long shot. She was wondering how to respond when Gerard appeared at the door of the porch.

"Ah!" he said, "*Bon soir, madame!* Please excuse my interruption. I did not know that Alice, she receives the visitor this evening."

Kori smiled, shaking her head. "Oh no, Monsieur Gerard, I am the one who interrupted your evening and Mrs. Ott's too. I apologize! I know it is very late."

Five minutes later, Alice had reassured Kori that she agreed that the planning needed to be much more detailed, and that all of them would keep thinking things through.

After Kori left to spend the night in her temporary home two doors down from them, Alice realized belatedly that the young woman probably felt frightened, but she was tired enough to drop in her tracks like a pack horse. She curled up in Gerard's arms, trying to put all worries from her mind. But Kori's concerns seemed to have amplified her own misgivings about their plan for Touch-Stone. Exhausted as she felt, she wondered if she could sleep.

She guessed that she might have fallen asleep briefly before she was awakened by the sound of the van returning. Warp had gone out right after dinner, reminding them that he had errands to do before he left the next day for his journey home to New England.

She listened to Warp come into the house and then get his make-shift air mattress bed set up on the porch. He had been sleeping out there for the past four nights. She guessed he fell asleep the second his head hit the pillow.

After another restless period of tossing and turning and worrying about their plans, Alice got up to use the bathroom. She decided to quietly get herself a small dish of ice cream, although she worried she might risk waking Warp. The screened porch could function as a third bedroom, but it was not ideal since both light and noise from the kitchen could easily awaken a light sleeper. Luckily, as she had anticipated, Warp was snoring loudly; he was a champion sleeper. RubyStarr had complained about that often enough for Alice to know this for a fact.

Now she wondered where Warp had parked the big van. Felicia probably left their new used car in the driveway when she had returned from her own errand-running, and then gone off to bed early, leaving the car in Warp's way.

Alice went to the front of the house and peered out the front window to see if the van was parked in the semi circle of road in front of the duplex. She was relieved to see that it was parked in the driveway where it should be. Even though she knew it was silly, she decided to check the garage to make sure that when Felicia had parked the Prius in there for the night, she had remembered to turn off any lights.

She opened the door from the kitchen to the garage, shining her flashlight for her routine check. The garage was empty!

Now she was wide awake.

Where on earth was Felicia? Surely she wouldn't have left in the night without telling someone where she was going! Because she had claimed that she was going off to bed early, it was quite worrisome that the car was missing.

Or maybe she had slipped out before Warp came back, and made a run to buy extra strength pain reliever or a thermometer or something. Felicia would not want Alice to find out that she was turning to Western medicine! That would explain her leaving the house without letting Alice know, but where was Felicia now?

Having imagined Felicia with severe enough symptoms to drive off in search of drugstore remedies, Alice suddenly worried that

Felicia was developing COVID. If one of them got COVID, they all would probably get it, she thought, even Warp.

Alice, stop imagining the worst! Alice could just hear Felicia scolding her. *You're just giving energy to the negative possibilities. They could grow into something real!*

She couldn't decide if she should wake up Gerard to discuss Felicia's disappearance. She decided against it, and made herself settle down in the living room to read until Felicia returned. Maybe she just took the car to the beach for a late night moon walk.

At three o'clock in the morning, Felicia crept into the house and found Alice asleep on the small recliner in the living room. She gently covered her with a blanket and went into her bedroom to catch at least a few hours of sleep.

Chapter Thirty-eight

As Alice and Gerard sat cozily in the living room the next morning to drink their morning coffee, Sue knocked at the front door.

"I have an idea!" she said enthusiastically through the screened door. "Not too early, I hope."

Alice took this as a statement rather than a question. "Come on around to the back," she said, "we can talk on the porch and have more fresh air."

Alice hoped that Sue had brought her mask with her. She would have to remind her to wear it before she came into the Florida room.

If their new neighborhood reflected Florida's casual approach to COVID prevention practices, Alice wondered how safe any of her little pod would remain even if they kept their period of strict quarantine. People around here tended to be unmasked and seemed to forget social distancing altogether. Alice wondered what she could to ensure everyone's safety.

"You remember I told you about the lady over on Kingfisher Lane who works for one of the big healthcare companies that specializes in nursing home care?" Sue said as soon as she had donned her mask and settled into the porch recliner. "Well, Pearl is willing to come over this morning and tell you what she can. But before she gets here, I should warn you that she's in kind of a negative space these days. I think she's planning to retire soon, so she may still want to get you interested in the company but she also might make you think twice.

"She's worked for several of the big companies down here over the past twenty years, and she knows a whole lot, but she's not too happy with the terms of her coming retirement or with the workplace generally."

Gerard frowned as if he wanted to be excused from this conversation. He was determined to follow up with one of his contacts who, as far as Alice could tell, was no longer tracking potential COVID sources.

Recently he had joined a group of online sleuths whose focus was identifying right wing, white supremicists who were organizing militias around the country. It didn't seem to bother Gerard that the subject of his investigation had changed. He was apparently avid about conspiracies of almost any stripe these days.

No, Alice decided, she was not letting him off the hook this morning. Whatever it took to learn more about the nursing home businesses, she wanted him there to listen even though he wasn't supposed to ask questions to keep his cover as a victim of dementia. She would be as relieved as he was when they could stop the pretense that he was suffering from dementia. In the meantime, she needed his good mind to analyze whatever they could learn about TouchStone from Pearl, their potentially useful new neighbor.

"What does she know about us?" Alice asked, looking meaningfully over at Gerard.

"Oh, not much except that you're down here to explore options for your husband," Sue said. "Everyone in the neighborhood has experiences to tell you about, but they have lots of opinions, of course, so you don't want to get swarmed. But Pearl is the real expert. Just don't let her scare you off any one place until you check with some of the rest of us."

Without further conversation, Sue whisked back out the door.

"I think you have not enjoyed your rest," Gerard commented, looking at her carefully. "You did not sleep well, my Alice?"

"No, I did not," Alice admitted. She wondered if Felicia was sleeping off her adventure from last night. Perhaps she had never returned! Suddenly Alice felt alarmed. She really should check to make sure Felicia was in there.

She went to the bedroom door, and tried to open it very slightly to peek in. "Oh my!" she said, jumping backwards and closing the door again. "I didn't mean to startle you, Felicia!" she called. "So sorry!"

"Not a problem!" Felicia called after her. "I'm just doing my naked yoga! You can put some water on for tea, please. I'll be right out!"

"I do not want to view the naked yoga," Gerard said. "You remind her, *s'il vous plait*, that I am sitting here also."

Less than a minute after Felicia appeared fully clothed in the living room, the doorbell rang. Alice looked at Felicia pointedly. "It's probably the neighbor who's come to tell us about nursing homes," she reported. "Sue just now stopped by to tell us Pearl was coming. She may be even more valuable than we expected! Sue reports that Pearl is in some negative space about the corporation and is soon to retire."

The doorbell rang again, three loud rings. "Anyone home in there?" a woman's voice called loudly.

Alice hopped up and went to the door. "Hello!" she said. "You must be Pearl! Can I invite you to come around to our screened porch at the back of the house? We'll have lots of fresh air, so we can all be safe."

The woman on the other side of the screen door peered in at her. "You worried about the sickness?" she asked, sounding slightly irritable. "I thought you'd be like that, being from up North and all. Sue told me you all wanted to ask me questions about the nursing home, but she warned me you were fussy about wearing masks. So I'm wearing my mask! You don't have to be afraid of me. Maybe we have to be afraid of the young ones who still think they can party all night at the beach. Worry about those silly kids, if you want. But you're safe here. Nobody around here has COVID!"

"Oh I am very sorry!" Alice said, her efforts at contrition sounding hollow in her own ears, "I know we're a little on the cautious side. But I do want to protect you from us! We've only recently travelled through eleven states to get here, so we're the ones who could have been infected. We could be carrying the virus even though we aren't sick." She stopped, worrying that she was ruining their chance to make this potentially valuable connection with Pearl.

Felicia came to peer over Alice's shoulder through the screen door.

"Could I make you a nice cold glass of iced tea?" she asked. "Or I could fix you hot tea and bring it around to the screened porch. And we could have delicious fresh French pastries in just a jiffy if you can stay a little while." She opened the door so they could all at least see each other.

Pearl looked at the two women, and then past them at Gerard

who was rather unhappily putting down his coffee cup. He stood up, and bowed slightly. "*Bonjour, Madame!*" he said. In his lovely deep voice was the sound of genuine welcome, and finally Pearl smiled.

Alice stepped back and went over to take his hand. "He still remembers how to make the most delicious pastries, don't you, my dear?" she told Pearl. "But I do need to give him the ingredients to get him started. Felicia will meet you on the porch with whichever beverage you prefer, and I'll help Gerard get started. I'll join you very soon." She waved her fingers at Pearl as she tugged at Gerard to come with her into the kitchen.

"I'll have that cold tea," Pearl said, "with extra sweetener. Whatever you've got." Felicia quickly offered to walk with her back along the side of the house to the porch.

It wasn't until Warp jumped up from his air mattress on the back porch that Alice realized her mistake. Felicia was ushering Pearl into the temporary bedroom on the porch! Warp fled in his t-shirt and shorts into the kitchen. He frowned sleepily at Alice and Gerard in passing.

He was sharing the second bathroom with Felicia. Alice hoped he had some clothes in there. "Oh dear, Warp!" she called after him, "I didn't remember you were still sleeping out there! I am so very sorry!"

"No worries," he mumbled over his shoulder as he disappeared into the bathroom. "Overslept. Need to hit the road soon anyhow."

Alice grabbed some frozen croissants Gerard had made the morning before and put them into the microwave to thaw, despite Gerard's complaints that she would ruin the texture of the pastry.

"Can't be helped!" she said. "Remember when we go out to the porch that you're supposed to have lost all your English! But don't hesitate to continue to charm her with your European courtliness!"

"I think you take her *les croissants* and *le café*. You and Felicia, you have the pretend conversation not with me," Gerard said firmly. "I will come later to listen to what you learn about the homes, but you and Felicia, you begin *sans moi*!"

Pearl seemed quite amused by entering the young man's temporary sleeping quarters while he was still asleep. "Travel gets you all discombobulated, doesn't it!" she said, brushing aside Alice's apologies about their awkward beginning.

She looked at each woman thoughtfully. "You still haven't told me which one of you is the lucky grandmother," she said. "Don't we all wish we had a grandchild visiting us these days! I haven't seen my grandkids for six months now because of the quarantine and everyone so fearful about getting the sickness. I got a grandson about the age of your young man, he's up in Ohio, and two more teenagers, one boy and one girl, in Virginia. Haven't been able to have any of them down here yet. I sure do miss 'em! But let's get back to why you wanted to talk to me.

"So you're looking to place your husband down here?" she asked Alice. "You planning to stay here in Florida to be near him?"

"Yes," Alice said. "Of course. I am broken-hearted that I even have to consider enrolling him in a nursing care facility but I can't really manage him at home anymore. Gerard has lost all his English over the past year or so, and I can't manage all of his needs anymore. We thought the climate down here would be easier for me also. I won't have to cope with all that cold weather and snow. I can't really drive in the winter at home anymore."

She realized she should explain something about Felicia's presence. "Felicia's here to -"

"I'm her best friend," Felicia interrupted, "so I was planning to come and help anyhow. It's actually a double pleasure for me to help Alice because I'm a journalist and I'm working on a feature piece for *Splash!* magazine. It's about nursing homes in the time of COVID. I thought it would be interesting to see how things are down here, where families can visit their loved ones outdoors even if they are institutionalized. We want to make the article really upbeat! There's been so much depressing news about how everyone is suffering from COVID's impact. *Splash!* wants to highlight places where things are going well."

Pearl looked at her, her frown a challenge to Felicia's airy optimism. "I don't know about that," she said slowly, "I don't know if I'll be much use to you in regard to the article, that is. There's not much joy and light going around for the older folks, at least the ones they've got in the nursing homes my company runs."

"Oh really?" Felicia said, looking inappropriately animated, "that's very interesting! Why do you say that?"

Once again, Pearl contemplated Felicia with a mix of doubt and resistance. "I never heard of this *Splash!* magazine," she said suspiciously. "Where do you get it? Could I buy it at the supermarket?"

"Oh it's still quite new," Felicia said, "but I'm surprised you haven't seen it. It's based down here, and I'm working with a very well-known Florida photographer. I can get a copy for you later today, and drop it by your house."

Pearl turned back to Alice. "I wanted to come over to give you some help with your questions," she said. "I've been working for TouchStone Healthcare for the past ten years. And I have a girlfriend I play cards with on Thursday nights, she works for The Good Shepherd corporation and they manage some nursing care places too. She's right here in the Cove, over on Blue Heron. Between Kathy and me, there's a lot we can tell you. But I have to be honest. It's not all good news."

Alice tried not to look as excited as she felt about the 'not good' news. She reminded herself that she still needed to appear to Pearl as a worried wife, still on the brink of deciding whether or not to put her husband in a nursing home. She should be looking especially worried about what the ratings might be.

Felicia, by contrast, was fully embracing her role as developer of the magazine article.

"Well, we know that there's no such thing these days as a nursing care facility without some hard stories," she said brightly. "At *Splash!*, we specialize in finding silver linings, no matter what we're covering. Even in this terrible time of COVID, there are so many human interest stories that make you believe in the goodness of humanity, don't you think?"

There was an awkward silence as Pearl looked out the screen window at the neighbor's bird feeder, ignoring her hostesses.

"I kinda prefer birds and dogs," she said finally. "Take our resident great horned owls right down the street from you. Once the couple makes the babies, and the mama bird starts sitting on the nest, there's nothing like the parental devotion you can see. They'll stick with their jobs as parents 24/7, through heavy rainfall, terrible high winds, unseasonably cold weather, you name it. It takes at least three months until the babies get born and then fledged. I could tell you stories about the owls here that would make you weep for the beauty of their devotion. Human beings are a whole other story."

Alice wasn't sure whether Pearl could be drawn into the details of the nursing homes' failures so early in their acquaintance. She had been told by Nancy Warren about the closeness of this particular neighborhood, and how everyone watched out for everyone else. Did that mean that as brand new residents of the Cove, they would be protected by hearing information that might get Pearl in trouble at work?

"You seem so young to be retiring," she said strategically, "but if you don't mind me asking, are you leaving your job because you can get early retirement benefits or are you unhappy with your working conditions?"

"Oh believe me, honey, I'm no spring chicken!" Pearl said. "No, Kathy and me, we're competing to see who quits her job first. We're both about to hit sixty-five, and it's going to be a race right down to the hour, if not the day, for which of us gets sprung first. I can't wait!"

Felicia looked even more ecstatic. "Oh how blessed!" she exclaimed. "We'll get to feature the two of you and your glorious futures in retirement, along with the happy stories of the senior citizens enjoying the comforts of your employers' nursing homes!"

"Ha!" Pearl exclaimed mirthlessly. "Not in TouchStone's nursing homes, you won't. The PR department might manipulate the facts to tell you some story full of bull pucky, but you won't get that kind of la-la story from me and you probably won't get it from the nursing home employees or the residents!"

There seemed to be a train wreck happening right under Alice's nose! Pearl was looking as if she couldn't wait to get away from Felicia's relentless positive spin. How could she coax this exciting new potential source to stay in the conversation long enough to gain access to TouchStone's secrets? She decided to bring up the federal grant to see how Pearl reacted.

"My friend here who invited us to Florida," Alice said, "told me something exciting about one of the healthcare companies that runs several nursing homes in Central Florida. She said the company got a big federal COVID grant! That's one of the major reasons we came down here. We thought my husband would get extra good care from a place that's been awarded such a big grant. Do you know anything about this?" she asked ingenuously.

"Oh you betcha!" Pearl said."That would be TouchStone, my company. Yup, there was a whole bunch of hoopla when it came out in the newspaper that we got that big grant. Everyone was over the moon about it, of course. Kathy started giving me such a hard time about it, telling me how I should apply for a raise because they got all that money.

"I told her, Kath, you know I'm not going to see a penny of that money! And you know who else is never going to get a penny from the big pot of money? The patients and the staff at Sunset Villages! TouchStone will put all the grant money into their rich folks facility, Serenity Place."

Suddenly Pearl stood up. "You girls mind if I have a smoke?" she asked. "I'll go right outside the porch here and we can keep talking."

Felicia's eyebrows almost reached her hairline! She shot Alice a look of acute desperation. Her reactions to second hand smoke were off the charts. Alice would call her friend's tirades about smoking close to apocalyptic.

For Alice, it was personal. Her fragile lungs had to be protected when it came to someone smoking in her presence. She had to say no.

"I'm sorry, but I have COPD," she said gently, "so I can't be too near anyone smoking. But we could go back to the front of the house and continue our conversation for you to have your smoke. I'm afraid even there I have to ask you to go down to the end of the driveway."

"Well," Pearl said, "I have to get going soon. I got a bunch of errands to do, and then Kath and I are going to a birthday party later at a bar up the road, in South Daytona. They have axe-throwing contests and free sweet potato fries with every order of beer!"

Alice tried not to leave her mouth hanging open at the reference to axe-throwing parties. Pearl didn't seem to notice.

"But anyway, before I go, I was telling you about when they got that grant. Kath told me and the other girls at our card game that she heard they never got what they were supposed to at Serenity Place either! Her son's girlfriend works there and she was saying everyone's just about ready to go on strike because they never got their money for PPE or their overtime."

She looked sorrowfully at Alice. "I apologize that I haven't been much help to you. I know you can find a decent place for your husband down here. And don't get me wrong, it's not all bad. But there's some shady stuff going on too. And now, ladies, I have to get my smoke!"

The three of them trooped along single file, and when they got to the front of the house, Pearl turned so she could face them both. She lowered her voice, stepping dangerously close to Felicia. "You best not do anything with what I just told you before I learn more about your magazine. I can get you in the door if you decide to go ahead with your feature, even after what I told you. I'll support your article, and you can just go ahead and sprinkle whatever happy dust you want over the nursing facility and what it offers. People need good news.

"But you better believe that if you dare to quote me on anything I told you just now, I will deny it and tell the lawyers to sue your ass! I mean it! But don't worry, I'm real close to another gal from the PR office, and she'll be over the moon when I tell her about your plan.

"So you go ahead and drop off the copy of the magazine at my house. Get it to me sometime before Sunday evening, so I can take it to work Monday morning. I'm over on Kingfisher Lane," she added, "next to the house with the turquoise truck parked on the grass. If you forget, Sue can point you in the right direction. She knows everyone and she knows everything. She's our own national treasure!"

Alice and Felicia watched Pearl cross the road and make her way down to her house at the other end of Kingfisher Lane.

"I think we have found the golden path into the magic kingdom," Alice said cheerfully. "I am looking forward to the meeting this afternoon with Charles and Daniel, aren't you?"

Felicia looked at her for a minute. "I'm just surprised that woman made it so easy for us," she said. "It feels almost too easy."

"The hard part," Alice said, "will be to figure out how to get more information without quoting her or getting her in trouble. She deserves to get that retirement package she's owed, even if it means we have to do the nitty gritty work of verifying this without her help."

"I hate it when you're right!" Felicia said, and draped her arm over Alice's shoulders as they walked back into the house.

Chapter Thirty-Nine

Charles felt responsible for bringing Felicia and Daniel together. The meeting to plan their magazine interview was carefully constructed. Daniel understood that the magazine article was becoming a multi-purpose vehicle for some very risky investigative action, but Charles still wanted to protect him. He needed to have at least some control over who said what to whom.

Felicia insisted that Alice be present, and Charles thought Kori should be there too. How could they leave out the person who was the original organizer of the investigation, as well as someone with a very precious family member in Sunset Villages?

The big question was whether or not Pearl should be invited.

Alice and Felicia were following their collective hunch, or their female intuition as Felicia told it. They both felt that Pearl could give them tips on who to approach to get the interview, what to say and who to avoid.

Charles was more skeptical. They had just met Pearl a few hours earlier. He couldn't understand why the others believed she would collaborate with a plan to dig up the dirty secrets of the missing grant money.

"Don't worry so much!" Daniel said. They were enjoying a late lunch before the meeting. "I can take care of myself, remember? I'm a former Marine! You can take the boy out of the Marines – and believe me, they do that! But you can't take the Marine out of the boy."

"What if Felicia starts some kind of really risky snooping while you're there? She's the kind of person who's likely to jump the gun, do some impulsive thing that could get you in trouble."

Felicia made Charles totally anxious. Even though she had quite skillfully handled their confrontation after she broke into his house, he still thought she was a flake. He hadn't decided when he should tell Daniel about her appearance the night before.

"Why do you think I'll take any responsibility for what she's doing?" Daniel said. "I've hired her to fill in for our regular writer, and I can play dumb as well as anyone. Her behavior is not my responsibility. I'm just the photographer."

"You're also one of the three owners of this magazine," Charles said stubbornly. "Have you told the other two owners? Are your finance person and your convalescing writer on board?"

"Hey, listen, I'm not telling anyone anything until we get this interview done. We'll see where we are then, and I'll decide what to tell them, based on what happens. If Felicia totally screws up, it's no big deal. I'll just find another nursing home and health-care corporation and start over."

Daniel was clearly getting restless. "Still want to take a quick walk on the beach before the meeting?" he asked hopefully.

Charles wasn't ready to let the discussion go.

"What do you think about the idea of inviting that neighbor to the meeting? She could end up giving you all a bad name at Touch-Stone if she really understands what you're conspiring to uncover. She could lose her job and she could cost me my job if I'm part of this planning meeting, by the way. Who knows what she might tell someone at Sunset about the plan."

Reaching across the table to squeeze Charles' hand, Daniel's voice became much more patient.

"Why didn't you tell me that you're worried about your job?" he asked gently. "You have a very good reason to be absent from this meeting. In fact, now that you're putting your concerns out there, I'm embarrassed that I didn't realize what a risk this is for you. You're the one who should not go to the meeting, Charles, especially if someone who still works at TouchStone is there. Absolutely! You should not be at the meeting.

"Now, let's breathe a little sea air and then I'll send you off to wait for me at your house, ok? I'll come over after the meeting and give you a complete report, and I'll even bring dinner!"

"Um, I'm not staying at my house right now," Charles said. "Everyone decided it's not safe, so Kori and I are renting a nice little Airbnb in Edgewater. Right down the street from where the New Englanders are staying."

"Oh, OK," Daniel said, although he looked a bit rattled. "Well then, I'll text you to come over to my place when the meeting's over?"

Alice thought it was a terrific idea to involve Pearl. She was hopeful that they had a new collaborator in their undercover operation. Pearl could give some real depth to the magazine story, including her awareness that the grant money still hadn't shown up in either of the nursing homes expenditures. She wasn't too sure about what Pearl herself knew or didn't know about the dispersing of funds, but she thought it would be helpful to have some guidance about where to look.

Fifteen minutes before the meeting was going to start, Alice's phone buzzed. When she saw Pearl's name on her caller ID she was prepared to be disappointed. Contrary to her fears, Pearl sounded very upbeat. So this was not going to be a cancellation phone call after all.

"Hey, it's Pearl! Just wondered if I could bring another of my girlfriends to this meeting. She lives here in the Cove, and she works at TouchStone. She's been there even longer than me. She can give you an earful too, maybe more than you even want to know!

"At first I didn't think about asking her to get involved because she's been real sick with a bad cancer. But then I was thinking it would give her a boost to get involved. She's always telling me how small her life is, you know, because of the cancer? I think she'd be excited to have something to contribute, and something else to think about besides being sick. That OK with you?"

"Oh my, well, yes, of course!" Alice said, wondering how complicated this might be. "Can she leave her house?"

They had decided to meet at the little pavilion down by the community dock. But could they meet there if the newest arrival was too sick to be out in the wind?

The pavilion had seemed ideal for their purposes. It had a couple of picnic tables and eight brightly colored Adirondack chairs. They could be as far apart as they needed, and be in the fresh air. It seemed to Alice that, so far, whenever they walked down there to enjoy the river view, they had never seen anyone using the pavilion. She hoped this meant that they weren't likely to be joined by curious neighbors.

"Oh sure," Pearl said. "I can drive her over if you're OK with her joining us."

How could Alice say no to a woman who was very ill and needed a new mission to distract her? Maybe this venture really would give her new energy.

"She's very welcome," Alice said, trying to sound more certain than she actually felt. "What's her name?"

"Her real name is Lolly, but she goes by Bud," Pearl said. "I can't even remember where she got the nickname but she's been Bud a long time, I know that." She hung up without further ado.

The first people to show up for the meeting were Alice and Felicia, soon joined by Kori, and then Nancy Warren. No one seemed to know if Flo was planning to come or not, though Kori had invited her. The next arrival was Daniel who pulled up in his shiny red sports car and trotted up the walk with an enthusiastic greeting for them all.

They were having an animated conversation about the Cove and its lovely little dock on the river when an old Buick pulled up behind Daniel's car, and Pearl got out of the driver's seat. She moved very slowly. She waved at them before she went around to the passenger side to help her friend Bud hoist herself up out of the seat. With great care, Pearl supported Bud, her walker and her portable oxygen tank progressing slowly along the walkway toward the closest chair.

Daniel was on his feet immediately. Alice was hoping Kori had filled him in on their invitation to include both Pearl and her friend Bud in the planning meeting.

"Here," he said, "would you like a little help getting into this chair? These Adirondack chairs are so big and good-looking but they can be hard to land in."

Pearl nodded her appreciation as she and Daniel lowered Bud into the chair.

Alice pulled down her mask for a second or two to smile at the emaciated woman seated across from her. "Glad to see I have another member of the oxygen tank club!" she said, with a wink at Bud.

Their newest recruit was bundled up in several layers of sweaters, a shawl and a winter cap. She was very pale, and seemed thoroughly depleted by the short walk from the car. Despite her obvious discomfort, she smiled radiantly at everyone in the circle.

"Thank you so much for including me," she said in a hoarse, whispery voice. "I will put my mask on now, but I wanted to speak before I disappear into anonymity."

"I thank you for including me also," Pearl said, looking at the others. "This is the most excitement we've had here in the Cove for years, right Bud?"

"What about the owls?" Bud retorted in a hoarse but audible whisper.

"We're hoping to have owl babies," Pearl explained.

"This is our third year! They're great horned owls! Big gorgeous birds with the funniest looking cartoon babies! I'll take you to where you can easily see the nest, unless Sue's already done that. They're right in your front yard!" she told Kori.

Kori giggled. "Oh I know! I only moved in yesterday, but I've watched half the neighborhood from my living room window. They're all out on my lawn looking up into the tree! I'm hoping to bring my Gram to see the owl tree when I move her in tonight. She's going to love it!"

"Where's she coming from?" Pearl asked.

"Oh," Kori said, hesitating suddenly. "Well, she's coming out of a nursing home." Then she looked at her feet and went silent.

Before anyone could change the subject, Pearl grinned at Kori. "Well, all I can say is God bless you, baby! A granddaughter who loves her gramma enough to have her move in! We need more young folks like you in this world. Don't you worry, we'll all take good care of her! She's going to love all the company, with everyone coming over to see the owls. There's a bunch of us who like to gather over there and have a glass of wine, and the owls are the guests of honor at our five o'clock cocktail party. Don't be shy, now. You just bring your grandmother right out there to join us. Everyone's welcome in the Cove!"

"Oh lovely!" Felicia exclaimed. "Now, shall we get started? I'm Felicia and this is Daniel and we're doing the magazine feature for *Splash!* magazine.

"And this is my friend Alice. Alice and her husband Gerard have just arrived from New England. They're looking into assisted nursing facilities. Alice and I are long-time friends, so I came along for the trip since I'm doing research on elders living in nursing homes in the time of COVID. Kori's friend Charles introduced Daniel and me, so we're just now planning our article.

"Do you want to say more, Daniel?" she asked.

Daniel cleared his throat and smiled, his eyes moving around the circle to each person until he came back to Felicia. "I'm really happy this is finally happening. I've got a few copies of our first publication of *Splash!* to give you at the end of the meeting.

"We just got started last spring when COVID was closing in, and lucky for us, our debut feature article on the many faces of Volusia County was very well received. But then my writing partner got sick, so the business wizard and I have been kind of stuck without her.

"I already had the concepts outlined, we even have the story boards for the feature piece on COVID and the local nursing homes. But I had to find another journalist to do the interviews and the writing. I'm only a conceptual vision guy and also the photographer. Though we have been lucky enough to hang on to our business manager, we needed a journalist. Then, bingo! Like magic, here Felicia is! Just who we need to make this work. Pretty amazing coincidence, right?"

"There are no coincidences!" Felicia said brightly. Daniel grinned, ignoring her unsolicited commentary.

"Now we're ready to make this happen," he continued, "and this meeting is to help us figure out the best way to make connections with the administrators and PR people at TouchStone Health. Once again, the fates have been smiling on us and we happened, through another of your neighbors, to find out about you, Pearl. Then Pearl suggested that her co-worker Bud could also be part of the meeting. Having two staff from TouchStone gives us another window into how this whole thing is working in the time of COVID, with the nursing home lockdowns and federal assistance and so on.

"So I guess the fates have decided that this article is supposed to happen, don't you think?" Daniel smiled again, and looked over at Felicia to continue.

Pearl raised her hand.

"Please," Daniel said, "go ahead!"

"Off the record, I think you all should know that I'm not going to give you a glowing report on how TouchStone is doing a fabulous job running its nursing facilities. I'm about to retire, and I want my pension and all, but as I've said before, the situation is not all sweetness and light, not from where I sit."

"Oh that's perfect" Felicia bubbled enthusiastically. "I want this to be a story that looks at issues from various points of view. Everyone knows that nursing homes in the U.S. have had the largest concentration of deaths from COVID of any population. We don't want to sugarcoat that.

"And remember," she said, looking at Alice, "my friends are looking for the best place for Gerard to live, and they're looking at what Alice's situation might be like, how will she be welcomed, informed, and consulted concerning her husband. We want to know whatever you can tell us."

Kori leaned forward, speaking so softly Alice wasn't sure she could understand her. "I'm taking my Gram out of Sunset Villages today," she said, "and I have mixed feelings about that. My friend Charles works there and he couldn't have been kinder to Gram, plus most of his staff have been wonderful. But in spite of these wonderful people, there are not such great things happening. I want the magazine to tell the truth."

Pearl and Bud looked at each other, then Pearl nodded. "We're both getting out of there. I'm ready for retirement, as you know. And Bud is, well, she's too sick to work at this point. She's not likely to be staying much longer. We both want the whole truth to be told, the good, the bad and the ugly, you know?

"But we also need the benefits that the company owes us, so we don't want to be directly quoted. How's that going to work?"

Daniel nodded thoughtfully. "We want to be open, disclosing what we find," he said. "And we want to respect your confidence and not put you at risk for any kind of retaliation. My friend Charles who works at Sunset, where Kori's grandmother lives? Well, he's been consulting with a lawyer who's representing some TouchStone employees, folks who are unhappy about some issues that haven't yet been made public. Among other things, I'm referring to the big federal grant for COVID relief. The rumor is that overtime pay and safety equipment promised by the grant, have never materialized at either Sunset Villages or Serenity Place.

"So, as you can see, this won't just be a feel good story."

"That's a relief!" Pearl said. She glanced at Bud. "Bud wants to see some real justice happening over there before she dies, right, Bud?"

Bud nodded, her eyes filling with tears. "I'm not going to make it. I'm too sick. My doctors have told me I'm not likely to keep going much longer. Before I die, I want to do the right thing, and see some justice done. I want to help expose the corruption I know for a fact is going on there."

Alice and Felicia looked at each other, then glanced over at Kori. This was almost too much good news to take in.

"Oh my goodness!" Alice said. "Will your plan for an upbeat story still work with a dark cloud like this, Daniel?" Then, remembering that she was supposed to be playing the desperate wife looking for the softest landing possible for Gerard, she tried to look appropriately worried. "I don't know what to think, personally," she added.

Bud turned to her, her eyes filled with compassion. "Oh, honey," she said in a hoarse voice, "don't worry! There are still good people who work there, and the same for every other nursing home. And plenty of the good ones stay, no matter that they're not getting paid for their overtime and they're not getting the equipment they need. They're dedicated. It's not all bad."

Alice was embarrassed to be getting undeserved comfort.

Felicia stepped in quickly to provide distraction. "Who do you suspect of stealing that grant money?" she asked Pearl and Bud, point blank.

Daniel coughed and shifted uncomfortably in the big yellow Adirondack chair. "Don't feel you have to answer that," he said, raising his eyebrows in a warning to Felicia.

"I've worked in accounting since I came to TouchStone," Pearl said, ignoring Daniel. "I can tell you there's a new special account that was set up soon after we got the federal grant. That new account received only one deposit, but it's a big one. Exactly one million dollars!"

Pearl paused to give her listeners a meaningful look.

"Since that account was opened, there have been a series of checks paid out to a mysterious research institute that I can't find in any search I've done.

"And listen to this!" she continued, glancing around before she spoke. "There's the account that was set up for the federal grant for two million dollars. There are small payouts from that account to Sunset Villages and Serenity Place," she continued calmly. "But that grant account went from two million dollars to one million almost immediately. The head honcho, the top CEO, told Bud to put the other one million into the mysterious account that sends checks every week to some kind of research institute. The CEO told Bud when she asked about that mysterious institute that it was for special COVID research. Well, I can tell you, that research place sure is keeping a low profile because when I say I've done a bunch of searches to try to find it, I'm not exaggerating!"

"Whew!" Daniel said, at the same moment that Felicia exclaimed "Ah ha!"

"We don't know if other employees know about these transactions," Bud said, "although it's hard to believe that the head of the accounting department doesn't know."

There was a long silence. Alice wondered if they were all holding their breath, the way you might do if you saw a rare bird land on your bird feeder.

"What I can't quite figure out," Pearl continued, "is how to show you the proof of all this so you can see for yourselves. You could maybe take some pictures of some of the documents I could show you. So I'm still figuring out a plan. If we do this right, there's no way they can prove it was me or Bud who leaked the documents."

She stopped for a brief pause. "We gotta figure things out fast," she said, "because your magazine won't even have time to hit the stands before I'm out of there!"

That evening as they sat outside the house eating a late meal, Daniel was already thinking ahead to the next steps.

"I can easily imagine getting us an appointment to meet with the PR people, assuming they'd jump at the chance to get some good publicity right about now. But I'm trying to figure out how we could get copies of anything that could prove the allegations those two ladies are claiming? That's going to be tricky."

Kori stretched her arms above her head. "I'm too tired to think about all this tonight," she said. "Alice, should I check on the cat, make sure he's adapting to his temporary home with you, or are you OK with taking over? I need to bow out soon, and get a real night of sleep."

She glanced at Warp. "Would you be willing to give me a little bit more of your time? I want to double check to make sure I have everything set up for moving Gram tonight."

Warp took the last bite of his sandwich. "Sure," he said. "Let's go over the checklist to see what you still need to pick up."

"Want to come over to The Nest now?" Kori asked. "I just want to make sure the rental equipment we got today is where it's supposed to be, and is in working order."

Alice watched Warp and Kori walk down the street to the Airbnb where Warp's van was now parked. There was a small group gathered at the foot of the tree watching the owls and enjoying their happy hour.

"Good thing it's going to get dark soon," she said, "or poor Kori would never get that sleep she needs."

Felicia turned to Daniel. "Do you want to plan our interview now?'" she asked.

Seeing Daniel nod eagerly, Alice turned to Gerard. "Maybe you and I can take a little walk down to the dock and watch for dolphins," she said. "And I can tell you about the meeting, if you want to hear it?"

Gerard had already risen to his feet. "First I clean the plates, then we walk to the dock?" he suggested.

The stroll from their little house down to the dock was a very short one. It took less than five minutes unless they stopped at the owl tree. Gerard reached for Alice's hand as they sauntered along. "This *petite village* and the warm nights of Florida, *ç'est agreable!*" he said cheerfully.

Alice herself was feeling surprisingly pleased by their new world, temporary though it was. She was beginning to understand why people loved coming to Florida for the winter. As she looked at the wide beautiful river and leaned against Gerard, she wondered what it would be like to have nothing else demanding her energy and attention. Could she be in such a beautiful place and just kick back and read, write emails, and chat with friends near and far? Perhaps.

"I am sad we do not have a special au revoir saying to Warp," Gerard told Alice. "I will miss him!"

Alice nodded. They would all miss Warp. Things were moving along so fast she hadn't really had a chance to think about making a little space to say their goodbyes. She promised herself to leave him a quick note in the van so if he left before they all were up, he would know how much he had done for them and how much they would all miss him.

"You will tell me about your meeting now?' Gerard asked. Alice dove happily into the highlights. She had just come to the best part, the moment when Pearl and Bud made their commitments to help with the expose, when her phone buzzed. She glanced down unhappily, resenting the intrusion until she saw the caller ID

"I must take this!" she told Gerard.

"Mrs. Ott, this is Pearl and I need to speak with you immediately. Your house or mine?"

"Well," Alice said, hesitantly, "I'm actually down here at the dock with my, ah, my husband Gerard."

"OK then," Pearl said. "I'll meet you there in one and a half minutes!"

"We are about to have Pearl, one of the neighbors who works at TouchStone, come to us right this minute!" Alice told Gerard. "She gave me no choice. Just remember that you are supposed to be suffering from dementia and you've forgotten all your English!"

Gerard nodded. Looking quite serene, he turned to watch the river.

Pearl's old Buick pulled into a parking spot at the pavilion, a small half circle just off the road as it curved from Pelican Lane onto Blue Heron Drive. Pearl made her way slowly out to the dock where Gerard and Alice were waiting. "Take a seat," she said pointing to the little bench that faced out to the river. "This will take a few minutes."

She nodded at Gerard, and then launched directly into her message."It's complicated," she said, "but Bud and I have a plan. What are you and Felicia doing Monday at eight o'clock in the morning?"

Alice stared at her, glanced at Gerard, then shrugged.

"There's a special program happening at the TouchStone company, and we think it will be a good way to get you in the building with a bunch of other people who aren't employees. It's the best chance to get in to take photos of those records and documents you need, while everyone is attending the hoopla in the auditorium.

"Goodness gracious!" Alice said. "What kind of program is happening?"

"Oh, the governor is coming and they're having all kinds of special guests. They're doing a big production about how great the state has done with keeping nursing homes and assisted living facilities safe from the virus. It's just the governor trying to show how much better he's handled things than other states.

"Anyway, they'll be honoring some of the employees, and introducing the oldest residents, and probably some of the officials from Volusia County will be there. Other press people will be there, for sure, so if Daniel and Felicia have press badges, they won't be noticeable at all. They could be anywhere in the building and not draw attention to themselves!"

Pearl looked very pleased with herself.

Alice was so startled by this fortuitous addition to the plan for infiltration that she was speechless. Gerard was playing his role and smiling sweetly at Pearl as if he had no idea what she was talking about. Actually, Alice thought, that could be real.

"Bud is ready to provide a distraction in case there are any surprises," Pearl continued, "but I won't spoil her story. She wants to keep her plan secret until that morning! She hasn't had this much energy in months, and she only wants to tell you the details of the plan when we drive over to the TouchStone building. She and I agree we should fill you in, but she doesn't want to get too specific until she sees how she's feeling. Plans for her part in this could change, depending on her strength.

"I'll drive over there Monday morning with Bud and you, Mrs. Ott, and your husband as my passengers. Daniel and Felicia should arrive separately. If our plan goes the way we hope, there will be no one else in the accounting office for about an hour.

Chapter Forty

Monday morning was hot and sunny, and everyone was ready for their adventure. The first activity on the group's agenda was for Bud to disclose her part of the plan.

Once again, the group met at the pavilion. They had agreed to meet at eight a.m.

Alice thought that she and Gerard looked a bit drab compared to Daniel and Felicia. Daniel's shirt and fashionable skinny jeans were a contrast to Felicia's lovely flowery Florida-wear dress. He was the young charming photographer and she the older, extravagantly gracious journalist. Both were wearing press credentials tucked in a clear plastic pouch hanging from a colorful lanyard. Daniel had taken Felicia's picture for her very own *Splash!* press pass.

"Your job is easy," Pearl told Daniel and Felicia. "All you have to do is meet me at the big convocation thing in the auditorium. We are getting there early enough for me to find the head of PR or one of her underlings, introduce you, and tell her that you're covering the event because you want to do a feature for your *Splash!* magazine.

"Great work on the press passes! I'm glad to see you remembered to bring the debut copy of the magazine, Daniel. It looks adequately glossy to get her attention. She'll say she's much too busy to see you today, but at least it gets you in the building, and you can always come back to do your interview another day. The crucial thing is to make sure that if something goes wrong up in accounting where Bud will be with Mr. and Mrs. Ott, we'll get ourselves up there and figure out how we can help!"

Daniel looked distinctly nervous, Alice thought, but Felicia was glowing with excitement.

"Now, let's see what Bud has in mind for you two," Pearl said, looking at her friend with only a hint of concern in her smile.

Alice was glad that Bud pulled down her mask when she began to speak, otherwise she would never have been able to hear the woman's soft whispery voice. The rest of them were fully masked, and she and Gerard were double masked to be as careful as possible.

Everyone moved in a little closer as Bud began to describe her strategy for the morning.

"When we first get there, I will leave you in the lobby so you'll be part of the crowd heading for the auditorium. But in fact, you won't go in.

"If anyone tries to usher you into the auditorium, you say that you're waiting for me, and that you so excited for this exciting chance to hear the governor! Tell them I'll be coming any minute to join you. If anyone tells you the event isn't open to the public, you just act like a confused little old lady, Mrs. Ott, and tell them you're hoping Mr. Ott will become a resident of Serenity Place, and you came to see what the governor might have to say. No one will want to miss getting in their seat before the event begins, so they won't waste much time on you.

"Everyone on the entire staff is required to attend the gathering," she said, "so even though I'll be upstairs in accounting, I'll tell anyone who asks that I need a little extra time in the bathroom when everyone else heads downstairs. After Pearl introduces Daniel and Felicia to someone from PR, she'll find you outside the auditorium and she'll get you into the elevator and you'll come to the tenth floor.

"I'll meet you at the elevator on the tenth floor and bring you into the Accounting Department, which should be completely empty. We'll begin immediately to look over the documents I'll pull up for you. You can take pictures with your phone of whatever you think you can use."

"Are you sure no one will be around?" Alice asked. "Couldn't someone decide to skip the event with the governor in order to catch up on their work, and then surprise us?"

"Very unlikely!" Bud said. "It's a corporate command performance. But of course we can't be sure of anything. I'm counting on myself to be good at diversion, should we have unexpected company. I will know anyone who might come back into our department offices, so my plan is to do something dramatic, using my illness as the distraction. Something will come to me, I'm sure, if we have to deal with a surprise."

"Let's just believe everything will go as we hope," Pearl said. "We are doing this for a good cause so God is on our side! We're all smart people. We'll make it work!"

"OK," Daniel said, "but what about getting the interview for the article, and getting some pictures too? Seems like a shame to waste time since we're going to be over there."

Pearl shook her head. "They're going to be too busy to do an impromptu interview, but you can get some shots of the governor praising the CEO. That should be a winning moment once the covers get pulled off the big scam, which is the real story, right?"

Daniel looked uncomfortable. "This is such a long shot," he said, "and if things get crazy upstairs because someone blows the whistle on you, I can't really see what Felicia and I could do to help you out."

He was looking very unhappy with the plan for the day. Alice feared he might take himself out of the action entirely.

"Oh Daniel, don't worry! We could be helpful by creating our own set of distractions, should things go wrong," Felicia said, with growing enthusiasm. "It will make the magazine feature even more exciting, and give it more depth. Let's just go with the flow! I can't wait for it all to begin!"

Daniel suppressed a groan, and Alice imagined that Charles might get quite the earful whenever he and Daniel got together after this was over.

Alice wondered as they drove toward the TouchStone building if she could get Gerard to take the photos of the documents. He was so much better than she was with the phone camera. Even if he had to continue to pretend he had dementia, she wondered if maybe the part of the brain that knew how to take pictures might last a little longer than, for example, remembering how to speak English.

She tried to think how to discuss this with him in French so as not to tip off Bud. But she was missing crucial vocabulary words. She told herself not to worry so much about keeping Bud in the dark about Gerard's fake dementia.

"My husband is a very good photographer," she said to Bud. "Maybe he will be able to help with that part of our mission. Do you have any idea how many documents we'll be looking at, or end up needing?"

"Well, it depends," Bud said. "If I can find what we want quickly, then you can help me figure out what's most useful."

"What will you say if another employee comes in?' Alice asked.

"It depends on who it is,'" Bud said. "Most anyone I work with will be primarily concerned about how I'm feeling. They know I'm not coming in regularly anymore because of my illness, and some of them even know that I'm going to die soon. I think they'll be surprised to see me up here, and of course they'll be curious that you're here with me.

"I'll tell them that you're my auntie – I came up with that last night," she said with a smug little grin. "I'll say I wanted to show you the price range and some of the various packages you could choose for my poor uncle. I'll say we're up here because the crowd downstairs was just too much for you, and for me too, even though we had so longed to hear the governor's speech! So we came up here to wait for the other people we came with, and I seized the opportunity to help you look over the cost packages, and so on."

Alice nodded. "Will we have to stop if we're interrupted?"

"It will depend on how intrusive they are, whoever it is. If it's my supervisor, I'll have to figure out something a little bit more complicated. I shouldn't really be showing you anything on my work computer, and she's a stickler about stuff like that. Even with all my seniority, she has never ever treated me like I'm her equal."

"What's her name, so I know who we're dealing with?" Alice asked.

She was starting to get nervous as they talked. This company had made a serious effort to hide some questionable financial transactions. Showing someone potentially sensitive files wasn't something Bud's supervisor would take lightly.

"It's Mari, short for Maribel. She's not likely to miss a moment of fawning over the top brass and the governor, but she might come back upstairs to get something, I suppose. Anyhow, if things are getting tense, I'm all set to buzz Pearl on speed dial. She and Felicia and Daniel will come upstairs immediately and help create whatever diversion we need. Don't worry, we're getting what we came to get, come hell or high water!

"The big thing is we have to do this fast! We don't have more than an hour, probably, before the other employees start to return. So we'll do the biggest stuff first, like the other half of the grant account and the checks to the so-called 'research' company. I also want to see if we can find records of how much money the two nursing homes actually received each month for PPE equipment and for overtime. That's going to be more time-consuming, but I'd love to at least get documents from the first month or two when they started their miserly pay-outs."

Alice was impressed by how capable Bud was, sick as she seemed to be. Again, she wondered about the brain's capacity to function in certain ways even when the body and other parts of the brain seem to be dimming. Bud was fast becoming her favorite local hero. There had been many over her long life.

When they arrived at the building, even though they were a full thirty minutes early for the event, there was a long line of traffic waiting to turn into the parking garage.

"Oh fiddlesticks!" Bud said. "I forgot how long it takes to get into the garage when there's something special going on! Just take us around the block and see what you can find for parking. I don't want to park too far from the building or I'll never make it. My stamina isn't great."

Alice smiled brightly and fished in her purse to pull out her handicap pass. "You can put this on your rearview mirror and use a handicap spot," she told Pearl.

"Hallelujah!" Pearl exclaimed, and pulled into a spot so close to the front door of the building that Alice wondered if Felicia might be right about the validity of divine intervention.

"My friend Felicia would say it's a God thing that we got a parking space so close to the building," Alice confided.

"'*Ahh, ma chèrie*, this is not *le Dieu* but it is the brain! The brain, it is *très* smart!" Gerard said suddenly.

Alice glanced at Gerard in alarm. He was supposed to keep up his pretense of dementia until they had gathered all the information they needed about TouchStone. How could he forget at a critical time like this? She thought fast.

"Gerard has moments like this that catch me by surprise when he remembers some English. I know I should speak French more of the time so he doesn't forget that too," Alice said nervously, "but it's getting harder and harder for me to remember my French. I don't know what we'll do if we get to the point where we can't use either language to communicate!"

Bud shrugged."You'll figure it out," she said, clearly intent on directing them into the building now that they were reaching the door. A swarm of well-dressed people were entering the building at a surprising rate of speed. Several people stepped aside to allow her and Gerard to go in before them, smiling benignly at them.

Alice realized that she and Gerard were considerably older than most of the people headed for the event. It was good to be reminded of how very harmless the two of them probably looked to young people. This should work to their advantage if they were surprised in the midst of their espionage efforts.

When they got into the lobby, Pearl went to find Daniel and Felicia. There was such a crowd that Alice could hear nothing that Bud was saying. She took Gerard's hand protectively and followed Bud over to the far side of the lobby.

Bud waved a quick goodbye and got into the elevator which, Alice had learned, could only be activated by an employee pass. She and Gerard stood docilely, waiting for Pearl to appear and get them into the elevator once Bud had signaled that the coast was clear.

For a moment, Alice wondered if this was Charles who was now greeting her. She had only met him a few times, and she was quite sure that he had decided not to participate in this event for fear of losing his job. And yet this handsome man in front of her had to be Charles.

"Good morning, Mrs. Ott!" His dazzling smile confirmed that she indeed was standing there with Charles.

"Well good morning to you too! This is quite a crowd, isn't it?"

Charles nodded. "I decided I had to be here," he said, "and now I'm going to go in and get a seat. I want to be down near the front. Wish me luck!"

Watching Charles push his way through the crowd, Alice was very curious about what was going to happen. From what she knew of him, Charles was brave and committed, but he was the kind of person who preferred not to be in the limelight. Now he wanted to be down in the front of the auditorium. This was very interesting!

She hadn't caught sight of Daniel and Felicia yet, and she wondered where they were seated. She assumed that the governor had not yet arrived since there were no obvious security people hovering around the lobby. Then a somewhat chilling question popped into her mind: Would it be guards working for TouchStone or city police who would be most likely to come for her, Gerard and Bud if they got into trouble on the tenth floor?

She couldn't imagine that any normal law enforcement or security types would want to arrest two very elderly people and a deathly ill woman for snooping in the Accounting Department. She hoped that, at most, they would face minor trespassing charges.

But this was no small thing they were about to do. The Touch-Stone executives might want the charges to be more serious once it was determined what Bud and her accomplices were doing.

"There you are!" Pearl said, appearing out of the crowd. "I haven't gotten the go ahead yet from Bud. The coast must not be clear. But I managed to get three good seats on the side aisle in the auditorium, so Daniel, Felicia and I can all slip out and come rescue you if you get a bad surprise up there!

"And you're sure Bud will buzz you?" Alice asked. She wasn't sure if she could feel completely confident in these two women who might never have broken a law in their lives. Accountants seemed likely to be the epitome of rule-following people.

"You know, I really believe she will call for help," Pearl said, "but we've never engaged in anything even approaching illegal behavior before today, not either one of us. So we're pretty green at this. I'm just going to hope that no one will pay any attention to us, and that we'll all be in and out of here within the hour."

"Well, let's look forward to celebrating then!" Alice said, not wanting to dampen anyone's enthusiasm.

Gerard leaned over to whisper in Alice's ear that he needed the men's room. "Do you think we have time to use the restroom down here?" Alice asked Pearl.

Pearl frowned and shook her head. "Better to wait until you're upstairs," she said. "There'll be a line down here with a crowd like this."

"Even the Men's Room?" Alice asked.

"Well, maybe. But I'd like to get back to my seat after I get you delivered to Bud," Pearl said. "Can he wait a few more minutes?"

Just as Alice was wondering if she should be making a decision like this for Gerard, there was a rustling in the crowd as the governor's entourage entered the lobby. Several serious-faced men with very short hair and tight suit jackets with muscles bulging, moved through the crowd with the governor right behind, smiling and waving greetings.

He came right past Alice and Gerard and stopped to beam at them. He bent over to take Alice's hand and smiled broadly.

"I'm so glad to see you out here, dear! We're going to keep taking real good care of you, hear?! And this must be your handsome husband! You sure do have a beautiful head of hair, Grandad," he said admiringly. "You must have all the ladies chasing you, am I right!"

He winked obscenely at Gerard, who stared back at him disapprovingly.

"We're running a little late, sir," the young woman at his side told him.

"She's the boss!" the governor said, and the group moved on into the auditorium.

"Oh good, she's calling now!" Pearl said, glancing down at her phone. "I think I won't ride up with you since they're likely to get started with the program right away."

As the elevator rose quickly up toward the tenth floor, Alice reached up to stroke Gerard's cheek. "You have made a great impression on the governor! And I guess I'd better get ready to fend off all the ladies who are going to chase you around the nursing home!"

Gerard squeezed her hand. "You are the only lady I chase," he said, with a little wink.

Bud was waiting as the elevator doors opened on the tenth floor. "All clear!" she said. "I've peeked into every office in the department to make sure no one's lingering. I even checked the restrooms. Here we go!"

After she showed Gerard where the Men's Room was, she led Alice into her office.

"They have a system so that you have to enter a password that only works in the building. This works to protect anything they want to keep secret. The password only works on the computers that have been cleared for use, but luckily I've been here so long that I'm cleared for just about anything. So let's dig in, and you can get as many pics as you want."

They were startled as Gerard slipped back into the room. He smiled calmly. "*La toilettes sont très grandes!*" he said.

"Is he saying that the toilet is grand?" Bud asked. "Like it's fancy or something?"

"That could be what he means," Alice said vaguely. She was so anxious to get their mission underway that she felt as if she couldn't wait another second.

Bud opened her computer, and clicked numerous times before she summoned Alice to sit next to her. "Here's exhibit A!" she said, smiling so cheerfully that Alice could see for an instant what she had looked like before she became so ill.

While Alice and Bud zoomed through a series of documents, Gerard was wandering around the clusters of offices. He found his way into the largest office, which had a glass wall that allowed the occupant to view all the other work spaces.

When Bud happened to look up and noticed where he was, she gasped audibly. "Oh no! No one goes into Mari's office unless you're summoned to appear before her. Do you think he understands not to touch stuff in there?" she asked Alice.

It was all she could do to take her eyes away from the screen, but Alice finally looked up to see what Bud was so worried about. "I think he'll be careful," she said vaguely, then focused on the computer.

"Maybe you could tell him not to touch anything?" Bud said, her voice tight with anxiety. "Maribel once got someone fired because they went in there and looked through a pile of papers in her Inbox, trying to find something they were sure they'd sent her. They did it while she had gone to speak to someone in another office, or maybe she had gone to the restroom, I don't know. But she came back into the main office area here and let out a yell that could have caused birds to fall out of the sky, it was so loud. The person was fired immediately and tried to contest it. They lost," she concluded."

"Gerard, my dear, please come. I need your help!" Alice called.

She actually was ready for him to come and start taking pictures with her phone now that she was viewing what they needed to copy.

"He understood you!" Bud said excitedly. "You were speaking English, and he understood!"

"Oh I think he can still understand quite a bit of English," Alice said, nervously winging it. "He just can't speak in English any more. The words don't seem to come to him. But he can still respond, thank goodness!"

Gerard had obviously found something he wasn't quite ready to leave behind. He looked at Alice, and pointed to something, then gestured for her to come into the office.

Alice was very frustrated. She was trying so hard to keep scanning all the budget items that they needed to prove the deception, and she knew time was short. "I need to keep working here," she called to him. "Bring me whatever it is you want to show me, all right?"

A moment later, Gerard was standing just outside the office, a triumphant grin stretching his mouth so that his mustache moved like a live creature across his face. "*Voilà!*" he said.

He was holding up the draft of a banner. The text announced the *Gannet Research Institute, Great Falls, Quebec*. Clearly an artist had been given the task of creating the images. The logo was for an Institute that seemed to be related to bird research. Why was Gerard so gleeful? Alice wanted to know, but there was no time for little side trips.

It was a strange image, she thought, looking more carefully. It featured a long blocky building instead of waterfalls or birds. Anyhow, this was simply the wrong time for him to be exploring, and she needed him to stay out of the dreaded Mari's office.

He looked at her, still excited as a child finding a treasured object in a random backyard digging project.

"This Gannet Institute, this is the research institute one they pretend, *oui*?" he called to Bud, who continued to insist that he vacate the forbidden office.

Bud stared at him, drop-jawed with surprise. "He's speaking English!" she said to Alice.

"The place, it is not the place you go to find an Institute!" Gerard said, stroking his mustache happily. "The Great Falls of Quebec, it is a *grande* waterfall in *le parc* in the *cite du Quebec!*" I think there is no city of Great Falls, Quebec, not anywhere."

He pointed to the drawing that was featured on the banner. "This is the same image for *la researche* building at Fort Detrick, in Maryland where I work for many years!" he said. "The artist, he make the logo for your institute from the places and the images he, ah, he take from something real, *oui*? But this is not a real town and not the correct image for this institute. It is a photo of *la bibliotheque*, the library and laboratory *chez* Fort Detrick, Maryland!!"

"Well, you are right about that!" Bud said. "No wonder I googled it every way I could and I couldn't find it. But it looks like they made it up and then Maribel had someone designing this banner so it could be displayed for events like the governor's visit!

"Uh oh!" she added. "I wonder if Mari was planning to bring the governor up here after his speech to see the banner and hear more about the research that the grant seems to be funding?"

"It's still less than half an hour since they all went into the auditorium," Alice said. "Let's keep going."

Gerard agreed to help with the photos, and they developed a relatively speedy process for gathering the many pictures of the withdrawals that kept being paid out to the Gannet Research Institute of Great Falls, Quebec.

"Don't you think we should get some of the budget going from the money in the grant account to document how little has been spent to cover PPE and overtime for the nursing homes?" Alice said. "That's the story I think we want to focus on even more than the phony research institute."

Bud switched them to another account, and more photos were quickly documented by Alice's phone. "You know that finding that banner in Mari's office is a big deal!" she said. "It means Mari's in on this swindle, helping to divert money to a research institute that possibly doesn't even exist. Gerard, could you take a picture of that?"

"Shouldn't you be the one to do that?' Alice asked. "What if she comes back? You could make up something about why you were in there, but we'd never be able to explain Gerard."

"But if he puts the banner on the floor, he's the tallest one. He can get a better pic than I can," Bud said.

"I go now and I take the photo rapidement!" Gerard said, glad for the chance to stretch his legs.

He moved as quickly as he could, but there was no way he could go at the speed that would satisfy Alice. "Hurry, Gerard!" she called to him. Her watch was beeping, telling her that the agreed upon window of time was up. Forty-five minutes had to be their limit. Any additional time became dangerous. They had agreed on this.

She buzzed Felicia, who texted back immediately. "Questions now. Better get moving!"

Suddenly Bud's phone buzzed. "It's Pearl!' she said. "They must be on their way. We've got to get out of here! Why don't you two go to the elevator and press the button. I'll close down here, and be with you by the time it gets up here. With everyone riding the elevators back up to their offices, it could take some time. With a little luck, we'll be just standing and waiting to go back down in the elevator if Mari or some other employee shows up."

Alice and Gerard walked as quickly as they could to the bank of elevators and pressed the Down button. They could see that lights for the Up arrows were on for all eight of the elevators.

Just as Alice started to think she might hyperventilate, Bud appeared and the elevator nearest them dinged as it stopped on their floor. At least ten people got out and flowed around them.

"Bud, I'm so glad to see you!" said a heavily-perfumed woman, resplendent in a tight lavender dress, her eyelashes and make-up also shimmering. "But why are you only now going downstairs? Did you miss the governor's speech?"

"Oh Mari, I am so sad!" Bud said, her voice starting to shake. "I got myself here, and I was all ready but I brought my special guests up to just peek at where I work. They're so proud of me! And then I had a really bad attack, so I went into the bathroom, and I just couldn't get myself out in time. And it was extra sad because I had brought my guests - my auntie and her husband all the way over from Ocala - because they were so excited to hear the governor talk. My Auntie Alice, she wants my Uncle Gerard to consider Serenity Place. He could get such good care there, couldn't you Uncle Gerard? And they were both so excited and then I ruined it all! We just couldn't get down there again, I was too weak and …"

Bud stopped talking and suddenly dropped backwards so that Gerard was forced to catch her in his arms. "I need to lie down," she whimpered, covering her face and beginning to sob loudly.

Maribel looked horrified. Others who had gotten off the elevator were watching the scene unfold in stunned silence. But the last three people who exited on Floor Ten, moved to help the stricken woman.

Pearl stepped forward and signaled to Daniel to help Gerard carry Bud to a loveseat that was conveniently positioned at the end of the elevator hallway. "We've got this," she said, waving Maribel and the onlookers away.

The circle around Bud dwindled to just a few. Maribel seemed to feel the need to oversee whatever happened on her watch. "Do we need to call an ambulance?" she asked Alice, who at that point seemed to be the closest to next of kin. Alice shrugged. She had no way to know if this was part of Bud's plan to create a distraction, or if she was in serious medical trouble.

Pearl was kneeling next to Bud. "What do you think, pal?" she asked. Bud seemed barely conscious. "Want to go over to the hospital so they can help if we need emergency intervention?" she continued. "Or should we call your own doctor to see what she thinks?"

Bud opened her eyes for a moment and stared at Pearl. Then she whispered something that Alice couldn't hear.

"I'm ready to call in whatever emergency services we can get in here," Maribel said, and pulled out her cell phone.

"No," Bud gasped. She struggled to keep her eyes open. "Pearl..can..take..me..to..hospital."

"OK, then!" Pearl said firmly. "Daniel, if you'd be so kind to help me get her downstairs and to my car, I'd be so grateful. Are you comfortable with that? I don't want to ask too much, but it would be a help."

Daniel nodded, and stepped forward. "Ma'am," he said, "I'd like to help get you on your feet. Do you think you can do that with me? Pearl's going to help me get you sitting up, then we'll take it from there."

"Is there a wheelchair anywhere in the building for emergencies like this?" Alice asked. It was a healthcare corporation, after all.

Maribel looked at her as if she'd requested a parachute. "Why would you think we'd have a wheelchair?" she asked irritably. "This is not a nursing facility!"

"We do have a small gym and lots of healthy snack and non-sugar beverage machines in the basement," Pearl said helpfully. "Employees are encouraged by TouchStone to stay healthy."

"May I quote you?" Felicia asked, tapping away on her phone as she asked.

With help from both Pearl and Daniel, Bud was finally able to stand. "If I keep my arm around your waist and Pearl supports you on the other side, do you think you can walk to the elevator?" Daniel asked.

Alice was impressed with his bedside manner. He must have had some care-taking experiences in his journey.

Bud nodded, and the threesome moved very slowly back to the elevator.

"You sure you can do this?" Daniel asked Bud while they waited for the elevator to arrive at their floor. "There are still going to be quite a few people down in the lobby. Once we get down there, I'll stay with you, and so will Felicia and these two, while Pearl goes to get her car."

"Yes." Bud said, and tried to smile. "Onward!"

Chapter Forty-one

Although it was slightly chaotic when they reached the lobby, the transportation problems were eventually solved.

Bud remained conscious but barely able to speak, so a trip to the hospital was actually necessary. She was adamant that she wanted nothing to do with an ambulance, so they finally negotiated that Charles would come and help Pearl get Bud to the hospital if Daniel was able to reach him.

In less than five minutes, Charles appeared. Not only was he willing to be their medical angel, but he switched cars with Daniel so Daniel could give Felicia, Alice and Gerard a ride back to Pelican Cove.

"We'll just hang out there on your nice screen porch, and wait for Charles and Pearl to get back, and maybe Bud too," Daniel said, confidently maneuvering Charles' big car into the busy traffic. "Felicia, you and I can get to work right away on what we've got for the magazine."

Alice leaned her head back against the back seat and closed her eyes. She didn't think it was fair to tell the story of what they had accomplished earlier without Bud, the star of the show, taking part in the victorious tale. Her exhaustion was more powerful than her desire to replay the infiltration operation. She wanted everyone present before they recounted the thrill of getting access to the sensitive financial records and uncovering the fraudulent Gannet Research Institute of Great Falls, Quebec!

Since it was getting toward lunch time, they stopped at Gary's Meats, a little market and sandwich shop in the small strip mall at the entrance to Pelican Cove. Alice had been surprised that the small strip housed the meat market, a childcare center with an outdoor playground, an Elks Lodge, a veterinary practice, an herbal healing store, a cell phone repair place, a golf cart business, and a gun shop.

They decided to get extra sandwiches for when everyone returned from the hospital, and Kori and the Warrens joined them.

Everyone could finally be together to hear about their adventure.

Felicia initially opposed patronizing a business with the name Gary's Meats. Her vegetarian sensibilities were offended. But she was pleasantly surprised by the variety of cheese and bread choices, and fresh Florida farm tomatoes.

"I will make you the best grilled cheese sandwich you've ever had!" Alice promised her. "All you have to do is order the cheese and bread of your choice, and I'll grill it for you when we're ready to eat. Maybe you could at least give us a sneak preview of how the governor's event was, and how the PR person responded to the magazine article idea," she suggested to Felicia while they waited in the car for the take-out sandwiches.

"Something quite unexpected happened," Daniel said. "It could be that Charles will end up being the cover boy for the winter issue of *Splash!* We'll see what happens next, of course, but he really stole the show from the governor!"

Felicia literally wiggled with pleasure. "Charles surprised Daniel and me both when he showed up, and we were even more surprised when he stood up in the aisle to ask the governor a question. The questions preceding his were really just general, neutral topics. Of course the governor gave one of those "we here in Florida are doing the best job ever!" kind of speeches.

"The lady who went right before Charles had just said what wonderful care her mother was getting at Serenity Place, and a guy before her talked about how great they were at Sunset Villages, keeping the residents and the staff healthy, and how wonderful the governor was to have won the big grant for Florida's nursing homes, blah, blah, blah!"

"Wait!" Alice said. "It's just hitting me. Charles spoke? I was sure he wanted no part of what we were doing today because he was afraid of losing his job. Of course I supported his choice to protect his job, and leave this risky stuff to the rest of us."

"Yes!" Felicia said. "Exactly! But you can't imagine what a shock it was to everyone packed into that big fancy auditorium when Charles stood up and started talking about how a granddaughter's love for her grandmother had moved him, and made him feel like he wasn't doing enough to protect the rights of every elder in the care facilities who was vulnerable. Then he told the audience his name and what his job was at Sunset Villages, and how upset he had been over the past four or five months because they kept being short on PPE. And he talked about the employees who put the welfare of the residents ahead of their own, and worked overtime, hours of overtime, and they still hadn't been paid!"

"I was so proud of him!" Daniel said. "I couldn't believe he had come to the event after all. Then when he nailed TouchStone for failing to provide adequate PPE or pay their workers for overtime, I jumped up and walked up the aisle as close as I could get. I just kept snapping picture after picture of him! He was glorious!"

Alice was thrilled to hear about Charles' act of bravery. At the same time, she was very worried for him. Not only did she expect that he would lose his job, but whoever was attacking the other whistle-blowing employees might be looking for Charles right this minute to try to silence him!

"Is anyone besides me worried for his safety? What if someone followed him and Pearl and Bud to the hospital? Someone could be stalking him, waiting for him in the parking garage or even within the corridors of the hospital. Shouldn't we call him and tell him not to go off alone anywhere out of sight of hospital security staff?"

"No worries about that," Daniel announced. "There was plenty of media there... newspapers, local radio guys and all three Orlando TV stations plus Spectrum's *News 13* crew. This is going to be all over the news up and down the state, on all their social media as they all try to beat each other with the story. It's out there right now! Here, look at the Facebook and Twitter feeds from the different media."

Felicia's eyes grew wide with excitement over the whole ordeal.

"Oh Alice! There were so many different media there! In fact, I might even get quoted in one of the local papers."

Daniel hadn't known about Felicia talking to other media. He was too busy doing his job photographing it all.

Felicia noticed his disapproving frown. "It's all good. I gave us a plug, but the only way they'll use it is if they can't get a comment from anyone else."

Alice jumped right in, almost dismissing Felicia's news. "This is perfect! Even if we're not the first to break the story, the sooner the news gets out about Charles' allegations, the sooner he'll be protected. TouchStone doesn't want this kind of publicity, and it would be a much bigger story if he gets roughed up or turns up dead!

"Let's go in and pick up our sandwiches and get back to the house to wait for word on Bud."

The four of them became increasingly restless as they waited to hear from the hospital. "Didn't Bud say that she was nearing the end?" Felicia asked Alice.

Alice nodded. Today could well be another giant step toward Bud's imminent death. It certainly had been stressful for all of them, and undoubtedly had taken a major toll on Bud. She was trying to think positive thoughts, even without Felicia prompting her.

Maybe Bud was already feeling better. Maybe, as they waited for a doctor, Bud was regaling them with her own account of the successful collection of revealing documents.

The fact that neither Pearl or Bud herself had called or texted made her feel pessimistic. If Bud was relatively stable, then surely one of the others would have slipped out to give them an update. Her phone buzzed, and her pulse began to race. She was disappointed to see that the caller ID was unknown to her, but she decided to answer.

"Hi Alice, it's Kori. I'm over here with Gram and she's fine. She's sleeping off the excitement of yesterday, I guess. Just wondered how you guys are doing. I've been getting nervous, not hearing from anyone. I couldn't even reach Charles, and he was supposed to come over here late this morning to get his stuff arranged. He hasn't called either. I'm getting kind of worried."

"Kori, I'm so glad to hear from you!" Alice said. "You know how we split up into two teams for the action this morning? There's quite a lot to tell you, but right now both of the neighbors, Pearl and Bud, are at the hospital, and Charles is with them. They're there because at the end of our reconnaissance mission at Touch-Stone, Bud had a medical emergency. So Pearl and Charles went with her to the hospital.

"Gerard and I and Felicia and Daniel are all safely back here, and we're about to eat lunch. We got enough sandwiches to feed an army, but we haven't heard a word from the three at the hospital. We want very much to include you in our post-event lunch. Maybe we should just move ourselves over to your front patio so you can hear your Gram if she calls out to you? It's easy enough for us to do it that way. We can watch for the other three to arrive from there."

Alice was glad when Kori agreed to the plan. As they gathered up the food, she saw Kori out on her patio, arranging chairs to seat them all.

They had started eating when Alice's phone buzzed again. "Alice, this is Charles. We're leaving the hospital with Bud, and we should be over at your place soon."

"Wonderful!" Alice said. "Don't stop for food. We've got plenty here, and I have a big pitcher of iced tea. And by the way, we're outside Kori's place so she can hear if her Gram calls for her.

"Charles, Daniel and Felicia told us all about what you did at the event this morning, so Kori's the only one who hasn't heard about it. But when you get here, you get to re-tell it your own way. May I say that you're up for Hero of the Century in this crowd!"

Just as Alice clicked off the phone, Sue pulled in on her bicycle. She looked over the group, and frowned.

"What happened to Pearl and Bud? I thought they were with you for your big scoop over at TouchStone. Did you already drop them off? Not like Pearl to miss a social gathering. Are they OK? Must have been a big push for Bud, given how sick she's been. But I would've expected her to be hanging out with you, celebrating whatever it was that you were intending to do. At least you're not locked up in the county jail!"

Alice smiled. It was a good thing there was not enough evidence to convict any of them since their exploits already seemed to be known beyond their immediate circle.

"Bud and Pearl are on their way, after a brief visit to the hospital, but don't worry. Bud seems to be OK."

"So did you get everything done that you hoped?" Sue asked.

"That, and then some," Alice said. "Would you care to join us for lunch? Pearl and Bud and Kori's friend Charles will be here any minute and then you can hear all about our day!"

Chapter Forty-two

"Hey Charles!" Kori called out as she came in the next morning with the local daily paper. "You're an overnight sensation, little brother! You're the headline in *The News-Journal*! You calling out the corporation in front of the governor and all the big shots? It's the top story! There's a great photo of you!"

Charles groaned, but put down his coffee so he could look at the newspaper Kori was waving around. "Good thing you quit your job in front of the governor and that big crowd, because today Touch-Stone would be firing your ass!"

Kori dropped down onto the love seat so they could read the story together. "Woo-hoo! Go Felicia!" Kori crowed, a few minutes into the article. "Felicia Wetherington, a journalist for *Splash!* magazine, says that she was shocked to learn that the TouchStone Corporation had diverted funds from the recent $2 million federal COVID relief grant. Taking the money away from its intended purpose has left the company's nursing homes without essential PPE supplies and hundreds of hours of unpaid overtime salaries," Kori read aloud.

Charles stopped reading over Kori's shoulder to stretch and take a sip of his freshly ground morning wake-up brew.

"I'm kind of surprised about Felicia giving a statement to *The Daytona Beach News-Journal*," he said. "I thought this was going to be an exclusive story so *Splash!* was going to get all the glory."

"I can see why she did it," Kori said. "You had already spilled the beans about the corporation doing all this, so you were the big news story for the local papers. She's there, watching the *News-Journal* guy trying to get more of the story from you, and you're brushing him off. So she probably wanted to get the *Splash!* name in the reader's minds. This way, people will be watching for the exclusive story as soon as it hits the stands so they can get the whole scoop."

"I guess so," Charles said. "I just hope Daniel feels OK about it and can get this next issue out soon. Felicia has written a terrific story, and Daniel took some powerful pictures. I love the ones he got of you with your Gram, by the way! But he and his business manager have to get all their ducks in a row ASAP and get the issue done, complete with advertisements, and then send it to the printer. I told him I've got plenty of free time right now, so he can count on me to help with phone calls or errands or whatever."

Two days later, it was looking like he wasn't going to have that leisure time after all.

Charles had been invited for an interview with the CEO of TouchStone's biggest competitor, Ascension Health. And he'd already gotten through a preliminary series of interviews.

Daniel was looking over Charles' wardrobe, scanning for the right look, professional but not too trendy. The skinny jeans were ruled out. He was trying to persuade Charles to get a new pair of shoes.

"You need to look more corporate," Daniel said. "They want to offer you a job that's all about oversight, about big new visions for new compassionate and transparent healthcare. This is in a different ballpark from your management job for TouchStone.

"These guys like it that you're this new poster boy for ethical practices in healthcare, so they want you to say yes to their job offer. But they'll want you to be the face of reassurance and stability for their rich clients who are considering putting their parents into the Ascension nursing homes. Your New Balance trainers just won't cut it!"

"Do you think I'd like a job like what you're describing?" Charles asked. "I feel like I'm kind of in a trance or something. The salary they've already mentioned in the Zoom interviews yesterday is more than twice what I've been making. But I like the patient contact I have now. I don't know if I can actually do something so different."

Daniel thought for a moment. "Well, you can give it a try, and then if you hate it, you can find another job like the one you've just left. Think of it this way: Alice Ott and her activist pals must have times they don't really enjoy everything they're doing, at least that's what I imagine. But they know they're doing something worth doing. They're making a difference. That's what you'll be doing,

Charles. It's your time to be a hero, man!"

Charles laughed. "I don't know about the ladies," he said, "but Monsieur Gerard loves what he's doing! He was happy as a pig in mud, tracking down that fake institute! He loves doing investigative research the way some people love to buy antiques! When he determined that the Gannet Research Institute of Great Falls, Quebec was a total scam, he got all excited about finding and exposing other fake research so-called institutes. You've given him a whole new boost, asking him to do that short piece for *Splash*!"

"Speaking of Gerard," Daniel said, "we're supposed to go over to their backyard in about twenty minutes to get the update on the documents Bud and Alice and Gerard accessed. Then Felicia can turn it into Part Two of the lead article and we can go to the printers. You ready to take a break before we go shoe shopping?"

The gathering of the TouchStone 7, plus Kori and Nancy Warren, was arranged once again in the small yard behind Alice's temporary home. The nine of them were grouped to observe social distancing, but also trying to ensure that everyone could hear what was being said.

Pearl was the first to speak. "I've got big news," she said. "I've gotten all my paperwork in and approved, and I begin my life as a retired person next Monday! So I hope that fits with the magazine schedule, Daniel? I loved being interviewed and I love going public as a whistleblower, but I just want to make sure I've got my retirement benefits locked in first.

"I think we're on schedule to hit the newsstand next Wednesday," Daniel said, "so hopefully you'll be fine!"

"Congratulations to you, Daniel and Felicia!" Nancy Warren said, "and to you, Charles, for your incredible bravery! This wouldn't be the same if you hadn't had the courage to call out the corporation in front of the governor the way you did. This story is making national headlines, and when *Splash*! comes out, there will be more news coverage in response, I'm sure!"

"And, Pearl, I want to congratulate you and Bud for your amazing courage!" Kori added. "I didn't even know you ten days ago, and now I feel like we're all part of a family and two of my aunties have just turned into super women!"

Pearl and Bud beamed proudly. "And here's to Mrs. Ott and Mr.

Ott for being totally great at doing their sleuthing under pressure, and for also being incredibly brave!" Bud said.

"Speaking of magic powers," Charles said, "can you believe all that our Neighborhood Protectors are doing? Kori and I feel almost over-protected, but I am also very grateful to them. What can we do to thank them?"

Sue had organized the neighbors with help from Chuck and his wife Susan. A group of trustworthy neighbors were committed to driving around the neighborhood and keeping watch over the endangered household.

The Protectors, as they called themselves, were scheduled for two-hour shifts, 24/7.

There were four houses to protect: Pearl and Bud lived near each other on Kingfisher Lane, and the other two households were close together on Pelican Drive.

There wasn't much the Protectors had to do except hang out in their cars and listen to the radio, read, play games on their cell phones or call friends or congressional representatives. The big part was not falling asleep, and remembering to keep watch while engaging in this variety of entertainments.

Chuck, his wife Susan, and their beloved dog Zoey were dedicated supervisors of the Protector team. Under their giant live oak tree where the baby owls would eventually emerge from their nest, the Protectors had held a quick meeting and declared they were in for as many days as it took until all four households felt safe enough to suspend the drive-by. They had enlisted a few regular dog walkers to help with the surveillance.

Elizabeth was their star Protector on Kingfisher Lane. Every time she walked Dusty the Dog and Buddy the Cat, she glowed with an energy that no one had seen since she began struggling with brain fog a few years earlier. And Alice's new next door neighbor Betty was on watch all day and into the evening, watching over all of the neighborhood she could see from her front window.

"It's an honor to watch over you after you've risked your jobs and all," Chuck told the group when they gathered to hear about the plan.

"You've even risked your lives because you believed in doing the right thing," Susan added, as Zoey wagged her tail energetically.

If anyone approached the at-risk homes, excluding bonafide delivery people with visibly labeled trucks and uniforms, the Protectors would immediately contact the person who might be at risk and determine if the visitor was known to them. If that person didn't respond, the Protector would continue to keep watch until the suspect was no longer in the neighborhood.

"They're committed to looking out for us as long as we think there's reason to be worried for our safety," Kori said. "I've gotten to know Sue, and she says they're all really devoted. They're mostly all retired, and as long as they rotate the eleven pm to seven a.m. shifts among themselves, no one's on for two nights in a row. She says it makes everyone feel like they're doing something meaningful."

Pearl glanced at Bud. "You want to tell everyone what's up for you?" she asked.

Bud nodded. "You all know how sick I am," she said. "I don't want to wait any longer. I intend to make a detailed record of everything we found, and go to the newspaper with it. I'll ask them to interview me and I'll tell them how the whole diversion of grant money emerged. And I'll turn this record over to the police, the F.B.I, and Channel 13. I will take full responsibility for the photos of all the documents, and if they ask, I'll just say I've been keeping track, and taking pictures. I'm going to throw my cell phone into the river right after this meeting! Then no one can retrieve anything from our little adventure.

"They may try to arrest me and charge me, but I'm ready for whatever they do. I want to die knowing I did something to make things right."

Alice was moved. She wanted Bud to do this her way. She hoped everyone involved would feel the same.

Kori's eyes filled with tears, and Charles looked stricken. Daniel bowed his head.

Felicia seemed to be more cheerful, animated by Bud's announcement.

"You are a shining light!" she said, her smile radiant. "We all honor you, and bless you. I would be delighted if you would consider calling on me for any herbal or spiritual support as you go through your passage."

She paused for a respectful moment. "You will wait a few days at least, though, won't you, so that the new *Splash!* issue is on the newsstands soon after your bombshell disclosure?"

"I'll do my best, but I'm running out of time now. Whatever happens next is not necessarily in any of our hands."

Startling them all, Sue materialized from behind the bushes that bordered the backyard. "Oops! Sorry to bother you," she said, "but Chuck has just apprehended a woman who has been sitting in her car outside your house, Alice, for at least thirty minutes. She finally has told us her name, but she won't say anything else."

"And what is her name?" Alice asked, imagining all kinds of possibilities.

"She says her name is Bernice," Sue said, "and she's not leaving until she speaks to you."

Chapter Forty-three

Everything seemed to accelerate from the moment Bud announced her plan to go public.

Nancy Warren had reminded everyone that at this point, Jake should be involved since there was nothing illegal planned.

Now, in Jake's large conference room, Kori, Charles, Pearl, Bud and Daniel were designated as the individuals who were all variously at risk of retaliation. If anyone had known how to find him, Mitch too might have been included in the meeting as an at-risk player.

"What about all the others who have committed themselves to being plaintiffs in the lawsuit?" Kori asked. "Will they be part of a meeting with you, Jake, once we sort out what we're doing? Will those folks still get the chance to be part of bringing TouchStone to justice?"

"Absolutely!" Jake said. "We'll go over the list to see if those I still am representing are up to date, and try to come to some decisions about whether or not to add to the list. There probably will be a number of folks who want to jump on board now that the situation has become so public. They're welcome to join, but we'll have to decide what the cut-off date is, and that will depend on a number of legal deadlines. Is that an adequate answer, Kori?"

Kori glanced over at Charles. "What do you think?"

Charles hesitated. "I think I still have lots of questions. But I need to hear from Jake about what happens next in terms of the specific crimes we're naming and what we want to get out of the lawsuit."

"Great!" Jake said. "That's basically our agenda for this meeting." He turned to Daniel. "I'm going to begin with you, Daniel. We'll go over what you'll be covering in your magazine, and what kinds of legal risks you're willing to take. I understand that there are two other partners in *Splash!* magazine? After we wrap up the work for this morning, I'll give you a checklist to go over with them to make sure they agree on the legal risks you all are taking.

Then I can meet with the three of you before you send your new issue to the printer."

During a somewhat tedious discussion involving rights for various types of printed word products, Alice's mind wandered off to review Bernice's sudden appearance. She still couldn't quite believe that Bernice had driven all the way to Florida to visit her without any warning.

Bernice had taken them all by surprise, and it was challenging to persuade the Protectors that Bernice was really a harmless visitor.

Chuck had immediately requested a private word with Alice even before she finished her meeting. "I can see that you know the lady," he said softly, speaking into Alice's ear to make sure she could hear him. He wiped the sweat off his forehead and cleared his throat several times. "But you did seem to be caught off guard."

He lowered his voice to a stage whisper that Alice could scarcely hear. "I need to let you know the lady has a gun in her car. Two guns, in fact. One's a handgun in the glove compartment, and the other's on the floor in the back seat. Just thought you should know."

"I've known her for quite a while" Alice said. "She's not a danger to us," she assured him. "She's retired military who feels safer with a gun."

"I can keep my eye on her while you finish your meeting, if you want. We could have her come over to wait on our patio. Susan and I will just hang out with her for awhile, give her something cold to drink, whatever."

Alice realized now that everyone was looking at her as they turned from Jake's big conference table toward the little group of witnesses. "Pardon me," she said, "did someone ask me something?"

"We were just deciding whether Daniel could be excused from the rest of the meeting so he can contact his business partners to see how soon they can meet with Jake," Felicia told her. "Then Jake asked if any of you had anything else you wanted to ask Daniel, or tell him, before he left."

"Oh I am so sorry!" Alice said. "My mind wandered off for a second. Well, I can't think of anything urgent."

Gerard raised his hand to speak. "I ask you, Monsieur Daniel, do you need references for the biological statements of fact you make in the magazine?" he asked. "I do not know if you talk of the COVID, but I have many references from scientific journals that I give you if you have need of these references?"

Daniel smiled broadly at Gerard. "I will check with you, and ask you to look at the final draft of the article before it goes to press. You can tell me what you think we need to include to make our case even stronger, starting with scientific references. Thank you for thinking of it!"

What a relief it was to have Daniel treat Gerard with such respect, Alice noted. She was relieved that Gerard no longer had to pretend dementia and could share the inner workings of his wonderful brain.

She wondered if Charles and Daniel would continue to date each other, or whatever people called courtship these days. Daniel was a good man, she thought. Charles was, too.

"OK," Jake said briskly, "let's keep going. The next question is how we can protect you, Bud, once your story gets into the newspaper. Are you planning to resign or retire before you give your story to the press, or will you wait to see if TouchStone fires you after the fact?"

"I really don't think there's much more time left," Bud said in a thin little voice. "I really want to turn over what we have now. Then I can die quietly on my own terms. Perhaps I should write a brief letter of resignation before I give my story to the press."

She was looking very ill today, Alice thought. Maybe among the assembled group, they could find someone from the local paper to hear her story, do some fact-checking, and then publish the interview as soon as they got the word from Daniel that the timing was coordinated with *Splash*!

"Sounds good. I know that Daniel and everyone here will do all we can to let you rest."

"I could share my letter of resignation with you," Charles said, "and then, if you like, I'll type your letter for you. You just sign it and I'll make sure it gets delivered the second we get the green light from Daniel."

"Thank you, Charles," Bud said, and closed her eyes.

Jake looked worried. "Let's finish up. I've already gone over Felicia's article, and read the report of what Charles said to the governor, and gone over his letter of resignation. What we will be charging the corporation with depends on what Bud, with help from Alice and Gerard, can prove TouchStone has done with the funds diverted into the alleged research Institute. Also Bud's report will determine what can be proven regarding the lack of PPE and overtime pay.

"It seems likely that we can claim fraud and negligence, misuse of federal money, and serious endangerment of a very vulnerable population. If we could somehow find out whoever beat up Kori, then killed Rufe and threatened Mitch, we'd have additional legal charges, but I'm not sure what to do about that right now. We don't have much to go on.

"Here's another thing to consider. If there happened to be an outbreak of COVID in either of the residential populations of Sunset Villages and/or Serenity Place, then we would have a very big addition to our suit. We could tie it to the absence of necessary funding for the PPE and overtime worker hours. It's just something to keep in mind.

"What we have now is plenty to get into motion, and Bud's fragile health is what speeds all this up. It's better this way, no time wasted," he said enthusiastically to Bud, and she smiled weakly.

By the end of the day, the work group had put together enough evidence to satisfy the paralegal from Jake's office, and Felicia's article had been added into the mix. They were ready for action just as soon as the magazine was ready to go to press.

Chapter Forty-four

"I'm finally free!" Bernice had told Alice during the first few minutes they had together. "I have a story for you, but it can wait until you've wrapped up whatever it is you're so busy with."

She had gulped down the iced tea Alice brought her as they sat quietly on the porch. Alice was surprised at Bernice being so relaxed about the time table, not her friend's usual response to having to wait for Alice's attention.

Felicia came out, saw Bernice, and let out a squawk of surprise.

"Bernice, what are you doing here? How did you get here?" she blurted out, her eyes wide with surprise as she stared at their unexpected visitor.

Bernice seemed genuinely happy to see Felicia, and she even smiled warmly at Gerard who was more than ready for his afternoon nap.

One day later, Bernice had already found a small apartment that she could rent by the month, not far from Pelican Cove. It was attached to the home of an elderly woman who had been putting off moving north to live with her son's family. She was happy to have a tenant who was willing to rent monthly, and Bernice was delighted with the arrangement.

She was more relaxed than Alice had ever seen her.

Today, Alice had promised herself she would make time to find out what was going on with Bernice, and try to fill her in on everything that had been happening since they got to Florida. Bernice had dropped in for an afternoon visit, bringing fresh Florida strawberries and half the batch of homemade cookies she had made to share with her new landlady.

Alice and Bernice sat on the screened porch, eating strawberries and enjoying the birds who came in splendid rotation to their bird feeder.

"What on earth is that magnificent little thing?" Bernice asked.

"It's a male painted bunting!" Alice said. "This is one of the only places in the U.S. where they live. Any minute now, another male will come. These two almost always feed together."

Sure enough, within a minute there was another shining blue, red, and green bird arriving for his snack. They pecked at opposite sides of the feeder as if synchronized.

"Are they a couple?" Bernice asked.

Alice glanced at her. "I don't know if birds ever choose same sex mates," she said. "But these two seem to be together whenever I see them."

Bernice took a deep breath. "This is a sign. I want to tell you now what I drove all the way from Massachusetts to say!"

Alice braced herself for a possible renunciation of Bernice's complicated past.

Instead, Bernice smiled cheerfully. "I've left that ex-husband of mine for good!" she said, grinning at Alice. "He started up with all the old bullying and putting me down and ordering me around. All of a sudden I understood that I had the power to make myself happy and to protect and free myself! I just stood up and told him I was leaving him, and not to waste his breath arguing with me!

"I packed up my things, the stuff I really needed, and drove away. After about an hour, I realized I had no idea where I was heading. So I stopped along the Connecticut River, and got out and stood there watching the water. Then I decided I was going to find you in Florida and give you the good news in person.

"I drove and drove and drove, and thought about everything I had been running away from. Then, when it was getting dark and I couldn't drive another hour, I found a place to sleep. When I woke up in the morning, I knew I was heading the right direction.

"I wanted you to be the first person to hear me say that I'm tired of running away from who I am! I love women, I have always loved women, and I'm not wasting anymore of my life being lonely or taking care of a self-centered man's every need!

"So I just kept driving, and now here I am, ready to start a new life."

Alice beamed at Bernice and pantomimed a great big virtual hug. "I am so happy for you! And whether you stay here in Florida, or go back to New England, or even go somewhere I've never heard of, I am sure you're going to have a wonderful life! And you know, I believe you will find a woman who loves you as you deserve to be loved."

Her phone buzzed, interrupting this remarkable moment. She sighed when she looked down at the caller ID "I think I have to take this," she told Bernice.

"Alice," Felicia said, "you're not going to believe this! Jake just called me when you didn't answer your phone. TouchStone has agreed to settle out of court! Here's the scoop!"

"Wait just a minute, Felicia," Alice said. "I'm in the middle of something important."

"I'm sorry to interrupt this wonderful conversation," she told Bernice, "but apparently the corporation we've been working very hard to expose has settled out of court. I need to hear the details, but then we'll have lots of time to talk more about your new freedom. Please bear with me."

Bernice smiled graciously, gesturing her permission for Alice to focus on Felicia's news.

"Go ahead, Felicia!" Alice said, popping another ripe strawberry into her mouth as she prepared to hear the news.

"TouchStone is going to give two million dollars to be divided among the employees who had remained plaintiffs in the lawsuit. The money will be awarded anonymously through Jake's law practice so that the corporation will not be able to target anyone and retaliate against them. There are ten people who remained plaintiffs, so that money will be divided evenly among them.

"The second good thing is that the corporation is also giving two million dollars to a Florida organization that funds healthcare for elders who need services but want to stay at home as they age. There are no strings on this gift, so TouchStone is not expected to profit from it in any way.

"And, ta-dah! They're restoring the original two million from the federal grant so that it can be used for PPE, overtime pay, and anything else COVID-related that the two nursing homes need most!"

Alice was speechless.

"Kori already knows," Felicia added, "and she will tell Charles when he gets in tonight from his new job. Do you want to tell Gerard, and the Warrens, and will you call Warp too? Besides justice prevailing, he'll be so happy that we're all safe and sound.

"I'll call Pearl and Bud now! I'm so happy that Bud can finally give herself over to really resting and saying her goodbyes, knowing that what she did has made all the difference. And what a wonderful thing at the end of life, to know that she did the right thing without worrying about her own comfort. I know that Pearl will also be thrilled with this outcome!"

"This calls for a celebration!" Alice said. "Shall we gather everyone together at sunset for ice cream or something else festive? We can tell everyone to bring their own chairs and we'll celebrate in our front yard. I'll make sure that Chuck knows that all our Protectors are invited!"

That night, after the boisterous celebration, Alice realized that she wanted to have a private conversation with Kori. She asked her to stay a few minutes to talk.

First Kori and Charles checked on Gram and determined that as long as Charles was there with her, Gram would probably continue to sleep deeply. She had been sleeping most of the time since her rescue from the nursing home, no doubt exhausted from her long wait for Kori to reappear.

In just a few minutes, Kori came back to join Alice out back on the screened porch.

"I love living under that giant live oak tree," Kori said. "I like knowing that the baby owls will be sleeping peacefully up there in their nest in a few months."

"Kori," Alice said, "I want you to know that since I've been engaged in this enterprise with you and the others, I have been deeply impressed with you! I wanted to tell you that you are a real treasure among organizers. You make space for everyone's voice, you think outside the box, and you give courage to everyone working with you. I could go on, but I just wanted you to know that I see you as an extraordinary leader!"

Kori smiled slowly. "Wow! I don't exactly know what to say! I'm very honored to get this kind of praise from you, Alice!"

They sat for a moment of silence. Alice wondered if she had been wrong to ask Kori about the future when she needed time to recover from all that had happened.

"I know you need some time to rest, and of course to figure out what you need to help care for your grandmother. But once all the pieces of the puzzle are in place, I wonder what you see in your future?"

"After what Nancy had told me about you, and what I've experienced working with you, Alice," Kori finally said, "you're kind of a legend as an organizer yourself. I'm honored and all, but I still have so much more to learn."

She stopped, and there was a long silence.

"You know," Kori continued finally, "until I got really upset about what was happening to Gram because of the resources the staff at Sunset Villages wasn't getting, I thought all I wanted to do was political work, like get folks registered to vote, and work to get Flo elected. You know, like that? But then when I started figuring out what we had to do to make the TouchStone corporation be accountable, I got caught up in this bigger picture of organizing. I hadn't experienced anything like it, working to force justice from a big corporation with all that power.

"And then, when things just got hard and scary, we all just did what we had to do. I haven't had a second to think about my future at all, really. I'm just glad we're all OK, except for Rufe of course." She paused, and they both sighed, thinking about Rufe and the awful sacrifice of his life. "I'm so glad Gram is safe. I don't know what happens next."

"Do you picture yourself staying here in Florida?" Alice asked.

"I need to be wherever Gram needs to be," Kori said. "I'm not sure if I can manage taking care of her without some serious help, so we'll see how quickly TouchStone gets its act together with the funding for seniors who want to stay at home. Beyond that, I don't know."

They could hear the sounds of an adult owl hooting, probably calling her mate back to the nest.

"What about you, Alice?" Kori asked. "What's next for you?"

Alice realized that she, too, hadn't had a chance yet to imagine the next thing that might happen.

"At this stage of my life, I don't make many long range plans," she told Kori. "But I've promised Gerard something that even his discerning French palate has not yet experienced – a piece of the best Florida key lime pie in the state."

"I know exactly where to take you!" Kori said. "Let's plan on it tomorrow, OK? We'll get enough to bring home for Gerard, and Felicia, and Gram, and Charles.

"Alice, I have a feeling we're going to become long-time friends!"

"Besides that piece of key lime pie, I can't think of anything that would please me more!" Alice said.

Acknowledgements

I will be forever grateful to Frances Crowe (1919 -2019) and Ann H. Wilson (1929 - 2016) who both inspired and shaped the character of Alice Ott. They are always with me.

Dorothy Cresswell continues the journey with Alice and me, offering thoughtful editing, brilliant plot suggestions, and invaluable support and comfort every step of the way. Savanna Ouellette also has been an extremely insightful reader and consultant, and has continued to help me with Gerard's unique blend of French and English.

Cindy Casey and CCE Publications have given new life to the Alice Ott series. Cindy has opened a new world of possibilities, helping to get Alice out into a bigger world of distribution, making the Alice Ott series accessible to a wider world of readers, and providing superb editorial and graphic skills.

Thanks also to White River Press and to Levellers Press, Amherst MA, for publishing the first four books in the Alice Ott series over the past nine years.

I would also like to thank my magical neighborhood in Florida. My friends in Pelican Cove have been supportive and delightfully distracting. Most of the neighborhood characters in Danger Within are real people: the neighborhood's deep affection and willingness to help out in a myriad of ways morphed right into the pages of this book.

Other Florida friends, especially Betty Bowne, Cindy Casey, Vern Whittenburg, Gerie Spencer, Bill and Marsha Cox and "the Smallies" have continued to teach me about the depth and diversity of human kindness. I am so grateful for all of you.

Thanks to ivy tilman for what you have helped me understand about Black lives in America today, and for the many African American writers whose work has opened my eyes and heart.

Thanks to the medical workers who have worked so faithfully

through the pandemic to protect and support residents of nursing homes, and many others elders. My appreciation in particular for what I have learned from Don Ahrens (and Theresa), and to Hospice of the Fisher Home for allowing me to be part of their community of care.

Deepest gratitude to Nzinga Hall and Vern Whittenburg for allowing me to use their images on the cover of this book, and to photographer Cindy Casey for getting exactly what I had pictured.

Author's Note

When I finished the fourth Alice Ott mystery, *Danger in the House*, I wrote in the "Author's Note" that I was wrapping up the Alice series, and told my readers about a new mystery series, set in Florida.

But when the changes brought by the COVID-19 pandemic hit me, I realized I needed to keep Alice Ott and friends in my life. And so I wrote *Danger Within* to comfort myself with Alice's steadiness and clarity, and also to shine a light on how I saw the virus threatening the elder population of the U.S.

I was horrified by the devastating number of deaths that ocurred suddenly at a local nursing facility for veterans. I listened to what it was like for medical workers who were caring for elders in nursing homes, assisted living facilities, rehab centers and emergency care hospital settings. I thought what this could mean for Alice Ott and the other aging characters in the series, and I thought about my own experiences as an elder. Out of this awareness, *Danger Within* was delivered.

I didn't forget my promise to expand the settings of my mystery adventures to include Florida. My wife and I live in Florida for half the year, and return to our New England home in the warmer months. In both locales, neighborhood connections are very important to me, and in *Danger Within*, I have loved sharing Pelican Cove, my Florida home.

If you want to share your thoughts about any aspect of the Alice Ott books, from characters, to settings, plot and/or social issues, please go to my website: dustyjmiller.com. I would love to hear from you and get your reactions to *Danger Within*.

If this is your first book in the Alice Ott Mystery Series, I hope you will go to my website to learn more about the other four Alice Ott books. The website also will keep you up to date on book events and Readers Theater productions.